PRAISE FOR THE NOVELS OF SHAYLA BLACK

"Scorching, wrenching, suspenseful."

—Lora Leigh, #1 *New York Times* bestselling author

"A Shayla Black story never disappoints!"

—Sylvia Day, #1 *New York Times* bestselling author

"Shayla Black inspired us to write, and now inspires us to do more, get better. She is a master of her craft: a wordsmith, a storyteller, and an undisputed genre trendsetter."

—Christina Lauren, *New York Times* bestselling author

"Wickedly seductive from start to finish."

—Jaci Burton, *New York Times* bestselling author

"The master at writing a steamy, smokin'-hot, can-I-have-more-please sex scene."

—Fiction Vixen

"The perfect combination of excitement, adventure, romance, and really hot sex . . . This book has it all!"

—Smexy Books

"To die for. [A] fabulous read!"

—Fresh Fiction

"This one is a scorcher."

—The Romance Readers Connection

Holding on Tighter

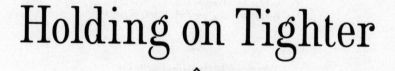

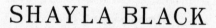

SHAYLA BLACK

BERKLEY SENSATION
New York

BERKLEY SENSATION
Published by Berkley
An imprint of Penguin Random House LLC
375 Hudson Street, New York, New York 10014

Library of Congress Cataloging-in-Publication Data

Names: Black, Shayla, author.
Title: Holding on tighter / Shayla Black.
Description: First Edition. | New York : Berkley, 2017.
Identifiers: LCCN 2016039286 (print) | LCCN 2016044645 (ebook) |
ISBN 9780425275481 (paperback) | ISBN 9780698164017 (ebook)
Subjects: | BISAC: FICTION / Romance / Contemporary. | FICTION / Contemporary
Women. | FICTION / Romance / General. | GSAFD: Erotic fiction. | Romantic
suspense fiction.
Classification: LCC PS3602.L325245 H65 2017 (print) | LCC PS3602.L325245
(ebook) | DDC 813/.6—dc23
LC record available at https://lccn.loc.gov/2016039286

First Edition: February 2017

Printed in the United States of America
1 3 5 7 9 10 8 6 4 2

Cover photos: Man © Claudio Marinesco / Ninestock
Back cover photo: Textured background © Pakhnyushchy / Shutterstock
Cover design by Alana Colucci

To all the dedicated fans of the Wicked Lovers novels who have been with me from the time Jack Cole jumped onto the page, through the stories about characters I never intentionally planned to become heroes or heroines but still stole their way into my heart, all the way through to the end, focused on another sighworthy bodyguard, Heath. This close-knit group of characters have been through love, hate, birth, death, terror, tragedy, laughter, and joy. And you readers have been with me every step of the way. It's been an enormous pleasure for me to tell these stories. I hope from the bottom of my heart that you've enjoyed reading them. I'm looking forward to the next story in this wonderful world that leaves me with warm fuzzies. I hope you'll join me there, too.

Acknowledgments

I have so many people to thank who have been beside me in every way with this series. First and always, my family. My amazing husband and daughter have supported my dream in every way imaginable. Nothing in my writing life works properly without Rachel Connolly. I'd be lost without you, so thanks for being the best assistant and friend a disorganized author could have. I can't neglect to thank some people who have had a tremendous impact in my life over the years but especially during this book: Lexi Blake, Liz Berry, Jenna Jacob, Isabella LaPearl, Chloe Vale, and Kris Cook. Y'all are some of the best friends a girl could have. I am blessed to have great people and readers in my life. Hugs!

Chapter One

Rule for success number one:
Pay attention—to the right things.

October

AFTERNOON sunlight streamed through the wall of windows as Jolie Quinn hustled down the hall of her North Dallas office, ready to make things happen. Which probably meant she had to bust some asses. It wouldn't be the first time . . . nor the last. But keeping her small, slightly offbeat workforce focused during crunch time was critical.

Her entire future was riding on it.

To her left, Gerard hovered over the latest copy of *Vogue*. Accessories for the summer collection she desperately needed sat half drawn as he swayed to the rhythm of Mozart blasting through his earbuds. Rohan hunched over his keyboard, his fingers flying, as he scanned his screen, working his E-Trade account far more intently than he coded her new website. Wisteria, her receptionist, was fresh from another breakup. She looked somewhere between contemplative and maudlin as she shuffled the mountain of customer records on the credenza behind her. Arthur, her accountant, wasn't even at his desk. He'd probably hooked up his PlayStation to that little flatscreen in the break room again. And the latest addition to her staff, her gorgeously distracting security contractor, never inhabited his desk. Instead, Heath Powell constantly cased the building and asked questions, watching everything and everyone with a dark, focused stare.

He unnerved her.

Jolie dismissed the thought and got back to business.

Hands on hips, she regarded her assistant designer. "Where are we with the sketches?"

Gerard's head snapped up as he yanked the buds from his ears, looking like a quintessential Frenchman with Continental sensibilities. "I am looking for inspiration. You cannot rush creativity."

"I have to. You know I don't have a choice."

He grimaced as if the situation was out of his control. "Nothing flows as it should, yes?"

She understood. When she'd designed the office attire for the upcoming line, it had come to her quickly. Admittedly, the casual wear had stumped her for weeks.

"Imagination, Gerard. You've got it. I need those handbags." Jolie glanced down at the sketchbook on his desk. "Off the top of my head, these look too much like last summer. Fashion is change. And I want more texture. Let's review everything you've got. My office. Ten minutes." Conversation over until then, so she turned to Rohan with a raised brow. "Do I pay you to build a website or work your stock portfolio?"

Rohan had already shuttled the day-trading site and retrieved the code he'd previously written. "I took five minutes to investigate an interesting stock tip."

She hated being lied to.

Jolie leaned into his face. "You were tapping away about the same small cap's historical data when I took my call in the conference room an hour ago. Planning for the future is important, but do you grasp that if my potential investor walks because I can't show him a working mockup of the new website, we may all be out of a job? It has to be done by Friday. That's in two days." She held up a pair of fingers. "If you've got some obstacle preventing you from finishing, let me know. I'll remove it. Otherwise, I don't have time for your personal financial health during my business crisis."

"Sorry." Sweat beaded on Rohan's olive skin. He swallowed audibly. "You know deadlines freak me out, but I can do it."

"You can or I wouldn't have hired you. Show me what you have ready on the new shopping cart and tax tables. My office in thirty minutes."

"I'll be there. I think you'll be pleased with . . ."

Jolie didn't stay to hear the rest since he would present everything relevant shortly. If the site wasn't functional and top-notch in time, it could mean the difference between her business flourishing and folding.

As she strode toward her office, she spotted a new pot of red tulips on her sister's desk and frowned. Karis was often taking in strays. Had she shifted her attention from cats to plants?

With every step, Jolie's stomach rumbled. Damn, she'd skipped lunch again. Maybe she'd munch on some crackers at her desk while she met with her employees and compiled the presentation for her prospective investor. During their upcoming dinner meeting, she intended to show Richard Gardner a complete strategic plan, new website functionality, current financials, and finished sketches of her summer collection. Right now, she was nowhere near ready. Food really didn't fit into her schedule.

Of course she hadn't had time for much of anything in the last four years—not waiting for inspiration, or her personal finances, and certainly not fun or games or romance. After waiting tables to put herself through FIT in NYC, she'd earned a bachelor's in fashion design. Then she'd gone straight for her MBA, focusing on merchandising, and studied feverishly to graduate at the top of her class.

Afterward, Jolie had refused eight high-profile job offers. They had been flattering, but she'd already spent enough time building someone else's name during her internships, thank you. Her dream had never been about working her way up from the bottom or limiting her income based on someone else's arbitrary pay structure.

So she had forged a different path, starting her own line of chic yet comfortable fashion for women of all sizes. She'd also launched a completely different distribution channel at the same time, merchandising exclusively through home-based parties. So far it was working because her company had grown ten-fold in the last four years. Jolie had recently been named an up-and-coming designer by Fashionista and one of the top ten businesspeople to watch in Dallas. A popular nighttime drama would begin dressing their popular, stylish heroine, played by Shealyn West, in pieces from her spring collection after their winter hiatus. Sales were predicted to skyrocket.

Jolie intended to build Betti into a brand as recognizable as Coke, as sought after as Apple, and as far-reaching as Starbucks.

It was a tall order for a thirty-year-old woman short on capital. She needed this investor and all the building blocks in place to take the next step.

She didn't want to think about what would happen if she failed.

Jolie ducked around the corner and peeked into the break room. Sure enough, Arthur was shooting a blue laser at both feral ghouls and raider scum in a post-apocalyptic wasteland. Currently, his character was fighting off a horde of enemies, along with radiation sickness.

"Arthur?"

He didn't turn to her, just pressed buttons on his controller like a madman. "Um, yeah. Two minutes. I'm almost done with these guys."

"You're done now."

Her accountant performed a quick save, pausing the game, then turned to her with a sheepish expression. He shoved the shaggy brown hair from his face and pushed his glasses up the bridge of his nose. Slender, brilliant, and a bit on the anxious side, he often seemed more like a slouchy college student than a CPA pushing thirty. "Sorry. I get involved. It's just that RooskieGamer posted a great YouTube video about how to defeat these guys and earn a trophy. I wanted to test it out."

"After hours. At home. I need the financials ready for my investor meeting ASAP."

"They're almost done," he assured her.

"I want to review them at tomorrow's staff meeting."

"Totally." He peeked nervously back at the TV, as if the screaming goons and trigger-happy baddies could somehow reach through the screen and annihilate him while he wasn't looking. "I'll have it done by end of business today."

"Good." She turned away, then thought of one more thing. "Don't spend the evening here playing that crap. Seriously. Go home."

He frowned. "My roommate is constantly shagging his girlfriend. They're so loud."

And Arthur was annoyed because he wasn't getting any. Not her problem.

"Turn up the volume on your game. The screeching ghouls alone will kill their mood," Jolie suggested.

"But—"

"No. Last time you stayed here all evening, you cooked raw fish wrapped in foil in the microwave. The place almost caught fire and reeked for days."

Not to mention that she'd had to buy a new microwave.

"I'm not much of a cook." He pushed his glasses up again. "I'll leave by six."

Mission accomplished, she gave him a sharp nod and turned for the door.

"Jolie, before you go, I've got a question. Ten minutes, tops."

"Do you need an answer to finish your part of the presentation for my investor?"

"N-no. But I—"

"Then let's talk next week. I've got more meetings now. Sorry. Everything else is back burner at the moment."

Jolie didn't wait for him to object, because it was probably another one of his causes like cleaner urinals or organic coffee. She headed to her office.

On the way, she passed Wisteria at her desk. "All that paper has to be scanned, filed, and locked inside the proper cabinet by the end of the day. I know you have a lot on your mind, but customers' addresses and credit card numbers shouldn't be lying around. If we mishandle their personal and financial information, they'll shop elsewhere."

"You're right." Wisteria looked appropriately contrite. "I'm not in a good head space but I'll get it done."

"I'm sorry he hurt you. But he's a man, so if he hasn't already, he'll be moving on soon. I suggest you do the same."

Jolie strode into her office and shut the door. She couldn't exactly tell Wisteria that she understood because she'd been there. Jolie refused to give a man that much power over her heart. She intended to build something more lasting than "love."

Leaning against the wood, she shut her eyes and basked in the moment of silence. In part, she blamed herself for her employees' lack of urgency. She'd given each a job because she'd believed in their talent, but they didn't quite grasp that, despite Betti's growing profits and impending opportunities, she would be unable to finance the company's expansion for years without an infusion of capital. And if she waited that long to get ahead, the competition would undoubtedly have passed her by. She shielded them from the daily dog-eat-dog rigors of business so they didn't see the throat-cutting happening all around them. Just last week, a man had initiated a hostile takeover of a growing cosmetics corporation and wrested it from the owner—his own mother.

Jolie wouldn't rest until her dream was secure. Some might not understand her methods, but experience had proven her staff was most productive when she was professional but exacting. Gaining respect as a female CEO hadn't been easy. Some misogynist, fidiot, or hack was always waiting to tear her down.

She refused to bend for small-minded people.

With a sigh, Jolie opened her eyes to tackle the mountain of work on her desk—only to be stopped short. Her younger sister, Karis, sat in her chair, staring out the window overlooking the parking lot. The girl's dreamy expression tightened Jolie's gut. She loved her sister, but as the baby of the family—and the one most like their mother—Karis didn't have many practical bones in her body.

"Tell me how you're working with that male god every day and not tearing your clothes off. He's so hot." Karis fanned herself. "And so British. That accent . . . Hmm. I want him."

Jolie held in a groan. She didn't have to ask who *him* was. Heath Powell. Her security contractor was incredibly male and terribly attractive. She refused to let him become a distraction.

Unfortunately, Karis lacked her willpower.

"Mr. Powell has been hired to make sure we don't suffer a catastrophic security-related event, whether that's industrial espionage or the burglar who's been hitting all the businesses in the neighborhood. He is not here to make your vagina tingle."

Karis huffed. "Not everything can be about business all the time."

"It has to be until we secure this investor. While you're getting your ass out of my seat so I can get back to work, let's talk about expectations. I've counseled everyone else in the last five minutes about getting the job done. It wouldn't be fair if I gave you special treatment because you're my sister. You're a hell of a graphic artist and I think you'll make a great project manager. Stay on top of Rohan. He's behind on his milestones for the new website. You're lagging on your deliverables, too. You all need to be caught up by close of business tomorrow."

Karis's mouth tightened in mutiny. "I had plans this evening."

"So did I." Jolie really wanted a few hours of extra sleep but that would have to wait.

"Fine. But I'm not letting that hunk of a spectacularly single man pass me by indefinitely. Jolie, you should find someone. You're sacrificing every shred of your personal life and future just for a job. Don't you want more?"

"It's *not* just a job." Her blood pressure ticked up twenty points. "It's my dream."

"Yeah? Maybe my dream looks more balanced, with work I enjoy *and* an amazing guy. That's exactly what Heath Powell is."

Did such a man actually exist? Her mother had been searching for one her whole romantic life, despite her three divorces and a copious number of live-ins. In Jolie's estimation, the odds of any woman finding the perfect man were right up there with saddling a rainbow-hued unicorn. "How would you know? You met Heath when he started here two days ago."

"I spent some time looking into him this afternoon."

Now the pieces of the puzzle fell into place. "On my computer?"

"You have more bells and whistles on your machine, plus the software that checks backgrounds."

And Karis knew how to uncover personal information online because she'd recently dated Ben, a hacker who had taught her how to dig into anyone's background, including his university dean's. Jolie was pretty sure the dirtbag had blackmailed his way into a degree.

"My office also gave you the privacy of a closed door so Heath couldn't see what you were up to." She raised a brow at her younger sister.

"Yeah, it came in handy, especially when I called Ben for help," she admitted. "Oh, don't make that face. He's a white hat . . . mostly. He walked me through bits of cracking and a back door or two. Some of it looked like top-secret stuff."

"Yeah, Heath is obviously a great guy." Jolie rolled her eyes. She didn't want to know how much of Karis's productive time that had wasted. "Looking into Heath's background isn't in your job description. Don't make it your top priority."

"But what if he's the 'one'?" She rose and grabbed Jolie's hands, her excited tone like a teenage girl's waiting for the football captain to give her a sweeping "promposal." "I needed to know more about him."

"Be real. That concept is an old myth perpetuated by fairy tales and exploited by Disney. Sis, he's sixteen years older than you."

"Age is just a number," Karis protested.

Jolie snorted. Only someone naive actually believed that. Then again, that described Karis well. So the difference between her sheltered twenty-three and Powell's well-lived thirty-nine might as well be a century. "Bullshit. Back to work."

"You're my sister. Why don't you want me to be happy?"

"I do." It hurt that she'd actually believe otherwise. "But your happiness shouldn't be dependent on a man."

"It's not dependent," Karis argued. "I'm just saying, he would help the cause."

"Well, I'm also your boss who thinks you could be very happy accomplishing great things here. So please start caring about your job as much as some guy you barely know."

Karis finally looked chastened. "I care."

"Then don't let me down. I'm counting on you."

"I won't. But will you hear me out first? Please."

Why was she a sucker for her little sister's pleading? "You've got two minutes."

"Did you know he's former MI5?"

And Karis clearly thought that having an ex-spy for a boyfriend would be somehow romantic. "That did come up in our conversation, yes. I know how long he was employed by the British government, the types of missions he completed, and some of his other relevant job experiences. He was candid about his professional background and seemed extremely qualified."

Callie Mackenzie, her friend from Yoga Oasis, had recommended him, based on her handsome husband's word. Sean was a former FBI agent and obviously knew his stuff. She was grateful to have friends like them.

"Qualified?" Karis blinked, her chocolate eyes wide with incredulity. "I know you like to pretend that you're dead from the waist down but surely even you must have noticed Heath Powell is scorching hot."

Jolie let her sister's jab slide as she took her seat. Of course she'd noticed the man. The moment he'd walked in her door and shaken her hand, he had rattled her with his big presence. He spoke with an economy of words she appreciated. He'd obviously catalogued everyone and everything around him with a single glance. And he'd been so damn male, she couldn't deny he was shiver-worthy.

But this emotional shit wasn't her speed, so she tucked it away as she reached for her computer. "Karis, I love you, but I'm only going to say this once. Mom isn't a role model to aspire to."

"Just because I'm interested in a guy—"

"You've been interested in far more than one, and you're not listening. You have to be a complete person before you can have a meaningful relationship with someone else."

"I am," she defended.

Jolie shot her younger sister a skeptical stare. "You don't know your father. God knows I'd like to forget my biological dad. Like you, I can count on one hand the number of times I've seen that scumbag. They didn't want either of us, and that hurt, but expecting some father figure with a penis—no matter how attractive—to fill the void in your heart now won't work. Ask Mom. Ten bucks says she's headed for divorce number four."

"I won't give up on finding someone to share my life with." Karis whipped out her phone, tapped a few keys, then sent Jolie an accusing stare. "I don't know what happened to you. Maybe you had to sacrifice too much of your childhood to raise me and Austin. Maybe you enjoy being miserable and alone. Or maybe you're too afraid to risk your heart. I just emailed you everything I found about Heath. Read it. He seems like a great guy. And I think he needs someone to make him whole." She raised her chin. "He needs me."

Jolie tried not to let her sister's barb hurt. "I'm not afraid. I'm ambitious. Why would I want to surrender my heart when I could conquer the world? Now get back to your desk and start giving me your deliverables."

Her sister sniffled. "I won't confide my feelings to you anymore. I know they're a terrible waste of your time, and you don't give a shit anyway. I'll enjoy the flowers he sent me earlier and ask him out the first chance I get."

Heath better not have given Karis flowers. "That's against company policy. You know that. I'll remind Powell he can't cross that line, either."

"Why? So you can make sure I don't have anything in my life but work? Or because you can't stand him pursuing me when you want him for yourself?" She held up her hand. "Never mind. I don't care."

With that, Karis slammed the office door. The sound reverberated in the otherwise silent room, echoing off the walls. Hurt sliced through Jolie's chest. She blinked away the acid sting of threatening tears and retrieved the spreadsheet she'd been working on. There was a reason people called it tough love. If it was easy—either to give or receive—it would be called something else. More importantly, Jolie knew she was right. Romance always let a woman down. Ambition never would.

But if she had to break up the budding office fling between her temporary security contractor and her sister to ensure no one's heart was broken and shit got done, Jolie had no problem doing it.

* * *

AT half past nine, Heath Powell stared into his Scotch. The bar around him was dark and loud, a press of perfumed bodies, despite it being a Wednesday night. Then again, it was smack in the middle of a trendy area a few blocks from Betti's offices. College students from nearby SMU rubbed against single professionals and a few overgrown partiers. The place thumped with Fall Out Boy and drinks flowed freely. With his back to the wall, he watched people coming, going, smiling, flirting, and hoping for a good time tonight.

He was the oldest man in the room. From experience, he knew that could be an advantage. He liked his odds. More than one pretty girl slid her inviting gaze his way. Now if he could just muster up more enthusiasm. Damn difficult to do when his mind was on someone else.

When he'd accepted the job with Betti, the position had been short term—perfect for his current needs because he didn't have a home here in Dallas. Hell, he didn't even have a country at the moment. This job gave him a few weeks to decide if he wanted to stay or start over elsewhere.

With forty breathing down his neck, Heath wasn't certain anymore what he wanted out of life.

Seven years ago, it had been simple. Anna, his wife, had been his world. He'd give anything now to go home to her and the small brood of children they should have had. But an afternoon of tragedy had wiped away that possibility. Six months later, he'd begun working for Marshall Mullins, the world-famous movie director, bodyguarding his daughter after their move to London following her headline-making abduction in L.A. Mystery had been sweet and reserved—at first. She'd given him her trust slowly, blooming gradually, and awakening more than a protective instinct inside him. He'd fancied himself in love with her—and told her as much. Mystery hadn't felt the same. Instead, she'd paired off with the soldier who had once rescued her. She and Axel would be married soon. And Heath would still be alone.

After losing in love twice, he wasn't in a mad rush to fall again. But he enjoyed sex and missed a woman's touch. So tonight, like many others, he found himself in a lamentable cesspool of booze and desperation. Only now he had a completely new reason to find a distraction.

Jolie Quinn.

After a summer spent in London and encountering constant reminders of Anna whilst running into Mystery, doting fiancé in tow, Heath had headed back to the States. Once in Dallas, Mitchell Thorpe, Axel's former boss, had called asking for a favor. Thorpe's submissive, Callie, did yoga with this lovely up-and-coming clothing designer, and would Heath be interested in shoring up her security, just temporarily of course? He hadn't turned down the quick cash or the chance to earn a reputation locally for his work. Now he wished he had because he couldn't get the bloody woman off his mind.

Blisteringly quick, acerbic, and ambitious, Jolie wore her confidence like a sexy sequined dress. Bright and sparkly, it hugged her every womanly curve and dip—and made her madly attractive. She never bothered with feminine wiles or coy flirtations. When she wanted something, she went after it. She was a green-eyed shark. Damn if he didn't want to swim in her waters until he got her under him and made her surrender to the bigger fish in the tank.

A brilliant but risky notion. He wasn't interested in anything that lasted more than a night. On the other hand, neither was she. But Jolie fascinated him as no woman had in years. He suspected that his desire to stay after the sheets had grown cold might exceed his will to walk away.

So he'd come to Nite Time, this terrible excuse for a watering hole, looking for a woman who would neither intrigue him nor linger in his memory.

A few feet away, a young woman sidled up to the bar with a glance from under a thick honey curl. Blue eyes. A smattering of freckles. Slightly crooked front teeth. A little scar on her chin. Given the way she leaned against the surface, she was slightly tipsy but not incapable of making a rational decision. Her short skirt and sky-high heels indicated she'd come looking for something more than a cocktail.

"Hi," she murmured. Her lashes were fake. Her breasts probably were, too. But he wouldn't know for certain until he wrapped his fingers around them.

"Hello."

"Your voice . . ." she said with a hint of a soft, southern drawl. "You aren't from around here."

"I'm not." He didn't elaborate because he really didn't want to talk. He doubted she did, either.

"Oh, I love your Aussie accent."

Heath didn't bother correcting her, merely glanced down at her empty wineglass. "Drink?"

"Sure." She smiled and stood, teetering slightly.

He took hold of her glass, sniffed, then downed the last swallow before motioning to the bartender. "A glass of merlot for the lady."

The bartender nodded, and Heath felt relieved that, even after a few visits, the man knew his routine. Helpful to have something of a wingman pouring. "You got it. Another Glenfiddich?"

"Please." Heath tapped the bar and turned to the girl with a smile. "Here with friends?"

Her smile faltered as she glanced toward the dance floor. "I came with a coworker and her boyfriend."

"They look busy." The couple she watched clung to each other like overgrown vines.

"Yeah." The girl's glum voice said she'd soon be having a pity party . . . unless he distracted her.

When the bartender delivered their drinks, Heath paid, then took hold of his tumbler, waiting until she did the same with her stem. "To finding your own fun."

She smiled brightly again. "I'll drink to that."

They clinked glasses, and Heath sipped his Scotch, watching the woman over the rim. She chugged half the glass, then set it down, sending a coy glance his way. "You want to dance?"

"If you'd like. It's not what I do best."

A little smile tipped up the corners of her lips. "And what is it you do best?"

He eased closer, sending her a weighty glance filled with manufactured seduction. Then he brushed his knuckles down her cheek before sliding his thumb over her mouth. Her eyes widened and her lips parted to form an "O" as his meaning sunk in. She drew in a shuddering breath.

Now that she understood him, she seemed nervous. He wouldn't push, of course. Everything he did with any woman was completely consensual. If she declined, another would come along. But so far, she wasn't walking away.

"How do I know you're not bragging?" She studied him, her eyes glittering.

Ah, the good girl who longed to be bad. By day, she probably had a very responsible job. She paid her bills on time, called her mother at least once a week, and had always done everything expected of her. Tonight she was feeling a bit envious of her friend and didn't want to be the wally who couldn't snare a man. Based on the smudges under her eyes and the slightly droopy cast of her lids, he'd bet she hadn't been sleeping particularly well. Lack of REM, coupled with alcohol, could heighten people's emotions. She obviously felt more than a bit lonely tonight, so she'd worn the "slaggy" dress she'd likely bought in a moment of weakness or impulse, torn the tags off, tossed on whatever daring shoes she owned, and come to this bar to prove she was both attractive and merely alone by choice.

"Talking to me, you don't." He sipped his Scotch again.

It didn't take her long to draw a conclusion. "You're saying I have to sleep with you to find out what you're best at?"

Her glance had turned slightly disdainful, as if she wanted him to think that men in bars regularly propositioned her. The pulse throbbing at the base of her neck said otherwise. "Not at all. In this instance, sleeping would be rather a waste of time."

The woman's jaw dropped in shock. "You've got balls."

"I do, indeed. I assumed you hadn't mistaken me for a female."

She tsked at him. "I meant you've got a lot of nerve."

"You will never have anything you want if you don't pursue it."

The cleavage above her plunging V-neck rose and fell rapidly. Heath grabbed her wrist. Her pulse hammered under his fingertips. Already, her eyes were dilated. He stepped closer and wrapped a hand around her nape, tilting her face to his.

"And you want me?" she breathed.

"You're a beautiful woman." He caressed his way down the graceful column of her throat. "A man would be very lucky to touch you. In fact, I daresay it would be a pleasure."

"Really?"

A thread of guilt tugged at him for playing on her loneliness. But in truth, sex would benefit them both. He could make her feel treasured and gorgeous for a time. She could distract him—he hoped.

He downed the rest of his Scotch. It did nothing to quell the ache in his cock he'd been fighting since meeting his new boss.

"Of course. But everything is up to you," Heath told the stranger. "We can stay here and have another round. Or I know a quiet spot where we could . . . talk privately."

The woman bit her lip as if she couldn't quite decide. She sent a sideways glance at the couple she'd come with. They danced their best imitation of vertical sex whilst moving to the beat of the music. Desire fused their lips together in an interminable kiss. Heath doubted they would be coming up for air soon.

The woman beside him tensed, her gaze skittering back to her wine. She swallowed the last half quickly as if downing liquid courage. "Let's go. And for the record, I don't want to talk."

"Excellent."

He led the blonde across the room, toward a cordoned-off staircase. On the far side, he glanced back, swearing someone watched him. But across the loud, smoky bar, no one in the crowd seemed to pay him much notice.

Heath shrugged off the feeling as he led the woman up to the private area of the club. The sounds below them faded to a dull roar. The lighting grew even more dim. The scents of sweat, alcohol, and desperation choking the first floor gave way to cologne, money, and sex.

"What's your name?" she asked with a shy glance when they reached the landing at the top.

"Does it matter?"

She hesitated, glanced down the stairs, then back to his face. "No."

"Right, then." Heath led her toward a quiet, poorly lit corner, then turned her to face the wall. He lifted her short skirt and lowered her knickers just enough before reaching into his pocket for a condom. "Brace your hands and feel free to scream."

Chapter Two

Rule for success number two:
Instinct isn't synonymous with impulse.

D AMN it," Jolie muttered as she watched Heath and a young blonde disappear up the stairs.

Not surprising that under his seemingly refined British demeanor lay a seasoned skirt-chaser.

For the past few minutes, she'd watched the two from just inside the doorway, blending with a group of revelers celebrating someone's birthday. Almost instantly, she'd spotted her security contractor. She wasn't at all shocked the woman looked willing to spread her legs for Heath after exchanging barely a hundred words.

But the casual ease with which he'd picked up a stranger just reinforced all the reasons Heath Powell would be bad for her naive sister. Jolie intended to stay right here until she made it perfectly clear that Karis was off limits.

In her pocket, her phone rang. Probably work, and whatever she didn't take care of tonight would only be waiting for her in the morning.

Sighing, she plucked the device from her pocket, glanced at the display, then winced.

"Hi, Mom," she shouted over the music as she made her way to the door, then out into the breezy October night. "I'm sorry I haven't called back."

"I'm glad I finally caught you. I've been trying for days."

Yeah, the three missed calls in the last forty-eight hours kind of spelled that out. "Work has been a zoo. I don't have much longer to persuade this investor to come on board."

"You'll manage. You're the smartest, hardest working woman I know." She gave a self-deprecating laugh. "By the time I was your age, I hadn't accomplished much except a handful of disastrous relationships and having you three kids."

Her mom had never been the ambitious sort, and Jolie wondered if she ever regretted that. "How are you?"

"Not very good, baby."

Jolie froze. She knew that voice. Diana Quinn-Michaels-Weston-Gale had marital problems—again.

"Are you and Charlie getting divorced?"

"How did you know?" Her mother sounded surprised by her insight.

Jolie couldn't imagine why. Mom had been married to Charlie Gale for nearly six years, which was as long as any of her mother's marriages lasted. Jolie had suspected from the beginning that husband number four was a philandering bastard. After all, he'd hopped into bed with her mom while she was still licking her wounds from a previous breakup—and he'd still been married to someone else.

"You sound sad, so I guessed what might be upsetting you. Did Charlie find another woman?"

Her mom sniffled over the line. "I should have known when he started eating at that diner every day that it wasn't the mashed potatoes he liked. Apparently, her name is Destiny. She sounds like a stripper." Her mom huffed. "She's definitely a husband thief."

"I'm sorry." And Jolie was because her mom was clearly hurting. Still, she kept hoping Diana would learn that she couldn't count on men. "When are you going move out and find a place of your own? Do you need anything?"

"I already moved out. Charlie's brother, Wayne, helped me get back on my feet. He's been a great . . . comfort."

Jolie groaned. "Please don't tell me you're sleeping with your soon-to-be ex-husband's brother."

"I—um . . ." She sounded as if she didn't know how to work around saying yes. "He's really wonderful. You'll like him."

If he was anything like his brother, she wouldn't. "Isn't he married?"

"To a terrible cow who doesn't appreciate him. She's a doctor. She's high and mighty, if you ask me. Wayne is a man with needs, and she isn't meeting them."

Apparently her mother was and didn't realize that Wayne was no better than Charlie or see the irony of calling Destiny a husband thief.

Jolie sighed. Berating her mother wouldn't do any good. Nor would pointing out that she was making the same mistakes she'd already made. Jolie had tried to reason with her during the last torrid ending. She'd have had better luck talking to cement. She loved her mother, but Diana was a grown woman and inclined to do whatever she thought would make her happy, whether or not it made sense.

"Did you get the money I sent?" Jolie asked instead. "I mailed it to Charlie's address—"

"Yes. I waited to leave until I received it. Thank you for understanding I had to quit my job. Working for the florist sounded lovely but it was a lot of long hours and grouchy people. I promise I'm looking for a new job and I'll pay you back as soon as I can."

Doubtful. Mom always needed a little more time to get her feet back under her again, then she inevitably met a new man and had a few unexpected expenses before she decided it wasn't working out and had to keep the money she'd tucked away—and borrow a bit more— to look for happiness elsewhere. But the woman had given Jolie life and a lot of love. She'd done her best by her kids in difficult circumstances. Jolie didn't understand her mom but she also didn't begrudge her a few hundred bucks here and there.

"Sure. Whenever you're ready." Jolie smiled to herself.

"Thanks. I paid off one of my doctor bills with the money. They were getting insistent."

"And you moved out with the rest?"

"No, Wayne helped me with that, so I lent him what was left to buy a new hunting rifle." She laughed nervously. "He's a manly man but such a sweetheart. He had an empty rental and he's letting me stay here for free until he and his wife separate. He's going to leave her soon. And before you say I've heard that line before, Wayne really means it."

Jolie shook her head and didn't say a word. How could a nearly fifty-year-old woman who'd been disappointed over and over still be so blindly optimistic? Granted, people often accused Jolie of being too cynical but she didn't let anyone take advantage of her. She worked her ass off, kept her eyes open, and always expected the worst. That way, if something better happened, she was pleasantly surprised.

"For your sake, I hope he's everything you've ever wanted."

"Oh, I think he is, baby." Her mom sounded giddy.

"That's great. Hey, can we talk later?" Jolie glanced up to make sure Heath hadn't already finished with his conquest and headed out the door. But other than a few suits returning home to their wives after an evening of booze and bimbos, no one entered or exited the building.

"Sure. Call me next week?" Diana asked hopefully.

"Yeah. Will do."

"Where are you?" her mom asked, concern lacing her voice.

"At a bar. I'm hunting down a lothario I intend to keep far away from Karis."

"Please watch out for her. She's still so young and doesn't understand men."

Karis wasn't the only one. Her sister had definitely inherited their mother's dreamy disposition, often choosing to overlook the probable shittiness of a relationship in favor of embracing all its wonderful possibilities if the stars aligned, hell froze over, and gold rained from the sky.

"I will," Jolie assured. "I love you."

"I love you, too, baby. Bye."

They rang off, and she shoved her phone back in her pocket, heading for the door. As soon as she ducked inside, the music thumped so loudly, she swore it made her organs vibrate. Having given up the club scene after college, she was a little disgusted that she had to pull a grown-ass man out of a meat market she'd heard he scored in almost nightly.

The bartender nodded at her, and she ordered a Grey Goose and cranberry, more so she wouldn't stick out rather than from any desire for alcohol. And vodka would help combat her boredom while she waited for her British Romeo to finish his business upstairs because he was either too impatient or impersonal to find a bed.

Yeah, she probably shouldn't have tracked him down at his favorite hook-up joint. But what she had to say to him had nothing to do with business and didn't belong in the office. She wanted Heath Powell to know that she understood exactly who he was so there'd be no misunderstanding about why Karis was off limits.

The bartender set her drink down. Jolie paid him and took a sip, glancing around. God, she did not miss this, the sizing up potential bedmates for the night over the rim of her drink and wondering if he was taken, terrible in bed, a mama's boy, or in some other way lacking. She'd been so much happier giving up on "romance" and focusing on work. Diana Gale wasn't going to grow up, but Jolie still had hope for her sister.

After witnessing a lot of bumping and grinding on the dance floor, she turned her back on a wannabe Casanova who'd stared her way when she saw Heath's bimbo finally stumbling and giggling down the stairs. One of the spaghetti straps of the woman's dress hung off her shoulder. Even across the room in the dim light, the blonde's hair looked mussed and her face incredibly flushed. She was still breathing hard. And she wore a loopy smile.

A pang of annoyance settled in the middle of Jolie's chest. She didn't want Heath. Scratch that. Some impractical part of her craved him. She refused to lie to herself. He would probably be fantastic in bed. Powell was blisteringly hot. And clearly he'd had lots of practice. Being near him made her heart rate ramp up and her palms damp. When he looked at her, she remembered that he was male, that she was female, and that chemistry could be a powerful force. No man had interested her for more than an hour in the last few years, so she gave him credit. But her attraction didn't go any further.

A few paces behind the blonde in the micro skirt, Heath emerged. With a satisfied swagger, he descended the stairs, finger-combing his dark hair laced with silver and zipping his slacks.

Jolie told herself to remain calm against the rise of irrational anger.

Unfortunately, that ship had sailed.

She tossed back the last of her drink and made a beeline for him, pushing her way through the crowd. When she reached them, Jolie looked past the midtwenties twit and over at Heath. "I want to talk to you. Now."

He met her hostility with a shrug. "About what?"

His dismissive attitude annoyed her more.

"Who are you?" The blonde glanced between them, blinking as she thought through the situation. "Is she your girlfriend?" She gasped. "Your wife?"

Neither of them answered, Jolie because she didn't owe his "date" anything. She could only assume Heath remained mute because now that he'd nailed her, he no longer cared what she thought.

"You son of a bitch!" Short Skirt screeched. "You took advantage of me when I was vulnerable."

He cocked a brow at her. "You failed to mention feeling vulnerable during any of your three orgasms."

"You're an asshole." The woman's face flushed red as she stormed away and left the bar.

Though he'd been nothing but professional to her, Jolie had suspected he had a ruthless side. She felt somewhat sorry for the blonde but took an odd comfort in the fact that she'd been right in her assessment of Heath Powell.

"Do we have a problem, Ms. Quinn? I can't imagine another reason you followed me here for the obvious purpose of delivering a dressing down that apparently couldn't wait until morning."

A ragtag band took the small stage then, and he had to shout so she could hear over the music. A couple of people lingering near the stairs nursed their beers and watched intently. "Come outside with me."

She turned and headed for the door. Her sixth sense told her that Heath wasn't following. When she whirled back, sure enough, he leaned against the banister, watching her with a dissecting stare.

Jolie marched back in his direction and tossed her hands in the air. "I know you speak English."

"The Queen's English, thank you."

His condescension about being British and obviously better annoyed her, too. She tried to put a lid on her temper and focus on Karis. In her head, she kept hearing him remind his temporary honey about her three orgasms and wondering how good he must be in order to get that reaction from a stranger in fifteen minutes.

Totally not important. "Will you please follow me outside so we can have a civilized discussion that doesn't require shouting at one another?"

"Of course. But I suspect, given your agitation, there will be shouting, regardless." With an acerbic smile, he gestured her toward the door.

Jolie resisted the urge to huff and threaded her way through the crowd. He would not get the better of her.

Once outside, she headed away from the parking lot, putting a few dozen feet between them and anyone loitering outside. Heath followed, watching their surroundings as she paused at the opening of an alley.

He shoved his hands in his pockets as if he didn't have a care in the world. "I hope you're here about a security issue."

"Stay away from my sister," she warned.

He frowned, looking genuinely perplexed. "Your sister?"

"Karis."

Heath barely responded. His brows gathered, but he gave no other reaction. "I'm aware of your sister's name. I'm merely expressing surprise that you think I'm . . . what? Sexually interested in her?"

"That's exactly what I think. I watched you work over the young blonde in the bar. It didn't take you long. A glass of wine, a few well-placed words, a soft caress, and she was yours."

"Why does that bother you, Ms. Quinn?"

"You're targeting Karis because you pick the doe-eyed girls too naive to know why they shouldn't spread their legs for a playboy like you." She scoffed. "You didn't even challenge yourself with tonight's conquest."

"I'm fascinated by your unsolicited opinion of my character," he drawled, letting her know he was anything but. "What's prompted this charming discourse? Do you always tell those in your employ what you think of their personal lives or are you making a special exception for me because you think I intend to debauch your sister?"

"Leave Karis alone. It's against Betti's policy to date another member of the staff."

"I did read the guidelines you provided. But I'm guessing your rationale for this conversation is more personal."

"Fine. She's got some breathless adoration for you. Karis is looking for a grand romance, and she's likely to pin her foolish hopes on the first man who makes her feel protected and treasured. I doubt you want that."

"Her attitude bothers you," he observed, studying her like a bug he'd pinned to a corkboard.

She bristled. "Women shouldn't be looking for someone to 'complete' them; they should be a complete person by themselves. And you prey on women with those misguided fantasies, don't you?"

"I provide single women with mutual, if temporary, companionship and pleasure."

"That's as misleading as calling tooth extraction without Novocain 'natural dental care.'"

He cocked his head at her. "You have some unsubstantiated notion that I'm mad for your sister, so you followed me after hours and saw me find a woman with whom I chose to spend a few pleasurable moments. Therefore, you've branded me a sociopathic predator. That's quite a leap."

Jolie had watched men behave this way her whole life. "I merely understand you, Mr. Powell. I see past the gentlemanly facade to the manwhore beneath. You must have loved your last position, guarding the pretty body of that world-famous director's daughter. How fabulous for you that she paid for everything in your life while you enjoyed the fringe benefit of taking her to bed."

That finally riled him.

"I never touched Mystery Mullins once." His eyes narrowed in furious warning. "Don't speak when you know absolutely nothing about either of us or the situation."

As much as Jolie hated to believe him, Heath's biting reply convinced her he'd told the truth. Fine, she'd drop that accusation. But she refused to let up about Karis until Heath agreed to leave the girl alone.

"All right. But I won't have you targeting my sister. I expect you to tell her tomorrow that those flowers you sent to soften her up were a token of your . . . professional esteem. Pick a reason. I don't care what you say as long as you gently discourage her."

Nothing overt gave away a change in Heath's demeanor but Jolie felt his surprise. "I did not send your sister flowers."

"Red tulips. I saw them on her desk earlier. She told me you left them for her. And now she likes you. Stop romancing her."

He leaned in, and she saw the faint hint of a scar bisecting his stubbled cheek. "You just witnessed my version of romance. If I want a woman, I don't bother with flowers, merely a condom. Your sister is utterly, one-hundred-percent safe from my attentions. You have my word."

"Is that supposed to mean something to me?"

"I've given you no reason to doubt me, Ms. Quinn." He studied her with a cynical gaze. "This is about you. Why are you hostile? Did a former flame tell you he would fulfill your little-girl dreams, then leave you broken hearted?"

"I don't believe in love, especially in it lasting. Karis is another story, and I'm intensely protective."

"Clearly. But I genuinely have no interest in your sister."

He said the words with all sincerity. Jolie weighed them. Maybe . . . Karis had misunderstood who had given her the flowers or why. Or she had wanted to believe they were from Heath so she'd convinced herself of that. It was even possible that, somewhere in Karis's offbeat brain, she'd wanted to see how her older sister would react to the idea of her in a relationship with the man Jolie had the hots for.

Heath Powell might be experienced, calculating, and totally male, but he'd come highly recommended as a security consultant from people she trusted. Her gut told her that—at least in this instance—he wasn't a liar.

"Excuse me for a second." She whipped out her phone and texted Karis.

Are you sure Heath gave you the flowers? Did he leave a card?

Her sister replied almost immediately. The card wasn't signed, just said that he thinks about me day and night, and he doesn't care who disapproves. Who else could it be?

So you don't know for sure that Heath sent them? She wrote back.

No.

Jolie tucked her phone away with a sigh. Mortification rolled through her in a hot flush. She'd have to apologize, damn it. "Apparently my sister isn't sure now who sent the flowers. I'm sorry that I accused you and disturbed your evening. Good night."

She whirled around and headed for her car. God, she'd all but jumped down his throat, and Jolie felt ridiculous for not asking Karis more questions before she confronted Heath. She never went to any meeting unprepared, damn it.

"Wait." Heath grabbed her arm.

Something electric arced between them, and she gritted her teeth against the sizzle.

The reaction made her even more prickly. "What?"

"Since we're off the clock and we've clearly set aside our working relationship for the moment, I think it's only right that I have the chance to say what I think of you."

She swallowed. If he was this hip to give her his opinion after she'd hurled a bunch of insults at him, she couldn't expect anything but ugly. Jolie sighed. It sucked but she'd earned it. "I'm listening."

"Excellent." He released her, his fingers curling into a fist as he began walking around her, studying her, drawing conclusions. "You don't trust men and that runs deep. It colors your decisions and prejudices everything you say to me. If you've never been in love, then your deep-seeded distrust must come from the lack of any stable father figure in your childhood."

"Thanks, Freud," she snapped.

Heath jerked back to face her and leaned in so close their noses nearly touched. "Am I wrong?"

She refused to stroll down that memory lane. "Does it matter?"

"I daresay it does. But we'll come back to that. If you were merely mistrustful of men, you would have waited until tomorrow and delivered a well-placed warning to keep me away from your sister. Instead, you came after me. And when you found me with another woman, your temper flared. If I merely lived up to your expectations of being a womanizing prick, that shouldn't make you angry at all, simply smug at being right. But you were livid. I doubt all that displeasure is on your sister's behalf. In fact, I suspect, Ms. Quinn, that *you* have more than a passing interest in me. You were jealous."

Apprehension raced through her veins. He was uncomfortably close to the truth. "You're egotistical."

"But I'm right." He gave her a tight smile. "For the record, if I intended to disregard policy and pursue a woman in the office, I wouldn't bother with your sister. As you say, she's naive and provides no challenge. But you . . . You would be far more interesting. Pretty, strong, smart, not easily bendable. Color me intrigued."

She tensed. "I'm your boss."

"Temporarily. We're both adults. Surely neither of us are prone to torrid emotional attachments. We could keep business separate from personal, couldn't we?"

Normally, she'd say yes. But working with him constantly buzzing around her, asking questions, and watching her every move had already dented her focus. "I have no intention of becoming your next conquest."

"I never planned to pursue you."

Jolie wondered why, then dismissed the question as she buttoned her red coat. "Perfect. There's nothing left to say except I'm sorry for intruding on your evening. I hope we can forget this by morning."

She had to get out of here. She'd overplayed her hand and needed to regroup, to think about how to treat him tomorrow. The last thing she wanted was for Heath Powell to decide she was a challenge he should convert into his next bed partner after all. Normally, the sexual urges of a man wouldn't concern her unless she was interested. If so, she found a way to have him for a night or two, then ended it.

Something told her that nothing with Heath would ever be that simple.

But when Jolie turned her back on him and headed for the parking lot, he snaked an arm around her middle and pulled her against his big, steely body. "I never planned to pursue you . . . but I've changed my mind."

Those soft words against her neck rolled a shiver through her. "Get your hand off me."

"I'll bet the bitch act has scared off a man or two in your past."

She jerked away and cocked her hand on her hip. "Why is it that when a man is assertive, he's hailed as alpha and take-charge. But when a woman is equally assertive, she's a bitch?"

"Oh, let's be clear. I don't believe you're a bitch at all. I think that under your steely exterior is a woman with a soft heart. You take in stray employees the way other people foster animals. Their former employers have all cast them off. They aren't perfect but under your leadership, they're productive again. You make them work hard—as they should—but you're fair. You don't wheedle effectiveness out of them by pretending to be their friend. You tell them exactly what you expect. But you're chilly with me because you fear that if you don't guard against what I make you feel, I'll slip under your defenses and bruise that untried heart of yours."

God, he'd seen way too much of her. "Don't touch me again. If I want to be psychoanalyzed, I'll hire a shrink. Other than that, I expect you to be professional and do your job. You have my promise that I won't contact you after hours unless there's an emergency. Now we're done. Don't forget we have a staff meeting tomorrow morning at eight."

She pulled her keys free from her purse and walked away as quickly as her high heels could take her.

"I felt you trembling against me," he called after her.

Jolie clamped her lips shut. No sense in acknowledging that. The best way to handle a man like Heath Powell was to ignore him.

It took every bit of her will to follow her own advice. Why did he have to be right?

As she marched to her car, she fought to catch her breath. Once inside the vehicle, she shut the doors, locked them, then glanced out the window to see the man still standing where she'd left him. He watched her every move. Swallowing down a shiver, she gripped the wheel and dragged in a breath, unable to dodge the suspicion that she had poked a sleeping bear.

Her phone buzzed in her pocket. Another text from her sister. She ignored it and launched her e-mail instead. A dozen new messages poured into her inbox but she sought the one Karis had sent a few hours ago. The one she'd sworn she had no interest in. The one she'd never intended to open.

The report Karis had compiled on Heath Powell.

Her finger trembled as she tapped the screen. The attachment took its sweet time downloading before it finally opened. She scanned the document because she needed to know her potential adversary on a personal level. Well, in part. She also felt a dangerous fascination she couldn't shake.

Jolie let out a breath. That admission had been tough but necessary. Lying to herself served no purpose. Heath's words had been like a crowbar, prying past her defenses and uncovering troubling facts she hadn't wanted to face.

Her business needed him. Tomorrow morning, he would tell her all the vulnerabilities in her physical and cyber security after observing her office and its habits. She had no doubt he'd found many, and she would address them all. If that was the extent of their interaction, Jolie would be relieved. But the unspoken attraction shimmering between them was like a genie. Now that it was out, she couldn't force it back in the bottle.

Damn it.

The words of the report swam before her eyes. Born outside of Liverpool. Upper-middle-class upbringing, lucky him. Decent student with a penchant for ferreting out information better kept hidden and working the system when it suited him. Jolie hadn't known that but she could picture it. After some time in university, he served for a few years in the military, including a tour in Afghanistan, before he suddenly appeared on MI5's payroll, just as he'd said during their interview.

But he'd failed to mention the bit about his wife being gunned down in broad daylight in the middle of an open-air market in London seven years ago. Jolie gasped. The case remained unsolved but the government suspected home-grown extremists. Based on what Karis had tracked down, Heath hadn't been involved in any lasting relationship since. There was more but she didn't need it.

Against her will, empathy softened her resolve. Were those women Callie said he frequently picked up a balm for his grieving heart? A way to pass the time? His attempt to forget the pain of his wife's loss?

The sound of Jolie's breaths echoing in her head mingled with the loud thump of her heart. She wished she could take back every word she'd said to him tonight. She had no excuse except the one he'd already discerned. Her reluctant personal interest had clouded her brain, and when he'd given another woman his attention, she'd handled it badly.

Jolie stared out the windshield, then turned to glance back at the alley.

Heath still stood there, unflinching, unmoving.

She owed him a genuine apology.

With a sigh, she pushed her car door open and stood, shoving her phone in her coat pocket along the way. When she reached him, he didn't say a word, just raised a brow, his dark eyes dissecting and undressing her at once.

"I'm sorry. Really." She didn't dare tell him that Karis had dug into his background. Jolie doubted he'd appreciate knowing she'd read about his tragic past. "You didn't do anything to deserve my outburst. I've had a bad day. I meant to protect my sister. You pushed some of my buttons."

"Still telling me I'm wrong about why?"

Of all the things that had passed between them tonight, he zeroed in on that. "Why are you fishing to hear that I want you?"

He drilled her with those dark eyes. "Because I want you, too."

With a silent gasp, she stared, the moment still and sharp. "Forget it. I've given you reasons for my earlier behavior. I promise it won't happen again. Can we be two professional adults and move forward?"

"In the office? Certainly. I never bring my personal life to my job."

"Good. That makes two of us."

"But I'm not letting this go. Girls like the one in the bar tonight are a way to get through an evening, but they don't actually interest me. You reminded me that I haven't challenged myself in far too long."

She'd walked right into that trap. Unless she wanted to suddenly declare that she was unable to separate the personal from the professional, she had to figure out some other way to combat him.

"Take your challenge elsewhere. I have too much going on now to handle a fling. I don't do friends with benefits. I'm even less interested in anything lasting."

He sent her a faint smile. "We're on the same page."

"Perfect."

"But it doesn't matter. Consider this fair warning: I'm coming after you and I intend to have you underneath me. I won't rest until I do. So shore up your defenses and work yourself up tightly. That way when I seduce you, it will be even sweeter."

"It's not a competition," she grated out.

"It's not."

Then why bother? Because he needed another conquest to make

himself feel big? Because he wanted to use her so he didn't have to think about his late wife's murder? "Fixate on something else. Try yoga."

Heath opened his mouth to hit her with some witty rejoinder, she was sure. Instead her phone buzzed insistently. She glanced at the display. Her sister. As ticked off as she was with Karis right now, Jolie might have declined the call but it gave her an excuse to pause this conversation with Heath until she got her head together.

She pressed the button and lifted the cell to her ear. "What?"

"Did you get my text?" she whispered. "I was hearing noises just outside the building but now I hear footsteps *in* the office. Heading down the hall. They're coming toward me."

Chapter Three

Rule for success number three:
Not everything will go your way.

STANDING inches from him, Heath couldn't miss the way Jolie froze. Panic widened her eyes, and whether she realized it or not, she looked to him, her mossy gaze silently begging for his help.

Something had gone wrong.

He cupped her shoulder in silent comfort. Yes, he was here for her. If she hadn't been so worried, she wouldn't have appreciated his gesture.

"Where are you?" Jolie asked, then yanked the phone from her ear and enabled the speaker.

"—Turned off the lights, left my desk, and sneaked into the break room when I heard what sounded like someone messing with the door to our suite," Karis panted. "Then I heard footsteps in the hall, so I eased the door closed and called 911. They told me it would be another ten minutes. I'm scared."

Heath had heard all he needed to. He grabbed Jolie and hustled her to his motorcycle only a few paces away.

As he tossed her his helmet, she tried to set Karis at ease. "I'm with Heath just down the street. We're on our way."

"Do you know where the intruder is now?" he asked the girl on the other end of the line.

"I think in Jolie's office." Karis's muted voice trembled.

"Are there more than one?"

"I-I didn't hear any others."

"Good. Get out of the break room." She couldn't reach the lone door out of the suite, which led directly to the parking lot, without passing the intruder, so he could only do his best to keep her safe. "Duck behind the cubicles and dash to the file room at the end of the hall. That door has a lock. Use it, then quietly wedge one of the chairs inside under the doorknob and wait until help arrives."

"Okay."

He turned to Jolie. "You have to disconnect the call and hold on to me."

Reluctantly, she nodded and told Karis to stay safe. As he started the motorcycle, anxiety bit into his gut. He refused to let anyone else die on his watch, especially not someone whose loss would crush Jolie.

He didn't want to think about why that mattered to him.

Though rattled, she quickly straddled the bike and settled onto the seat behind him, wrapping her arms around his waist. Then Heath bolted out of the parking lot and zipped toward the office. Tomorrow he'd planned to present his recommendations for a more secure workplace to Jolie and hopefully get the measures in place quickly. He wished now he'd simply bypassed her approval process and installed the equipment he knew she needed.

Streetlights blurred on either side of him as he dodged cars, speeding toward Betti. His head spun with all the scenarios he might encounter once they reached the office. Behind him, Jolie clung tightly, her whole body stiff. He suspected she'd never been on the back of a motorbike, and he'd love to take her for a long ride, gauge her mood after being plastered against him for an hour or two with the purr of the motor between her legs.

Yes, he should leave his boss alone. But she'd sparked something inside him he didn't think he could simply snuff out. He couldn't recall the last time he'd felt this alive merely being near a woman.

Dangerous thoughts, and he shoved them aside. Only saving Karis was important now.

Who the devil could be in Betti's offices? That burglar who'd been reported in the area seemed the most likely suspect. The coward apparently waited until after hours when he wasn't likely to encounter anyone who'd put up a fight. He intentionally hit small businesses without alarm systems and quickly thieved all their technical gadgets, probably having some black market buyer ready and waiting. But no one had ever reported coming face-to-face with the prowler, so Heath didn't know if the man was armed or would be dangerous if confronted.

As they reached the parking lot outside of Betti's offices, he saw Karis's blue compact still in the lot and dimmed the headlight of his cycle, putting the engine in neutral and coasting around the side of the building, away from the door to Jolie's suite.

She tore off the helmet and shoved it at him, then darted for the door. With one hand, he hung the helmet on the handlebars. With the other, he gripped her arm and gave it a yank. "Stay here. You can't barge in."

"My sister—"

"Won't be any safer if you dash in half-cocked. Wait here."

"Like hell." She jerked from his touch. "I'll stay behind you if that makes you feel better but I won't let you leave me altogether."

Heath pulled his gun from his holster and gritted his teeth as he took her hand and crept toward the building. "If the situation weren't dire, I'd take you over my knee."

She sent him a sideways glare. "I'm not a misbehaving child."

"No, you're a bloody stubborn woman."

The light bulb seemed to go off in her head. "I don't submit."

She might not think so . . . but interesting that her mind had gone there. Given all the responsibilities she juggled and how tightly she was wound? Heath would bet she did. "Let's go."

Now that he suspected they had a mutual interest, he didn't simply want to touch Jolie, he felt compelled to.

"Is that thing loaded?" She nodded at the semiautomatic.

"It won't do me a whit of good if it isn't."

"Thank god."

Heath liked that she understood the need for a firearm in moments like this and didn't act squeamish that he kept one. Then again, Jolie seemed practical if nothing else.

He palmed the gun in one hand and gripped hers with the other. "Stay behind me."

For once, she didn't argue. He approached the front of the building, peeking through the wall of windows that overlooked the cubicle area, searching for any lights that shouldn't be on or obvious beams from a torch. Nothing, which meant the intruder likely wasn't sneaking around the employees' desks. He probably wasn't bothering with the break room, either. No electronics there except a less-than-stellar coffee pot and a TV worth sixty pounds at best on eBay. That meant the burglar could only be in the file room he'd told Karis to barricade herself in, the conference room with the projector, or Jolie's office—near the suite's only exterior door.

He wished like hell the willful woman behind him would stay outside but she was determined. So he tugged on her hand and led her toward the office.

Heath glanced at his watch. Another six minutes before the police arrived. Jolie's sister could be in deep peril now. They couldn't afford to wait.

"Stay down," he whispered.

She nodded and crept toward the door, mirroring his every move. Through the wall of windows toward the end of the building, the intense beam of an LED flashlight suddenly arced through Jolie's office. Moments later the glow from her computer shafted the room with a softer glow, and the intruder clicked off the torch.

Cursing under his breath, Heath peered through the windows again and spotted someone in Jolie's chair—short hair, broad shoulders, definitely tall. Male. That didn't surprise him. But the sight of the man hunched over the PC, studying it intently, did.

"Why is he reading my computer?" she hissed.

Good question. "Anything sensitive on the hard drive?"

"The sketches of the summer collection I'll be launching soon, along with my manufacturing sources. That's probably the most valuable information."

When she'd suggested industrial espionage to him during their initial interview, he'd been hard-pressed to believe that a bunch of fashionistas could be cutthroat enough to steal intellectual property. After a few hours of research, he'd rethought his position. Now it looked as if she'd been right.

"Is the computer password protected?"

"Of course." She hesitated. "But after I had the flu last fall, Arthur insisted I leave someone the password in case he has to generate payroll in my absence. I keep everyone's electronic time cards secure because they include Social Security numbers. Wisteria has the password taped to the desk, under her keyboard."

Heath nearly groaned. They'd definitely be talking about that vulnerability, along with a list of other items, at tomorrow morning's meeting. Provided, of course, everyone survived tonight.

"Is your computer secured to your desk?" he asked.

"No. Someone could unplug it and walk off. God, that sounds ridiculous when I say it."

"We'll discuss precautious later."

"I don't see Karis." Jolie texted her sister and stared at the phone, her apprehension thick in the air. "She's not answering."

"She may not have reception in the back of the building," he reminded.

Under normal circumstances, Heath would slip in, take down the intruder and wrestle him into cuffs, then ensure Karis stayed safe while he waited for police. With Jolie beside him, the scenario had to work differently.

He counted down with his fingers, maintaining silence. When he reached one, he pointed toward the office entrance and began creeping forward. She followed, crouched low so they didn't throw any shadows inside from the streetlights behind.

The opening to the suite sat slightly ajar. The intruder had picked the lock, and there'd been no alarm to disable. Just inside, the door to Jolie's office was closed. Heath peeked through the sidelight window to see the intruder still sitting in the computer's blue glow. He hoped the thug was too focused to notice the two of them sneak past.

He gave the door to the main entrance a gentle shove and slipped inside, weapon drawn and pointed at the portal to Jolie's office. She stayed right behind him.

His knees protested crouching, and he was feeling every one of his thirty-nine years, but adrenaline kept him upright and sharp. With a wave of his hand, he motioned Jolie toward the back of the suite and the file room he hoped Karis had been able to reach safely.

Before Jolie could head back, Heath heard the first peal of the police sirens.

He peeked through the sidelight again and saw the moment the intruder heard, too. The man jerked and leapt to his feet, the chair rolling across the industrial rug before he yanked on the computer's cords. The beam of his flashlight jerked and circled again. Footsteps pounded toward her office door.

A few feet away, Jolie froze. Damn it, she would be one of the first things the burglar spotted once he emerged from her office.

"Hide!" Heath hissed, pointing at Wisteria's big wooden desk.

With a shaky nod, she dove under the monstrosity, out of the burglar's sight.

A moment later, the stranger emerged from her office. He was too busy stomping his way to the door, trying to escape amid the sirens drawing closer, to notice anyone hidden in the nearby shadows.

Heath waited until the man inched past him, obviously carrying a computer in his latex-gloved hands—and no weapon in sight.

As soon as the man tried to sneak out the suite's door, Heath tackled the thug from behind.

The burglar grunted as he went down. Jolie's computer clattered to the carpet as he came up swinging, twisting to dislodge the unexpected weight on top. Heath wasn't about to let go.

He pressed his gun against the ski mask covering the intruder's head. "Don't move."

The man beneath him froze. Heath glanced back to ensure Jolie was safe. He spotted her, still curled beneath Wisteria's desk.

"Should I find something to tie his hands?" she asked, her voice surprisingly even.

"The police should be here any moment. You did well," he praised her before focusing on the thief again. "What are you doing here, wanker?"

Silence.

"I suggest you talk to me. I daresay I'll be more reasonable than my SIG Sauer."

Still not a word. Heath knew the man hadn't passed out. Every muscle beneath him felt tense and poised for action. He could almost feel the trespasser's thoughts racing, most likely plotting a viable method of escape.

The sirens drew closer, and Heath shifted his interrogation into high gear. If he wanted to know what this criminal had been up to before the police took the man away, he had to act fast.

"Talk now or I'll shoot your fingers off one at a time. You've got five seconds."

Suddenly, every light in the office flipped on, temporarily blinding him.

"Jolie!" Karis screamed and darted down the hall.

"Stay down," he growled at her.

"Karis?" Jolie sounded downright desperate to reassure herself that the girl was all right.

They might seem as different as two sisters could be but they loved each other.

During that distraction, the intruder elbowed Heath in the ribs, squirming before giving him a mighty shove. As Heath toppled back, the thug scrambled to his feet and darted for the door, drawing a semiautomatic and pointing it Heath's way. With the other hand, he bent to retrieve Jolie's laptop.

Adrenaline making him sweat and his heart pound, Heath found himself staring down the barrel of a gun. He pulled the trigger first, firing at the assailant. The bloke feinted right but grunted out a curse and dropped the computer to clutch his arm. As the machine plunked to the ground, the burglar fired back into the empty doorway a few times, then ran.

After a bullet whizzed past his ear, Heath darted after the intruder as the sirens drew closer, now a mere block away.

"Stay here," he barked at the sisters, then took off after the thief, his feet pounding the pavement.

Why the bloody hell had the man been in Jolie's office? What had he sought? And why had he tried to take only her computer? Did it contain more secrets than she let on?

The questions raced through Heath's head as he pursued the dark form, gripping his weapon and ready to shoot. He sized up his foe. Fast, athletic, smart. Not quite the amateur he would have expected from a typical burglar.

As soon as the prowler could, he disappeared into a cluster of trees behind the building. The foliage shrouded the ambient light, swallowing them both up in darkness.

Heath gripped his gun and followed, shoving leafy branches from his face, pursuing where the rustling ahead led him. A dozen steps later, when he shoved his way through a thick wall of brush, the man was gone. Heath scanned the sidewalks dimmed by shadow. The sound of nearby cars drowned out footfalls.

Behind and beside Betti's offices sat industrial buildings and warehouses. They should be locked tight. Beyond that lay a major road. Pedestrian traffic less than two-tenths of a kilometer down that street would be heavy around the area's bars and restaurants.

Heath followed his gut. If he'd planned this job, his exit strategy would have been to blend in on the busy street and disappear.

Once he covered a few blocks east and people milled about everywhere, he holstered his weapon. The criminal could easily be swallowed by the crowd. He would find it equally simple to steal one of the many cars parked along the curb and disappear.

The police would be with Jolie and Karis by now. As much as Heath hated to leave them, he refused to let this thieving prick go without giving chase.

He dodged pedestrians as they strolled from restaurant to bar, headed to their cars, walking hand in hand. Many paused to stare at him. Some jumped out of his way as if they sensed the urgency and adrenaline pouring off him. Heath fell back on his training, scanning everyone he passed. Finally, he zeroed in on a man fumbling his way into a black sedan at the curb, holding his forearm awkwardly.

Heath kicked into overdrive, reaching the vehicle just as the man dove inside, yanked down his ski mask again, and started the engine. Heath didn't dare shoot now or he'd risk hitting a bystander. Instead, he dove for the back of the car as the vehicle lurched into traffic.

Launching himself onto the trunk, Heath tried to hold on but as the car accelerated, he lost his grip and tumbled onto the street.

He came up with a curse. This wasn't over. His legs might not run as fast as when he'd been twenty-five but there was nothing wrong with his eyes. Even without the car's taillights engaged, he'd managed to see every number and letter.

He hoped that would be enough to nail this bastard because he didn't want Jolie in danger again.

* * *

HEATH jogged back to Betti's offices, multitasking with a phone call to Mitchell Thorpe's friend and Callie's legal husband, Sean Mackenzie. As a former FBI agent, the man had contacts Heath needed.

"Hello?"

"Not to be rude, but I need to bypass the small talk. Will you run a license plate for me?"

Sean didn't hesitate. "Sure. I'll pull a few strings. What's the number?"

Heath rattled it off, still dragging in deep breaths, and explained the situation. "I chased the wanker all the way to his damned car but I'm determined to find out who he is and why he broke into Jolie's office."

"Give me a few hours and someone will get back to you. Callie is having contractions. She's not due for another three weeks. If Thorpe and I take her to the hospital, I'll put this in good hands."

Heath couldn't ask for more. "Thank you. I hope Callie and the baby will be all right."

"Thanks. If you need any more help, call Jack Cole or one of the Edgington brothers. I'll text you their numbers."

He'd met them once briefly after returning from London. He hoped he didn't have to ring reinforcements but he would if danger warranted it.

They rang off as Heath trekked through Betti's parking lot. The door to the suite stood wide open. A couple of patrol units had skidded to a stop, bracketing an unmarked car. The officers were obviously inside, probably taking statements from the sisters.

As he approached the door, a patrolman stopped him. "Sorry. Only witnesses allowed."

"I fought the intruder before I chased him down the street. He managed to get away but—"

"That's very dangerous, sir. You should have waited for the police. We're trained for this sort of thing."

Heath didn't have the patience for this young cop's posturing. "I served three years in the British military, then another ten with MI5." He'd been well trained longer than this officer had been out of puberty. "Where's the detective in charge?"

"Heath!" a woman screeched across the office.

While he didn't think Jolie would keen so loudly for any man, he whirled around. Instead, Karis barreled down the hall and launched herself against him. She stunned him even more by throwing her arms and legs around him, then pressing an urgent kiss to his lips. He was still trying to process why the devil she meant to suck the air from his lungs and how to gracefully extricate himself when Jolie strolled into view with a scowl.

Damn it all.

With a firm grip, he pried Karis away and set her on her feet, clearing his throat. "Are you both all right?"

"Yes." The younger sister looked at him with something uncomfortably akin to hero worship as she pressed a hand to his chest and blinked at him with big brown eyes. "Thanks to you. I was terrified out of my mind but knowing that you were coming to save me, I kept calm."

"I'm fine," Jolie answered in clipped tones. "You?"

Obviously, she'd been worried about her sister. But did she imagine that he'd come to Karis's aid and chased the intruder to earn the girl's adoration and seduce her? Perhaps. Jolie was a cynical creature. He understood that well.

But as he'd already pointed out, she wouldn't be annoyed by any potential lover of his if she didn't care.

Heath put more distance between himself and Karis. "Excellent. I'm sorry I didn't catch the prowler. But I'm working another angle."

And he refused to say more within earshot of the police. If their intruder had been the burglar common to this area, the Dallas PD had sought him unsuccessfully for weeks. Heath intended to investigate on his own and figure out who'd broken in and why—without sticky bureaucratic red tape. Jolie had hired him to keep Betti safe. He intended to do his job.

Still, her attitude remained chilly. "Thanks."

He held in a curse. Even if Jolie believed he had no designs on Karis, she might cut him cold. Besides being driven, she was wary of letting men close.

Heath wanted to understand her.

"I was so worried about you, chasing down that awful burglar who cornered me." Karis pressed close. "I was afraid he'd hurt you, shoot you. Oh . . ." She gasped. "I couldn't have lived with myself."

He gave her a brotherly pat. "As you see, I'm perfectly well."

"The police are still asking questions. Excuse me." Jolie stepped away.

He lunged into her personal space, wishing he could take away the worry and displeasure pinching her mouth. "Are you certain you're all right?"

Before she could reply, a fortysomething female detective approached and "invited" him to the conference room so she could ask all the usual questions. The interrogation told Heath they had already decided the neighborhood burglar was their man. The detective also demanded he show his permit to carry a firearm in Texas, explain his spent shell casings, and hand over his gun for a quick examination. The one bit of good news? The intruder had bled enough for them to capture his DNA, and they intended to run it through their systems. Sadly, that could take months.

Heath feared the Dallas PD would be useless in this investigation.

Finally, the woman finished interrogating him. When they emerged from the conference room, he spotted a lanky male detective standing with Jolie and Karis. He spoke a few words meant to be reassuring. The police would, of course, investigate fully, check in, have units canvass the neighborhood, and all that rubbish.

Then both of the detectives disappeared into Jolie's office to hover around the CSI unit, who wrapped up their examination. As they gathered their things, Jolie ducked into her office, straightening the room to her usual pristine standards.

Heath couldn't stop himself from watching her every move. Obviously, she wasn't happy. Besides her earlier anger, the disarray now all around agitated her. The sense of violation that someone had broken into her space did, too. He understood her conflict. Her beloved sister had been in danger. Her worry churned. Her adrenaline pumped. Then the moment the peril passed, that same coddled sibling put a lip-lock on the man she was reluctantly attracted to. The entire evening must have jarred Jolie's meticulously balanced world. Right now she couldn't hide behind investor reports and design sketches.

Though he wished it wasn't necessary, he had to set her even more off-kilter tonight.

Karis tugged on his sleeve. When he turned to her, she blinked at him with big brown eyes brimming with tears.

"Will you hold me?"

He hesitated, turning over possible outcomes and consequences. Finally, he shook his head. "I'm the big, bad wolf, the sort who would eat you alive for sport and leave your bloody carcass in the dirt. Choose wisely. Pick another man."

She reared back. "You're not like that. You're brave and wonderful and—"

"Not interested in your white lace and promises."

Karis blinked innocently. "I-I didn't . . . I'm not—"

"Looking for your Prince Charming? Yes, you are. I've no wish to hurt your feelings but I did not leave you flowers."

"Oh." She looked crestfallen, then she sent him an intent little frown. "Would you, if you had thought of it?"

"No. The last woman I had sex with, about an hour ago, was someone whose name I still don't know. She's hardly the first such stranger. I have a very simple iron-clad no-repeat rule. So even if you were foolish enough to let me whisk you to bed, I would never touch you again. For your sake, don't flirt with me, don't pin your fairy-tale hopes on me, and don't kiss me again."

Karis swallowed, looking hurt. "You don't have to be harsh."

He softened his tone. "I'm being honest. I'm not good for you."

"You could be," she whispered so earnestly, it almost made a dent in his cynical shell. "And I could be good for you."

"I'd only hurt you."

And he didn't want to discuss it anymore, especially when he turned to find Jolie talking to the male detective, a tall, athletic man in his early thirties. The suit smiled at Jolie as he passed her his card and patted her hand.

Heath had no right or reason to be jealous. She could probably gut a man with her tongue and leave him trembling in a pool of his own blood. But damn if he didn't want to shove the detective's balls down his throat until he understood that Jolie was off-limits. Heath only refrained because he hadn't touched her—yet.

Why did he want her so badly? She wasn't his usual. His wife, Anna, had been beautiful but reserved, soft. She'd needed his steady hand and guidance. Mystery, though more spirited, had been much the same. Jolie would eat a man for breakfast. In fact, this morning, he'd watched her bark into the phone at a supplier who had displeased her. She'd laid down the law with a sharp rebuke and some hardball. He'd been fascinated by the pursing of her full lips, the sassy flip of her dark tresses sweeping away from her striking face to brush her shoulders. She did everything with passion, conviction, and a feminine confidence he'd never seen.

More than his interest had risen. The meaningless hookup with the blonde had done nothing to take the edge off his desire. Heath feared very much that, until he had Jolie, only she would do.

With a trembling lower lip, Karis turned toward her desk, pretending to fumble for her purse and keys so she could avoid the embarrassment of looking at him. It probably made him a bastard, but that suited Heath. She might have taken his words more firmly than he intended but she'd finally gotten the message.

Once the police had left and Jolie closed the door behind them, she approached, glancing between him and her sister with a frown. "What did you say to her?"

"Not to touch me again."

Satisfaction settled on her face before she blanked it. "Thank you for being professional."

He drilled his stare deep into her. "I wasn't. I warned her away because I want you."

"It's not happening, Romeo. If you don't leave it alone, I'll fire you."

"You could do that but you would be putting yourself and everyone who works here at greater risk. I have pages and pages of recommendations that you can—and should—implement to keep your business and employees safe. If you have to start over with another security specialist, that will set you back weeks, maybe more. I'm not sure you have that sort of time before whoever this intruder and what he represents strikes again. So, you can either cut me loose because you feel threatened or you can work with me."

"I don't feel threatened, just annoyed."

Rubbish. I've got your number. "You're the one most at risk."

With a roll of her eyes, she anchored a hand on her hip. "How so?"

"This intruder didn't make a grab for every technical gadget in your office, merely your computer. Those policemen who dusted your office diligently for prints? They won't find anything. He wore surgical gloves. He wasn't stealing in order to afford his next fix. Nor was he terribly rattled after being confronted by unwanted company. He had a weapon and a quick exit strategy. So I doubt very much he was your neighborhood burglar. He was, however, a professional with a target."

She hesitated. "So what do you think is going on?"

"If tonight's break-in was about industrial espionage, you're the brains behind the operation. You hold the capital and connections.

You *are* the brand. If your competitors want you out of business, they would start with you."

"Agreed. What do you propose next?"

"I need more time to get to the bottom of this so I can protect you."

She sent him a sideways glare. "If you stop trying to wheedle me into bed, I'm on board. But I don't date where I work."

"I don't want to date you."

Her lips tightened more. "I don't want to fuck you."

"Liar," he accused softly.

"I won't be one of your conquests."

"You can't be. Those, once scaled, are easily forgotten. You're different. I want you far more than I'm comfortable admitting."

"Well, now I know which sister you'd rather hit on. Why didn't you just say so?" Karis gripped her keys, shooting Jolie a pouty stare. "Good night."

Even as he cursed the girl's timing, he stepped in front of her, blocking her exit. "Not so quickly."

"What?" The younger sister flounced.

"Because you were the one in the office when the intruder broke in, I want to ensure he's not waiting for you at home. Let me follow you there and make sure your apartment is clear."

Karis shook her head. "I'll be fine."

"Don't put embarrassment before safety," he chided.

"Whatever." She grabbed the strap of her purse. "Keep up."

"You're coming as well," he murmured to Jolie. "The intruder might have barged his way in while Karis was working here alone but he focused on *your* office. If he was looking for something in particular, it's quite likely that he'll look next at your place."

Jolie's expression told him that she wanted to disagree but couldn't fault his logic. "Five minutes. You look, then you leave."

"While I'm there, I intend to make sure your security is up to snuff."

Reluctantly, she gave in. "Then be quick. Once I lock up my computer, we'll go."

They made their way to the car park. Heath took Jolie on the back of his bike to her vehicle before they all caravanned to Karis's little apartment. She parked, and he did the same before he followed the younger sister into her flat. Within seconds, he knew no one had disturbed it. Still, he searched carefully before declaring her clear. The windows of the third floor unit would be difficult for anyone to climb through. Her door seemed solid, her deadbolt relatively sturdy.

"You should be safe here tonight," he told Karis.

"You don't care."

"Don't confuse a lack of romantic interest with a lack of concern for your safety."

She looked away, visibly chagrined. "I'll be fine."

And she would be. Karis was stronger than she thought.

He cupped her chin and raised it, peering down into her eyes. "You're lovely and young and someone far less cynical will scoop you up someday. I'm simply not that man."

"You'd rather have my sister." And she sounded glum.

He wasn't going to justify who he wanted or why. "That simply means you're intended for someone else. If you see or hear anything suspicious, you have my number."

Karis nodded. "Be good to Jolie. Very few people have been."

He and Ms. Quinn might be terrible for one another in the long run but he wasn't thinking about tomorrow now. "Sleep well."

Heath headed out the door, then followed Jolie. He intended to make sure she arrived home to an empty place and stayed safe. Whatever happened after that . . . happened.

Chapter Four

Rule for success number four:
When opportunity knocks, answer the door.

As they approached the front door of Jolie's chic condo complex, Heath scanned the lobby for anyone who looked too watchful or out of place. Nothing but hipsters arguing politics and young professionals on their mobile devices. The building was everything trendy he didn't subscribe to. Nearby coffee bar, twenty-four hour gym facilities. Sleek and chrome and gray, lacking all hint of character.

He'd lived in Britain with its traditional architecture, quirky layouts, and pokey rooms for too long to understand, he supposed.

Beside him, Jolie looked tense. "Was my sister all right?"

"I assured her that her apartment was clear. She locked up behind me. I gave her my number just in case." He volunteered information because Jolie would never ask. "I didn't touch her."

She punched the button for the elevator. "I didn't think you did."

"Really?"

"You were in her place for less than five minutes. That would be working fast, even for you. Besides, you'd already told Karis no. She would never have pouted that way if she hadn't been sure you meant it."

"You asked me to gently discourage her. I tried not to upset her."

The elevator arrived with a ding. She climbed into the empty car and pressed the button for the sixth floor. "I know. And if you toughened her up a little, maybe that would be good for her. Some heartache might help her mature."

Heath couldn't disagree, based on what he'd seen. "I'll bet you were never naive."

She shook her head. "I'm too pragmatic."

"Indeed. Because your father broke your heart somewhere along the way."

As the doors slid shut, enclosing them alone in the lift, Jolie stiffened, then tried to steady her temper. "Why do you keep digging at me?"

It was a fair question. He simply didn't have an answer she would like. "I want to understand you."

"That's not necessary for you to do your job."

"It's not." But he had no intention of backing down.

Jolie Quinn compelled him. If he learned her well enough, maybe she'd lose her shine. Or he'd figure out how to get her into bed and fuck her out of his system.

"Here's what you need to know: I like to win. I've always wanted to be my own boss. I have an eye for fashion and seeing trends come. I'm a good negotiator. Betti was a perfect fit for my passions and talents."

She hadn't boasted, as far as Heath could tell. "Before you hired me, I looked into you. You doubled your profits after your first year in business and every year since, despite a difficult economy. In fact, last year you increased that percentage even more."

"I'm proud of my accomplishments, but money isn't the goal. It's a means to prevent being beholden to anyone else and to keep score with the competition. No denying it's nice, but what I've been able to make won't support my expansion plans in the necessary timeframe, which is all I really want. So I clearly didn't do well enough."

He scowled. "You're awfully hard on yourself."

The lift stopped, and the doors dinged open. "If I'm not, a few dozen competitors and fashion bloggers are always willing to be. It's better if I anticipate their criticism and counter before it's too late."

Something drove Jolie to succeed. She had a thirst to thrive without relying on others. Her strength intrigued him, but more, he wanted to see if he could scratch her hard surface and find the soft woman beneath. He wanted her vulnerable to him.

So fucking dangerous.

When she strode from the elevator and down the hall, she bent her head to dig in her purse for her keys.

Heath couldn't resist proving she needed him for something.

Once they jingled in her hand, he rushed her from behind, grabbed the ring from her grip, and jammed the key in the lock with one hand. With the other, he grabbed her hair and tugged. Before she could do more than gasp, he shoved her inside and slammed the door.

Heart racing, he pushed her against the adjoining wall face-first, then covered her back with his body.

God, he couldn't wait to take every one of her curves in his hands and caress her until she begged for him.

"What the hell are you doing?" Her breathing accelerated. No doubt, her heart rate did the same.

"When you approach your door, you should never bury your head in your purse. Have your keys in hand well in advance and be alert. Otherwise, you've made yourself an easy target."

She struggled to dislodge him but he'd wedged her against the wall, fist in her hair, rendering her essentially immobile. "Let go. The intruder, whatever he wanted, didn't come after me physically."

"Yet. But he might. You have a lot to learn."

"Check my condo for intruders and get the hell out." She struggled to shake him off.

Her anger fired Heath's blood even more. "We do this my way.

You design the clothes, lead the staff, and run the office. This is where I'm in charge."

"Security, fine. That's why I hired you."

"And sex," he vowed in her ear. "I'm always in charge there."

She bucked again. "I'm not having sex with you."

"You'll find I can be persuasive."

She scoffed. "With naive little doormats, sure. Sadly for you, that's not me. Let go."

Heath didn't want to. He burned to hold her. Oddly, her refusal only made him more determined to change her mind.

For now, he released her and stepped back. "Lock your door."

Jolie did, but when she raised her hands to her deadbolt, he saw her shaking.

"Did I scare you?" he asked.

"Pfft. No."

Good. That meant he affected her on a deeper level. He shook her foundations, made her aware, aroused her in a way she didn't understand. The same was true for him.

"Wait here. I'll check the rest of your flat."

He inspected every room, closet, and cranny in the next two minutes and learned that she was, indeed, alone. And she kept her personal space every bit as tidy as her office. He smelled her everywhere, something citrus with a hint of musk—teasing and feminine. Imagining her in the queen bed with all the fluffy pillows or the big glass-walled shower turned him on.

As soon as Heath finished in her bedroom, he sauntered into the kitchen to find her pouring a glass of red wine, seemingly determined not to look at him. "Coast clear?"

"Indeed."

"Good. See you tomorrow."

Normally, he'd take his cue and leave. But nothing that had happened tonight had been normal. "I'd like to ask a few questions."

"The police have already done that."

"You're paying me to get to the bottom of this break-in. Do you really worry so much that I'll seduce you that you're willing to let your burglary go unsolved?"

Jolie slammed her glass on the counter. "God, your opinion of yourself is high. You don't do that much for me."

"So I misunderstood your trembling earlier. If you aren't afraid of me—and why should you be?—the only other explanation is that I get to you."

"I'm hungry and tired," she bit out.

"That makes your heart race?" He stepped closer, determined to have her look at him. "Makes your nipples bead?"

Instantly, her head snapped up and she flipped an angry stare at him. "Okay, so I noticed you're a man. I don't sleep with every guy I'm attracted to."

Heath liked flustering her. Just like a bit of heartache would help Karis, a little loss of composure would do Jolie loads of good.

"I thought I didn't do that much for you," he teased.

"You don't. If you did, I would have already slept with you."

She was determined to keep the upper hand. He was equally determined to show her that she didn't have to with him.

"Why do you think you need to control everything and everyone around you?"

"What?" As soon as she spit out the word, she shook her head. "I don't."

"The absolutely meticulous apartment? Control."

"I like things neat and orderly," she countered.

"The way you run the office, manage projects, negotiate deals. You're always in control. I've watched you." He swiped a finger across the fastening at the neck of her blouse. "You control your employees, your schedule, your appetite, your temper. You even control the thermostat—"

"I'm a doer, Mr. Powell. I maintain order so there's no chaos. Ask your questions about the break-in and leave."

"Do you think you can control me?"

She didn't answer right away. "I wasn't trying to."

But some part of her wanted to give it a go, at least long enough to make him stop digging into her psyche. He suspected she'd grown up with chaos, minus a strong male figure, and now sought order to keep ugly surprises to a minimum.

"I'm not the enemy, Jolie," he assured softly.

Their exchange had only served to put her on edge and increase her need to manage the situation. She'd had a difficult evening. If he wanted to find out more about her so he could exorcise his attraction, he had to set her at ease, focus on his job. Then maybe they could see where that led.

She glared at him, all green eyes and fire. "Then stop harassing me. I don't need it."

"You don't. But you bring out something primal the man in me can't ignore."

"Well, you shouldn't be too primal now since you've already scratched your itch with . . . what was her name?"

"No idea."

"Lovely," she said tartly, then downed more wine. "You and I don't have a personal interaction, just to be clear. Ask your questions, then go home."

He wouldn't mention just now that "home" was a room at Dominion, the BDSM club Mitchell Thorpe owned. If he decided to stay in Dallas, he'd rent a place of his own, but this served his purpose for now.

"Of course. Shall we sit?" He nodded at the spotless white sofa on the other side of the breakfast bar.

"All right." Then, as if she realized she hadn't offered, she held up the bottle. "Wine?"

"I'll take a glass. Thank you."

She poured. "You're welcome."

As soon as she handed him a stem, he stepped back to allow her to pass. She settled into an oversized gray chair, so he took the right third of the couch and sipped his vino. Lush and dense, layered with notes of berry and plum. "This is a good cab."

"You know wine?"

"That surprises you?"

"Most men I know drink Jack Daniels or light beer."

He raised a brow. "Maybe you should improve the caliber of the men you spend time with."

"I didn't choose to spend time with them," she corrected. "My mom did."

Yes, he remembered reading that her mother had a checkered love life. "She's been divorced three times, as I recall."

"Soon to be number four, with lots of live-in boyfriends in between. Thanks for invading my privacy."

"Occupational hazard." He shrugged. "Does your mother leave them or do they leave her?"

"They leave her. She has this self-esteem issue I don't understand. She's convinced herself that she doesn't deserve better. I sometimes wonder if losers just look at her and know that she'll let them take advantage of her."

Now Jolie's need for control made perfect sense to Heath. Too much upheaval as a kid, of course. But she obviously strived every day of her life to be nothing like her mother. "You're worried Karis will follow in her footsteps. That's why you warned me away."

"Yep." She took another sip of wine, then sloshed it around her glass. "She's teetering and could go either way. I want her to develop a sense of self-worth and responsibility, to realize that every choice comes with a consequence. That ambition will never let her down."

"She isn't you. She's not driven."

"It can be a learned skill." Jolie raised her chin defensively.

Heath shook his head. "Your burning hunger to succeed is a passion that comes from within. You want to be someone. She simply wants to be happy."

Jolie sat back, studying him. "I don't understand you. You're a soldier and a secret agent, but you drink wine and psychoanalyze me . . ."

He didn't fit into any of those neat boxes she sought to compartmentalize him into. "Your sister will find her way. She's a smart girl."

"She is or I wouldn't have hired her."

"Let her figure it out. You can't control that obviously, but once she learns her worth, I think she'll bloom."

She sighed. "It's not your problem. Ask me your questions."

Subject closed. Heath let it go. In truth, Karis wasn't any of his business, and he knew Jolie wanted him out of her condo. He wished like hell he didn't ache to reach her so badly, that he could look at her as another job. But almost from the beginning, something about her had made him crave more.

"I assume our intruder isn't a simple burglar?"

"I think we've established that. So we have to ask ourselves what he wants and why."

"Either he sought the scans of my sketches—"

"But if he's been hired by a competitor, wouldn't you know who stole your work the moment you saw a similar collection?"

Jolie shifted in her chair. "Unless he or she alters it significantly. Or merely meant to bury it."

"What else could one of your rivals want?"

She scanned the room absently, biting her pillowy lower lip. The sight made him hard again. "My customer database, my supplier information, my business plan." Then she paled. "The details about my potential investor."

"Tell me about him." Heath wanted to look into the man, ensure he wasn't part of the problem.

"His name is Richard Gardner. He's the son of a recently deceased

Texas business mogul who inherited a mind-boggling amount of money. Even a fraction of that could make my business a household name almost overnight. He's agreed to be a silent partner. He's really involved in local LGBT causes. We've spoken over the phone. He understands the financial arrangement I'm proposing: In exchange for his up-front funds, he'll receive twenty percent of the profits for the next five years."

If the break-in had anything to do with Gardner, maybe Heath could pinpoint why someone would steal Jolie's computer. Or dig up useful information. "Do you know of anyone else courting him?"

"No, but who doesn't want an investor with deep pockets and no interest in interfering?" She tossed him a wry stare. "I met Gardner a few weeks ago at a fund-raiser, and because his sister loves my clothes, we decided to talk. We'll see where it goes. It's a first meeting. We haven't agreed to anything beyond bare bones. So I doubt anyone would break into my office because I'm having dinner with him on Friday. And before you ask, no, I can't think of any other enemies."

Heath tended to agree with her about the investor but he'd double-check. He felt less certain that she didn't have a nemesis somewhere in the shadows. "A disgruntled ex-employee?"

"I've never needed to downsize and, until tonight, I've never had a violent or unpleasant incident at the office."

Good to hear, but Jolie could be very direct and not at all shy about expressing her opinion. Just because no one had lashed out or talked back didn't mean she hadn't earned a foe. "To be safe, I'd like a list of all former employees."

"I'll have Wisteria compile it in the morning."

He'd figure out if any were capable of picking locks, firing weapons, and selling her secrets. "Brilliant. What about former neighbors? Classmates? Friends? I'd like lists of those as well. Any have a reason to hold a grudge?"

"None who'd want to steal the contents of my laptop. They have no interest in my business, so why would they bother?"

Exactly what Heath wanted to know. Something about this situation set off his senses. "If we figure out who, we may find out why. If the worst happens to you, what becomes of Betti?"

"Everything goes to Karis. We've talked. She knows I'd want her to take care of my mom and brother, but one person needs to run the organization."

"Can your sister do that?" he asked.

"No one else in my life is even remotely qualified." Jolie sounded tired.

"Point taken." Another reason she pushed the girl so hard. Someday, she would likely leave Karis her legacy and she wanted her sister to keep it thriving. "What about former lovers? Would any of them want to do you harm?"

"If any man raised a hand to me, he'd find himself without balls."

Heath wondered about her experience with domestic violence but didn't ask now. "Rightly so. How about a less physical form of retaliation? Did you end a relationship and break someone's heart?"

She downed the last of her wine in a few long swallows. "None of those men meant anything, and I'm sure they felt the same about me. So I can't imagine they'd be harboring latent animosity. Besides, I never kept any man around long enough to learn about my business."

So none of her ex-flames should care about the contents of her laptop. Good to hear.

He tapped a toe, glad his sturdy boots hid the nervous tic and wishing her former love life didn't matter to him.

Jolie stood and wandered restlessly to the kitchen. "More wine?"

"Please." He brought her his glass.

As she poured, Heath couldn't dismiss the facts that they were alone, that in the near silence he could hear her breathe, that the longer he stared the more he could see a faint flush crawl up her cheeks.

She finished and handed him the glass. "I really have no idea who's done this. Guess you'll have to earn your paycheck."

As she brushed past him, Jolie wouldn't look at him. But he couldn't take his eyes off her. Nor could he help but notice how pale and exhausted she looked. "I look forward to that. Did you eat dinner?"

"I never had the chance. Oh, well. It's not the first time."

Heath already knew she'd skipped lunch and he doubted she'd made time for breakfast.

He grabbed her arm and pulled her close. She looked up at him with a surprised gasp.

"Listen to me," he said. "I find your ambition sexy as hell. I don't fault you for skipping a meal now and then. But there is no fucking way you should be neglecting to eat for an entire day."

She frowned. "It's fine. I'll eat a good breakfast in the morning. Let go."

"You'll eat tonight if I have to hold the fork and feed you myself."

Jolie gritted her teeth. She looked as if she wanted to spit in his face. "Don't tell me what to do."

"Then don't be ridiculous. Eat. I'll even cook. What's in your refrigerator?"

His offer clearly surprised her. "A little of this and that. You don't have to—"

He shoved the wine in her hands. "Sit. I'll bring you something."

After scrounging up some pre-cooked chicken strips, snow peas, and mushrooms, he made a little stir-fry and added a touch of ginger and soy before pouring the mix over some instant rice and settling it all on a plate.

When he handed it to her, she looked at him as if he'd come from another planet. "You can cook?"

"A man should have skills beyond a firing range, a tool bench, and a mattress. Eat." He headed back to the kitchen to wash the dishes.

"Where's your plate?"

"I ate before carousing." He sent her a caddish smile.

She rolled her eyes and took a bite. "Thanks. It tastes amazing. Mmm . . ."

Heath enjoyed hearing her pleasure. He'd like to give her more.

"I'm surprised you find my ambition sexy." She swallowed another bite. "Most men are intimidated."

"They're fools whose small minds match their other undersized attributes."

She stifled a laugh. "Strong mother?"

"In her way, I suppose. Very much a homebody, really. She loves to cook and spend time with the family. I think she merely raised her children to be secure in themselves. I don't feel less masculine around an ambitious woman who has achieved something fantastic. Any wanker who does needs to figure out where he's lacking."

"But you don't date strong women, I guess. If tonight's . . . companion was anything to go by."

"Typically, I don't date at all."

Jolie didn't ask why. Instead, she finished up the last few bites as he slid the pan in the dishwasher. After another swallow of wine, she brought everything to the kitchen. Heath downed the last of his vino, then set the glasses on the top rack.

"Thanks for cooking. It tasted great."

She looked as if she'd caught a second wind now that she had some calories and vegetables in her. He really didn't have any other questions for her tonight. No doubt they both needed sleep before what was likely to be a busy day ahead. Yet he was loath to leave her.

"It was my pleasure. Now, for the sake of your safety, I intend to sleep on your sofa tonight. Where can I find a pillow and a blanket?"

* * *

JOLIE stared. Yes, she'd feel safer with someone here tonight to watch over her but . . . "No. Not happening."

After the wine and food, she'd felt mellow, almost happy. With one sentence, the attraction that had been simmering between them heated to something near a boil.

He crossed his arms over his wide chest, the dark cotton of his

T-shirt stretching to accommodate every bulge and ripple. "I won't negotiate on this. You have no idea who broke into your office or what they sought. Until I can investigate a bit more, I'll be the sentry between you and danger. In order to reach you, any robber, rapist, or killer will have to go through me."

Who would save her from him?

His protective mien made her belly tighten and flutter. Stupid female response. She appreciated the offer. Busy love life aside, he was a decent guy, so he didn't want to see her hurt or dead. That didn't make him her hero. That didn't mean they should get involved.

Heath could be polite. He could be confrontational. He could be a pain in her ass. She also suspected he could be dangerously seductive.

"I have an alarm system," she argued. "It's wired directly to the police."

"It's standard-issue shit. If I wanted you dead, I could bypass it in thirty seconds and kill you in the next five."

"Stop trying to scare me."

"I'm merely giving you a fact, not a ploy to stay the night. Say yes."

"No."

He stared at her as if he could see right through her and enjoyed rattling her. "The only reason you would refuse is because you're less afraid of physical danger than how I make you feel."

Jolie managed not to grimace. He was right and she didn't want this . . . whatever they had between them to cloud her head. "If that's what you think, then stay. Tonight only. I have to be on top of my game tomorrow for my staff meeting. It's the last big investor prep session before Friday's dinner. Wait here."

When she turned and scurried to the linen closet in the hall bathroom, she realized her hands were shaking. The first man to intrigue her in forever would spend tonight sprawled on her sofa just down the hall. Would she actually sleep?

Grabbing a fluffy pillow, Jolie put a crisp white case on it and snatched a spare blanket. Was Heath the sort of man whose scent would swirl in the air after a night's rest? She'd bet so because she often caught whiffs of something masculine and woodsy when he walked by. Just this morning, he'd let himself into her office to ask about keys and passwords, and she'd been so distracted she could barely answer.

Totally unacceptable. Time to get her shit together.

Yet as Jolie headed back to the living room, she couldn't help but wonder what sort of five o'clock shadow would darken Heath's face come morning. Already, the stubble covered the sharp angles of his jaw and the severe ridge of his chin as if his masculinity wouldn't be denied.

"Here you go." She shoved the linens into his hand. "Help yourself to whatever's in the kitchen. You know where everything is now. Guest bathroom is the first door on the right. Towels are under the sink. Good night." Before she could turn away, Jolie realized that he'd volunteered to inconvenience himself by sleeping on a sofa too small for his frame in order to keep her safe. He might want to get in her pants . . . but he was also helping her out. "And thanks."

When she tried to escape, Heath dropped the linens and grabbed her wrist. He stared through her bravado. Was there any part of her his dark stare couldn't dismantle? "I'll take care of you."

Was he talking about her safety? Or her sexuality?

"I know. That's why I hired you."

Maybe she only felt vulnerable tonight because she was tired, not thinking straight. Tomorrow she'd be ready to tackle everything. And it would be a cold day in hell before she ever made herself as vulnerable to a man as her mother did.

When he released her, she sent him a little wave, grabbed her phone from her purse, and headed back to her bedroom, easing the door shut. It didn't help. The knowledge that only a thin piece of wood, some drywall, and a few feet separated them plagued her thoughts.

Feeling his big presence was worse. Heath Powell was like a beacon she couldn't help but home into. Right now, he was probably stripping off his shirt and pants and—

The pipes clinked. Water rushed into the hall shower a moment later. Jolie bit back a groan. He really was getting naked. Somehow, that only reminded her that she hadn't bothered to take her sex drive out for a spin in months. But more than a neglected libido unsettled her. The fact was, she actually liked Heath. Besides being attractive, he was insightful, confident, and interesting to banter with. He also seemed perfectly comfortable with himself. And really hot. Jolie didn't find that combination often. Try never.

Damn it. Listen to her waxing poetic. She sounded a lot like Karis just before she'd chastised her younger sister earlier this afternoon.

Dropping her clothes into the hamper, she eyed her favorite La Perla nightie, a lovely splurge made of black silk. It whispered over her skin. Sheer white lace cupped her breasts, making her feel feminine and sexy. Yeah, she didn't need more of that tonight.

So she donned a plain gray cotton cami she'd picked up at Target as a poor college student.

After washing her face, she fell into bed, plugged in her phone, and flipped off the lights. She turned on some soft instrumental music to help her brain wind down and closed her eyes. Almost instantly, Heath crashed into her Zen. She liked his smile. It never failed to make her jittery, just like that dark stare of his. Why did the man get to her? Never mind that. She knew. The better question was, why did he seem so determined to provoke her? To understand her?

Maybe she mattered to him against his will and better judgment, too.

I want you far more than I'm comfortable admitting.

Those words skittered through her memory. The moment he'd confessed that her body had flashed hot, reacting almost as if he'd touched her.

"That makes two of us," she murmured to herself.

With a grunt, Jolie threw off the covers and paced. It wasn't as if she hoped that she and Heath would share some fairy-tale happily-ever-after. On the other hand, their attraction wasn't going away. So she had two choices: keep trying to ignore it—which wasn't working—or confront it head-on.

Jolie wasn't one for avoidance. "Let's get this over with."

With a squeak, the faucet shut off. She heard him yank back the shower curtain and step from the tub. She imagined him naked and hard and wanting her as badly as she ached for him.

"Damn it," she muttered as she stripped off her cami, pulled open her door, and marched down the hall.

Chapter Five

Rule for success number five:
Passion. It's all about passion . . .

ONCE she reached the living room, Jolie braced her hands on her hips, her naked body illuminated in the soft glow of the kitchen light, and waited.

The cool air caressed her skin, puckered her nipples. Seconds ticked by. She couldn't deny that she'd never felt more like a woman. Why did even the thought of Heath Powell make her feel so damn alive?

Chemistry, an unsolved mystery of the universe. Or something like that. If she had sex with him tonight, tomorrow she'd no longer wonder what it would feel like if he touched her. She could satisfy her curiosity and libido at once. Same for him. Then whatever this attraction was between them would be over. Done. Finished. *Poof!* By tomorrow, everything would be normal again. She would be in control of her life once more.

Down the hall, Heath jerked open the bathroom door. He entered the living room with a white towel wrapped around his lean waist. Water beaded on his broad shoulders that tapered down to ridged abs. He held his clothes in one fist, his gun in the other.

He was unbearably sexy. Jolie found it hard to breathe.

When he caught sight of her, he stopped, stared—and dropped his clothes where he stood. He set his weapon on the arm of the sofa, still within reach. He didn't even try to bank the hunger on his face.

Jolie panted, aware of how completely naked she was. The feeling went far beyond mere flesh.

He prowled closer, stopping when their bodies nearly brushed and she smelled soap on his skin. "Is this an invitation or are you tempting me with what I can't have?"

Once she answered him, there would be no going back. "Spend the night with me."

"You've decided I do something for you, after all? Is that why you're seducing me?"

The words she'd tossed at him earlier had come back to haunt her. Jolie wasn't surprised he hadn't let that go. She hoped he wouldn't turn her down but he might. Heath had chided her for having control issues, yet he'd already admitted he wanted to be on top in the bedroom. Not being the one to initiate might grate his masculinity or rub the in-charge man in him wrong.

"Do you want to analyze my invitation or have sex?"

"I want to have sex. I've wanted that since I laid eyes on you."

Then why had he screwed the blonde at the bar?

It didn't matter. This was a hookup, not the start of a romance. She had simply cut through the crap and made it easy for them both to scratch their mutual itch.

"I wanted you, too. My bedroom is down the hall." She headed toward the back of her unit.

Heath didn't follow. "I said I want to have sex with you. I didn't say we would."

She stopped midstride, grateful that he couldn't see her face. His rejection hurt. She would never reveal how much. Better to pretend that she could simply shrug it off.

"I guess since you've already had a piece of ass tonight, I shouldn't be surprised you're not ready to go again. I mean, you're getting older so you must need eight hours of sleep and a little blue pill in between your meaningless fucks."

"Look at me." He waited until she turned to face him. His eyes glinted with a biting desire that left her breathless. "Let me rephrase. It's likely we'll have sex, probably for the rest of the night. In fact, if we do this, don't expect to be well rested for your meeting tomorrow. I simply wanted to be clear that you don't order me to fuck you. You don't say when or where or how. That's my role."

She braced her hand on her hip. "Because you're the big, dominant stud muffin? Look, that whole taking-orders thing is not how I roll. If you want me, come to the bedroom and we'll be two consenting adults choosing to have orgasms in a way that mutually suits us both. Or we can drop the idea and you can go find some other nameless bimbo tomorrow night at that meat market of a bar." She shrugged and tried to pretend his answer didn't matter. "Your call."

Heath didn't say a word, just grabbed his gun and stalked closer, unwinding the towel from around his waist and dropping it to the floor. She gasped, her stare glued to his body. His olive skin, which she suspected was a throwback to some Italian or Spanish ancestor, stretched over bulging muscles, lean sinew, and hard bone. Everything about him looked powerful and determined. His body, his expression, his cock.

Jolie had hit the sheets with some hot guys in her life. Athletes, a few models, some high-powered business executives. Not one had made her breath catch or her heart race like this.

Had provoking him been a mistake?

She couldn't think clearly when he urged her back against the wall and braced his forearm above her head. The gun clattered against the plaster as he leaned in and loomed above her. The nine-inch difference in their heights suddenly made him seem like a mountain. Though he wasn't touching her anywhere, he bore a hole through her composure with his midnight eyes. They stripped her resistance while vowing untold pleasure.

Jolie heard rapid little pants filling the silence between them and was horrified to realize they were hers. She couldn't make them stop. Instead, she settled her fingers on the hard slab of his chest, as if some part of her thought she could push him away if he overwhelmed her. But his stare told her it was too late for that.

With his free hand, he curled his fingers around her nape and pulled her closer. "You must be the most opinionated, guarded, difficult woman I've ever met. And I want you so badly."

Heath bent into what was left of her personal space. His lips hovered just over hers. His hot breath caressed her. He didn't kiss her, merely waited, studying her. She trembled, her heart thumping wildly, as he surrounded her with his scent, his masculinity, his desire.

"Are you ready?" he asked.

No.

But as much as he overwhelmed her, Jolie couldn't deny the desperate ache for him. "Yes. Hurry."

"Maybe this first time. After that . . ." He smiled, leaving her imagination to run wild. "It's going to take me all night to fuck you properly."

Heath turned just long enough to set his weapon on the hall table beside her, then closed the distance between them again, bracketing both hands around her face. To her shock, he didn't push his way into her mouth and plunder. He employed stealth as he slowly settled his lips above hers. He paused, breathing her in as if he wanted to catalog everything about her before he decided how to proceed. His patience nearly made her scream. They were naked. Her body was humming. She was breathless and aching and needy, damn it.

That had to stop.

He was getting to her too fast, but she didn't know how to stop reacting. And he hadn't actually kissed her yet, merely teased. Her reactions were unacceptable.

Jolie jerked her face away. Almost instantly, she missed the intimacy of their closeness. It made sense, she reasoned with herself. She'd worn out a couple sets of batteries since she'd been this near another human being.

But trying to fool herself was pointless. This desire eating at her composure and sucking her resistance dry wasn't like anything she'd ever experienced. Towering and terrifying, yes. But damn if she didn't feel beyond eager to melt into this man and let him take whatever he wanted.

Heath didn't pull her mouth close to his or chide her coyness. Instead, he pressed long, lingering kisses to her cheek, her temple, her forehead, then back down to her throat. "I don't think anyone has ever properly worshipped your body. I intend to change that."

Jolie's blood caught fire. She swallowed.

Anticipation. Apprehension. Arousal. The mix bloomed in her belly, burst in her head.

She couldn't stop herself from angling her face closer and rubbing her cheek against his. He cupped her face and she exhaled, pressing herself to his big, solid form.

He'd barely touched her and he was already undoing her. Normally with a guy, she got naked, enjoyed half an hour of adult time, managed an orgasm or two, and was mentally scrolling through her to-do list before she'd even finished dressing. With Heath pressing her into the wall and his lips working against her jaw, his breaths in her ear, she could barely remember her own name.

"Just kiss me already," she managed to get out.

Heath cradled her face. With a burning, solemn gaze, he held her still. Every cell in her body strained for more. He tsked. "So impatient."

Before she could shoot back a snappy reply, he bent and brushed his lips over hers—a second of bliss. Then he backed away, dragged in a shaky breath. His battle-hardened hands still held her in an inexorable grip, trapping her against the wall as he hovered over her and inhaled her slowly.

Jolie couldn't stand it anymore. She clutched his head, thrusting her fingers into the dark spikes of his hair, and surged up to cover his lips with her own.

She could almost sense his triumph, and Jolie realized he'd played her, ramped her up. And she'd tipped her hand, walking right into his trap.

A moment later, he forced her lips apart and surged inside as if it was his right to take every inch of her. He swept through and slid deep, savoring her like she was the sweetest morsel he'd ever stroked with his tongue. He kissed her as if he refused to let her go.

With a whimper, she melted, clinging, in desperate need of an anchor. She'd worry later about how she would recover from this total breakdown of her defenses. Right now, his touch felt once-in-a-life-time. This thing between them engulfed her, consumed her whole. She craved even more.

Heath eased back, nipped at her bottom lip, then dragged in a harsh breath. "Wrap your legs around me."

Jolie didn't question him. She let Heath drag her up his body and clutched him with her thighs as he snatched up his gun from the nearby table and stalked down the hall.

Inside her bedroom, her relaxing music had given way to something with a dark, steady beat. It sounded primal. Sexual.

As he dropped her onto the bed, he set his weapon on the nightstand and bent to her. Jolie didn't wait. She surged up to meet him halfway, arms tangling around his neck, legs hooking around his waist again, as she crashed her lips onto his once more. Hungry and urgent, she devoured him, demanding everything he could give her.

Heath had other plans.

He jerked free from her embrace and grabbed her wrists in an iron grip. Then he pinned her arms to the mattress and pressed his forehead into hers while he held her down and settled himself in the cradle of her thighs. "You're very impatient."

"You want me. I want you," she panted. Every hard inch of him covered her. "We agreed to have sex."

"Yes, a night of it. But you can't control this. It won't happen on your timetable. I won't put my cock inside you in the next three minutes because you're too twitchy to wait. I'll fuck you when I'm sure the only thing you'll give me is your utter and complete surrender."

His words detonated inside her. Jolie had never been afraid she would give a man too much of herself.

Until now.

"You didn't demand all that from the blonde earlier tonight."

"This is about *us*, you and me. And I want you to spread your legs wider."

Heath may not have meant to but he'd answered her perfectly. He wanted her more than the blonde, more than his usual hookup. She wasn't the only one shocked that every touch between them felt as if it burned into both psyche and soul.

Jolie refused to comply. "Not until you find a condom. Top drawer of the nightstand."

"Oh, we're nowhere near that. I intend to learn you first. Where you're sensitive, where you ache, where you're ticklish, where you liked to be touched . . . and where you don't. I'm going to map every inch of your flesh until I know it as well as my own name. Once I'm satisfied I can arouse you to a frenzy, then . . ." He dragged his lips up her neck. "Then I'll fuck you."

Oh, god.

She drew in a deep breath. Did he feel that way because she was a challenge he wanted to conquer? Because he would enjoy the triumph of seeing her every day for the next few weeks and know she'd given him every part of her? Or because, for some crazy reason, she mattered to him?

Jolie wasn't sure she wanted to know. In fact, she should stop this—for many reasons.

But she didn't think she could.

"You talk too much." Somehow she managed to keep her voice even. "Let go of my hands so I can touch you."

"You're not in charge. Shut off your brain. Give yourself to me."

If she did, he would completely unravel her.

"I don't need you in my head, Powell. Just my vagina. The point is orgasm, and we're wasting time."

"You're not listening. Or learning. But I have all night to fix that."

Before she could reply, he eased off her enough to flip her onto her stomach. She yelped in surprise when he pinned her to the mattress with his body once more, hard chest pressed to her back, his fingers curling around her wrists. His breathing sounded rough in her ear.

She struggled beneath his big body. "Get off."

"I suggest you get comfortable. We'll be here for a bit."

She didn't even have time to question what he meant before he transferred both of her wrists to one meaty hand and clamped them together above her head. Then he nestled his erection between her cheeks and rocked, nipping at the sensitive spot between her neck and shoulder. With his free hand, he wedged his way between her body and the mattress to cup her breast.

She felt overpowered. Taken. Dominated.

And—oh, hell—she liked it.

Jolie didn't even think about fighting back. With a shuddering gasp, she tossed her head back until it met his solid shoulder. She arched her nipple into his palm.

He ground against her ass again and set his lips to her ear. "You're sexy as fuck. I like you available for my hands, my mouth, my cock."

Jolie couldn't answer when he grasped her nipple between his thumb and finger and squeezed while he skated his lips up her neck in a slow tease. A shiver rippled through her. Heat flashed in her bloodstream. The heavy ache of desire gathered between her legs.

His touch felt so searingly intimate.

"Now let's try again, shall we? Spread your legs for me. Your pussy is mine tonight."

No man had ever talked to her this way. Her head told her she should hate it. Her body didn't give a shit.

She opened herself a fraction, then hesitated. If she gave too much, he'd take the rest—especially her sanity.

"More," he demanded.

"I'm not a contortionist."

He grunted in her ear. "I'm not a tosser. If you want this, open up. Give yourself to me."

Jolie was debating whether she'd rather have this pleasure or her wits. He ended her indecision when he worked his hand from her breast, down her stomach, finally sliding his fingers across her swollen sex, pausing over her most sensitive spot. "You wanted this. Let me give it to you."

"I wanted it my way."

"A polite, meaningless fuck. We've both done that with too many others to settle. Now stop fighting me or I'm going back to the sofa."

He gave her a spine-melting incentive, brushing a lazy circle over her hard clit.

She bit her lip to hold in her cry but the tingling bliss was more than she could fight. She parted her thighs.

"That's better." Satisfaction laced his gruff tone. "Just a bit more, then I'll see about getting as deep inside you as a man can be."

That sounded like heaven, and Jolie didn't have the strength to resist.

She spread her legs even more and lifted her hips, gyrating up on his thick staff still planted between her cheeks. His low, masculine groan tore through her body. Goosebumps covered her skin. The heavy throb between her thighs demanded more of him.

"Do something." She didn't know whether she was begging for mercy or ecstasy.

He settled his palm possessively over her mound, his fingers pressing her sensitive button again. "Move with me. Show me the motion you like. Let me feel what gets you off."

She barely managed a little moan before her hips rolled in a slow, grinding glide that quickly undid her. Jolie found herself gasping, gripping the blankets, falling apart. Every moment only multiplied the staggering pleasure until she couldn't breathe, until she surged faster and held her breath, waiting for the moment she'd finally know satisfaction at this man's hands.

He didn't disappoint.

With skillful fingers, he rubbed her and amassed a heavy knot of need between her legs. The swell of sensation was big. Huge. And as it began to crest, Jolie knew it would be unlike anything she'd ever felt.

Then he sent her over the edge in a cascade of beautiful agony that gripped her entire body and shook her to her core. The pleasure held her immobile as she howled out a scream of satisfaction. It morphed into a low, agonized groan as it went on and on. It was unlike any sound that had ever fallen from her lips.

The ecstasy wouldn't let go. She had no control because Heath forced her to accept every sensation while he pinned her down with his powerful body and clever touch. He held her captive even as he gave her exactly what she needed to soar.

"That's it." He kept strumming her clit. "Take it. Let me hear how good I make you feel."

No way she could refuse him, so she merely rode the wave of sensation for those long, incredible moments, crying out as the rest of the world fell away.

Slowly, the euphoria tapered off, dissipated, leaving her a heap of humming gratification. She melted into the mattress as her breathing recovered slowly. Crap, he must have turned her brain to goo. Nothing mattered now except bliss.

When had orgasm ever been that intense? He put anything battery-operated to shame.

"You're gorgeous." He rose and she heard a whisk of a sound that vaguely registered as a drawer opening but she was too wrung out to investigate. A ripping sound commenced a moment later. "But I want to look at you when I slide my cock inside you and fill that snug pussy with every inch I've got."

Jolie lacked the energy to tell him how badly she wanted that, too. Or to move. But when he rolled her onto her back and eased between her legs, towering over her, his closeness wired her body all over again. Sexual need blazed from his midnight eyes. With one hand, he stroked his sheathed cock. With the other, he gripped her thigh.

She gasped helplessly, wanting once more.

"Look at you. Cheeks flushed, muscles lax, cunt swollen. I don't know when I've seen a sight so pretty. If you want more, open to me. Spread your legs wide."

"You say that a lot," she mumbled.

"Because that's how I want you."

For once in her life, she didn't argue, just complied, planting her feet wide and dragging a fingertip down the valley between her breasts as she sent him a come-hither stare.

His glittering gaze followed her movement as he covered her with his own body, sliding his lips up the swells of her breasts, to the sensitive column of her throat, before he took her mouth like he had a fever only she could slake. A second later, she felt the thick head of his shaft probe her opening. Once he found the fit, he began to push in.

The climax had swelled her flesh, and she'd already seen that lack of size wouldn't be an issue with Heath. She relished the challenge of taking all of him.

She groaned at the feel of Heath easing deeper and clutched his shoulders, refusing to let go.

Gripping her hips now, he shoved with an impatience that fed hers. He reared back again, plunging even farther inside her. She mewled out her approval, wriggling for more.

"Give me your hands," he insisted.

Jolie had no illusions about what he wanted. She shouldn't like being held down, overpowered, used. Heath was the only man she'd ever met with the guts to do that to her. A warning voice in her head told her she was giving him too much of herself.

She'd worry about that later.

When she unpried her fingers from his shoulders, he gathered them in one hand and shoved them to the mattress over her head as he slammed inside her, filling her up completely.

Her flesh burned as she stretched to take him. With the head of his cock, he prodded a tender spot deep within her no man had ever touched. It set off a pain-to-pleasure chain reaction unlike anything she'd felt.

With a keening cry, she arched her back, writhed against him, and rocked her hips.

He tucked his arm around her waist, palm at the small of her back, and held her immobile against him. "You're not dictating how I fuck you."

"Hurry." Jolie wrapped her legs around him. "Please . . ."

"Ah, there it is, the pleading. That's so sweet, love. Have you ever begged a man?"

Briefly, she considered distracting him with a kiss or telling him it was none of his business. But he eased out almost completely, then in once more, bottoming out at the hilt. Sparks lit her body. Jolie closed her eyes and let sensations overtake her. She didn't concede defeat very often, but tonight she admitted he had far more experience and know-how in the bedroom than she could fight.

"No," she gasped out as he nudged that sensitive spot again.

"You've never let a man have control of you." Satisfaction laced his voice.

"No."

He hissed out a breath as he stroked deep. That knowledge was clearly a pleasure to him all its own. "You like it. I can tell. You're so wet. And already tightening around me. I hate that I haven't had the chance to suck one of those plump nipples yet but I will. I'll make you feel my mouth all over your body before I fuck you again. That's a promise."

His words destroyed her. Involuntarily, her flesh clamped down on him harder. Yes, she'd always enjoyed sex but . . . this didn't feel like mere intercourse. He was making a statement.

Even fearing he was ruining her for other men with every word and each possessive push inside her, Jolie couldn't stop herself from yielding to him.

"I want that," she gasped, seconds away from another screaming climax.

"I do, too. You're so close."

Yes, his climax must be nearing, too, right? His accent thickened. His cock swelled. His heart slammed against his chest as his pace quickened.

"Don't hold out on me," he coaxed. "I feel you arching. You're ready, aren't you? Let it go. Give it to me."

Jolie would give him her pleasure; she didn't see any way to stop that. The question was, how was she going to keep him from taking something she could never have back, like her heart?

* * *

PASSION rushed like a raging river in his head, thick, strong, swift. Heath pulled back, then ground into Jolie again. Bloody hell, he'd never experienced a desire so overwhelming it nearly drowned him. He couldn't breathe, couldn't escape. So he gave in—and quickened his pace.

With every thrust, he inched her up the mattress. The bed frame squeaked. Her cries turned high and sharp. His gut torqued up. The orgasm would tear him open but it was too late to pull back. Too late to stop.

Heath threw everything he had into possessing Jolie Quinn. This might be their only night together but he intended to make damn certain she never forgot it.

He clenched his teeth, breathing roughly against the raging pleasure. "Open your eyes."

Her hands curled into fists. She squeezed her eyes shut even more tightly as her little whimpers filled the room. She rocked beneath him in perfect sync, wanting the ecstasy every bit as badly as he did.

But she failed to do what he'd asked. Like in everything else, Jolie tried dictating the terms. He intended to make sure she understood she couldn't control this. He would take care of her.

If Heath had more willpower, he would have made her wait, forced her to burn in the fire between them before he let her scream in release. But the fuse on his imminent explosion already felt too short.

Still, he'd be bloody damned if he came before her.

"Look at me," he growled, hearing the Liverpool of his youth slip into his voice.

Again, Jolie didn't comply. Every part of her body clenched and coiled as she strained against the explosion that would splinter her control. Her silence felt like a barrier between them, as if she shied away from sharing this startling, searing ecstasy with him.

Not bloody happening.

With a curse, he nestled deep inside her pussy and went utterly still.

Her eyes flared wide with shock, then panic. That beautiful begging he'd wanted from her once more returned.

"Heath?" Her breath hitched.

"Do you feel the burn?"

She arched, struggled to writhe under him even as he held her still. "Yes."

It took every ounce of his restraint to slide back and in again with a slow stroke designed to kindle her senses, rather than plow deep and send her over the edge. "Want me to relieve your ache?"

"Yes."

"You want to come?"

She nodded frantically, eyes squeezing shut again. "Yes!"

"Then look at me. Watch me while I fuck you."

For once, she gave into his demands, lashes lifting to reveal those startling green eyes. In reward, he ramped up the pace of his thrusts until tingles skittered over his skin and up his spine, until her little cries slid over his senses like a lick to his cock, until he saw her pupils dilate and her mouth fall open and ecstasy begin to transform her face.

God, even in pleasure the woman looked fierce with a burning stare and gritted teeth. She was a warrior fighting for what was hers. Heath liked that. He loved watching the moment the full brunt of ecstasy rolled over her senses and crushed her mental armor. Finally, he glimpsed the vulnerable woman beneath.

It set him off like nothing else.

Heath rocketed inside her again, plagued by a need he didn't understand to take her, affect her, mark her, own her. Make sure she only ever wanted him.

Before he could tell himself how foolish and unrealistic that was, his pleasure catapulted up and orgasm roared through him. The overwhelming crest of sensation clawed through his gut, overtaking his system. She screamed again, clamping on him like a vise. Then he cried out in sublime ecstasy, knowing Jolie wasn't the only one moved by this night.

Even as satisfaction rolled heavy and languid through his body, Heath withdrew, rolled over, and stared at the ceiling, panting wildly. What the bloody hell had just happened? Despite the fact they no longer touched, he felt her keenly beside him. He knew what she smelled like, sounded like, looked and felt like when she cli-maxed. He didn't know how he would ever stop wanting her again.

"That was great," she said, swallowing. "Thanks."

He turned to stare and found her face almost devoid of expression. She'd thanked him with all the passion of someone showing appreciation for a coworker who'd done her a favor.

Did she actually think he believed her impassive shit? Or would accept it?

"Yes, it was. Should I thank you as well?" He rolled onto his side and propped his head on his elbow to stare at her. "Should we have a meeting later and compare notes about how much we both enjoyed it? Perhaps analyze it for its merits and drawbacks and come up with an action plan on how to improve the next fuck?"

"Don't be ridiculous." She rose and reached for her plain gray top.

As if they were through for the night. Not even close.

What she needed was a giant dose of intimacy. If she could erect her defenses moments after the orgasm ended, then he had to keep tearing them down. Tomorrow, she could go back to her bossy, charming self. But tonight, by god, she belonged to him.

Heath leapt to his feet and stepped on the cami before she could reach it. "You promised me a whole night."

Finally, she turned to stare at him. "Surely you don't mean . . . again?"

"That's precisely what I mean." He tore off his condom and deposited it in the nearby bin. Then he grabbed her little gray cotton scrap and tossed it out of the room and down the hall before he shut the door and faced her. "I want to taste you. Right now. Fresh from the orgasm I gave you." When she hesitated, he raised a brow. "It's more personal, intimate that way. You're not afraid?"

Jolie looked terrified. But she lifted her chin and soldiered on. "Of course not. But we've kept the neighbors awake long enough and we both have a meeting in the morning."

"I don't care about the neighbors or meetings right now. I care about getting between your legs." He sauntered toward her, watching a fresh glow creep up her chest, pinken her cheeks. "I care about making you feel good. I care about being inside you and hearing you scream for me again."

He maneuvered her down to the bed, onto her back. When she lay blinking up at him, torn and aroused against her will, he fell to his knees and took her thighs in his hands, spreading them wider.

"I don't think—"

"Precisely. Right now you shouldn't think at all." He couldn't resist baiting her because he knew she would give in. "I'll make that possible. C'mon, love. Give everything to me."

Chapter Six

Rule for success number six:
Get your head in the game.

HER concentration was nil this morning. Whenever Heath spoke, Jolie remembered every dirty, amazing thing he'd said he would do to her body—just before he lived up to his word and performed way beyond her expectations. Despite the importance of this meeting, she could hardly think about anything else.

For all the times she'd chastised her friends, her sister—especially her mom—for being too wrapped up in some guy, she was finally understanding how a man could wreak havoc on her concentration. And karma was paying her back in spades. When he said, "Lack of proper security protocols around all entrances and exits," what Jolie somehow heard was Heath commanding her to take him deep again. As he demonstrated the proper use of the security card readers he advocated for the office suite, she zoned out to memories of him sliding his tongue through her sensitive folds before he settled on her clit and ate her to screaming climax.

Damn it, she really needed to focus, but she couldn't seem to stop squirming in her seat and reveling in the delicious soreness pervading her most intimate places. Could everyone else look at her and know that she'd spent the night with Heath buried inside her?

"What do you think, Jolie?"

Startled out of her thoughts, she peered down the table at Karis, who stared expectantly. When had she projected that mockup for Betti's new website, complete with graphics, on the screen?

Blinking and resolving to ignore the hot British sex god across the conference room, she focused on the image. Immediately, she spotted Karis's handiwork in the visual elements. Slightly whimsical, a little bit retro, yet somehow cutting-edge and chic, the splash page dazzled.

"It looks fantastic," she praised, smiling at her sister. Then she noticed the girl's dark smudges and drooping lids. "Are you all right? You don't look like you slept much."

Karis blinked, her expression startled.

Her sister couldn't be surprised that she cared. But openly expressing concern during a business meeting was definitely unusual. At the office, Jolie focused hard on Betti and its problems, leaving her personal stuff—what little she had—at the door.

"I'm fine."

But Karis wasn't. Besides looking pale and tired, she seemed agitated. She glanced at Heath, then back Jolie's way, her face now sharp with speculation.

Jolie tried not to wince. Not once last night had she stopped to think that sleeping with the man Karis currently mooned over would hurt her sister. Remorse slashed her. Yes, Karis probably felt nothing more than a crush, and Heath wasn't interested. It took two to tango, right? But she could have let the girl's feelings wane before she jumped on the sexy Brit.

Jolie bit back an apology. Now wasn't the time or place. "Just checking."

Karis set her mouth in a flat line. "I'm guessing you got even less sleep than me."

She looked down at the papers in front of her so no one could see the blush heating her cheeks. "I never sleep much. Show me more of the site. You've done a great job with the home page. Do you have the fall collection ready to display here?"

Rohan jumped in to click the link, explain the coding, and talk through some options with her. After that, they slogged through Gerard's accessories and Arthur's financials while Jolie struggled to concentrate. She really should rethink the concept of the eight a.m. staff meeting.

No, she should stop sleeping with the man she'd hired to keep her company safe and pay closer attention to the most important meeting of her career.

When it was over, everyone began to gather their belongings and rise. Heath stared at her like a man with something to say. Jolie had to think about Karis first. Sisters before misters, and all that. She didn't want a confrontation now. Honestly, she didn't have time. But she'd never been one to push something uncomfortable off until tomorrow when she could tackle it today.

"Heath, let's talk more in depth about the security system this afternoon." She glanced at her phone, shocked to discover that it was nearly noon. "I'm going to take my sister to lunch now."

He nodded. "One thirty, all right?"

"Perfect."

"See you then." He sounded professional but his gaze lingered a fraction too long before he sauntered out of the conference room.

Karis jammed her phone on top of her notebook and shoved the pen in the wire spiral before heading to the door with an exaggerated huff, glaring Jolie's way. Poor Arthur watched, looking like he'd rather be killing a super mutant in the wasteland than watching this awkward exchange.

"Wait!" She followed after her sister, who utterly ignored her. "Karis."

"I'm busy," she called back over her slender shoulder.

Arthur chose then to step in front of her. He adjusted his glasses and cleared his throat nervously. "Um, I know you asked me to wait until next week—"

Karis was getting away, and Jolie didn't want her leaving mad.

"Sorry. Not now." Then she darted after Karis, catching up to her in the hall and wrapping a gentle hand on her arm.

Her sister jerked away. "What?"

"Let's go to lunch and try that new Indian place you've mentioned. My treat."

"Like I said, I'm busy." Karis folded her arms across her slight chest.

Jolie dropped her voice to a whisper. "If you want to talk about this, then come to lunch. I'm not discussing it in the office."

Her sister hesitated for such a long moment, Jolie expected her to refuse. Or worse, threaten to quit. The girl could be sweet and fun . . . and so damn impulsive.

Thankfully, Karis sighed, her spine losing some of its starch. "Fine. I'll get my purse."

Neither said a word in the car or as the hostess showed them to a table tucked into the corner of the cavernous restaurant. Dark and atmospheric rather than trendy, the place wasn't particularly crowded.

That would be a bonus today.

The moment the waiter took their drink orders, Jolie glanced at the menu to confirm they had chicken tikka, then set it down to find Karis glaring at her.

Jolie didn't drag her feet. "Yes, I slept with him."

"You knew I liked him." She looked both angry and hurt.

"I did. And I handled it badly. I'm so sorry." Jolie tried to say the next words gently but diplomacy really wasn't her forte. "But your feelings . . . You know they aren't reciprocated."

"Yeah," Karis said glumly. "But that might have changed in time. You never know. Maybe he just needed to know me better. Now I have no chance. The way he looked at you during the meeting, like he couldn't wait to strip you down and devour you—"

"He didn't," Jolie protested. But she feared he actually had. The few times she'd dared to peer at him for more than a moment or two, his stare had darkened, lingered.

She'd flushed hot every damn time.

"Oh, please. It was so obvious. Everyone noticed." Jolie grimaced but Karis kept on. "Even Gerard looked crushed. He really hoped Heath might swing both ways—"

"I can wholeheartedly vouch for his heterosexuality."

"Yeah, my gaydar is pretty accurate and I told him Heath was straight as an arrow when he walked in on Monday morning. Gerard still didn't want to believe me but he didn't ask Heath out because of your policy forbidding dating among the staff. Remember that?"

Jolie remembered when she feared office romances would be a distraction. Now she knew they were. "He's a contractor, not an actual employee."

"Aren't you splitting hairs?"

Probably. So in addition to Karis thinking she was a man thief, now she sounded like a hypocrite. "You're right. I really am sorry if I hurt you. That wasn't my intention."

In the past, Jolie had chided women for their weaknesses when it came to men, but last night she'd become that bimbo willing to do something desperate and stupid to be with a hot guy. Damn it. How had she gotten so turned inside out by a stiff penis and her softening heart? She didn't like it. Worse, she knew she should take a step back from him. But she wasn't sure how. She'd never had to fight her feelings before.

Was this desperate giddiness what her mother felt when she thought she was falling in love?

"You seemed really off your game at the meeting this morning. Did he upset you? Hurt you?"

The concern in her voice touched Jolie. She and Karis hadn't been really close since they were kids. Back then, they'd banded together to survive a chaotic life with a fickle, almost gypsy mother. During college, Jolie had worked nonstop to afford her tuition and books. She'd scraped enough together to afford a crappy studio apartment she shared with a cash-strapped med student. It had been a tight squeeze that really only worked because Melanie had been gone more often than not. Jolie hadn't visited her family a lot. In truth, she hadn't wanted to. By the time she graduated—with honors—Karis was fifteen and headstrong and unwilling to listen to anything her big sister had to say. She'd hoped this job would make them closer . . . but that didn't look promising now.

If Jolie wanted that to change, she had to make it happen.

"No. He didn't hurt me." She sipped her tea. "But I wish I could have a bottle of wine right now, KK, because he shocked the hell out of me."

Karis smiled a little at the childhood nickname. "Was he kinky?"

"Dominant."

"I'm surprised you didn't shred him with your tongue." She gasped. "Oh god. You *let* him boss you around?"

Jolie squeezed her eyes shut. Was she actually talking to her sister about her sex life? "When everything he wants you to do gives you the most amazing orgasms, it's not that difficult to comply."

It was only later that she'd had serious second thoughts about being so vulnerable to him. What was supposed to happen between them next? They hadn't ended the night with promises, which was fine. But they also hadn't started their morning by talking. Jolie had never before found herself in the position of caring if she had a tomorrow with a man.

Her sister giggled. "Seriously? That good?"

"Incredible." Jolie covered her face with a hand and shook her head. "I sound like a starry-eyed girl."

Karis cocked her head. "Is that bad, to be human? To be a woman?

I've often thought that, if we weren't related, you would have drifted out of my life long ago because you've never let yourself care too much about anyone. Maybe he's good for you."

"I'm pretty sure it was a one-night stand for him." Jolie lifted one shoulder, refusing to want more. "Besides, it's a really busy time for me. And hopefully, I'll be even busier soon. If I get this financing from Gardner, I'll be swamped with all the expansion tasks, including hiring additional stuff, overseeing a nationwide online marketing campaign, getting my suppliers ramped up . . . The list goes on. I can't get involved with anyone now. I don't think Heath wants to, anyway." She peered at her sister, whose brown eyes now looked sweetly empathetic. "I read some of the report you compiled about him. It's been seven years since his wife died. If he was going to get seriously involved with someone again, wouldn't he have done it by now?" She heard herself and groaned. "Crap, I can't be angsting about a guy I hooked up with once. We don't have a future together, and I'm okay with that."

"Are you?" Karis asked pointedly. "He may not have gotten seriously involved with anyone else because he's never met the right woman. Not saying it's you, but how do you know if you don't try?"

There was some wisdom to Karis's statement but . . . "Because I'm not anyone's perfect woman. I'm built for business. For my career."

"You're capable of more." Her sister raised a brow. "I think the real problem is that you're afraid to be like Mom."

"I love Mom," Jolie protested.

She did. But the idea of being dependent on a man or losing herself to one so completely that she forgot to be her own person terrified Jolie utterly.

The waiter set down their food and promised he'd check back shortly. Jolie dug in, hoping Karis would pay more attention to her tandoori chicken than to the turn of this conversation.

Nope. She shoved a bite in her mouth and kept the chatter rolling.

"But you don't call her on the shit you should. If I did that stuff, you'd haul me into your office and berate me until I admitted the error of my ways. It's as if you've accepted that Mom is just going to do whatever she wants, and you still send her money and listen to the plights of her romantic life. I know you love her. But you don't respect her. And you work hard to make sure you're nothing like her."

Jolie opened her mouth. Then she closed it. What was there to say when every word was true? She stalled by pushing the creamy chicken around on her plate. "Why does she get married and divorced over and over?"

"I'm not sure. She's looking for something she's not finding . . ."

"Perfection?" But Jolie didn't think that sounded like her mother.

"No," Karis agreed. "I don't think she has unrealistic expectations. I mean, she puts up with stuff that would totally piss me off."

Diana endured way, way more from her former husbands and ex-boyfriends than Jolie would. Of course, the moment any had stood between her and the success she'd yearned to achieve since sketching out her first designs at eight, Jolie had ditched the guy and spent more time on her dreams.

"Her self-esteem isn't the greatest. But I don't think she ever had any goals in life, either." Jolie took a bite of the chicken tikka and chewed. "I've never seen her strive for anything."

"Yeah. Are some people born without ambition?"

"Maybe. What about you? What do you want to achieve in life?" Since this was the most honest conversation they'd had in forever, she might as well see what Karis would say.

"I love my graphic art. Photoshop, Sketch, and Pixelmator all thrill me. I find an odd peace whenever I take my laptop to a quiet, pretty spot, turn on some good music, and just . . . be. Not everything I create is fantastic. But it's my art. My truth."

A subtle jab. Jolie enjoyed sketching but was a bottom-line woman. A childhood with too much responsibility had started her down that path. Her entrepreneurial spirit had honed it. For Karis, life wasn't about the destination but the journey. Her sister knew what made her happy and Jolie envied that. Success was fantastic . . . but she was beginning to wonder if life was about more.

"We all have ways of expressing our individuality. It's about being true to ourselves, right?"

Karis chewed on that, then grinned. "What you're saying is that you make choices that I wouldn't and I should back off preaching to you about how you should be relaxing."

Her younger sister was proving to be deeply insightful and more mature than she'd thought.

Jolie nodded. "Just like I should stop lecturing you about ambition, I guess. But this thing with Heath . . . I never meant to hurt you."

"You did at first; I won't lie. But he wasn't going to choose me. We both know that. I think I was upset you didn't consider my feelings more than I was that he didn't want me."

"I should have been more sensitive. I got lost in the moment with him and . . ." She flushed.

"This talking?" Karis sipped her tea. "It's good."

"Yeah. I've been trying to look out for you and guide you like I've always done."

"I appreciate it but I don't need you to be my second mom anymore."

"Point taken."

"So, what are you going to do about Heath? Take him to bed again?" Karis asked with a devilish smile, then her mouth gaped open. "Oh, maybe not. I just remembered . . . He has a strict no-repeat policy. According to him, he's Mr. Hit-It-and-Quit-It."

Disappointment spooled through Jolie. Yeah, he might have merely been telling Karis that to discourage her but it fit Heath's pattern. For the last seven years, he'd never stayed in any one place for long. He'd never stayed with any one person, either. Except Mystery Mullins. She'd been his employer and his constant—until she'd agreed to marry another man. But if Heath had never touched

Mystery, maybe—despite ruthlessly rushing to her defense—he'd never loved her.

That possibility made her happier than it should have.

"We didn't make each other any promises, and I have too much to do to pine over a guy, especially now. I'll write him off as a hot memory and move on." Jolie hoped it was that easy.

"Don't you want a family?"

"I've got one," she reminded. "You, Mom, and Austin keep me more than occupied."

"I don't mean parents and siblings. A husband and children. Don't you think about that?"

Sometimes. When she let herself, which wasn't often. "I'll just stand beside you at your wedding, hold your hand while you're giving birth, and spoil your kids rotten."

"You'd better." Karis squeezed her fingers for a sweet second. "But I'm hoping you'll let me return the favor. I'm not sure the path you're on will lead to the kind of happiness that lasts."

With that sobering observation, the waiter returned to collect their plates. After Jolie paid the bill, they headed back to the office. The clock on her dash told her she had only a handful of minutes before one thirty. "I'm glad we took the time for a sister lunch. We should do it more often."

Karis smiled as if she'd like that. "Yeah."

As Jolie parked the car, she grabbed her purse and jumped out. "I've got to run before I'm late for my meeting with Heath."

"Don't want to be late for that." Karis winked.

"I never want to be late for any meeting," she clarified. But no denying that she really anticipated this one. Just being near him made her blood pump, her skin tingle with life, even if she had no idea what she'd say to him once they were alone again.

"Right . . ."

As soon as they entered the suite, Jolie looked across the open space and spotted a box wrapped in brown paper with a floppy lace bow on her sister's cluttered desk. "What's that?

"I don't know. It's the right size for See's Candy." Karis looked hopeful.

"Do you see a card?" Jolie pointed to the little white square. "What does it say?"

She'd expected the note to read *You're pretty* or *Go out with me.* A romantic come-on of some sort.

What she saw seemed far more menacing.

"It says 'No one, not even your sister, will stop me from enjoying your sweetness.'" Jolie frowned at the obliquely ominous note.

Karis was too busy tearing into the packaging. "It *is* See's Candy!"

"Do you know who that's from?"

"No. I guess it's from whoever sent me the tulips?" She sounded unsure. "It's kind of cool that I have a secret admirer or something. I really hope he's more Henry Cavill than Dexter."

Jolie hoped so, too. But she refused to assume anything. Unfortunately, when she looked around, no one else sat at their desk. Gerard took notoriously long lunches, which promoted "maximum creativity." Rohan often attended get-rich-quick seminars. Wisteria and her on-again, off-again boyfriend were apparently speaking today, so she'd probably met him for lunch. Arthur got together with a group of gamers to discuss the latest cheats, hacks, and strategies every Thursday around noon. In other words, no one had been here to see anything.

"Would you mind if I shared this with Heath?" Jolie pointed at the card.

"Yeah. Sure." Karis handed it to her, then lifted the lid on the candy, inhaling the scent with a sigh of bliss. "Do you think it's safe to eat?"

Her sister's hopeful pout would have made Jolie laugh if the situation weren't possibly dangerous. "Taking food from a stranger? I don't think that's wise."

"It's like grown-up Halloween."

"It could also end up being *Real Stories of the ER*."

Karis shoved the lid back on the confections. "They're nuts and chews, too. I hate it when you're practical. And right. Ugh. Show the card to Heath. Maybe he can solve this so we can figure out if someone sane gave these to me and I can have an awesome dessert tonight."

Jolie had to laugh at her sister's slightly goofy side, especially since her own genetic makeup hadn't included anything like it. "I'll keep you posted. If not, I'm sure you can drown your sorrows in some merlot."

"Good call." She winked.

Jolie hugged her. "I'm glad we talked. Now I'm heading to find Heath. I'll let you know what he says."

"See you soon, sis." Karis kissed her cheek. "Have fun . . ."

Three minutes later, Jolie had gathered her stuff and headed into the conference room. When she opened the door, she found Heath inside, waiting. A barely banked fire lit his eyes when she walked in. He stood, watched her, his whole body tense.

"You're here. Good." He'd used that low, gruff voice on her last night and it had shredded her common sense. "Now close the door."

* * *

JUST like last night, Jolie complied almost instantly, naturally. As soon as Heath heard the click of the knob sliding home, he relished the thought that they were alone.

For having almost no sleep and fifteen minutes to get ready for work, the woman should not look that scrumptious. A dozen different ways he could take her on this table flashed through his head then. He'd love to spread her out, push inside her, and stroke her deep until ecstasy claimed them both.

Unfortunately, he couldn't touch her now. She seemed determined to keep the office strictly professional . . . but his thoughts refused to behave.

Sex with Anna had been like coddling a lamb. He'd held her and stroked her, reassured her of his love. She'd often indulged his desire for bondage and impact play but only if he served them up with gentle words and tender aftercare. Taking Jolie to bed had been like wrestling with a feral tiger. He had the scratch marks all over his back to prove it. Oh, she'd finally let him be the alpha—but only because it brought her pleasure. Orgasms certainly hadn't made her more docile. Heath wasn't sure anything would.

Surprisingly, he liked that about her.

In fact, he'd been inside Jolie last night for hours, taking her repeatedly with a hunger he'd been unable to slake. He'd had no chance to touch her since. Heath hadn't expected the craving to return today at all, much less with such a vengeance. Now he felt itchy and restless, like an addict desperate for another fix.

Her uneasy expression yanked him from his thoughts. "I've got something to show you."

He went on instant alert. "What's wrong?"

She hesitated, frowned, and gripped something in her hands. "Maybe nothing. But . . . well, yesterday someone left Karis tulips. Remember, she thought it was you? It wasn't, and we never really got back to talking about who might have left the flowers on her desk. Today when we returned from lunch, someone had left her a box of her favorite candy, along with this." She handed the card to him.

He scanned it. And froze. "Any idea what this means?"

"I have no idea. Neither does Karis. If he means it as a romantic gesture, why does he sound slightly like a rapist making a threat? And why is someone dragging me into this?"

"Good questions." They'd already covered the bases in Jolie's life around industrial spies, disgruntled former employees, and jilted lovers. She was too sharp to simply overlook or forget someone who might turn dangerous or deadly. "Besides me, you haven't warned anyone away from her lately?"

"I'm not her keeper. She's always been free-spirited, going where the wind takes her, romantically speaking. I keep hoping she'll learn from her mistakes and be more grounded."

He probably shouldn't veer into this territory when they had a potentially dangerous situation to deal with and he'd uncovered some troubling facts, but Heath couldn't turn his back on Jolie's concern. "Her mistakes?"

"The first was the wrestling captain in high school who thought it would be fun to see if he could get his personal number to one hundred before graduation. Karis was eighty-four. Apparently after plowing his way through most of the senior and junior girls, he started on the sophomores." And Jolie sounded as if she'd still like to throttle the prick. "Then came the guy who claimed to be a singer/songwriter. Baggy pants, plaid shirts, scraggly beard, unwashed hair—the whole bit. He also apparently didn't grasp that if he decided to move to Denver to start a marijuana farm with a new squeeze, he should break up with his current girlfriend first."

Heath tried not to smile. It wasn't funny, strictly speaking. But Jolie had a tart way of putting things that amused him.

"Most recently she gravitated to a guy she met at an anime convention," Jolie went on. "Turns out, Ben was really a hacker who did a lot of questionably legal things. Thankfully, the government recruited him and he moved to D.C."

"So Karis has made terrible decisions in the past, but no one you've tried to command out of her life in the past week except me?"

"Oh, I've scowled at a twerpy waiter and raised a brow at a leering UPS driver, but nothing serious. Maybe I missed something. I've been so busy."

Heath paced. He always thought better when he was moving. "You have no idea where the candy came from, then?"

"No. Someone hand-delivered it to her desk. Did you see anything while we were gone for lunch?"

He cleared his throat. "I popped back to my place for a quick shower since we ran out of time this morning."

Right on cue, her cheeks blushed a sweet pink. She pretended to stare down at the crisp, typewritten card with the oddly veiled threat. "What should we do?"

The whole situation gave Heath more than a little disquiet. Why would anyone send a gift to Karis but include a note threatening Jolie? The situation didn't look inherently dangerous but he especially knew better than to assume anything.

"Keep the office safe going forward. I have enough security card readers in my stash to install them at the front door, your office, and the hallway to the building's rear facilities—"

"You mean the restroom?"

"Do you really rest in that room?" he challenged.

"Fine. The toilet, as you Brits prefer." She rolled her eyes. "Are you saying that everyone will need an electronic badge just to go?"

"Yes. I plan to equip everyone with a lanyard. They should wear their badge on their person at all times, so going to the loo will require no more extra effort than the swipe of a card. I'll create the electronic access profiles today. I'll need a picture of every employee so I can laminate each to its respective badge. Once the system is in operation, it will keep logs and generate reports of access in and out of the suite, so everyone must carry their own badge."

"You'll be keeping track of our movements?"

"Indeed."

"So every time Rohan goes for a smoke or Gerard drinks too much water . . ." Jolie frowned. "I don't know. Security is important but this seems like an infringement of privacy."

"But if the system I've proposed had been in place this morning, Karis might not have received candy from a stranger. If she had, I'd already know precisely who had entered the suite and through which access point. I'd also have a log of when and where that person exited so I might be able to track him. As it stands now, we've no idea whether the culprit is someone working in one of the adjacent businesses, one of the cleaning crew, a random loon, the prowler from last night, or someone else entirely. These precautions will help keep us insulated from future incidents."

Jolie crossed her arms, wearing one of her stubborn expressions. "I recognize that I hired you to secure the facility, and I truly wish we'd been more prepared for the recent rash of problems. But I wasn't anticipating anything intrusive. Isn't there another way?"

"Would video and audio recordings seem less pushy? They're not much good for preventing a crime or stopping one in progress but are helpful in prosecuting after someone's already been attacked or killed. Is that what you want?"

"No. I thought you'd put better locks on the doors, maybe recommend a few more lights in the parking lots and a better firewall around our computers. This . . ."

"Is my area of expertise. Should I review my qualifications with you again?"

She sighed. "No."

"Fine, then. I've sent you a detailed e-mail with all the associated costs for the equipment I've recommended, as well as monthly maintenance fees. Let me know if you have any questions in the next hour. If not, I'll spend this afternoon installing everything."

"You can do that yourself?"

Why that surprised her, Heath wasn't sure. "For the most part. I may call in an extra hand or two but I never use any equipment I can't properly utilize. Too risky, otherwise."

She sighed and finally took a seat. "All right. When we're done here, I'll take a look and let you know whether to proceed. Let's get down to the rest of our business. Do you have any other recommendations to make the building and all our intellectual property more secure?"

Heath spent the next thirty minutes outlining those suggestions. He also returned her computer to her with added security and a mechanism that attached the machine via a locked cable to a bolt he'd have anchored in the concrete slab beneath her desk. She followed along, asked insightful questions, and picked apart his answers, negotiating for protocols she believed would balance the need between the safety of Betti's employees and their privacy. She frustrated the devil out of him because she'd argue with anyone about the color of the sky if she thought it would benefit her business, but she really was one of the brightest women he'd ever met.

Intelligence had never been a specific turn-on. Anna had been loving, joyful, and a bit reserved. She would rather have watched cute videos of puppies and babies and couples holding hands than anything about politics. She'd avoided discussing things like war, genocide, nuclear proliferation, the international economy, and terrorism. She hadn't enjoyed the mental challenge of a good crossword. Not so Jolie.

And he couldn't deny that he found his temporary boss a refreshing change from all the young party girls he'd spent his evenings with for the past six years.

Once they'd agreed in theory to his office security proposal, Heath sat back. Perhaps it would be more polite not to stare but he couldn't seem to help himself. Negotiation made her eyes glitter a dazzling shade of green. And how interesting that, as silence fell, she looked everywhere but at him . . . Now that she'd experienced how incendiary they were together, was she having trouble walking away, too?

That really made him wonder about her reaction to his next recommendation.

"Once you've approved the proposal via e-mail, I'll send everyone in the office the updated security protocols. In light of last night's break-in and another potential breach today, I'm implementing all the measures effective immediately. I'll be checking everyone's access and, of course, be here to answer any questions. Most importantly, I will monitor all the entrances and exits around the building and investigate anything out of the ordinary."

"There will be pushback," she warned.

"As their boss, you can give them a bit of encouragement."

"I'm paying for this, so you can bet I will." She gave him a sharp nod. "But none of that changes who they are. Gerard can't be bothered with anything practical. Rohan will be cranky with the extra two seconds it will take before he has his nicotine fix. Wisteria will lose her badge, guaranteed. Karis may make a sign protesting Big Brother—or in this case, Big Sister. Arthur will complain if we impede his access to that damn video game. I think he's got an addiction."

Jolie might not like to show that she valued their happiness. It probably didn't fit with her tough businesswoman persona . . . but Heath saw.

He hid a smile. "In Arthur's defense, the RPG he's immersed in now is quite well done."

"RPG? Never mind. I don't think I want to know what that means. I didn't know you're a gamer."

There was a lot she didn't know about him. "A casual one. In most cases, I'd rather read or go for a run."

Jolie wrinkled her nose. "Run? No thanks. If I'm going to sweat, I'd totally rather do yoga. Or Zumba. You like to dance?"

"The only time my feet have moved in any haphazard fashion, I was dodging bullets."

She laughed, then seemed to remember they were supposed to be having a professional relationship. After clearing her throat, she stacked her papers, then studied him with a carefully blank face. "Is that everything?"

"Not precisely. How much do you know about Richard Gardner?"

"Good family. Old money. His sister is a lovely woman. He graduated from West Point. He's worth nearly a billion dollars." She'd done her homework. "Gardner can afford to put a big stake in Betti and it would still be a baby investment for him. He knows nothing about fashion, just making money. He'll be a great silent partner."

"You've met him?"

"Socially. We had a long conversation at a recent AIDS fund-raiser, which is how we decided to explore Betti as an investment opportunity for him. He's a big advocate for LGBT causes."

"But he's not gay."

"I never said he was." Her eyes widened. "Tell me you didn't investigate him."

"And lie to you? I won't bother. So you know he's a skirt chaser?"

"It's ironic you should accuse him of that." Jolie leveled a sharp glance at him. "But I doubt Richard's first concern is what's under *my* skirt."

"Has he flirted with you?"

She shrugged. "He flirts with everyone, even his brother-in-law's ninety-year-old grandmother and his great-niece who just learned to walk. He likes females and has the kind of charisma many respond to."

Would she? The question disturbed Heath. "Do you want him to chase what's under your skirt?"

Jolie tilted her chin and sent him a measuring glance. "Would it matter?"

It shouldn't. Normally, it wouldn't.

He tried to phrase his next words carefully so he didn't sound like a possessive prick. "I think you need him as an investor far more than as a lover. I hope for your sake that he shares your priorities."

Brilliant. That didn't sound as if he might rip the man's balls off and shove them down his throat if he made a pass at Jolie.

Heath swallowed. Normally, he wasn't the jealous sort. Of course, he never stayed around long enough to care. Hell, he hadn't been half this angry when Axel had swooped in and stolen Mystery away.

"But you're not holding your breath?" she asked. "That's what it sounds like."

"Precisely."

"As it happens, I'm not interested in mixing business with pleasure. I'd rather not muddy the waters or deal with more distractions. Besides, if I'm in his bed, I'll be on his radar. I want a *silent* partner."

Heath felt some tension bleed away. Hopefully, that meant he wouldn't need to restrain an urge to commit murder tomorrow night.

"I'll be watching your back to ensure everything goes smoothly," he swore.

That put her on alert. She gave him a narrow-eyed glare. "At the restaurant? You can't be there."

"I will," he shot back instantly. "And I won't change my mind."

"Last night does not give you the right to follow me to my dinner with Richard. It's not a date; it's business."

"The purpose is irrelevant. I'm going."

Her face closed up. "No. You're not involved in my business, and I'm not discussing what happened between us last night."

Normally, that would suit him. He hadn't "repeated" once since he'd started hooking up about a year after Anna's murder. Normally, slipping away from a one-night shag was simple because he never saw the woman again. He never thought of them or missed them. He was never tempted to seek any of those women out once more.

Jolie didn't fall into that category. And he wasn't willing to accept her brick-wall attitude.

"Until we have more answers, I'm not comfortable assuming that whoever broke into your office won't return. I don't like the veiled threat in the note delivered with Karis's candy. So I'll not only be your security specialist, I'll be your bodyguard. As such, I'll be your shadow at dinner."

She shook her head. "But nothing violent has happened."

"This is non-negotiable, Jolie. I won't bend because you don't like it. The only way you'll be rid of me is if you sack me." Even then he didn't think he could merely leave. "And before you consider that notion, think about the safety of your other employees. Do you want them unprotected?"

"That's manipulative."

"But true. So if you pop out to the grocery store, I'll be there. If you decide to attend a yoga class with Callie, I'll tag along. If you hit a pub with the girls, if you shop for clothes, if you stand on your balcony, if you go on a date—"

"You can escort me from the office to my front door. I promise to go straight in and lock up for the night. Then you can go home, retrieve me the next morning, and take me to the office."

She wasn't comprehending, so Heath intended to make himself perfectly clear. "Break-ins happen. So do assaults, rapes, and murders. I'm now your bodyguard. End of discussion."

She huffed out a little sigh. "You're not spending the night again."

"I am. I won't touch you but I also won't leave you unprotected."

"How do I know this isn't some ploy to seduce me?"

"If that's all I wanted, I wouldn't be talking to you across this table. I'd be kissing you and reminding you that I know exactly how to make you scream in pleasure. Wouldn't that be more effective if all I wanted from you was sex?"

As if she didn't have a good argument for his logic, she switched gears. "And my sister? I'm worried about her safety. No one has tried to reach me, just my computer. But she was here last night when someone broke in. She's received gifts—"

"I've thought of that. I'll be calling in a few favors and finding someone to watch over her when she leaves the office."

"I don't want a stranger staying in her apartment while she sleeps. Besides, you've seen how small it is. Where would she put anyone?"

He stood and drew in a steadying breath. Jolie had worked herself up. Too much stress with all the unexpected lately. The anxiety of her investor dinner tomorrow night was likely weighing on her. He needed to calm her down, get her out of her own head for a bit. He had a fabulous idea how to accomplish that, but since they both had reservations about tangling the sheets again, he'd have to think of another way.

"Leave it to me. I'll make something work. You really don't have to control everything."

Jolie looked as if she wanted to argue. Instead, she crossed her arms over her chest. "What do you think is happening here? Are all these incidents related?"

He'd wondered when she would start asking the more difficult questions. Now that they'd settled most of the immediate issues, Heath figured she'd start digging for answers.

Pacing the length of the whiteboard, he chose his words carefully. "The timing is awfully coincidental. I have no proof . . . but with the facts we have now, I don't see another possibility. Someone is playing a head game with you. I don't know what they want yet. I also can't promise that whoever is causing this mayhem isn't violent. So I'll do everything I can to keep you safe."

"If he's playing games with me, why involve Karis?"

"Perhaps he's using her to get to you because he sees her as your weak spot." Heath knew well how those could be exploited. "Maybe the gifts are intended to butter her up so she'll influence you or lull her into a false sense of security so she'll help him with something intended to take you down. Without more information, I can't say. I only know I don't like dodgy pricks who threaten women in any way."

Jolie looked down pensively, as if she didn't know what to say. "If he could use her to influence me, then he'd probably suspect he could use her to hurt me."

"Precisely. Until I can assign someone to watch her, maybe it's best if she stays at your place so I can protect you both."

The suggestion clearly surprised her but she nodded in relief. "Thanks. I worry about Karis. Until we understand what's going on, better to be safe than sorry."

"That's the attitude. I'll need a list of all your appointments for the next week so I can be in sync with you. I suggest cancelling whatever you can, especially anything public. If you're a target, being out in the open makes you easier to reach. I also want to know the moment you receive any contact that seems remotely threatening. You won't leave my sight."

Jolie gathered up her belongings and stood. "Try not to get in my way. And don't think about seducing me again."

Heath knew he should let it go but . . . "Who surprised whom naked and waiting last night?"

She flushed, then turned to open the door. "Go to hell. I'll have your answer about the security equipment in an hour."

* * *

AT four o'clock, Jolie found herself frustrated and exhausted. After reading Heath's security bid and agreeing, he'd gone straight to work, barking at Wisteria to take everyone's picture. Now the sounds of power tools distracted her, and knowing Heath loomed nearby was killing the rest of her concentration. She had a few more finishing touches to put on her proposal for Gardner, but she could complete them at home later, in peace, with a glass of wine. And hopefully, Heath would still be here, installing the card readers and whatever else.

Looking for a change of scenery, she ignored her untended inbox and texted Callie. I need to skip yoga. Meet me for coffee?

Less than a minute later, Callie answered. Since I'm too pregnant to do much more than waddle to the bathroom, yoga is out of the question for me. Love to!

As soon as they agreed on a location, Jolie tiptoed to her office door, peeking out. Everyone appeared hard at work for once. Gerard perched over a sketch pad as if inspiration had finally struck. He swooped his pencil over his pad feverishly, looking like his fingers were doing their best to keep up with his brain. Karis and Rohan murmured together in his cubicle about something on his screen. Arthur frowned as he balanced receipts against his records. Wisteria typed at a slow but steady pace on her e-mails, working around her long, canary yellow nails.

And Heath had shucked everything above the waist except a tight ribbed tank while he installed the security equipment. As he drove a screw into the wall with a power drill, his biceps bulged. His shoulders flexed. Every bit of his lean torso bunched in silent power.

Jolie swallowed her tongue.

Why did the only man she'd ever craved have to be the one who made her feel so vulnerable?

Yeah, some time away from the office—and him—would help her concentration. Heath would be pissed but she really didn't need a bodyguard. The recent events had been admittedly unnerving, but no one had truly threatened her. Whoever had broken in seemed more like a desperate business rival hoping to steal secrets and use her sister's soft heart to get to her than a hardened killer.

Grabbing her purse from her desk drawer, Jolie tucked it against her chest and crept out the door. With a sigh of relief, she drove away. She needed to clear her head before making the biggest pitch of her career. She wouldn't get that if Heath was around.

Fifteen minutes later, Jolie pulled into an upscale coffeehouse in a well-established part of Dallas. Glass and chrome gleamed everywhere, accenting an open fire pit, dark wood, and sleek lines. Everyone here sipping coffee in the late afternoon looked incredibly busy, impeccably dressed, and reeked of money.

Jolie hadn't grown up with two dimes to rub together but she definitely appreciated having money now.

As she looked around, she spotted a gorgeous brunette in a nautical-themed maternity dress waving. The navy color suited her fair skin and made her blue eyes gleam even from across the room. The pregnancy glow only added to her beauty.

At the table beside her, her husband, Sean Mackenzie, sat glancing through the newspaper. At the back of the shop, her devoted lover and Dom, Mitchell Thorpe, lazed against the wall, watching everything around him while he talked on the phone.

Disappointment wound through Jolie. She'd hoped Callie would come alone, but since she'd met the woman six months ago, neither man was ever far from her side, and with the baby coming any day, they hovered even more.

With a hug and a smile, Jolie slid into the empty chair across from Callie. "Hi. Wow, you look fantastic."

She put her hands on her belly and laughed. "I look so pregnant. When I see myself naked now, I think that if I get any bigger, I'll need my own zip code."

"How much longer?"

"A few weeks. But the baby keeps trying to make an early appearance. I'm supposed to be on bed rest but I had to get out of the house before I lost my mind." Flipping her gaze back to Thorpe, then over to Sean, she leaned in. "I thought they were overprotective before but now they're downright exasperating."

"I heard that, lovely," Sean remarked without once looking up from his *Dallas Morning News*.

"And I'm sure Thorpe will know too as soon as he ends this call. You guys can let up a little. I'm not going to give birth the next time I stand up and accidentally drop the baby on its head."

Sean frowned skeptically. "We promised you thirty minutes before we took you home to rest. If you want to gab with Jolie, I suggest you get started."

How did Callie put up with any man taking so much of her control?

But the bubbly brunette didn't let it ruffle her. Instead, Callie stuck out her tongue playfully. "Fine. I'll get you later."

Sean sent her a smoldering gaze. "I look forward to it."

The other woman giggled, then handed her a chai iced tea before taking a sip from her water bottle. Her huge diamond wedding ring winked in the light. "How are you, doll? Rough day?"

Rough forty-eight hours, actually. "You could say that."

"Is Heath helping you out?"

Jolie couldn't seem to stop herself. Heat crawled up her face. "He's fine."

"Oh . . ." Callie raised a brow. "So he gave you more than recommendations to shore up your security, huh?"

She ignored that question.

"We had a break-in at the office last night." Jolie filled her in on the details, along with a bit about Karis's odd gifts. "So I'm not sure what to think or do. Now Heath seems determined to stick to me day and night. I don't think it's a good idea."

"Because you like him despite knowing he doesn't ever occupy the same bed twice? Or because he got under your skin?"

Jolie grimaced. Callie had always been perceptive. "Gee, don't ask me hard questions or anything."

Her face softened with apology. "Sorry. I don't mean to overstep. I only want to help."

With a sigh, she sipped her tea and whispered so Sean couldn't overhear. "I know. The truth is, I'm not sure. And I'm even less sure I want to know the answer."

Callie hesitated. "That's new for you. If it makes you feel any better, he's a good guy."

"I didn't really want a guy at all. I don't need the distraction."

"You never get to choose when love comes your way." She and Sean shared a meaningful glance before she turned to Thorpe, who was still on the phone. As if he sensed her stare, the intimidating man in the perfectly cut suit gazed back with an adoring smile. Callie glowed with happiness. "I wasn't looking for it a year ago. But it found me. Now look." She caressed her belly. "Married. Happy. About to have a baby. I didn't plan this, but I wouldn't change it for anything."

"I'm thrilled for you. I know you've been through a lot. But I've never been in love and I don't plan to start now. I just needed some sanity."

And some space Heath Powell didn't inhabit.

Thankfully, Callie let the love thing drop. "What's making you crazy?"

Jolie explained the installation of the security equipment and Heath's insistence that he was now her bodyguard.

Suddenly, Callie's eyes went wide. "So you didn't tell Heath you were coming to meet me?"

"No. I don't need a keeper. I'm sure these incidents have something to do with the business, and Heath will figure it out. But I won't have that man breathing down my neck as if he owns me."

Her eyes flared even wider. "Um . . ."

"Unless you'd like me to make a scene in this posh little coffeehouse, I suggest you come with me now."

Jolie recognized that deep, clipped British voice. She froze.

Heath had tracked her down. And he didn't sound pleased.

Chapter Seven

Rule for success number seven:
Pick your battles.

JOLIE whirled around. Heath stood, muscled arms crossed over his wide chest. He didn't look mad but under the surface she felt him seething. Karis stood behind him, wincing with an apologetic glance . . . before she started checking out the twentysomething guy behind the counter who had a mop-top haircut, gauges in his ears, and a fresh tattoo. To Jolie, he looked like a cliché. Her sister was probably wondering if he could be her soul mate.

How had Heath known where to find her?

Obviously not from Callie but . . . Sean appeared as surprised as his wife, though his scowl at her was now laced with disapproval. After a scan of the back of the shop, Jolie had her culprit. Mitchell Thorpe held his phone in his fist, his expression more than suggesting she start answering Heath's questions—fast.

Irritation bit. She didn't like high-handed people and appreciated men who thought they knew better than the women in their life even less.

"Just a minute." She made her way to Thorpe. Power rolled off him but Jolie ignored his alpha vibe, refusing to be intimidated.

"Why the hell did you tell Heath where to find me? You're interfering."

"I'm helping a friend keep his charge safe. And I know a thing or two about stubborn women," he drawled, glancing at Callie. "Better to have you annoyed than dead."

"That's *my* decision to make."

"You hired Heath for a reason. Let him do his job."

Jolie gritted her teeth together when she felt a gentle hand on her shoulder. Callie.

"Mitchell meant well," she murmured as she pulled Jolie into a hug. "I'll torment him later for you, okay?"

When she might have argued, Jolie realized everyone in the coffee shop was staring. She backed away. "That would be great."

"I'll see you soon?" Callie looked worried that Jolie was too pissed to be her friend anymore. But Jolie couldn't stay mad at the woman.

"Absolutely. Let me know when you go into labor."

"You mean for real?" She laughed at herself. "Will do."

They'd barely broken apart from their hug when Jolie felt firm fingers wrap around her elbow. Heath stood beside her, looking perfectly relaxed, but his grip revealed his tension.

"Let's go," he growled.

Jolie snagged her tea and left. She wanted to argue but not in public and not where she'd potentially put Callie in the middle. Her friend hadn't known Thorpe would rat her out to Heath. No, she'd deal with her security contractor all by herself.

"Karis?" he asked.

Her sister flicked one last glance at the guy behind the counter as she paid for her coffee. "Yeah."

The three of them walked in silence to the parking lot. Karis jumped in her little compact. Heath was two steps off Jolie's ass as she made her way to her sedan.

The moment they were both in her vehicle and she started the engine, she turned to Heath with a glare. "You had no right—"

"You've paid me for the right. If I have to keep you safe from yourself, I will. But never mind me. Think of your sister. When she realized you'd gone, she was worried and insisted we find you immediately. She's not too stubborn to realize you could be in danger. Since you usually attend yoga on Thursday nights, I started with a call to Thorpe to see if Callie had joined you. Imagine my surprise to learn that you'd come across town to sip coffee in public and left your bodyguard behind. Did you stop to consider for a moment that you might be putting Callie, a woman thirty-seven weeks pregnant, in danger? You want to be independent, I know. But think of the people around you."

Before he'd even finished speaking, regret and shame burned her. She'd merely wanted some Zen. No, she'd wanted to run away from everything he made her feel.

Jolie hadn't been thinking about danger. She'd been thoughtless and reckless.

"You're right. I'm sorry."

"Say those words to your sister and Callie. I don't need an apology. I have other ways to get my point across to you."

With that ominous note, he fell silent, texting furiously for the next ten minutes while she fought the swelling traffic. In her rearview mirror, Karis followed dutifully, waving when Jolie looked back.

When they reached her condo, the three of them entered wordlessly. Tension poured off Heath. It made Jolie skittish and jittery. Some foolish part of her wanted to touch him, calm him. She didn't. She paid him, so he wasn't going to tell her what to do . . . Though knowing she'd worried her sister and inadvertently risked others, she vowed to start listening more.

After a silent dinner of pizza and salad, Karis borrowed a T-shirt from her, hit the shower, then emerged from the bathroom with wet hair and a pensive expression.

"Night, y'all."

Jolie hugged her sister. "I'm not mad. I hope you're not upset with me."

She sighed with relief. "No. I didn't mean to panic but when you disappeared . . ."

"I understand." And Jolie could see how, after the last couple of days, her younger sister would draw the conclusion that something terrible had happened. "I won't sneak off anymore."

Karis smiled, then retired to the futon in Jolie's home office, carrying her iPad and earbuds. Jolie was glad they'd cleared the air and her sister could sleep tonight in safety and peace.

But that left her alone with Heath, her frustration, and her thick desire for the man she could neither purge nor escape.

"I'm going to shower and take my laptop to bed. The pillows and blankets from last night are still sitting on the sofa. Help yourself."

"So that's it? You're going to avoid talking about the elephant in the room. Brilliant."

Jolie didn't pretend she didn't understand. "There's nothing more to say. I've apologized for leaving without letting you know. Things are right with my sister again. We've both agreed that we won't be having sex anymore, and I have to finish prepping for my meeting tomorrow night with Gardner. So we're done here."

He took a step closer until he towered over her. "We're not. I don't care how reluctant you were when you agreed to keep me as your bodyguard. We'd barely been out of that conference room two hours when you completely disregarded everything I said, went behind my back, and acted as if nothing I said mattered."

"Don't take it personally. I just wanted a coffee with a girlfriend. I didn't tell you to shove your security up your ass."

"Actually, you did. Without words, mind you. But your actions told me to sod off and that you don't give two shits about staying safe. Between your to-do list and your hang-ups, you're too wrapped up to think at all about the people around you who care."

He was uncomfortably close to right. "Why do you give a shit?"

Instantly, his face closed up. "I don't. I'm merely doing my job." The passion with which he gritted out the words—with fists clenched and tendons standing out in his neck—made a liar out of him. "But your sister was beside herself. No one knew where you'd gone, if you'd left voluntarily or . . ."

"My sister doesn't seem half so agitated as you. You want to talk about the elephant in the room, fine. Let's get it out there," she challenged. "I left because when you're near me, I find it harder to breathe. You make me want. You make me ache. I admit it. I'm sorry if I worried you, but it pisses me off that you're pushing your shit off on my sister because you won't man up to the fact that, for whatever reason, you don't want to see me hurt."

"I don't want to see anyone hurt." He came at her again, pointing a finger at her. "But don't make the mistake of thinking anything or anyone matters to me. I stopped caring years ago."

"In other words, don't read any emotion or meaning into last night. Great. That works for me," she shouted back. And she didn't mean a word of it. Last night had sure as hell felt like it mattered—even when she hadn't wanted it to. She suspected it had meant something to him, too. "Now I'm going to my room. We'll leave for work tomorrow at seven a.m."

Jolie grabbed her purse and swiped her iPad off the coffee table, then marched down the hall. By the time she closed the door between them and pulled off her clothes, she didn't want to think about why tears began to fall.

* * *

WITH arms crossed over his chest, Heath watched Jolie close her door between them.

No way he could simply brush off her actions today. He had to make her understand the world could be dangerous so he would be implacable when it came to her safety.

Because despite what he'd told her, he cared.

He also couldn't forget her words. *You make me want. You make me ache.*

She wasn't the only one.

Some obnoxious pop tune bled out from under Jolie's room, interrupting his reverie. A young male vocalist crooned, calling the female he sang about a generic "girl," as if he couldn't recall her actual name.

Heath shook his head. He didn't know precisely why Jolie had chosen to shut him out, but instinct told him that he couldn't allow that door to separate them for too long.

For now, he let himself into the hall bathroom for a quick shower, then headed to the front of the flat and checked each door and window, ensuring he'd locked the unit as tightly as possible for the night. Tomorrow, they'd discuss the security here at her condo and he would make some changes for the better.

Seeing a sliver of light spill out from under the guest room door, he knocked. Karis opened up enough to peek her head out. "You need something?"

"I'd like to check the window in here, make certain it's locked."

She stepped back and opened the door wider, revealing an oversized T-shirt, sans bra. She looked clean, innocent. Normally, he'd find her attractive. Lovely, impressionable, and clearly in need of a guiding hand. Yes, Heath knew his type.

With Jolie in the picture, the doe-eyed neediness that had always drawn him paled next to her vibrant fire. She never waited for someone to help her. She attacked life with a passion that burned him. Even in bed, she'd been a firework, blistering him as she burst loud and colorful all over him.

Down the hall, he heard running water. Jolie had stepped into the shower. He tried not to think of her naked. It would distract him, make him forget that he didn't intend to be her lover again.

Once he'd ensured the window was locked tight, he headed for the door. "Good night."

Karis lingered near the futon she'd covered with a sheet and blankets. Thank goodness Jolie had never tried to make him sleep on that miniature-sized chaise.

The younger sister bit the inside of her cheek, looking uncertain. "Wait. Jolie would kill me if she knew I was saying this but I think you're right. My intuition says something dangerous is going on. She knows she should listen to you. My sister has always been so fearless, the leader in every situation. She had to be. Me and my siblings all have different dads. None of them were ever around, and Mom was always working multiple jobs to make ends meet. Jolie was nine when she started parenting Austin and me. She's so damn independent because she's used to calling the shots. Because of her dad, she refuses to want someone in her life more than they want her."

It made sense, certainly. As a girl, Jolie had craved the father who hadn't shown any interest in her. So she'd learned to stand on her own two feet, proven to the world that she was just fine without him, and distanced herself from every man so none would have the opportunity to hurt her. "I understand."

"She's not trying to be difficult," Karis defended her older sister. "She's afraid. I think you must have really gotten to her last night."

The feeling was mutual. "I'll handle it."

"I know what you told me about your no-repeat rule, and I'm guessing that means you're not looking for a relationship. If that's the case, then leave Jolie alone. She claims to be perfectly happy single but deep down, in places where she won't even admit it to herself, she wants love. You could really hurt her if you slept with her again and walked away. That's why she's avoiding you."

Every word out of Karis's mouth was heartbreakingly honest,

and Heath couldn't fault the girl for making so many astute observations and wanting to protect her sister.

"I see." Heath wasn't sure what to do about Jolie. Circumstance had forced them together. Well, that wasn't precisely true. It *had* thrown them together but he couldn't simply leave because knowing Jolie only made him want her more. "I'll look after her."

"She knows you're hurting, too. I mean because of . . . your wife." Now Karis bit her lip, looking decidedly guilty. "I did a little digging about you yesterday. My sister was angry but I sent her the report I'd compiled and . . ." She sighed. "I'm sorry. I had no right to pry."

Heath couldn't very well fault her when he looked into the background of nearly everyone he met. "She knows about Anna?"

"Yeah."

Heath didn't like it but the damage was done. "Thank you for being honest. Sleep well."

Karis wanted to ask if he was angry; she wore the question all over her face. But she didn't speak it. "Night."

Back in the family room, Heath felt exposed. Anna's death was something very private he never discussed with anyone. The only person he'd ever shared his feelings with about that terrible afternoon was Myles Beaker, his partner during their MI5 days. His best friend at the time. Myles had lost his wife to the same senseless crime. He was the only other person in the world who understood what it was like to have woken up that morning happily married and thinking he held the world by the tail—and then have everything snatched away in a moment.

Shoving the memory aside, Heath retrieved the pillow and blanket Jolie had left him. Now he had to deal with the first woman to make him truly feel something in seven years. The only one stubborn enough to demand her independence when someone had his target on her back.

After tonight, she would understand the new order of things. Maybe they both would.

As he tucked the pillow under his arm and slung the quilt over his shoulder, he headed toward her bedroom, ready for battle. No doubt, that's exactly what he'd have on his hands.

Heath shut her door and locked it behind him. He'd barely set his pillow and blanket on the chair in her room and doffed everything but his underwear when he heard the shower taps turn off.

Setting his weapon on her nightstand, he sat on her bed, back propped against her padded headboard, fingers laced over his abs, and waited.

As she emerged from the bathroom in a cloud of perfumed steam, Jolie spotted him and stopped short, clutching her towel to her naked body.

"I said you could sleep on the sofa."

"I heard you. But when it comes to safety, you don't make the rules. You agreed on that. So I alone say what's necessary to protect you. Today, you disregarded me completely."

Heath tried to ignore the water gleaming down her velvety shoulders and sleek thighs in shimmering drops. Damn difficult when she looked so beautiful all scrubbed clean, hair slicked back. She had nothing to hide behind now—no clothes, no makeup, no inky hair curling around her face. Only the starchiness of her attitude.

The alpha male inside him wanted her to know that he believed in her. She had the power and conviction to conquer the world. But he wanted to be the man who commanded her body, her laughter, her—

Heath halted that train of thought completely. It was dangerous and derailed him from the point he must make. Jolie was his temporary employer and they'd had a one-night stand. He had to stay focused. Feelings were inconsequential. But as long as he was doing his utmost to save her life, she'd better fucking listen.

"And I apologized," she reminded. "You made some good points I hadn't considered. I promised not to worry my sister or put others in danger again. We have nothing more to say, and I want you out of my room."

"I won't touch you, if that's what you want. But I refuse to leave."

"You're not staying here tonight." Her lips flattened into a stubborn line.

Her defiance made him itch to toss her across his lap and let his palm have a go at her pert ass. He would never spank her against her will. He suspected her body would melt for it, but that fast, sharp mind would reject the notion. He definitely needed to set aside his urge and find another tactic. But the biting panic he'd felt during those minutes he'd been unable to find her wouldn't fade away.

"Do you understand the role of a bodyguard? If not, I'll be happy to take half the blame. Perhaps I didn't properly explain the concept, so let's resolve that now."

Her eyes narrowed. "I'm not an idiot."

"No, but you're a very stubborn woman." Heath said nothing more, merely stood and strolled to her closet, finding what he wanted immediately hanging from a colorful rack on the back of the door.

"Why are you rifling through my things?"

"To make a point." He wrapped a silky scarf in a vibrant shade of blue around his hand and stalked in her direction. "There are consequences for the disappearing act you pulled this afternoon. Do whatever you need to be ready for bed. You have five minutes."

"What? No! I still have to go over my presentation for Gardner again. I've got more fact-checking to finish, to make sure the details are absolutely correct, and—"

"Unless he's too busy wining and dining you into bed to notice your presentation, Gardner will be more than impressed. Get ready. Five minutes."

Jolie seemed to forget she was mostly naked when anger took over. "Listen, you high-handed bastard. It's my business so I get to decide when my presentation is done. Not you."

If she wanted to stay awake, that didn't dent his plans in the least. "As long as you've done everything but turn out the light when you come to bed, that's fine. Four minutes now. Ticktock."

She gave him a loud huff. "Fine. Put my scarf back."

Heath fully expected her to grab a nightie from a drawer, retreat to the bathroom, then avoid all further contact with him tonight.

He should never try to guess what Jolie would do next.

She meandered back to the bathroom. He heard the rustling of her towel, then the lights flipped off. She emerged again stark naked. He tried not to gape at how beautiful she looked with gleaming skin, irresistible curves, and forest-hued eyes that dared him to touch her.

Dared, hell. She was bloody well taunting him and his no-repeat rule while distracting him from his purpose. He swallowed. What would it be like to have Jolie again? Her soft skin. Her fierce passion. The fire in her eyes when she finally gave into the peaking pleasure.

Jolie took her time scrounging through her dresser to find just the right nightie. As she bent to the drawer, he had an unparalleled view of the straight line of her spine bisecting her narrow back, the smooth cheeks of her backside, the firm length of her legs—and a hint of everything pink and feminine in between.

Heath gritted his teeth and held in a curse. What would happen if he bent his no-repeat rule just this once?

Finally, Jolie selected something white and sheer, edged with lace. She made a great show of considering the delicate matching knickers, only to shove them back in the drawer. Then she turned to face him, lifting the lingerie over her head, letting him watch it slither down her body and hug every part of her he ached to touch and taste again.

When the garment reached the tops of her thighs, Heath still couldn't tear his stare away. Technically, she was covered but the darkened shadow of her nipples showed through, as did the dark curls protecting her pussy. He couldn't miss the outline of her nipped-in waist and the feminine curve of her hip.

Jolie was definitely taunting him, trying to strip his control. He couldn't let that stand.

With a come-hither sway, she strutted to the bed and crawled onto the mattress, letting him see the swell of her lush breasts that he shouldn't touch. Then she settled in beside him with an exaggerated stretch that accentuated her hard nipples poking the transparent fabric.

As she sent him a saccharine smile, Jolie settled against the headboard and opened her iPad, attached the matching keyboard, and tuned him out utterly.

Heath couldn't deny that she'd done a fantastic job of piquing more than his interest. A fine layer of sweat dampened his temples, sheened his back and chest . . . But the hardness of his cock astounded even him. As many times as he'd had this woman last night, he should have nothing left to feel for her, not even arousal.

He burned more for her now than he had the night before.

Gritting his teeth, he fisted the blue silk scarf. Yes, she might have done her best to drive him out of his mind, but he definitely intended to have the last word.

Tossing off the covers, he exposed their legs. He didn't give a fuck if she saw how hard she'd made him. Two could play her game.

Then he wrapped the scarf around her ankle. She'd barely had time to jerk her gaze up to stare at him with both shock and rebuke when he slid it around his own ankle and tied the two of them together.

"What the hell—"

"You've proven that I can't trust you not to sneak away, so I'm making certain that you'll stay put tonight. If you're difficult, I'll bind our hands together as well."

She glanced down at his sturdy knot, then back to his face. "You've done this before, tied a woman up."

"I have."

But he hadn't indulged in anything like that since he'd been widowed. He'd thought about it often but hadn't been able to tap into that part of himself with anyone else. Now the possibility shimmered between him and Jolie, and he felt his blood racing. The idea of her being tied to him while he teased and tormented her, slowly breaking through her defenses, roused him. The notion of stroking her into a pleading, shaking need before he ruthlessly fucked her nearly tempted him beyond his control. Even at the thought, desire buzzed through his body like an intoxicating chemical.

"Not with me. Never. I told you. I don't submit."

Because she'd never tried. She'd never trusted any man enough to give herself over that completely.

Stupid or not—against his one rule of engagement or not—Heath wanted to be that man.

"I'm merely making certain you understand the concept of staying beside me until I tell you otherwise."

She jerked her leg, testing the bond he'd tied. When she could only twist and turn a bit to find comfort, she huffed. "Whatever. If this gives you some peace of mind that I won't leave, fine. Just let me get back to work."

She tapped on her tablet again, swiping her fingers across the screen, scanning, reading.

Heath would rather feel his skin slide against hers. No, that wasn't precisely true. He wanted her to put that damn tablet down so he could roll her to her back, hold her down, kiss her with the passion blistering inside, and coax her to take him again in one relentless thrust after another.

After ten minutes of swiping, typing, sighing, and frowning, Jolie finally darkened the tablet and set it aside, then flipped off the light. As much as Heath wanted her, he could feel her worry, too. She wouldn't rest until she'd succeeded.

"You're ready for this meeting," he assured.

She rolled to her side, turning her back to him and dragging his leg along with her. "I've done everything I should. The rest is up to him."

"You're brilliant and driven. You've gotten this far because you believed in yourself. Don't stop now."

Heath felt Jolie's surprise.

She didn't say anything for a long moment. "Thanks."

He rolled up behind her, spooning her body and fitting his aching cock against her. He wrapped an arm around her waist, the tips of his fingers just a breath away from cupping a handful of her breast. Damn, he was a stupid bastard for tormenting himself.

She froze. "You said you wouldn't touch me."

"I can't be tied to you in a queen-size bed without brushing my skin against yours."

"This is more than incidental contact." With a wriggle of her backside against his erection, Jolie damn near made him groan. "So is that."

He banded his arm more tightly around her waist. "You think the way you dropped your towel and wore your peekaboo lingerie didn't feel like a provocation to me?"

Then Heath couldn't help himself; he rocked his hips, grinding into her. More than vaguely aware of the scarf around his ankle, he was dying to know how it affected Jolie.

"Oh, I see. Since I wore something you think is a little risqué, I deserve to be mauled?"

She might be arguing . . . but she sounded suspiciously breathy.

"No, I'm pointing out that you intentionally tormented me because I'm sure you know I never take the same lover twice. But I may change my mind . . ."

Heath slid his lips up the back of her neck. Fuck, she smelled so clean and womanly. Dragging in her scent made his head swim. He couldn't forget the crushing pleasure she'd given him last night. Almost of its own volition, the hand he'd wedged under her body raised up to cup her breast and tease the peaked nipple through the sheer fabric. The palm he'd thrown around her hip lowered, settling over her mound. Dampness instantly coated his fingers.

"Stop," she said even as she arched her hips, thrusting her pussy directly into his touch.

He rubbed her with slow circles and pressed his lips to her ear.

"Stop what, love? Stop making you feel good? Stop making you moan and ache for the orgasm you know I can give you?"

Jolie merely answered with a jagged cry, so Heath kept on, sliding his fingers between her slick folds and rubbing her sensitive flesh with methodical strokes.

Her clit hardened. Her flesh swelled. She gasped, writhed, gyrating back against him with a sensual sway that nearly undid him. He was an adult male; he'd had more than a lap dance or two. He'd had a lot of sexual partners. No woman had ever incited this sort of blinding need to tear away the few clothes they both wore and slide inside her immediately.

Against him, Jolie tensed and began to clutch the sheets. She tossed her head back to his shoulder, whispering his name. They moved together in complete darkness, but she lit him up in ways he couldn't fight. He heard nothing but her pants and cries, smelled nothing but the musk of her growing need, felt nothing except her sweet body wriggling against his.

When her moans turned desperate, Heath paused. Desire coated him with sweat. His thoughts raced. What now? Teach her a lesson? Or give them both what they wanted, consequences be damned?

Bloody hell, he'd allowed his pride and his dick to lead him into this mess. Now he either had to break his one cardinal rule . . . or suffer the torment of her nearness all night without relief.

"Heath!" she gripped his thigh, nails digging little stinging half-moons into his skin.

He nipped at her ear, wishing like hell he could see the pleasure on her face, the sheer beauty of her response. Damn it all, he didn't want to prove a point about who had the sexual control.

He simply wanted *her*.

Scrambling to one side, he rolled Jolie to her back. In the shadowed room, he searched her flushed face, her dilated eyes. She panted, and her lips drew his stare. The ache tightened in his gut.

Since losing Anna, he'd wanted sex but he hadn't wanted any particular woman. The no-repeat rule had been easy because he hadn't ever been tempted to break it.

As she had from the start, Jolie challenged him on every level.

He shouldn't touch her again. It wasn't smart. It wouldn't end well. But Heath couldn't seem to stop wanting her.

"What is it?" she murmured, her body tense, waiting.

He could have answered that a hundred ways. With a redirecting reminder that she needed sleep to prepare for her "big day." An alpha pronouncement that he wouldn't reward her running off with an orgasm. Either of those would squash the intimacy developing between them.

When he opened his mouth, something else came out. "Karis told me you know about Anna."

She exhaled away some of her sexual tension. Her face softened. "Losing her must have been awful."

"Devastating." Why the hell had he brought that up? He wasn't saying that he couldn't have sex because he was still too grief-stricken. It wasn't true, and she would know better.

"I'm sorry."

And she was. Jolie didn't often wear her emotions on her face but he saw her sincerity.

It struck him then exactly what he was trying to say. "I don't get involved anymore."

"I don't get involved ever."

That was a shame. Jolie had so much to offer, even if she didn't see it. She would light up someone's world. Life with her would never be boring, that was certain. Her sharp wit kept Heath guessing. If she wanted advice, Jolie would ask but she would never wait for his guidance to act. He appreciated her moxie and independence. She wasn't—in any way—a girl.

He should tell her that she had every reason to get involved with someone but he'd sound like a hypocrite. Worse, if she took his advice, he'd have to know another man touched her. He would have to imagine another man sliding his fingertips over the pale glow of her skin and looking into her eyes before he kissed her lips, inhaled her scent, then surged inside her soft silk body.

At the thought, Heath jerked away. He was surprised by his clenched fists.

The movement tugged at their joined ankles.

Jolie touched a tentative hand to his shoulder. "You okay?"

No. He was coming apart with want but too bound up to take her again. He liked her. He cared when he fucking didn't want to. In his head, he replayed finding her in the coffeehouse with Callie, silently challenging him. He felt her desperation when she'd clung on the back of his motorcycle as they dashed through the night to rescue Karis from the office break-in. He saw her taunt him just minutes ago with her transparent nightgown as she eschewed knickers. He remembered her face flushing with pleasure last night before orgasm while he drowned in her feminine heat.

"I didn't protect Anna when it mattered." His voice sounded hoarse. "I didn't see the threat coming, didn't put the pieces of the puzzle together. I still haven't. And I regret that every day. With you, there's danger on the horizon. Stop making it so bloody hard for me to do my job."

She swallowed audibly. "I wasn't trying to make it hard today. I needed a friend." She sighed. "I wanted less distraction. I can't look at you and not . . . want."

At her words, he squeezed his eyes shut, his entire body going tense. He understood precisely what she meant. The two of them together was like throwing oil on a bonfire.

Heath turned back to her in the dark, challenging. "What are we doing?"

She shrugged. "Let's . . . go to sleep."

Heath didn't know if that would be possible for him. His cock throbbed for her. His gut clenched. His chest ached. His thoughts were wrung inside out.

He prayed the answers would look clearer in the morning. "All right. But understand me." He zeroed in on her. "Whether you meant to or not, you put yourself at risk today. Don't make me live through the guilt of not being able to save someone else."

He almost choked on those words. It wasn't easy swallowing that much blame.

She didn't break the moment with words, merely nodded.

"Sleep well." He lay back and stared at the ceiling. It would be a long night.

Jolie hesitated, then curled up against him. Their feet tangled. He felt her warm breaths on his chest. This was her way of comforting him, and it touched him on a level that terrified him.

Even so, Heath wrapped his arm around her and closed his eyes. Since Anna, Jolie was the only woman with whom he'd actually slept, he realized. Sex aside, he'd relaxed enough beside her to fall into healing slumber. For once, being more than physically close to a woman hadn't felt wrong.

That idea terrified him, too.

"It's okay," she whispered, rubbing her bound ankle against his. "I won't go anywhere. I promise."

Chapter Eight

Rule for success number eight:
Steady your reactions.

AFTER sleeping better than expected, Heath was surprised to wake feeling restless. He untied his ankle from Jolie's, rose, and made coffee. Barely five a.m. Normally, if he felt this agitated, he hit the gym or went for a run. He couldn't leave her side now.

But with Jolie still sleeping peacefully, that left him alone with his thoughts.

Briefly, he thought about calling Mystery. She would talk to him. And she knew him, after all.

Well . . . did she really? He frowned. Perhaps it was more accurate to say he knew her. He'd made it his job to learn Mystery's every habit, quirk, and thought. But he'd never opened up to her. Since she'd gone from his day-to-day life, he realized he hadn't been in love with her as much as she had been a comforting fixture. She was smart, had a fun sense of humor. His life with her had approached something like normal. Knowing at the end of every day that he'd kept her safe to see another sunrise had given him satisfaction. After the past few days, he saw clearly that caring about her wasn't the same as the twisting, burning, ever-present ache to claim, comfort, and understand that Jolie made him feel.

Maybe that's why he'd awakened so agitated. Sleep hadn't changed his outlook. She was still the fever he couldn't shake.

Heath grabbed his phone from his pocket and turned it over in his hands. He'd heard a rumor a few weeks back that Myles, his best mate from his MI5 days, had remarried and was expecting a baby again. Good news for him. Great, in fact.

Heath thought back through the last half dozen years of random shags, the avoidance of letting anyone too close. How had Myles managed to work past the grief and guilt to let go of the tragedy and embrace the future again?

Once, he and Myles had done everything together—worked, caroused, drank. Eventually, they'd both gotten married. Anna and Myles's wife Lucy had got on right away and become the best of friends. Then one day they'd both been gone in the same senseless act of violence, leaving him and his mate struggling with grief and guilt. Heath hadn't called Myles much after they'd become widowed. The man reminded him too much of all he'd lost. Myles hadn't called a lot, either. Heath assumed that, like him, he hadn't been able to handle the memories.

In addition to losing his wife that day, Heath had lost his one real friend.

A couple of weeks after Anna's death, he'd quit his job and made it his mission to extract revenge. He had been successful . . . somewhat, learning the name of the thug who'd pulled the trigger, ending Anna's and Lucy's lives, along with the baby she and Myles had been expecting. The baby Anna had been so envious of. But their killer had been nothing more than a hired gun with a few low-level accomplices, willing to snuff out virtually anyone for a price. They'd been puppets before he had easily wasted them. To this day, Heath had no notion who'd been pulling their strings.

Revenge had solved nothing, and afterward he'd had nothing

left but to sink into the bottom of a bottle. Thankfully, a connection at MI5 had recommended him to Marshall Mullins as a potential bodyguard for Mystery. The job had probably saved his life.

Heath glanced at his phone again, then punched in the security code and flipped through his contacts. Though he'd upgraded devices more than once through various versions and countries, he'd never quite been able to let go of Myles's number. It remained one of his few links to the past. He hadn't dialed it in at least a half dozen years, had scarcely thought at all about calling in nearly five.

Now he considered it—hard.

It wasn't yet noon in London. Myles would be up and working. Rumor had it his old friend had a managerial role now. Oh, that was supposed to be classified but Heath heard whispers from time to time. Myles had been shot a couple years ago. He'd also turned forty a few months back. With his new wife pregnant, it made sense for the man to slow it down, play it safe.

Myles had likely changed his number in the ensuing years. If not, what were the odds his old partner and friend would even answer? Would he want to hear from the ghost of his past or stop his life to listen to an old mate's current woes?

"Heath?" Jolie stood in the opening of the hallway, wrapping a fuzzy bathrobe around her middle. Her hair looked adorably mussed. Concern wrinkled her brow.

He wanted to grab her, hold her, take her back to bed. Forget the world.

Instead, he stood and pocketed his phone again. "Morning." Calling Myles after all these years would only stir up the past. Dealing with the present was all he could handle now. "Coffee?"

"Sure. I'll need a tub of it today. I'd like to get into the office early and go over my pitch a few more times."

He nodded. "I installed as much of the security equipment as I could by myself yesterday. I'd like to finish the rest today. We should get moving."

"I'll wake my sister. I hate to. When I peeked at her, she was sleeping so soundly."

He sent her an apologetic expression. "We can't leave her alone just yet. She'll have opportunities to sleep in once I've assigned her a bodyguard. I'll get that done today as well."

Jolie woke Karis, and soon they were on their way to the office. Once there, Heath sat in a makeshift cubicle, testing the last of the card readers. To get everything operational by close of business today, he needed help, especially setting up the files that would log all the swiped activities, as well as enabling a redundant backup storage system for the data. He texted Sean Mackenzie. Moments later, his phone dinged with a reply. The former fed was stopping by with solutions to several of his issues. Heath sent back his thanks.

Callie's husband appeared at the suite's door about two hours later. Beside him stood another man. Blond and obviously military at some point, he looked watchful, war-hardened, and itching for action. Heath very much feared the bloke had come to the right place.

"Heath, this is Cutter Bryant," Sean introduced. "He works for Joaquin and the Edgington brothers. He has an assignment starting in Dallas a week from Monday, so they've lent him to us until then, if that's agreeable. It gives you a bit of time to find Karis someone more permanently, if necessary."

He held out his hand. "Hello."

Cutter shook it politely enough but clearly he wanted to get down to business. "What's up?"

"A dodgy situation I suspect could quickly turn dangerous."

When Cutter smiled, it wasn't happy or polite. "Excellent."

Heath liked him instantly. "Why don't I introduce you to Karis? She's . . ." How did he explain the sweet, slightly bohemian girl? "She's got a soft heart and she's trying to put on a brave face but I think she's scared."

"Roger that. I'll try not to raise my voice above a dull roar or startle her unless necessary."

"Great." Sean smiled. "Jack Cole is lending Stone to you for the tech help. He should be here in a few hours." He withdrew his keys. "I'm joining Callie and Thorpe for a late lunch since her contractions have stopped for now. Let me know if there's a change of plans or you need something else." When he turned to leave, Sean paused. "By the way, the license plate you asked me to run? That car came back as stolen. It's been recovered and local CSI swept it. Clean."

So a dead end. Damn. "Thanks for trying."

"Always. I asked Thorpe to put in a call. He knows people at city hall. They're going to look into the street cameras in that area, see if they picked up a face. We should have an answer in a few days. I'll let you know."

An excellent suggestion. Heath hoped that nothing dangerous happened while they waited.

With a handshake, Sean left. Heath turned to Cutter and sized the man up. In a perfect situation, finding Karis additional security wouldn't be necessary. But everything now was far from ideal. Jolie would be lost if something happened to her sister. Heath would never be more than her temporary lover, but while they were together, he intended to keep her as safe and happy as he could. The world would be a less interesting place if grief dimmed Jolie Quinn's light.

And wasn't he sounding like a philosophical shit?

"Come with me." He led Cutter down the hall to a conference room and shut the door.

Heath filled him in on everything happening around Betti. He'd hoped that applying a fresh head to the situation would help him find new perspective but Cutter seemed as perplexed as he was.

"Why send gifts to Karis if Jolie is the target? If she's actually the target at all . . ." The guy scowled.

"Precisely. Nothing quite adds up. I would be less worried if these three incidents hadn't taken place so closely together and if the intruder hadn't been firing real bullets."

"What's next?"

"See if the police found any evidence, I suppose. The prowler wore gloves, so I doubt he left behind prints. If the official investigation is fruitless, I fear I'm in a position of waiting for something else to happen that will perhaps provide more clues. Both sisters swear they don't have any enemies. I'm not even certain what this man wants, so I haven't the faintest notion where to look next. Or even what to look for."

Cutter swore. "I've got nearly ten days to lend a hand. Hopefully, this situation comes to a head before then."

"Would you like to meet Karis now?"

"Let's do it."

Heath had a feeling the two would be like oil and water. Cutter seemed like the decisive sort, a man of action and few words. Karis fluttered her way through life, seeking out happiness like a moth searching for a flame.

Before they could make their way out of the conference room, Cutter's phone rang in a high-pitched chirp. "One minute. This might be an emergency."

Heath nodded as Cutter ripped the phone from the holder clipped to his belt, then turned away for some privacy. "Brea? What is it?"

A pause. A faint murmur of a voice on the other end sounded rushed and panicked.

"Slow down. It's okay. What's going on?"

Whatever she said made Cutter's entire body tense. A forbidding thunder suddenly rolled off him. "Have you seen a doctor?"

Heath went on high alert himself. Not that he tried to eavesdrop, but in a small room, he couldn't fail to hear. The snippets he caught made him worry for the woman on the other end of the phone.

"You need to make an appointment today. It's not going to go away."

Now Heath could hear the teary, pleading tone on the other end and frowned.

"You need to see the doctor first. I'll go with you. I promise not to do anything until then. After that, if you're right—" She interrupted him, and he shook his head. "No. I can't promise I won't kill him."

More sobs sounded over the line.

"It's okay, sweetheart." Cutter's voice took a gentle turn. "We'll figure it out. I'll take care of you. I always have. I always will."

A minute later, they hung up and Cutter shoved his phone back into its clip, grinding his teeth together as if his promise of temporary non-violence had used up a serious amount of restraint.

"It's none of my business, but was that your wife? If so, you should know that Karis is in love with the idea of love and may make a pass at you."

Cutter sent him a WTF glance. "No. Brea is my best friend. We've never . . . It's not like that."

Heath wondered if Cutter truly meant that or if he was deluding himself. "Is she ill?"

He hesitated, sighed. "A couple of months back, I got in a hostage standoff. I managed to get the captive released but I had no way out myself. I was outmanned and outgunned. The situation required the help of a world-class sniper. Brea and I know one, a complete asshole of the first order. He likes to be called One-Mile as a nod to his longest kill shot. She asked him to get me out of the bind. He agreed to do it . . . for a price."

Shock jolted Heath. "The bastard coerced her into sleeping with him in order to save you?"

"Yeah." He sighed long and heavy. "And now she thinks she's pregnant. I work with the asshole every single day. I can't wait to kill him."

"That option puts you in jail, mind you. Perhaps you could make him own up to his responsibility?"

"Oh, he'd marry Brea tomorrow. But the fucker isn't good enough for her. Lowlife scum-sucking asswipe. He'd make her absolutely miserable. *I'll* take care of her. Pierce Walker won't ever touch her again." Cutter seemed to shake himself from his anger.

"But that's another problem for later. Sorry. Let's get back on track so I can figure out how best to keep Karis protected."

"Very good." Heath led the other man down the hall, in search of Jolie's sister.

Instead, he found Arthur standing in the girl's cubicle looking slightly flustered. "Have you seen Karis?"

As far as he knew, the sisters had planned to run through the investor pitch together. "No. I escorted her and her sister to work this morning. Maybe they've gone to her office."

With long strides, he made his way to the reception area at the front, Arthur and Cutter following. Jolie's office sat empty, her computer dark.

If the sisters weren't in her office, where the hell had they gone? Heath frowned, his senses sharpening.

Arthur scratched his head. "That's weird. I saw Karis thirty minutes ago. I heard Jolie in her office, on the phone. I wonder where they went."

And whether they'd gone voluntarily. Last night, Jolie had promised not to leave him. She might be many things—driven, stubborn, headstrong—but she was a woman of her word.

Fear nicked Heath's composure.

Damn it, he hadn't yet finished installing the last bit of the security system, so he didn't know the door through which she might have gone, in which direction to begin the search.

Taking a breath and fighting for calm, he peeked through the suite's windows and into the lot. Karis's little car still squatted next to her sister's. If they'd gone, who had driven them away? Jolie hadn't mentioned an appointment off-site. He would have insisted on going.

Yanking his phone from his pocket, he launched the app he'd secretly installed to trace her mobile, only to realize moments later it was somewhere in the building. He sent a text. The device dinged not two feet from him.

She was not where she should be and had no way to contact him if someone tried to hurt her.

Fear began to chill into panic.

Visions of her body limp and lifeless on a morgue table, waiting for identification, ran through his head. Heath had done that once already. He'd be damned if he ever endured that again.

"We've got to find them," he barked at the men.

"Let's fan out," Cutter suggested.

"Check the break room on the east side of the office and bathrooms through the door to the south. I'll hit the file room at the west." He turned to Wisteria, who meandered to her desk just then. "Did Jolie and Karis leave?"

The blonde shrugged. "I don't know. Jolie asked me to clean up the break room and organize the supply cabinet. I've been back there for the last hour."

Heath held in a curse and forced himself to breathe. But his heart revved. Fear burned. "Keep looking, everyone."

As Cutter darted away, Heath tore down the hall toward the back of the suite, a vision of life without Jolie assaulting his brain. He imagined her as prey of a killer, imagined standing over her remains sealed forever in a casket while people sang, the scent of too many flowers choking him as he wondered when everything had gone so fucking wrong. How he would cope without her?

Bloody hell. He was falling for her. And now he might lose her.

"Jolie . . ." he called. "Jolie!"

A moment later, the door to the file room opened and she poked her head out. "What?"

His relief in seeing her was a bleeding, palpable thing. His breath rushed out with a shudder. He tried to grab hold of himself, waited for calm to return.

Nothing. He still felt shaky and worried and overwrought.

"Is Karis with you?" Arthur asked behind him, sounding somewhere between concerned and confused.

The door opened wider, and her younger sister stepped out. "Yeah, I'm just helping Jolie with her pitch for tonight."

"In here?" Heath demanded.

"You were in the conference room with that hot—" Karis stopped herself. "That other guy."

"And my office phone kept ringing since Wisteria was busy in the break room and couldn't answer." Jolie frowned. "So we came in here and locked the door. Is that a problem?"

"It is when you don't tell me and don't take your phone with you."

"We didn't go far," she argued.

"Um . . ." The accountant looked ruffled as he focused on Karis. "The invoices for the . . . ah, the photographer who took the website pictures? I'd like to go over them today." He directed his attention to Jolie. "And I have a question for you, boss. Can you spare a minute?"

"No, she can't." Heath couldn't wait another second to get to Jolie. He knew all too well that life could be short and he intended to seize this opportunity now. "She's busy." He marched toward her, pausing to peer at Karis. "You're all right?"

She looked bewildered. "Yeah. Why wouldn't I be?"

"Excellent. Will you excuse us?"

Karis glanced between him and Jolie. Understanding lit her eyes. Her voice dropped to a whisper. "Go easy on my sister. She's really nervous about tonight and—"

Heath stepped into the little room and shut the door in her face. Then he locked it.

"What are you doing?" Jolie's voice shook.

She must feel the tension pouring off him, couldn't possibly miss his restraint hanging by a thread.

He dragged in a breath, then another. Every urge running through his head was foolish and mad and irresponsible.

Heath didn't care anymore.

He took two long steps toward her and pulled her stiff body against him. "What I should have done last night."

His lips crashed over hers. He was so far past worrying whether this was right or wrong, whether he should break his own rule or not. He only knew that holding Jolie felt perfect, and in that moment he needed her alive and warm and welcoming in his arms.

She met him halfway, opening to him instantly. He ate at her mouth as if he was both starved and half-crazed. She was there with him—every breath, every touch, every heartbeat. She pumped his veins full of need, fired his blood with warmth.

The last eighteen hours he hadn't been inside her had felt like the worst sort of hell.

As Heath reached for her skirt and lifted the hem over her hips, he brushed his lips across the swells of her breasts. "Give me your knickers."

"What?" Her voice shook, her expression puzzled. "No. Heath—"

"I thought you had disappeared. I thought . . ." He clenched his jaw tight and swallowed the words. "I thought the worst. I don't want to think now. Take off your whatever you're wearing under that skirt."

Somewhere in the back of his head, Heath suspected she would balk because his kneejerk response was out of line. But he couldn't stop it. To lose Jolie to violence—hell, to lose her at all—would do something to him. Heath didn't want to consider what that meant.

He should slow down, scale back, but the blinding, primal urge to have her against him, around him, holding on to him, and crying out his name wouldn't be banished.

"I'm here," she assured, not moving to do his bidding. "I'm fine. But I can't have sex with you now, in my place of business." She frowned. "You can't have sex with me again, either, remember?"

He no longer cared about his no-repeat rule because he'd found a good reason to break it.

He bent to her ear, softly commanding, "I want your knickers, Jolie. Give them to me."

"We're supposed to be working," she argued but now sounded breathy. "My sister and I—"

"Hand them over or I'll take them. Unless you're saying no. Say that, and I'll stop."

She swallowed, blinked, stared as if trying to figure him out. Maybe it was the barely leashed need pinging off his body. Maybe it was her own hunger.

He didn't care when she bit her lip, then bent and removed her panties. Then she gave the silky scrap to him.

His fingers closed around the warm softness that had just graced her skin. "Thank you."

He held the garment to his nose. Her breath caught as he inhaled her scent. *Hmm . . .*

Her nipples beaded under her white blouse. He wanted that—and her standard bra beneath—gone.

Heath shoved her lacy knickers in his pocket, then he brushed his knuckles over the curve of her breasts before settling his fingers at the top button of the filmy shirt. "Tell me you want this."

She hesitated for a moment before she gave in. "I want it."

That should make him happy, satisfy the requirement for consent. Instead, the words only made him ache more. "Tell me you want *me*."

By god, if he was going to break his one rule for her, he was all but admitting—to her and himself—that she meant more than a fuck. That she was important.

Her breathing turned choppy. Jolie stared, searching his face. "Will you resent me later?"

She worried that he'd blame her for giving in and distance himself afterward. She feared he'd hurt her, just as Karis had said. "I think I'm way past that."

A wariness he wanted gone gleamed from her eyes. "I'd be taking a chance."

"You won't regret it. I need to feel you." That was bloody hard for him to admit.

Jolie hesitated, clearly grappling. "I still don't want anything lasting. I'm not looking for love."

She might believe that, but she was fooling herself. Still, Heath didn't argue because he had to have her. "I understand. I want you here, now, mine in this moment. Can you give me that?"

"Yes."

Heath didn't think for a single instant that would be the end of the passion between them, not when it gripped him in the sort of chokehold he'd never experienced. He didn't think he affected her any less. His head reeled with the possibilities and implications but the last thing he wanted to do now was pry the attraction apart and examine it.

"Is that a yes? You want me?" he demanded.

Her lips parted softly. "I don't know how *not* to want you."

That was all he needed to hear.

He began tearing into her blouse, unfastening one button after the other with ruthless efficiency, then pushing the pearly silk from her shoulders. Jolie shrugged it off the rest of the way, letting it skim down her arms, then onto the floor.

Her bra was built for efficiency, not seduction. Heath didn't care what her lingerie looked like. She was still unbearably sexy to him. And that white cotton was in his way. "Bra off."

"I don't like it when you give me orders."

Her breathless anticipation made her a liar. She loved it when he gave orders. It was only afterward, when they weren't in a haze of passion, that the strong female in her had second thoughts. Jolie would soon learn he had no desire to strip her power, just her body.

"I promise to make it worth your while, love."

Jolie flushed softly. Her lips parted. After a long moment, she reached behind her back and unhooked the garment. When she relaxed her shoulders, it fell away. Heath didn't bother to watch the garment hit the floor. He was too busy staring, seeing her body soften, her nipples harden, her gaze cling to him as if he alone held the answers to her burning questions.

Her pale skin fascinated him. Over the years he'd had sex with women of nearly every race, color, and creed. But Jolie wasn't like any of them. The night they'd shared passion, he'd taken her repeatedly in the dark, not really savoring the pristine, milky flesh.

Now wasn't the time, he knew. The office wasn't the place. But if he was going to break his no-repeat rule once, he could do it again and again, until he satisfied his desire to consume every part of her.

Heath turned her toward the wall and lifted her businesslike skirt as his hungry gaze ate up her alabaster shoulders, the smooth expanse of her back that led to the gentle sway of her hips. He could grip them, tell her to spread her legs and brace her hands against the wall and scream at will. He'd done it hundreds of times with hundreds of faceless women.

But he couldn't make himself speak those practiced words to Jolie. He'd fucked so many women standing up and from behind precisely because it was impersonal. He never had to look into a woman's eyes and care what she was thinking during sex, never risk knowing her beyond a shared orgasm.

Taking Jolie like that would never satisfy him.

"Talk to me," he skimmed his lips up her neck and murmured in her ear. "Tell me what you like, what you want."

He ached to satisfy her in the way she wanted to be pleasured.

"Touch my nipples. Kiss me. Make this burning go away."

A little smile tugged at his lips. The burning was never going to go away, he feared. But he didn't mention that now. He merely gripped her hips and turned her to face him again. "In that order?"

"Yeah," she challenged. "Hurry."

Of course she'd have an assertive side when it came to sex. That was Jolie.

Caressing his way down her chest, he cupped the firm weight of one of her breasts in his palm, thumbing the nipple. Then he lowered his head and swallowed the sweet sound of her gasp before he delved deeper and possessed her lips utterly.

Sweet honey surrender. He savored her texture as she opened to him, tasted her tongue. The pleasure was like a riptide, pulling him under until he didn't care that he was drowning.

Jolie threw her arms around his neck and jumped into the kiss with a passion that had his body tightening, his cock hardening, his head reeling.

He pinched her nipples, worked them, dragged his knuckles over them, then started the cycle again. They stiffened. She whimpered, digging her nails into him, sharp even through his T-shirt. He reveled in the fact that he could seemingly get under this amazing woman's skin and make her stop thinking long enough to feel.

"Heath." She pulled away with a gasp, reaching for his all-too-eager shaft.

Once she touched him, he'd be inside her in less than three seconds. He wasn't ready for that yet. Jolie didn't know it, but neither was she.

Swallowing a curse, he lifted her onto the nearest flat surface—a forgotten desk—and shoved her skirt around her hips. Jolie didn't play coy; she knew what he liked. She laid back and spread her sleek thighs.

He found himself staring at her dark curls and feminine pink flesh.

Desire seared him as he bent his head and inhaled her scent with a groan.

Everything about her dazzled and thrilled him. Other people would argue that she wasn't perfect. She could be every bit as aggressive as any of her male counterparts. She had a temper, a ruthless streak, a desire to control everything. Yet she cared, she listened, and she was often honest even when it hurt her. She had a heady sort of feminine lure Heath had never experienced.

Gripping her thighs, he sank between them, braced over her as he pierced her folds with his tongue and raked his way up her wet slit. He lapped at her, focused on the little bud at the apex before he sucked it between his lips and drew it deep.

As he tasted her, his heart thrummed in his chest with a wild cant. Her flavor was so exquisitely sweet and tart and addicting as she melted around him. She responded artlessly, groaning as she threw her head back with a long, low wail.

Everything about her intoxicated him. He bloody loved this intimacy, the potent thrill of owning her. Vaguely, he wondered how he'd resist wanting to taste her every time he saw her.

When she spread wider and gripped his head with grasping fingers, another hoarse cry fell from her lips. "Heath!"

The rest of the office could probably hear them, but he wasn't about to quiet her or stop the glide of his tongue through her flesh. The urge to consume her utterly fired his blood.

He pulled her vulva apart with his thumbs to expose her, open her to him totally. Then he slid a pair of fingers into her opening, already swelling in pleasure. She clenched around him, clamping down tight as she bucked her hips in demand, disturbing the rhythm of his tongue. With his free hand, he held her down to the table.

"Stop thrashing. You can't control this orgasm. It's not for you to take. It's mine to give you."

"Then give it to me now." Her voice sounded like something between a whimper and a demand.

Perhaps he should remind her that he was in charge in the bedroom, but that would require him to stop exploring her succulent heat with his mouth again and have a conversation in which she'd merely argue. Or try insisting again that he hurry this pleasure along.

Talking was overrated.

"Once you hold still, I will," he murmured the silky vow across her skin. "If you do, I'll fuck you with my fingers and my tongue. I'll wring orgasms out of you until you're deliciously sore and sated. I'll work my cock inside your pussy, which I know will be snug and hot and perfect. I'll ride you until you can't scream anymore."

Almost instantly, Jolie stilled. Her body trembled in anticipation. Her eyes pleaded in a way her words simply didn't.

Heath smiled. Now he had her.

Gliding his fingers in and out of her tight walls, he lowered his mouth to her clit again, nudging, teasing, the slow drag making her breath shudder and her skin flush. Her fingers found their way to his head again as she tried to grip his too-short hair. Her nails dragged against his scalp with a little bite of pain that urged him on. He shuddered against the dizzying rise of need.

Around him, he could feel the swelling of her folds, the clenching of her cunt. She panted, made other sounds he barely recognized, welcomed him by opening even wider.

God, when had any woman ever been half so alluring?

Tasting a female was an intimacy he hadn't indulged in for years. It required not only time, a bed, and some privacy, but it implied a deeper connection than mere fucking. It meant that a woman had to share every bit of her body in a way that left her vulnerable. Since Anna, he hadn't sought anything but no-strings sex.

Jolie changed everything. Whatever the reason, whatever her lure, he couldn't seem to get enough of her.

"Oh, love. You're tangy and sweet on my tongue." He twisted his fingers in her opening and found a sensitive spot, then rubbed it ruthlessly. "I'm going to want this again. I'm going to crave you. We'll spend our lunches with my head between your legs. I'll need you again with evening cocktails. And dessert." He lapped at her again. "Especially dessert."

"That's too much, too c-crazy. Y-you can't . . ."

Since she couldn't speak without stuttering or losing her train of thought, Heath knew he could have her however he wanted her now. She would let him.

He smiled and dragged his tongue through her essence again. "Never tell me I can't. I'll prove you wrong. Over and over. You're going to come, aren't you?"

She whimpered and nodded frantically. "I . . . Oh, my god. I can't stop it."

"Let's have it. I want it. I want all of you."

"That's it. Yes!" She dragged in a huge gulp of air. A glance up the beautiful curves of her body proved her nipples tight, her lips parted, her dilated green eyes focused on him and widening with every uptick in pleasure. Then sensual shock splashed across her delicate face. "*Heath!*"

Her entire body convulsed with the force of her ecstasy, legs shaking, hips bucking, back arching, lungs working.

He looked up her body. She was positively stunning, and Heath only wanted her more as he ate at her like a starving man. He was determined to guide her into the sugary haze of aftermath so she'd be damn pliant when he impaled her and fucked her with abandon.

Jolie tried to close her legs, as if she'd suddenly decided to be embarrassed that she'd climaxed nearly hard enough to shake the walls. Heath refused to allow her that misplaced modesty now. He pushed against her tensed thighs and continued to lick, suck, and nibble, groaning when she somehow turned sweeter, diving in deeper when she softened and became accepting beneath him again. Ravenous when her breath became uneven and the little moans filled his ears. Harder than hell when she swelled with need once more and he realized just how bloody tight she would be.

Jerking away, he stood and fumbled through his pockets until he found a foil square—the last he had tucked away.

Fuck, he hoped once was enough to satisfy this craving. Since he was with Jolie, he had his doubts.

His movements were a blur and he blocked out her whimpering protests until he'd sheathed his cock and held himself at her opening. Then he shoved his way in with one savage thrust.

Jolie twisted her back and cried out in an impatient roar. "Yes . . . Fuck me."

Oh, he would do far more than that. And if she wasn't ready to admit that whatever they had went beyond mere sex, that was all right. He'd only just realized it himself. Being with her again, inside her, was undeniable proof. The rightness of her lit up his body, rolled down his spine in an electric shudder. He suspected Jolie also knew what they shared wasn't meaningless. But he'd be patient . . . for now.

Leaning over her, he balanced his forehead on hers. She exhaled against his lips, then she breathed in. Heath kissed her, letting her taste the passion he'd wrung from her. She didn't fight, so he grabbed her hair, changed the angle of the kiss to dive deep, and pressed his hips forward until she took every last inch of his cock.

He didn't move his body then, just filled her mouth, her pussy, her senses. It wasn't long before she wrapped her legs around his middle and arched restlessly, as if she needed everything he could give her.

He lifted his lips, narrowed his eyes at her. "You keep trying to control the way I fuck you, Jolie. Stop. It won't happen."

"Why are you teasing me? What are you waiting for?"

"Didn't you learn anything when I had my mouth on you? Didn't it feel better when you finally let me send you to climax? It wouldn't have been half so good if you'd taken it when you wanted it."

Jolie stared at him as if understanding that he had answers to questions she'd never thought to ask. "I know. But we shouldn't be doing this. I have work."

When she gave him a half-hearted push, he held her still. The last thing Jolie needed was for her brain to work overtime, for her anxiety to notch up before tonight's crucial dinner. Best if he drowned her in bliss, sated and relaxed her. Even better if he some-how helped her realize this crazy spark between them probably wasn't going to fizzle out.

Heath wrapped his fingers around the edge of the table above her head and gripped tight, using the leverage to pull himself deeper into her body, reveling in her gasp. "Enjoying the pleasure, love? How does that feel?"

She didn't admit aloud that he was turning her inside out . . . but she stopped arguing. Instead, she let him have his way, meeting him thrust for thrust as he pulled back to the sensitive head of his cock, only to drive in once more, ensuring that he hit every tender spot along the way. He ground his pelvis against hers at the top of the stroke, giving her awakened clit a press-rub that sparked more need.

Jolie cried out again. She was so damn responsive, fit him so perfectly. And once they passed the negotiations of the will-we-or-won't-we stage, she always gave him her total attention, complete arousal, and whole body.

In that moment, it wasn't enough. He wanted her soul. No, that wasn't all. He fucking wanted her heart. Her devotion. Her tomorrows.

That should have alarmed the hell out of him. At the moment all he could think about was how explosive the orgasm between them was going to be and how tightly he intended to hold her afterward.

"Take everything I'm giving you, Jolie. Every kiss . . ." He dragged his lips up her neck, then to her ear. "Every stroke, every inch. All my determination to make certain you crave me again and again."

"I already do," she admitted in a rush. "It's never been like this, so intense, so addicting, so distracting."

Drunk on triumph, Heath plunged inside her even harder.

She tightened on him again, and it drove him to new heights. Not just because the sensation shot down his cock like lightning or because the sheer force of his arousal felt like lava running through his veins. No. Somehow, they were connected deeper than their bodies.

Her arms tightened around him, fingers digging into his shoulders, around his spine as she dragged them lower—until she cupped his backside, rocking with him and urging him deeper with every thrust.

"Jolie," he gasped. "Love . . ."

"Yes." She nodded frantically. "Yes. Oh, hell. Yeeessss. Heath . . . *Heath!*"

Fire lit his blood, burned his flesh. He held her tighter as he felt her convulse around him then followed her into the white-hot ecstasy that blistered as much as it soothed. And as he plunged into her one last time, Jolie held tight to his hips and pulled him in even more, continuing to grind out her climax and proving what he already knew: She would give herself to the people in her life, the people she knew and trusted and cared about. But she would also never be a passive partner who laid back and allowed things to happen to her. Jolie was a take-charge woman.

Suddenly, despite his years with Anna and his attraction to girls who might never manage anything more ambitious than a grocery list, Heath couldn't imagine sex—or life—with a woman who didn't have her own agenda, goals, and demands. In short, he couldn't imagine life without Jolie.

Chapter Nine

Rule for success number nine:
Know your moral compass and stick to it.

JOLIE almost died of embarrassment when she and Heath hastily righted their clothes and emerged from the file room. The rest of the staff lingered near the door, pretending they had business in the vicinity but they were gawking. No, they were judging. And they were entitled to.

Mortification rolled through her. She'd been strict about workplace policies that encouraged maximum productivity, like no in-office dating. Her sister had once called her an automaton, an accusation Jolie had both denied and spurned. But she had to admit that until now—until Heath—she hadn't understood how people could be so swept away by their emotions. For the first time, she'd behaved all too humanly.

Being fallible, vulnerable was a brand-new feeling for her.

"Hi." She smoothed her hair, gathering her wits. "You're all here. Wow. Um . . . You're probably angry or shocked. What just happened was unprofessional. I owe every one of you a huge apology. I'm deeply sorry."

No one said a word, merely blinked or stared mutely.

They were shocked. Jolie wasn't surprised.

Hell, she should lead by example, which meant immediately relieving Heath of his duties. Once, she would have done that without a second thought. But the sex had been half her fault. She couldn't cast all the blame on him.

But fairness and staff safety were only minor reasons she was choosing to keep him. The truth was, she felt way too satisfied—happy, even—to let him go.

When had she become one of those women who allowed a man or romance to influence her mood? Her choices? Her thoughts? Betti was on the verge of greatness, and nothing else should matter, least of all a relationship that likely wouldn't last.

She cleared her throat, plowing through the awkward moment with her staff. "If you need to voice your concerns about what happened, I'll make myself available on Monday. Once this meeting with Gardner is behind me, I'll obviously be giving some thought to Betti's policies. I want to be as fair as possible. Again, I'm truly sorry. Anything else?"

More silence, along with a shrug or two.

Well, after such a colossal screw-up, she couldn't possibly expect open arms. At least no one was yelling.

"Thanks for listening," she muttered. "And now . . . I guess we should all go back to work."

"But of course. Good luck with your concentration." Gerard gave her a conspiratorial wink. Then he eyed Heath speculatively before heading to his desk.

Rohan followed, fighting so hard to keep a straight face, his mouth contorted comically. Apparently, he found the boss being a screw-up humorous.

Wisteria looked teary and envious of the "true love" she was clearly convinced they shared. Jolie didn't want to think about how uncomfortably beyond infatuation her feelings for Heath had become.

With a sly smile playing at his mouth, Arthur turned his focus to the tablet in his hands. Oddly, her sexual faux pas seemed to have earned her brownie points from the accountant. Or maybe, in his mind, her office romp cancelled out his video game playing.

That left Karis.

Jolie turned to her sister, who silently asked how she was holding up. Jolie gave a nod. Physically, she'd never felt better.

Emotionally, she was a mess.

Forget the dozens of reasons she should still be pissed at herself for allowing Heath to seduce her or horrified that she'd had noisy office sex within earshot of her employees. Thankfully, she didn't have to deal with any negative blowback from her staff. But that still left the tangle of her feelings for Heath. Somehow, being surrounded by him, impaled and wrapped in his arms . . . She'd felt even more drawn to him today. She was afraid to ask why.

Her sister leaned close, whispering in her ear, "Don't beat yourself up. You're human. It's okay."

When Karis left to resume her work, relief spilled through Jolie. She took a deep breath to process everyone's surprisingly accepting reactions when she realized Heath still lingered. A stranger—a seasoned soldier with a buzz cut of golden stubble—stood beside him. When the guy met her gaze, his hard hazel eyes softened with an amused glint.

Heath straightened his shirt and cleared his throat, then dropped a palm to the small of her back. Marking his territory? As if he'd need to at this point . . .

"Jolie, this is Cutter. He's going to provide personal protection for your sister while we figure out if she needs an asset long term. He comes highly recommended and . . ." He frowned at the other man. "Have you met Karis, then?"

"Yep." Cutter's poorly concealed smile deepened. "You didn't mention to her that you'd be assigning a bodyguard. So that was an interesting conversation."

"It . . . slipped my mind." Heath turned the slightest bit red. "My apologies."

"Clearly you've been busy," Cutter drawled, then turned to her. "Ms. Quinn, your sister will be fine. I'll protect her, take a bullet for her if necessary, and make sure she lives another day."

His words startled Jolie. Would Heath do the same for her? Give his life? It was their job, and Cutter seemed more than adept. But Heath . . . He'd volunteered—no, insisted—that she needed him to watch over her. It had sounded distracting and intrusive. Now it felt so personal.

Of course, it wasn't the first time he'd agreed to risk his life for another. He'd guarded Mystery Mullins's body for years. That made something angry rip through her. God, she hated being jealous of a woman she'd never met. And she was afraid of where this angst was stemming from. It felt suspiciously like her heart.

She shoved her hand in Cutter's direction. "Thank you. I worry about my sister. The mysterious gifts have all been for her and this odd admirer has an uncanny knowledge of what she likes."

Cutter shook her hand. "No worries. I'll make sure nothing and no one gets to her."

Jolie nodded and glanced at her watch to avoid looking at either man. Just past lunchtime. Normally if she'd had a tough morning, she'd splurge on a mani/pedi. No time today. Or she'd go home and take a hot shower. But if she did that, Heath would follow her, watch her, distract her. Seduce her again?

Why had he broken his no-repeat rule? She didn't think he was the sort of man to act without thought, to be provoked so utterly by the heat of mere passion. He already had too many regrets to risk adding to the list. But he'd gone out on a limb to be with her. No, that wasn't quite it. To make love to her. That's what being with him today had felt like. They hadn't shared mere sex in the file room. He hadn't had it with her simply because he'd been sure she wouldn't get clingy or attached.

Jolie sneaked a peek at Heath. He watched her, his dark stare intent, focused, possessive. It made her breath catch, her heart rev.

Damn, damn, damn.

It was too much for her to handle now. She didn't need distractions. "I'll be in my office for the rest of the afternoon, making sure tonight goes smoothly."

Hiding.

Jolie didn't wait for either of them to reply, she simply headed down the hall. As she passed Wisteria's desk, she regarded her receptionist, who was tucking away the remnants of her lunch. "Do you need to use the bathroom or get something else?"

"No."

"Then stay in your seat and don't let anyone in until I say so. Hold all phone calls unless it's blood, death, or Richard Gardner."

"Of course." Wisteria nodded. "I'll give you some time alone."

Jolie was bowled over by the woman's kindness and understanding. "Thanks. Really."

She marched into her office and withdrew a piece of paper from her printer. When she dug around her desk and located a black marker, she wrote out in big capital letters: DO NOT DISTURB. Then she taped it on the front of her door before shutting and locking it.

Now what?

No idea. She needed a breather. She needed some peace until she had an answer.

Jolie pulled up her notes and made sure that she'd memorized all the pertinent financial figures for tonight. The Wi-Fi on her tablet worked fabulously, so she could show Richard all the progress on the website. She had cherry-picked a few of the best sketches she and Gerard had already completed. She really was beyond ready. She wasn't worried that she lacked the necessary ingredients to wow Gardner.

Her inability to focus right now scared the hell out of her.

It was only two. Way too early to go home and dress since Heath would insist on being with her and god only knew what would happen if they were alone.

Out of desperation, she picked up her phone and texted her sister. Was it bad?

From listening, I'm pretty sure it was damn good, Karis responded immediately.

Jolie groaned. So it was loud?

Silence. She took that as a yes.

Can you come to my office?

Her sister answered that straight off. Be right there.

Tiptoeing to the door, Jolie peeked out. She didn't see Heath hovering but he was here, close. No way would he simply back off to give her some space, much less leave.

Then Karis made her way to the door, Cutter following not far behind. She motioned her sister in, past Wisteria, who nodded in understanding. Cutter took up sentry just outside Jolie's little office. Sighing, she closed the rest of the world away with guilty relief.

She and Karis stood staring at one another, her younger sister fidgeting. Jolie realized that her sister wasn't sure how much love or comfort she would accept.

It was a startling thought. Equally discomfiting? She didn't know the answer. She'd kept everyone at arm's length for years, and she would still be doing it now if she didn't feel scrubbed raw, her emotions both rusty and overtaxed.

"I don't know what to do," she managed to say. "He makes me feel too much."

Karis's face softened. "And you can't control that."

Her sister was too smart to phrase that as a question, and Jolie was glad Karis understood. "Yeah."

"It happens to all of us at some point, honey. You've guarded your heart for so long—"

"I don't want him near my heart!" But Jolie already feared she didn't have a choice.

Pity flitted across her sister's face before she schooled it. "I wish I had something to say that you wanted to hear."

"I don't get to choose whether he works his way into my heart." Jolie began to pace. "I know."

"You're not Mom. Hell, I'm not Mom. I may have gotten hurt before. And you may be hurt this time. But you would never sacrifice your future, your loved ones, or your ambitions for the euphoric high of what she considers love. I wouldn't, either. I know you think I'm guy crazy and believe in fairy tales, but I've walked away from relationships with men who were crazy-hot and made me feel so good in bed because I knew they weren't right for me. I haven't figured out exactly what I am looking for but I knew those guys weren't it. I won't ever get involved with anyone with the hope that I can change them with my love."

As her mom assumed every time. And Diana Gale had never managed to learn that, no matter how much she sacrificed, her husbands and boyfriends were flawed men who weren't going to become different people simply because she willed it with her martyrdom. From watching the cycle repeat over and over, Jolie had long assumed there was no such thing as love in the traditional romantic sense. Maybe she'd been right. What had Heath given her besides a whole lot of alpha attitude and his penis?

His support. His belief in her. His unwavering presence and protection. Despite having lost a wife to violence, he was having far less difficulty opening himself to the possibilities between them than she was.

She was pretty sure that said something terrible about her. She'd always seen herself as too driven to pause for a personal life. Now Karis held up a mirror to her soul, and she saw the damaged woman too afraid to attempt anything deeper for fear of ending up hurt and used like her mother. Jolie didn't like her reflection much at the moment. If she didn't change something, she knew she'd spend her life alone.

"You would never do that, either," Karis pointed out softly.

"I wouldn't." But that wasn't the worry that scraped her nerves raw. "I just envisioned filling my life with Betti."

"Heath is making you see an existence beyond that."

He was. And she didn't know how to cope because it absolutely petrified her.

* * *

"YOU look elegant," Heath murmured, standing beside her in the foyer of the well-established restaurant on Maple as she adjusted her black sheath and pearls. "Don't fidget. You know what to say. You've rehearsed. If he veers into the suggestive or personal, I'll be right beside you."

"I know." She did her best not to look at him. If she did, she'd only get distracted by how drop-dead sexy he looked in a tailored gray suit. His crisp white dress shirt magnified the hint of olive in his skin. His dark eyes gleamed with a knowledge that something more than sex lay between them. Jolie still had no clue what to do about that. "I can't believe you coerced the restaurant staff into adjusting the table layout simply to keep an eye on me."

"It's not the first time they've worked with a bodyguard. They were more than happy to put a pair of two-tops beside one another to accommodate your safety."

"All this can't be necessary."

"Are you willing to take that chance"—he raised a disapproving brow at her—"when your livelihood—maybe even your life—is at stake? And what about your employees? Your sister?"

He was right. But it was more. She hated how much the idea of disappointing him upset her. She'd never once given a shit about a romantic partner's opinion because she never intended to keep him. Jolie didn't want to have any desire to hang onto this one.

But she cared too much to let him go.

"Richard and I are in public," she tried arguing instead. "I'll be fine."

"We've been over this. I'm staying. That's final."

Jolie wanted to be annoyed but his protective instinct melted her. "You can't hover."

"I'll be at the table beside you but I refuse to let you out of my sight." When she opened her mouth to protest, Heath laid a finger over her lips. "This is my compromise. I don't want you in public at all, just in case whoever's broken into your office or given your sister gifts is watching. But since you scheduled this dinner weeks ago, I'm being flexible. I would be far happier if you met in the office. Wouldn't that be more conducive to serious business?"

Yes. In fact, Jolie had suggested that. Richard had insisted they spend more time "getting to know each other better" before diving into mission statements and income projections. "If this dinner goes well and we agree in both philosophy and principle, that will be our next step."

"I still don't like it," he grumbled.

"I doubt someone has been waiting for me to appear in public simply to kill me."

"But you don't know that for certain, and I prefer not to leave anything to chance." Heath's phone dinged then, and he glanced at it, then back at her with a thunderous scowl. "Brilliant. Gardner booked a suite at Hotel ZaZa tonight. He's already ordered champagne chilled as well."

Jolie didn't want to know how he'd learned that. "Maybe he has a date later. Or a mistress. It's possible he plans to celebrate in style alone."

"Rubbish. He's using your business pitch to get into your knickers."

She shoved down her disquiet, hoping that wasn't true. She needed this deal to go through. Time was running out. "You're cynical."

"Normally, you are, too. I know men. I'll bet every dime you're paying me for this job that he makes a play for you tonight."

Before she could reply, the heavy wooden doors opened, and the last of the day's golden rays slanted in. As Heath melted into the background, Richard Gardner walked in, smiling and looking urbane in a navy suit with a sharp red tie. Of average height, he had a killer smile, complete with a dimple in his left cheek. Despite having equal amounts of salt and pepper in his hair, he managed not to look anything close to the fifty she knew him to be. Normally, she wouldn't have noticed him as anything but a potential business partner. But Heath had planted the suggestion.

And Gardner was carrying a dozen red roses.

"Hello, Ms. Quinn." As he handed her the bouquet, he leaned in to kiss her cheek—and lingered. His voice dropped to something just above a whisper. "These are for you."

She took them because she couldn't risk insulting him before they'd even sat down. "Thank you. They're lovely but the gesture isn't necessary to conduct business. I'm sure we'll get along just fine."

"What can I say? I'm a bit old-fashioned. If I go out to dinner with a lady, I think she should expect flowers."

"I'm here tonight merely as a business owner."

"You can't chide the southern gentleman in me." He winked. "My momma simply wouldn't have it."

A glance behind her said that Heath wasn't pleased. He was probably ready to say that he'd told her so, but Jolie was determined to make Gardner focus on Betti and the investment opportunity, and get his mind off hoping she would do the mattress tango with him.

Jolie opened her mouth to politely put him back on track, but the maître d' approached to say their table was ready. Gardner gestured her in front of him. She hated to turn her back to the man. The primal instinct that she'd just made herself vulnerable to a practiced predator bothered her. She shouldn't judge his business acumen by his flirtatious manner, especially since she knew that was his norm. But when he slid his hand down her back, nearly to the top of her ass as he "escorted" her, Jolie stiffened.

She didn't want him touching her. Worse, she could feel Heath following behind them at a barely discreet distance, radiating a pissed-off male vibe. Jolie flung a cautious glance over her shoulder, around Gardner, and caught a glimpse of the tight fury all over Heath's face.

As they sat, Jolie took her menu with a plastic smile and tried to focus anywhere but on him sitting at the table beside hers with his back to the wall and a glower on his face.

"I hope you like wine. I've taken the liberty of ordering a bottle in advance." Gardner snapped his fingers at a passing staff member.

Jolie frowned. Was that man even their waiter? Did Richard care or did he simply assume everyone was at his beck and call?

"Yes, sir?" The waiter managed to sound ready to do Richard's bidding while still conveying a hint of annoyance.

"Could you bring me the Château Lafon-Rochet '99 I ordered earlier today? And two glasses." Then Gardner dismissed the waiter utterly and turned to her.

Jolie didn't like his attitude. She smiled at the waiter. "We'd appreciate it. And if it wouldn't be too much trouble, could I also have a glass of club soda with a twist? Thank you."

With a smile in her direction, the waiter nodded and left.

"You didn't need to order wine," she ventured. "I'd prefer to do business with a clear head."

He patted her hand. "We're just having a friendly conversation. I know you'll tell me all about Betti. But as I said before, I prefer to do business with people I know. Tell me more about you."

A spark of tension lit the air, and she glanced over to see Heath clutching his water glass in a death grip while glaring at Richard's hand on hers.

He looked a bit like a wild beast ready to defend his territory.

She swallowed nervously and pulled her hand free. "I'm a very driven businesswoman without a lot of free time on my hands. I'd prefer to begin the presentation I've prepared and give you time to ask whatever questions you may have about Betti, our cash position, our EBITDA, and our income projections. I have a mock-up of our coming website to show you and—"

"Whoa. Slow down. We'll get to all that when we're better acquainted." He grabbed her hand again. "Intimate . . . You know what I mean."

Yes, Jolie feared she did.

* * *

"WHAT a fucking disaster!" Jolie took another long pull from the ridiculously expensive bottle of wine Gardner had ordered and kicked her shoes off, discarding them onto the floorboard. She pulled her sheath up around her thighs and propped her toes on his dashboard.

She looked ready to spit nails and cry—at the same time.

Heath speeded down the virtually empty freeway and tossed Jolie another glance. "You did everything possible to focus him on business."

"You told me." She shook her head angrily. "You told me exactly what he wanted. Stupid me believed that a man with Richard's business acumen and supposedly progressive views would care about both profit and the gender equality gap, so of course he'd want to get in to business with Betti. Nope." She took another long swallow from the bottle. "He just wanted to get into bed with me. Do you think I scalded his penis when I dropped the steaming pea soup in his lap?"

Despite the disastrous evening, a smile tugged at the corners of Heath's lips. He was proud of his spitfire. "I'd rather you not think about Gardner's penis."

She wrinkled her nose. "Good call. I just . . . no."

"You made that quite clear to him, love. And I believe the answer to your question is, yes. Let's hope for blisters."

Jolie sighed. Her mojo seemed to leak out of her, along with her breath. "He can ruin me. He has the connections. He knows all the big-money people. Now my best option is to go to a bank. If they listen to me at all, they'll want so much control that it will ruin everything."

"Perhaps not," he consoled, wrapping a gentle hand around her knee. "But even if that's true, would you sleep with Gardner for the money? Because he made that ultimatum quite clear."

"Never. That's not who I am, despite whatever moral compass Carrington Quinn thinks I inherited from him." She took another long swallow from the bottle as if wanting to drown out thoughts of the man.

"Your father?"

She glared, her mouth in a stubborn line. "I prefer sperm donor."

Leave it to Jolie to say things as bluntly as possible. Then again, Heath rather liked that about her. "All right, then. When did you last see him?"

"Until recently, I hadn't seen him since I was five. Then about three months ago . . ." She gulped more wine, and booze began softening the edges of her words. "He showed up. It wasn't long after the *D Magazine* article naming me one to watch in Dallas came out. I was speaking at a local Rotary Club function. When the presentation ended, I headed to the ladies room. He was waiting for me in the hall. Seeing him was such a shock, and I didn't know what to say. All the careful speeches I'd planned in my head over the years evaporated."

"Of course. You weren't braced."

"That shouldn't matter."

He frowned. The woman was so damn hard on herself sometimes. "But it does."

She shrugged off his consolation. "He told me it was time to expand. I knew that but I resented the crap out of him telling me how to run my business."

"He's some sort of executive mogul, isn't he?" Heath had done his research.

"Oh, yeah. Big ol' bigwig. Upper East Side real estate coming out his ass." She giggled. "Well, not literally. But that would be funny."

Jolie was a bit beyond slightly tipsy. Normally, Heath would stop her from imbibing more, but he suspected that she'd never confess why her father impacted her so much if she was completely sober. If he wanted to understand her, he needed to hear what came next. Besides, she'd earned a little mental vacation from all her stress, and if she chose to get pissed . . . well, he'd rather she do it where he could watch over her and keep her safe.

"Comical, indeed," he agreed. "So he told you to expand?"

She snorted. "Yeah. Fucking bastard. First, he told me that I'd been delusional to believe that men smart enough to make hundreds of millions of dollars would invest in a pretty young woman expanding into a complex global operation. Most, of course, would just want a piece of my ass. So unless I didn't mind whoring myself, he said I would never accomplish my expansion without him. He told me the glass ceiling wasn't a myth and that, without spreading my legs for others or putting him at the helm, I had no hope. Either way, I was a foolish girl and I should stop swinging for the fences."

"That's ridiculous!" Heath wanted to wring the misogynist's neck.

"Of course it is. Women have successfully helmed companies like Kraft, PepsiCo, and DuPont. They've led countries. I told him I didn't see why I couldn't be a leader simply because I didn't have half my brains dangling between my legs."

Heath smiled, picturing it. "What was his reaction?"

"To ignore me, just like he has for the last twenty-five years. Where was he all that time, while Mom worked three jobs to make ends meet? When I was little, she used to stock shelves at a grocery store down the street from midnight til five A.M. She left me alone in our crappy little trailer to do it. A lot of people have judged her for that. But we didn't have family who could watch me. We needed the money to eat. Carrington Quinn sat fifteen hundred miles away in his posh apartment, sipping Cristal—or whatever the hell he drinks—not caring one whit if I was unsupervised all night or starving. So he can kiss my ass."

Heath couldn't agree more. And he understood now precisely why Jolie had sought a silent partner, so that when she succeeded, her father would know all the brain power behind Betti had been hers.

"He didn't pay child support?"

"The bare minimum. When he and my mother divorced, he had all the high-powered attorneys. She'd signed a prenuptial agreement, so what little she got went to pay her lousy lawyer." Jolie rolled her eyes. "I can't believe he had the nerve to tell me after that Rotary meeting that he was proud of what I'd managed to accomplish as a mere female."

Despite his ancient views and lack of tact, had the man meant to make amends? Or had he merely sought to belittle her in the hopes that she'd second-guess herself enough to turn over her budding empire to him? Either way, Heath was furious on Jolie's behalf.

As he pulled into Jolie's condo complex and killed the engine, he turned and watched her tip the wine up to her mouth again, the bottom of the bottle nearly brushing the roof of the car's interior.

She'd polished off the whole bloody thing?

Yanking it away, she slumped back against the seat and tried unsuccessfully to slot the bottle in the too-small cup holder. When she cursed, he took it from her and leaned in to kiss her forehead.

"I'm sorry he was an ass. But anything he said would have been too little too late, right?" At her miserable nod, his heart went out to her. "C'mon, let's get you inside."

Heath climbed out of the car, then helped Jolie back into her shoes and onto her feet. She staggered, and he eased her across the lot, toward her unit.

"Way too late." She emphasized her point with a nod. "Saying he was proud, despite the fact I lacked a penis, was probably the nicest thing he'd ever said to me. Of course, he killed any warm fuzzies I had for him by telling me next that I was in over my head. But he'd do me the 'favor' of investing in Betti so he could take over. I could still be in charge of creative, of course. But since I wasn't equipped to run with the big boys and ensure my company reached its fullest potential, I would probably crumble without him."

Prick. Jolie had built this company from the ground up, with the leftover funds from her student loans and the money she'd scraped together while working odd jobs in school. She had more than enough intelligence and gumption to grow her company and fulfill her dreams.

Heath opened the condo door, then eased her inside, locking up behind him and flipping on lights before he herded her toward the bedroom. She tripped on her own feet. He caught her, but she righted herself. Fury probably kept her going.

"I take it you turned him down?"

She scoffed. "Oh, I told him to go fuck himself. I promised I'd take Betti to the next level without him or a dime of his money."

As they made it into the bedroom, she stripped off her dress and tossed it to the floor. She stood before him wearing a bra, a thong, and a killer pair of heels. It was completely the wrong time . . . but Heath couldn't stop the bomb of desire from detonating inside him. Yes, he always wanted her. Had from the moment he'd laid eyes on her. But this was different. He wanted her not merely because she was beautiful—though she was. He wanted her not merely because he knew how explosive the chemistry between them was—more powerful than he'd ever imagined. No, he wanted her because he was seeing the real her, the vulnerable woman underneath the businesslike facade. He understood now where her ambition had come from. He could see the determination and moxie not just to succeed but to thrive, to be her most successful self. And he admired the hell out of her for that.

"I can't fail. I can't," she wailed, her frame crumpling. "A-all my life, I told myself that I would succeed, that I wouldn't have to scrape by like my mother, that I would someday prove to Carrington Quinn that he was wrong about me."

As Heath rushed to pull her into his arms, Jolie lifted her face to his. The sight of her tears hit him like a visceral blow to the chest. She never willingly made herself vulnerable. Was it an indication of their growing bond . . . or just her momentary vulnerability? Heath ached to make her world right. "You're the smartest, most amazing woman I've ever known."

Her face fell, her bottom lip trembling. "Why did I have to prove that I had potential? Isn't a father supposed to love his daughter? I tell myself that he was the deficient one. He had to be, right? What sort of man tells a five year-old that she was his stupidest trailer park mistake?"

Until now, Heath thought Quinn had merely ignored Jolie over the years and she'd resented him for it. But this was so much worse. Fury fired in his belly. "Whatever he said to make you feel unworthy is utter crap. Do you hear me? Despite the way he phrased his acquisition proposal, you earned his respect—"

"I don't want it!"

He suspected that, deep down, she did. And the fact that she'd even unconsciously sought it only upset her more. But he wasn't about to refute her. The elder Quinn wasn't important. Jolie was.

"I know, love. Forget him. Forget Gardner, too."

"I can't. Carrington called me last week to say that he intended to visit me in the next two weeks to discuss a takeover. He can't have Betti. That's *my* dream. I've worked damn hard for it."

Quinn had stripped away her dignity as a child, making her feel undeserving and unwanted. She'd spent twenty-five years overcoming his slight. And now the man intended to take her dignity again?

Over Heath's dead body.

"You don't have to sell to him."

"I've already started some of the expansion plans and now I'm a bit overleveraged. I knew it was a risk, but if I can work it out, the rewards will be amazing. I just need a year or two to realize Betti's full potential." Her shoulders slumped again, and this time he read defeat. "Since Gardner wanted what he saw as easy vagina more than he wanted to make a profit, I have no idea where my capital injection will come from now."

"We'll figure it out tomorrow, love. Why don't you lie down?" He angled her onto the bed, and for once, she did as he bid without argument. "How's your stomach? You didn't eat a thing. Can I get you a bite?"

She didn't answer, just looked at him with a puzzled expression. "I was a bitch when you first came to work for me because I wasn't sure how to respond when the attraction between us was so strong. Why are you being nice?"

Because she could use a break. Because she deserved it. Because he wanted to give her the world. "I like to see you smile. And maybe I've discovered that I quite like a bit of bitchy in my woman. Would you eat soup, if I promise not to make it split pea?"

She shook her head and tossed a careless arm above her head, onto her pillow. "I don't need food. Would you . . ." She sighed and looked as if she grappled for words. "Would you just lie here with me?"

"Of course." Heath shucked his shoes and shrugged out of his suit coat, draping it across a nearby chair. Then he lifted her sheet and slid in beside her, bringing her soft body against him. "That better?"

"Yeah." Jolie laid her head on his chest, closed her eyes, and relaxed against him. "I have to come up with a whole new plan. I have to shake some trees, find some investors—"

"Don't worry about it tonight. Why don't you take a shower and get ready for bed? I'll find you some water and an aspirin because I think you're going to have a doozy of a hangover."

"You said 'doozy.' That's funny." She laughed. "You know you're wonderful."

"I try."

"You're good at everything. I mean *everything* . . ."

Now she amused him. Heath didn't imagine for a moment that this debacle was over. In the morning, she'd be on a rampage to combat Gardner if he tried to discredit her, as he'd threatened. And to counter whatever nasty tricks Carrington Quinn might have up his sleeve.

For now, Heath parried in a tone that matched her lightness of mood. "That's nice to hear. Let me know whenever you need a reminder of some of my more singular talents."

Her smile turned wry. "I'll bet when you came to work for me you never pictured crazy crushes, sister drama, lecherous investors, or a crying boss."

"I'm afraid those are generally out of my wheelhouse, yes. But it's good to know I'm keeping up."

"You don't regret anything?"

Heath knew she meant the two of them. Jolie must be feeling off-balance, indeed, to expose her tender heart enough to ask that question. She was too smart not to realize he might say something terribly crushing. It wouldn't be the first time she'd endured verbal cruelty. Yet she simply kept showing him her backbone.

"Not one thing," he vowed softly.

"Good." She curled up to him like a kitten, and Heath had no illusions about how often she showed any man her soft side. He understood perfectly well why.

He curled his arms around her tighter.

"Me, either," she added. "Well, I regret letting my sperm donor get under my skin so that a stupid cocktail conversation I had with Richard Gardner a few weeks back made me decide working with him would be a great idea. And I regret that I hurt Karis's feelings by having sex with you the first time. I'm probably really going to regret the bottle of wine tomorrow. But even if this ends badly—you and I—I don't think I can regret you."

From Jolie, those were words of affection. He wasn't quite sure whether knowing she reciprocated his feelings should make him happy or scare the hell out of him. But like everything else about this connection with her, his heart decided for him.

Heath skated his fingertips down the lean curve of her shoulder, then made his way to her waist and glided over her hip. "You really should sleep, love."

She sighed and lifted her head with a seeking stare. She wanted something and he wasn't quite sure what. Affection? Reassurance?

"Sleep will be nice . . . eventually. Right now I'd rather you take your pants off and get inside me."

Chapter Ten

Rule for success number ten:
Sometimes you have to take risks.

HEATH froze and raised a brow at Jolie. Just when he thought he had the woman figured out, she surprised him again.

"Take off my pants and get inside you, is it? That sounds a bit like workplace harassment," he teased.

"You can sue me." She rose above him and doffed her bra, freeing her breasts in a bounce that stole his breath. Her nipples tightened. A sweet flush was already creeping up her skin. "Or make love to me."

Before he could answer, Jolie laid into the buttons of his shirt. Her coordination wasn't close to perfect since she was still a bit tipsy. And maybe he should stop her, wait for her to sober up, and ensure that she was making a responsible decision, et cetera. Doing that would be the worst mistake. He wouldn't lament the loss of sex. All right, he would. But he'd mourn the loss of this moment when her defenses were down; when she ached to be her raw, honest self; when she needed him to hold her.

"Suing you sounds like a dreadful amount of paperwork. Besides,

I hate lawyers." He helped Jolie with the last of the buttons and peeled off his shirt. "Too argumentative and expensive."

She nodded as she peeled off her knickers. "They never tell the truth. I had one on staff. He specialized in human resources. I fired him. He wrote Betti's cyber anti-porn policies, then proceeded to violate them in spectacular fashion. After seeing that video he downloaded, I'd never eat at that kitchen table again. Just eww . . ."

This sexy, complex woman sometimes frustrated him. She always tied him up in knots. But she never bored him. "Indeed. Do I want to know?"

"No." She shook her head emphatically. "Why would people do something so depraved with peanut butter and ricotta cheese?"

He laughed and shucked his pants, dropping them to the floor, unable to remember the last time he'd been this happy. Not getting by. Not somewhat content. Actually sublimely thrilled to be alive.

"I shudder at the thought," he murmured. "So if I'm not going to sue you, I suppose I'll simply have to make love to you."

"Yeah." She sat beside him, her hip propped against his, and leaned over his chest. "Let's see if we can make you shudder about something else."

Desire razed through him as she bent and took his cock in her mouth. She sucked with a desperation to be close to him. She caressed his thighs, cupped his balls, moaned in appreciation. She worshipped him.

Heath tossed his head back and hissed. No man in his right mind didn't love a warm mouth wrapped around him but this . . . He gripped the sheets. Jolie Quinn stunned him. It wasn't that she gave the best head he'd ever had. She simply gave the most sincere. Anna had done it to please him. The hookups with whom he'd bothered to share more than the standard screw had wanted to dazzle him with their "skills." Jolie simply wanted to be with him, to give him a part of herself. He felt the difference.

And he doubted he would ever want another random woman again.

In that moment, he didn't care about anything but the stunning pleasure she laid over his senses. Her soft breaths on his abdomen, her butterfly touches across his skin, the reverence of her tongue. He stuck his hands in her hair, wrapping the soft strands around his fingers, and fell into her rhythm.

"Jolie, love . . ."

She merely moaned, then lifted her lashes, glancing up his body and into his eyes. Her stare electrified him. Then she took another long pull on his cock. Sparks shot up his spine. He swore his legs had gone numb. Certainly, his brain had ceased thinking about anything but Jolie Quinn and how right being with her felt.

Her tongue swirled around him, something between a tease and an embrace. She closed her eyes again and sank into the moment. But he needed her with him in every way.

"No, open your eyes. Look at me."

For the very first time, she didn't hesitate before complying. She wanted this intimacy as much as he did. And as she dragged her lips up his shaft and kissed the sensitive head, his back arched, his spine rattled. Would he ever be able to let this woman go?

"Stop," he panted.

She licked up his erection again in a saucy little rebellion. "This feel too much like harassment in the workplace?"

He hadn't seen her sense of humor before tonight, and he enjoyed it—just not while his cock was on fire.

"No." His voice sounded gruff, harsh. "I want to be inside you."

She stroked the nerve-rich spot just under the head with her tongue again. "You always want to be inside me."

"You're damn right I do." He sat up and grabbed her arms. "Now."

Jolie pushed him to his back once more. "This is more sex than I've had in years. You've turned me into a maniac."

Heath opened his mouth to comment when she threw her leg over his body and straddled him. As if his stubborn dick had a mind of its own, his hips lifted. He rooted around until he found her opening. She smiled and began sinking down onto him with a sigh.

"Condom," he managed to choke out the reminder.

"Did you ever have random hookups bareback?"

Was she mad? "Never."

"Perfect." Perched on her knees, Jolie worked him down slowly, savoring every new inch her clasping hot silk pussy enveloped. "I need this, to be close to you."

"I do, too." God, did he ever.

He stopped resisting this incredible slide into heaven. Actually, he'd never had sex without a condom in his life. He'd been a careful youth. Anna had been a bit of a germophobe and had been unable to tolerate the thought of exchanging bodily fluids. Everyone else he hadn't wanted to really, truly touch.

He had no idea if Jolie was taking the pill or could get pregnant. But the idea of climaxing deep inside her, of leaving behind his seed to take root and grow . . . A week ago, that would have scared the fucking piss out of him. Now it made his desire flare hotter.

If she conceived, she couldn't simply toss him out of her life, right?

Slippery moral slope, mate . . .

"Jolie, are you sure?"

"Hmm . . ." She wriggled up his shaft, then slid slowly down, burning him with her heat. "Yeah. Probably the most certain I've been about anything in a long time. Don't leave me."

"I can't," he admitted.

She glided her way up his erection again, her walls gripping and clenching, her wetness making the ride buttery and smooth, before she put the force of her hips behind her next stroke and slammed down, jarring the bed, shaking his body. Stealing his soul.

He grabbed her hips and ramped up the rhythm of her thrusts, plunged deeper and harder, groaning so loudly the sound echoed off the walls.

Jolie braced her hands on his chest. "Let me. Let me do this. I need to be able to . . ."

With a frown, she searched for the right words, but Heath knew. After an evening where her careful plan had gone to hell, her future looked uncertain, and she might have to face the ghosts of her past, she needed to control something.

Normally, giving up power would chafe him. He was a man with dominant tendencies. He loved a compliant female whom he could make gasp and pant and beg. But tonight wasn't about him. Jolie had sought him for comfort, affection. He would be there for her in every way.

Heath dropped his hand to her thighs. "Whatever you need, love."

"Thank you," she whispered as she writhed, tossing her head back as she took him deeper than ever.

She looked like a goddess, all shimmering and lovely, even more beautiful in pleasure.

"I want to touch you." He requested, but tonight he wouldn't take.

"Please."

He settled his thumb over her clit. "Such manners. A 'thank you' and a 'please'. Shall I reward you, then?"

"Absolutely," she purred.

"Very good." He rubbed at her, reveling when her breath caught and a rosy flush pinkened her skin even more. "Maybe you could bend down and kiss me?"

Their shared tenderness seemed to peel back another layer of her softness, leaving her utterly exposed. "I don't think I can help myself. I've never been able to when it comes to you."

She pushed her hair behind her shoulders and leaned in, her green eyes wide and raw. Heath wondered if she was aware of her silent plea. He cupped one of her shoulders gently and cradled her cheek with his other hand. Her breath caught.

Her lips touched his in a slow, searching brush. She lifted back, stared in question. Was she uncertain of her welcome? Every inch of his aching erection was packed inside her and he only wanted more. But she was used to being turned away, belittled, and rejected. She usually had to forge her path alone.

Never again.

His chest buckled at the realization. He caressed his way to her nape and pulled her forward until he cemented their lips together. He tasted wine and woman and need—a dizzying combination.

Beneath her, he pressed up, burrowing deeper inside her. She moaned into his mouth and he swallowed her cry. He enjoyed taking her defenses down a little at a time, loved the slow dance of her surrender.

He fell into a rhythm, hips and tongue working in sync to drive her closer to the brink. But the bloody woman never did anything passively. She never simply gave over. No, Jolie pinched his nipples, which he would have sworn before now weren't sensitive, and nibbled at his bottom lip, sucking and teasing, absolutely driving him mad.

His need ratcheted up. Passion rose. Soon they were grasping each other, desperate to be closer. They panted in unison, shared groans and sighs, as they rocked together on her bed as if nothing and no one else in the world mattered.

She clung, tightened around him, her nails biting into his shoulders as she kissed below his ear, nipped at his lobe.

Damn it all, the burn of the desire was too hot to last. As he arched up beneath her with a shove, he hit a sensitive spot that had her whimpering and clasping his cock harder until she threw her head back with a wailing cry and came.

God, he'd never seen anything like her. When Jolie committed to something—work, an argument, sex—she did it completely. She didn't have polite, restrained orgasms. They weren't quiet. They certainly weren't manufactured. Everything she gave him was honest and real and fiery.

Jolie drove him to the brink. He strained to hold on to his composure, but as she gripped him completely and her mewls filled his ears, as her eyes slid shut and her nipples beaded inches from his face with a blushing rush, Heath couldn't hold out anymore.

"Love, are you using birth control?"

"What?" She kept wriggling and thrusting, lost to pleasure. "No, but—"

"Shh." He fucked her deeper, harder, wringing the last of the searing climax out of her. Every muscle of his body tensed as he shoved down ecstasy and tried to hold back. God, she was murder on his self-control.

Finally, the tension of her climax spent, she lay limp against him with a sigh. Relief rolled through Heath. His torment was over.

He rolled her to her back in a blink, then situated himself in the cradle of her thighs. How badly he wanted to stay deep and release himself in her snug depths. But Jolie had too many ambitions on her bucket list to get pregnant without careful consideration. This might have been her idea but she might not be ready for the consequences or sober enough to make the choice.

With a curse, Heath withdrew from her and glided his aching erection between their bodies, bucking against the pad of her pussy and rubbing his cock over her sensitive clit. She cried out, jolted again, welcoming him with open arms and legs as he felt fire lick up his spine, bliss roll through him, and the building orgasm crest just before it demolished him.

He shuttled his surprising disappointment that he couldn't be with Jolie completely and tie her to him for good.

* * *

ONCE again, Heath woke before dawn. He had to risk leaving a sleeping Jolie in their bed to stop by Dominion and pick up a few of his things, but he advised Cutter and made it quick. When he let himself back in Jolie's place, the quiet told him she hadn't awakened. That left him alone with his thoughts.

Yesterday morning, he'd contemplated calling Myles and asking the man how he'd moved on after tragedy had ripped his life apart. Today he didn't think he could wait anymore.

Of course Anna would have wanted him to be happy. She'd been selfless in nearly every way. Kind to a fault. Happy with friends and hobbies and a part-time job tending plants at a nursery. In the evenings, she liked cuddling on the sofa with a cup of tea and the telly. It had been a comfortable life, and he'd enjoyed his time with her. He'd mourned her loss and tried to pick up the pieces while making sense of it all.

He still didn't understand why his world had come crashing down.

What he did know . . . Jolie should be his future, and he had to figure out how to move forward without the nagging fear of losing her plaguing him. He'd avoided relationships because they could end suddenly and violently, through no fault of either party. The pain and devastation would be too much to bear a second time.

But walking away from Jolie was no longer an option.

Without hesitating or deliberating, he picked up the phone and hit the preprogrammed number he hadn't dialed in years. Myles answered on the second ring.

"Heath? Is that really you?"

"It is." And now he felt almost embarrassed that he hadn't stayed in touch. Myles had tried for a time but ultimately given up when Heath had not responded in kind. "How are you, old friend?"

"I'm well. Very well. Surprised to hear from you! Pleasantly, mind you . . ."

"Good. I hear you're still working and doing a bang-up job of it. I was sorry to hear that you were shot a few years back. But you've been promoted recently?"

"Yes. I won't ask how you know all that," he sounded amused. "You were always sly about your informants back in the day."

"A few still talk." But maybe tragedy might have been avoided if he'd had a better network when it counted.

"Indeed. Well, a desk isn't all that exciting but, as you've probably heard, I'm remarried now. Camille is a wonderful woman, originally from Dover. We met at a pub, I'm sad to say. But we've been married nearly a year now and we're expecting."

The cheer in Myles's voice made Heath's chest tighten. "I did hear. Congratulations! That's actually why I called. I know it's rather poor manners for me to ring you out of the blue like this, in the middle of your weekend, and ask you to give me some advice on how to carry on with life again. But . . ."

"You've met someone?"

"I have. She's amazing. I've never known anyone as passionate about her work or smart or determined to succeed."

"I take it you're not referring to Ms. Mullins since I hear she's engaged to that former soldier who rescued her."

"Yes. Whomever makes Mystery happy is the man she should marry, and it seems that's Axel Dillon. So all's well that ends well."

"Except for you. Are you uncertain about the lady you've met?"

"I've rarely been more certain about anything or anyone. I was so smug, believing I'd never fall . . ." Heath stopped before he said the next inevitable words.

"In love again?" Myles prompted, plucking the words from Heath's very thoughts.

God, that was it exactly. How? He'd met Jolie a mere handful of days ago.

But Heath was done questioning it.

"Something like that. How did you let go of your grief and fear and try again?"

"You've got to decide you'd rather risk your heart than chance being the sad sack who spends every night in some seedy pub, looking for a girl to shag so you can forget how bloody lonely you are."

His old mate was so close to the truth it hurt. "That's it?"

"I'm afraid so. No elixir. No mantra. No special affirmation. The therapy was shit, an utter waste of time. I had to figure out how to be single again and how to live happily without Lucy. Neither one of us were very good company after it all happened, and I know you've gone through hell without Anna. But at some point, I simply decided I wanted to live again. I didn't want to do it alone. It sounds as if you're there."

"I think so. It would be easier if we knew who ordered Anna and Lucy's deaths and why, if we had avenged them somehow, bashed skulls, or put the masterminds away for good—something. Every day, I'm haunted by the idea that my wife died and I didn't make the proper people pay."

"I won't ask if you had anything to do with the deaths of the triggerman and his accomplices." Myles sighed. "That sense of devastation and loss gives you some empathy for the families of victims, doesn't it? I've been over and over that day in my head, too, mate. The truth is, we were good at our jobs but that didn't make us omnipotent. We couldn't know everything. Terrorists and thugs attack all around the world. Civilians die. I miss the good old days when soldiers kept the battle to the fields but . . ." He sighed. "After Lucy was gone, it was awful. The darkest days of my life. I was haunted by the child I'd never meet, who never knew life because some maniac with a sniper rifle and a yen for explosives decided to blow up a marketplace as a criminal or political statement he never took responsibility for. But I realized the anger and the sorrow didn't make anything better and it didn't bring anyone back. You've grieved. Now it's time to live again."

Heath suspected Myles was spot-on. It sounded so easy, and yet making the decision was infinitely simpler than putting his resolve into practice. Still, he didn't think he could go back to being that numb cad carelessly plowing his way through the singles' bar scene to avoid the fact that he'd become a lonely widower.

"You've given me a lot to think about. Thanks, mate. I know it's been a long time and you could have told me to piss off—"

"Are you joking? I was just telling Camille that I wanted to ring you and find out how you were doing. So you're in Dallas now? I hear you're working for a gorgeous clothing designer. Is that who you're romancing?"

"I've had this job less than a week. I won't ask how you learned about it already." Heath chuckled, feeling truly light for the first time in years.

"Best if you don't," he drawled. "Seriously, keep in touch. Let me know how you're doing. The caring again . . . it's a bit overwhelming, but worth it. Call me anytime you need to chat."

That's what Heath had always appreciated about Myles; he'd been a genuine friend. "Thanks, mate."

They rang off, and he stared at the device a moment more. He'd been rolling an idea around in his head since the wee hours of the morning, when he was curled up beside Jolie as she'd slept restlessly.

In for a penny, in for a pound.

He scrolled through his contacts again and found his brother-in-law's mobile number. Heath's only sister had married some financial wizard. Jane had convinced him to turn the inheritance Anna's wealthy parents had left her and the life insurance money he received following her death over to Jane's husband. Because the money had almost seemed tainted by blood to him, Heath had done it, not caring whether he saw it again. But the last statement he'd received via e-mail told him it had grown to an amount that staggered him. Clarke had worked wonders, despite global financial uncertainty.

Heath hit the contact button on his phone and his sister's husband answered, the sounds of playing children in the background. They seemed happy, and he was certainly glad for Jane. But their domestic bliss had always disturbed him. Today he knew it was because he hadn't experienced that for himself.

After some chitchat and learning that his sister was currently playing Bunco—which Clarke referred to as Drunko—with some neighbors, Heath realized he'd best get to it before their three rambunctious kids tied their dad to a chair and set the house on fire—or something equally disastrous.

"I'm actually calling in a professional capacity, Clarke. I need your help." Heath rubbed at his forehead, caution setting in. His next step was the right one, but he had to do it carefully. "How quickly can I liquidate my money?"

"All of it? And do what?" His brother-in-law sounded horrified. "That's your future. Your nest egg, mind you. You can't still spy or protect people or anything quite so strenuous for another thirty years. You'll need this to retire on."

It was much more than he'd ever need, especially since he couldn't picture himself lying on a tropical beach somewhere by himself. Without a future—without Jolie—what did vacations or houses or worldly things mean? "I've got an investment opportunity."

"Send me the details. Let me vet it. I'll make sure everything is on the up and up—"

"I've already done all that. It's completely legitimate. This company is poised to make a fortune." And even if he never saw a dime of the money again, he wouldn't care.

Heath only wanted to make Jolie Quinn happy.

No doubt, he was in love.

"Then I'd like more details to—"

"There's no time, and I don't need to explain, Clarke. It's my money, yes?"

"Of course," Clarke conceded with a sigh as if it pained him to admit that now. "But it's growing so nicely. I have you positioned for some incredible profits by second quarter of next year. There are procedures I have to follow. There are penalties you'll be forced to pay."

"I don't care. Convert whatever I have into U.S. dollars and have it ready next week."

"Next week!" Clarke sounded aghast. "I don't understand. This isn't done. Do you need help? Has something happened?"

Now his brother-in-law sounded concerned. He would convey that to Jane. Heath took a deep breath and reminded himself that, to

Clarke, all this shuffling of funds might as well be life or death. "I'm fine. I really did find a company I'd like to invest in. But there's one catch. You'll have to create a dummy corporation before you contact the CEO. Make up a retirement fund. Do whatever you must to ensure she doesn't know I'm the one investing in her business."

Heath would tell Jolie the truth eventually, when she was ready to hear it. Until then, he would be her completely silent partner. She needed someone to believe in her, and he absolutely did.

"Why not?" Now Clarke sounded positively confused. "This is all highly unusual, and I'm uncertain of the ethics . . ."

Heath stopped listening. Jolie wouldn't want any investment from him. She would probably assume he pitied her—difficult, contrary woman—and refuse his "handout." She would take capital from a male investor she had chosen and vetted, as long as he was contractually obligated to stay silent. But Jolie hadn't chosen him as a business partner. Her pride would likely spur her to refuse his offer, even though he sought to fund her simply because he knew she could succeed. Bloody woman was determined to conquer the world on her terms, to spite her heartless prick of a father. Heath didn't want her to doubt herself for an instant; he just wanted to enable her dream.

Damn it, that wasn't all he wanted. "I'm going to marry her."

Clarke didn't say anything for a moment, simply sat in stunned silence. "You? Marry again?"

Heath had to chuckle. "Never thought you'd see the day, did you? My sister will be ecstatic."

"Beside herself," his brother-in-law agreed. "And your parents . . ."

They would be thrilled, yes. And they would all love Jolie.

He explained the situation with her business to his brother-in-law. "So that's why I need your help."

"Consider it done."

Chapter Eleven

Rule for success number eleven:
Pace yourself. You can't work nonstop.

I'M really sorry Gardner didn't work out," Karis said the following morning over the phone.

Jolie winced against the sunlight glaring through the window and turned over in bed. Damn, her head hurt and her mouth felt as if something fuzzy had taken root and grown. It had to be way past nine in the morning, and for a woman usually working by the time the sun rose, this felt downright lazy. She couldn't decide if she'd simply needed the splurge or was beginning the descent into mediocrity.

"Heath tried to warn me. I didn't want to believe Richard would waste my time and his for nothing more than a glorified booty call."

"He was literally willing to pay you millions of dollars for what's in your panties. Wow. That's kind of a backhanded compliment."

Jolie scoffed. "I would rather have had a serious investor."

"No doubt but at least someone wants your pink parts. I can't seem to give mine away these days."

"Don't tell me you tried to get busy with your new bodyguard."

Surely, Heath had warned Cutter about her sister's propensity to be man crazy. Still, Jolie hoped Karis would stop looking for her happiness in the men she met and start looking inside herself.

"Oh, god no. He's . . . like Oscar the Grouch in a hot dude's body. The packaging might be good. Okay, *really* fantastic. But I've had better conversations with my cat."

Jolie had to laugh at that. Thankfully, Karis had moved beyond the superficial attractiveness of the men around her in a way her mother never had. Diana Gale always went for the most masculine, charismatic guy in the room, as if snagging his attention did something for her ego. It was a step forward for Karis, but Jolie was relieved that her sister at least realized that she had to like the man she'd spend the rest of her life—or at least the next few years—with.

"Besides, I think he's got some woman in his life. And it sounds like there's drama, drama, drama. I'm okay that he's not interested." Karis paused. "Did I shock you?"

"A little."

"Good." Her sister giggled. "So what are you going to do next? Your days are numbered until your asshat of a biological father comes knocking, right?"

Jolie's stomach tightened with worry. "Yeah. I have to come up with something and get a new ball rolling quick. I'm just going to lock myself away with a pot of coffee and my laptop—"

"No, you're not," Heath said as he entered the room with a covered plate and a steaming cup on a tray. "You're going to relax and rejuvenate for the next two days."

She turned to scowl at him as if he'd lost his mind. What was he up to? "I have to go, sis. Take care."

"Sure. Before I forget, I got another 'gift' from my weird office admirer yesterday afternoon, after you'd gone. He left me a gift bag with my favorite candle, Yankee Christmas Cookie. It's as if he knew I'd just used up my last one and another would make me smile."

Jolie wasn't sure what to make of Karis's secret admirer, but it worried her more than a little that he seemed to understand her sister so well when they had no idea who he was. "Any card?"

"Yeah. Get this. *Burn this for me like I burn for you. I'll scorch anyone who tries to stand between us.*"

"He's not very poetic."

"He's not," Karis agreed. "But it's almost sweet."

"In a creepy sort of way." Jolie paused.

"I know but my gut says he's not dangerous or anything. Okay, you probably think that sounds like an excuse Mom would make, but he's the first guy in my life who's paid any attention to my likes and dislikes this carefully. That's got to mean something."

"Yeah, that he's a stalker. KK, he's pretty much threatened me."

Karis sighed. "I know it sounds that way and it bugs me, too, but I have to believe that if he had menace on his mind he wouldn't be capable of such sweet gestures."

"That definitely sounds like something Mom would say."

Suddenly, Heath set the tray on her dresser, then plucked the phone from her hands and engaged the speaker. "Are you all right?"

"Fine. It's a candle, not a bomb."

Heath didn't look convinced. "Cutter is still with you?"

"Closer than my shadow." And Karis didn't sound too happy.

"Have him look into your latest 'gift' and tell him to call me."

"Will do. Y'all never let me have any fun," she grumbled.

That finagled a laugh from Jolie. "See you later."

As Heath set the phone on her nightstand, he retrieved the tray and bid her to recline against the headboard. The sight stunned Jolie. "Breakfast in bed?"

He set the tray over her lap. "You've been burning your candle at both ends all week, not eating or sleeping enough."

And he wanted to take care of her. No one had ever done anything half so thoughtful. Tears closed up her throat and she tried to joke the feeling away. "The not sleeping part is your fault. I thought guys pushing forty were supposed to have a less active sex drive."

Heath scoffed. "I've no idea where you heard that rubbish."

"Don't know. I'm not complaining."

"Glad to hear it. Eat. Once you're done, I'm going to draw you a hot bath. You're going to relax, then we're going to sit on the couch and watch movies or read or whatever will take your stress down many notches."

"I'm fine," she insisted, lifting the lid on her plate. "French toast and bacon! Mmm . . ." She dug into her breakfast with a moan. Everything tasted fantastic. "One of my favorites. You're spoiling me."

And why would he do that?

"I prefer the word pamper, and you deserve it after the week you've had."

Jolie finished every bite, finding that, despite the disaster her business was now in, she had been famished. When she set her fork down on the empty plate, she looked at him with a sigh. "If this bodyguarding thing doesn't work out for you, I could make you my personal chef and sex slave."

Heath looked as if he didn't want to smile but couldn't stop himself. "The sex slave part sounds very intriguing."

He lowered his palms and one knee onto the mattress until he loomed over her, his face inches above hers. He kissed her gently, with a reverence that made her catch her breath, before he brushed his lips across her jawline and meandered up to her ear.

When Jolie shivered, Heath nipped at her lobe. "Very intriguing, indeed. We'll explore that." He pulled away and lifted her to her feet. "After your bath."

"I only shower."

He glowered. "My mother swears by a good soak for relaxation and restorative purposes. Try it."

"I'll relax once I'm working on a new plan to save my business. Breakfast was really fantastic and sleeping in helped—"

"Could you humor me, love?" He shook his head with a hint of exasperation. "Could you be less independent and stubborn for twenty bloody minutes?"

Her go-go-go way of life seemingly worried him. He wouldn't bother if he didn't care. Jolie had only patchy recollections of last night. She'd told him about her father. He'd been supportive as hell. Afterward, she'd all but rubbed up against the man like she was in heat. Through it all, he had remained deeply accommodating. Being with her probably wasn't easy. But Heath took everything she threw at him with a shrug and more steps down his doggedly correct path in life. He didn't let her moods, her ambitions, or her past bother him.

He was kind of perfect for her. Crap, was she in love with him?

"All right. I'll try it," she conceded. "Thanks for breakfast."

Heath seemed pleasantly surprised by her compromise as he lifted the tray from her lap. "You're welcome. Meet me in your bathroom."

As he returned the tray to the kitchen, she tossed on her robe and padded to her little spa-like retreat. She hadn't splurged a lot on decorating this place but she loved her bathroom. The quartz counters, the teak floor, the gray Shaker cabinets, and the soothing shades of soft aqua walls.

After brushing her teeth and pinning her hair on top of her head, she started the bath water. In books and movies, people always added salts or oils—something—to the tub. She'd never bothered, seeing it as an expensive splurge when she was a college student and a silly timewaster now that she'd become a business owner. And who wanted to sit in their own dirty water?

Heath hustled in a moment later, carrying a candle he'd found in her living room and a vial of some liquid, which he added to the steaming tub. It smelled divine.

He lit the candle, tested the temperature of the water, then held out his hand in her direction. "Get in."

Jolie doffed her robe and stepped into the tub. "Thanks. What is that?"

"A homemade recipe my mother mixes and sends to me. It's carrier oil combined with bits of sandalwood, rose, orange, pine, and lemon. It's for relaxation." He turned a bit red. "She also sends me one for happiness. My mother believes that a long hot bath with the right oils will solve whatever ails your mood."

"I see. She wouldn't send you this stuff if you didn't like it, would she?"

His flush deepened. "I grew up with it. These smells remind me of home. So . . . yes. Sometimes, if I'm in a flat with a decent tub, I climb in. Does that make me less manly?"

His challenging tone had her grinning as she sank into the water. It felt pretty damn heavenly. "Not at all. You sound evolved. Neanderthal two dot oh."

"Charming." He turned off the lights, then disappeared. A minute later, he returned with a loofah and a misshapen bar of scented soap. "My mother makes these as well."

Rather than hand them to her, he knelt close, the candlelight flickering over the strong angles of his face. He dipped both items in the water, then proceeded to bathe her from head to toe. At first, Jolie couldn't seem to relax. What did he see? Why was he taking such meticulous care of her?

As the gentle cleansing turned into a mind-melting massage of her tense muscles, those nagging questions dissolved. Two larger ones took their place. Had her mother ever had a man treat her so tenderly, causing her to believe that she was in love? And what would Jolie do when she no longer needed Heath for security reasons and he walked out of her life?

For the first time ever, the idea of letting a man go actually filled her with panic.

"Hey," he soothed. "Relax. Your prescribed twenty minutes of soaking aren't up yet."

She lay back and let him resume his ministrations. Yep, she very much feared this was love, and she was finally beginning to understand why people searched endlessly for it, went to great lengths to protect it, were willing to kill and die for it.

"I know you called it pampering but you really are spoiling me," she murmured, eyes closed. "What can I do to return the favor?"

"My demands are all sexual, of course."

She smiled. "Naturally. So what do you want? Should I play the braless sorority sister whose car is broken down and will do *anything* to persuade a stranger—that's you—to help?"

"While that might have interested me twenty years ago . . ." He grimaced. "I'm afraid that won't do now."

"Glad to hear it. So what do you want?"

"Later. Stop talking. You have fourteen minutes left."

"You're bossy."

"Do you think so? And here I thought I'd been on my best behavior. Damn it all."

She chuckled. "How is it that you never married again?"

Because from what Jolie could see, Anna must have been an extremely happy woman. Heath was very good not just at caring for a woman's well-being but making her feel utterly adored.

He didn't answer at first. A long moment went by, and Jolie began to worry she'd picked the wrong topic.

"I . . ." He sighed. "I couldn't—"

Before he could say more, his phone rang at his side. Heath stood and dried his hands, then answered his mobile. "Powell."

He motioned her to wait there and walked out of the bathroom. Jolie soaked for long minutes, letting herself revel in the scents, the steam, the utter feeling of needing to be nowhere and being required to do nothing. *Now* she understood the value of a good bath.

With her head propped on the edge of the tub, she dozed for a long minute, thoughts of Heath swirling in her head. He had been unable to remarry. She understood that now. He must have loved his late wife very much.

Maybe he'd never love anyone else.

The thought had her frowning as Heath returned to the room.

"Cutter is looking into the mysterious gifts your sister has received. He doesn't like them, either. Particularly the latest. How could he possibly know we've had so many other issues that I haven't yet finished the office security?"

"Good question. So what should we do to figure out Creepy McStalker's identity and get rid of him?"

"Your sister must know more than she's letting on. Cutter plans to grill Karis this weekend."

"That won't go over well," Jolie warned.

"He's a professional. He'll get to the bottom of it. In the meantime, he'll keep her safe so you don't have to worry."

She appreciated that. But she'd feel much better once they'd solved this riddle. "Are my twenty minutes up?"

"Not yet. Close your eyes."

With a sigh, she did as he'd demanded. The little protest was mostly for show. She hadn't relaxed in years and was actually enjoying it. But she couldn't let him think he was right that easily.

Jolie was about to drift off when she heard the sound of shattering glass followed by a loud thump coming from the front of her condo.

No one was here except her and Heath.

She gasped and sat up, only to find him tense and alert. "What was that?"

* * *

INSTANTLY, Heath went cold, focused. He grabbed a towel and tossed it on the edge of the counter. "Get up slowly. Keep the sloshing water to a minimum. Get dressed. Stay back here."

"You think someone's broken in?" she whispered.

It was a distinct possibility, and he didn't want to frighten her.

"Call the police." He headed out the bathroom door.

"Be careful," she called in a breathy, shaking voice.

"Always."

He drew his weapon from his holster, headed into her bedroom, and found it clear. Then he crouched and turned down the hall. The narrow walkway ran nearly the whole length of the unit. From here, he could see the hall bath and home office doors closed on either side. The family room straight ahead looked almost too still.

He crept farther toward the front of the condo, and the kitchen came into view. The pans he'd used to cook breakfast were still scattered around the stove and counters. He'd left the butter out. A few shards of glass peppered the floor, refracting sunlight from the surrounding windows. Those shimmering bits hadn't been there before. Heath pressed forward. The hair at the back of his neck stood up.

A disturbance to his left drew him toward the front of the condo. When Heath reached the kitchen, crouching and taking cover behind a pony wall, he peeked over and around the corner. Glass lay everywhere, littering the area rug, the formal dining table, its leather chairs. Shards glinted in the light as they poked up from the mat in front of the door.

Heath took stock of all the windows in the room and found the culprit. One to his right had been shattered, probably by a projectile, based on the splatter of the glass. An accident? A neighborhood kid with a ball?

He hadn't noticed many children in this complex seemingly devoted to single, career-minded adults.

Then he caught sight of a rock half under the table. He rushed over, glad he still wore his boots. Had someone pulled a prank? Did the neighborhood have an unexpected vandal element?

Determined to find the answer, he flipped the rock over with the toe of his boot. In red letters, the word BITCH covered the other side.

His blood turned to ice. This wasn't a poor joke or a local street thug. Someone knew where Jolie worked—and now where she lived—and he had anger and an agenda.

Footsteps echoed behind him. Heath whirled, gun poised, heart pounding. Jolie, wearing a pair of hastily donned yoga pants and a sweatshirt, gasped and froze.

"The police will be here in less than five. What's going on?"

"Someone seems determined to make a point that they'd prefer you hurt or dead. I won't have you in danger. Pack a bag. We can't say here any longer."

"Where are we going?"

Heath was relieved she hadn't argued but she asked a viable question. He knew few places in town that were truly secure. The one he could think of made him sigh. "I'll need to make some phone calls from the car, then I'll have an answer."

"I'll start throwing my stuff in a suitcase."

She was too smart to argue about staying here, and Heath appreciated her all over again.

"By the time I'm done with the police, be ready to go."

It didn't take long for the cops to decide that the rock wasn't menacing, just likely some prank from a kid in the complex. Heath mentioned the break-in at Jolie's office but the officer wrote him off. The exhausted cop doubted those two incidents, while unfortunate, were related. Heath's gut said otherwise but belaboring the point would get him nowhere.

And he was still minus a suspect.

After last night, Heath might have suspected Gardner of retaliating against Jolie for refusing to put out. But not only did vandalism seem childish for a man of his age and social standing, after the split pea soup Heath doubted Gardner was in much shape to threaten anyone. The man's sister had texted Jolie early this morning to apologize profusely for her brother's behavior. And apparently, Gardner had gone to the hospital for minor burns in some very sensitive areas. Now he was laid up, loopy on pain killers.

Heath was more than a bit happy. But that left him with a problem. If Richard wasn't able to vandalize her apartment, who had?

"That cop is an idiot," Jolie remarked as they shut the door behind the uniformed officer.

"I think somewhere between lazy and lacking imagination would be a more apt description. But I understand. At first glance, these two crimes don't seem related at all. Different location, different M.O. It could look like a string of bad luck."

"Until this past week, I've never had any occasion to call the police. My only brush with them has been a speeding ticket."

Heath grunted. No sense in staying here to discuss this potential threat. They only made themselves easier targets for whatever might come next. "Let's go."

After gathering the few things he'd brought in a duffel bag, they drew the blinds, patched up the broken window with a discarded cardboard box and some heavy-duty strapping tape, locked up, and headed out. As soon as Jolie backed out of her parking spot, Heath got to work on his mobile.

Sean answered after the third ring. "Can't really talk. I'm at the hospital. Callie has gone into labor for real."

And the last thing Thorpe and Sean needed now was for them to park danger inside Dominion, their club. Besides, while Jolie had been receptive to him tying their ankles together for sleep, he didn't see her accepting medical tables, ponytail anal plugs, or whipping posts quite so easily.

"I need a safe house. Jolie's place has been compromised. Any ideas?"

After a long pause and some shuffling of the phone, Sean returned to the line. "Yeah, Axel is out of the country, and Thorpe has the keys to his place. It's quiet, out of the way. It should have all the creature comforts. Swing by here to pick up the keys."

Heath memorized the address Sean rattled off. "We'll be there as soon as we can."

"We'll probably still be waiting for this baby. It's been a long few hours already."

Heath frowned. "Is Callie all right?"

"If cursing Thorpe and me then crying all in the same ten minutes is normal, then she's perfect."

He had no clue. "Good luck, mate."

The second he hung up, Jolie turned to him with a frown. "What's wrong with Callie?" As she pulled up to a red light, she dug into her purse and pulled out her phone. "Damn it, she texted me forty minutes ago to say she was in labor. We have to go."

Jolie sent back a quick reply, then took off when the light turned green.

"I'll be running in to pick up a key, then we're leaving the hospital."

Before he'd even finished speaking, Jolie was shaking her head. "No, we're not. I want to be there for Callie. She has no other family and she's one of my few female friends. Most other women call me a bitch because I'm assertive and I don't wear my insecurities on my sleeve. I promised her. I won't let her down."

"Danger could be following you."

"I'll be in a well-monitored facility where nothing will happen. I'm going to support my friend, hold her hand if she needs." She pressed her lips together mulishly.

Heath cursed under his breath. He supposed he should be mad as hell that she didn't want to do as he demanded for the sake of her safety. But he liked her loyal streak. It seemed nearly as long as her stubborn streak. He didn't relish the idea of having to be constantly vigilant in public but that was part of being a bodyguard. He didn't love her choice but he understood and respected it.

"All right, then. But you'll do what I say, when I say, without question. It could be the difference between life and death. Am I clear?"

"Of course."

Minutes later, they pulled up in front of the hospital. Jolie had barely killed the engine before she vaulted out, grabbed her purse, and dashed to the maternity ward. Heath had to sprint to keep up.

Once they reached the waiting room, he spotted Thorpe and Sean pacing.

Jolie skidded to a stop in front of them. "How is she? What's going on? Will they let you back with her? Is there a problem?"

Sean turned, face gentle. "No. She sent us out here to find you and bring you to her room."

"Are you certain you want to do that?" Heath looked at Sean pointedly. "Someone has Jolie on their radar." He summarized the incidents that had taken place over the past few days.

"None of that is life threatening. Trust me, man. It's in our best interest to keep our pregnant wife happy."

"Or she'll never let us come near her again." Thorpe rolled his eyes with an indulgent smile.

"Thank you. I want to see her," Jolie insisted.

Heath shrugged. Looked as if emotion was trumping logic today. "Lead the way . . ."

* * *

WHEN they reached the birthing suite, Jolie darted around Sean and Thorpe to Callie's side. "Hi. How are you doing?"

"I'm uncomfortable and scared as hell. But I'm so ready to hold my baby." Somehow, even with her face scrubbed clean and looking as if she hadn't slept all night, Callie was still beautiful. She balanced a cup of ice chips on her belly and had the remote control for the TV in her hand.

"How long have you been here?"

"Since three this morning. Apparently I'm dilating slowly. The doctor should come in to break my water in the next few hours, now that I'm at a five."

"So you're really having this baby today?"

"It looks that way. I don't know how much more I can expand to accommodate my growing little dynamo. The doctors think he or she will weigh about eight pounds. I don't care whether it's a boy or girl. I just want a healthy baby."

Jolie already knew Callie wanted the gender to be a surprise. But what amazed her was the woman's calm. Her life was about to change forever.

"I'll be here with you for as long as you need me."

Callie teared up. "Who knew that asking someone where a pregnant girl could find a yoga mat would lead me to such a great friend?"

"I'm glad you asked me. If it hadn't been my first class, too, I might have known the answer."

They laughed, then Callie winced and grabbed her belly, breathing in a practiced pattern with Jolie during the next thirty seconds. Finally, her friend sighed, her whole body going lax, then she looked at her men. "The contractions are coming about every five minutes. They're getting more intense."

They each rushed to one side and took her hands. Jolie could feel the palpable love between the trio.

"We're here, lovely," Sean murmured. "Those marriage vows said forever, and I meant it."

"I know, babe." Callie smiled faintly. "You both have been the best."

Thorpe leaned down to kiss her forehead. "You're doing well with your breathing."

She nodded. "I've been practicing."

"Good. Sean will work through it with you. I'll be behind you to help you push."

The nurse came in then, frowning at the trio as if she still didn't quite understand the relationship and didn't want to ask too many questions. She monitored Callie's vitals, took some blood, then returned with a clipboard.

"I've been sent to begin the birth certificate process. The exact spelling of your name?"

Callie answered, and the young woman froze, star struck. "The heiress Callindra Howe?"

"That one," Callie confirmed.

Jolie wasn't surprised by the nurse's reaction. Unless someone had been living under a rock, they'd heard the story of the little rich girl who'd run away after supposedly killing her family as a teenager. She'd been wanted for years and fought hard to prove that someone else had murdered her loved ones. When Jolie had first met the woman, she'd been shocked, too. But since then Callindra had just become Callie to her, and they'd turned into great friends.

"Yes. I'm Callindra Howe Mackenzie now."

"Wow. Nice to meet you. So the baby's last name will be Mackenzie?"

Callie shook her head. "Mackenzie-Thorpe, please."

The nurse, who looked just out of school, glanced between the two men. "Father of the baby?"

Thorpe stepped in then, his expression a subtle but effective warning. "We'll be swabbing the baby after birth to determine that. If you need anything else, ask Mr. Mackenzie." He pointed to Sean, holding Callie's hand across the bed. "Or me. I'm Mitchell Thorpe."

The wary nurse heeded his warning undertone to stay away from Callie. "I-I think that's enough for now. We'll complete the form once the child is born and tested. Excuse me."

When the flustered woman backed out of the room, Callie scowled. "Mitchell, behave. She was just doing her job."

"Not very politely, pet."

Callie sighed. "I knew it was going to be awkward. London Santiago warned me since she's also got two husbands." She turned to Jolie. "They recently had a baby girl, so she gave me some pointers."

"Is that why you're going to DNA test the baby?"

That hadn't been the plan originally.

"Yeah. She made some good points. We need to know the father for legal and medical purposes. Beyond that, we don't care. He or she belongs to all of us."

Sean squeezed her hand and looked at her as if Callie was his moon and stars. Thorpe brushed the hair back from her face and snagged her gaze, his full of silent promise.

Just then, another contraction hit.

One turned into another, and the next few hours slid by. Nurses changed shifts, and the doctor came by at lunch to check on Callie, who had dilated to a seven. When they told her to walk while they prepared to break her water, Jolie meandered up and down the halls with her friend, stopping to help her bend and breathe through the discomfort.

"How are things with Heath?" Callie asked between contractions. *Exhilarating. Complicated. Uncertain.* "Fine. Don't worry about me."

"I have to. He looks like he wants to beat back anyone who would dare to look at you, then gobble you all up for himself."

Jolie flushed. "He's been really . . . amazing so far. Helpful and reasonable."

"Then you must have some magic elixir because he's usually taciturn and remote—unless he's picking up a random woman." Callie cocked her head. "But he's not doing that anymore, is he?"

"He can't exactly slip away to exercise his sex drive when he's busy bodyguarding me."

But that wasn't the whole truth and Callie saw through her answer. "I'd bet my entire bank balance he doesn't want to anymore. He looks at you like he's hooked."

"I think maybe . . . yeah. It's not one-sided. I don't know what to do."

"Let it happen." Callie shrugged.

"The timing is lousy." Well, that wasn't her only objection. Would she have ever thought the timing was good? Probably not. "I wasn't looking for love. I never have been."

"I know you like order in your life, prefer to plan where you're going so you know what tasks to tackle next. Love isn't like that. At first, it's more like . . . grabbing a fast-moving train. The track can be wild and harrowing and a little slippery, but once you get some traction and figure out where you're going, it's the most amazing ride of your life. I know you're a results-driven woman, but there's no bottom line in love. Don't think about the destination, doll. Focus on the journey. That's where you'll find the beauty of love."

Yeah, Jolie was beginning to understand that, and it was a completely foreign way of thinking to her. Still, she suspected Callie was right and no amount of trying to filter romance through any preexisting experience was going to work. "Thanks. I don't know if it's love or anything close . . ."

She nodded. "I have a sense about these things. Or maybe it's just pregnancy hormones. Everything makes me cry now."

Callie hugged her. Jolie held on to the other woman in return and felt herself tearing up, too. She never had many female friends. She'd always been too ambitious for slumber parties, makeovers, and gossip. She couldn't have cared less about boy bands and crushes or cheerleading skirts in high school. The girls on the academic decathlon team had all been socially awkward, not to mention enthralled by sci-fi and gaming in a way she never would be.

Karis might be the sister of her blood, but Callie was the sister of her heart. And despite the belly bumping between them, Jolie was thrilled to be here for her on the day she would become a mother.

As they rounded the nurses' station and wandered back down the hall, Callie looked Jolie's way. "I heard through the grapevine that you had dinner with a potential investor last night."

"In other words, Heath said something about it to Sean?"

Callie laughed. "Yeah, Heath wanted some local connections at that restaurant to make certain he talked to the people who could get security things done. How did it go?"

"Richard Gardner is a manipulative manwhore."

"I could have told you that." Callie tsked.

"I'd hoped that the desires of his bank account would outweigh the desires of his penis."

"Nope. He made a pass at me once. I thought Thorpe and Sean were going to kill him in the middle of a cocktail party. Honey, if you were looking for an investor, why didn't you call me? I would have—oh!"

When she gripped her belly and squatted with a gasp of pain, Jolie dropped down beside her. "What can I do? Should I get a nurse?"

Callie didn't reply for a long moment, just breathed through the pain. "They're coming quicker now, getting more intense. I don't think it will be much longer."

Jolie agreed as she helped Callie back to her feet. "Let's get you back to bed."

"In a minute." Her voice sounded strained. "Why didn't you call me?"

"I didn't want to risk our friendship. I couldn't guarantee your funds." Jolie teared up. "I could find another investor but I couldn't find another best friend."

Callie didn't even try to hide her tears. "Oh my god, that's so touching, even if you're being a silly bitch."

Together they laughed as Jolie helped Callie down the hall. She looked up to find all three men watching protectively from the end of the hall. Thorpe and Sean jogged toward Callie, concern all over their faces. She took another halting step to reach them when a splash of clear liquid unexpectedly doused the floor between her feet.

"My water!"

That brought nurses running, had the men worrying, and Jolie panicking. She knew how to handle a company that grossed nearly ten million dollars annually. She had no idea what to do with a woman in active labor.

Thankfully, Callie was soon back in bed and fighting the first urge to push.

In between contractions, she held out her hand to Jolie. For the first time, she looked afraid. "I know it's a lot to ask, but since my mother and sister aren't alive anymore and can't be with me today and I . . ."

Callie wanted female comfort. Though Jolie had never been in Callie's shoes, she couldn't imagine going through such a momentous event without her mom and sister. Husbands were all fine and good, but sometimes only a woman understood what another woman was going through.

Jolie squeezed her fingers. "I'm here for as long as you need me."

"Thank you. That means the world to me." Callie looked slightly sweaty but a bit more at ease. Love glowed from her eyes.

After that, things progressed quickly. Callie's men took over the duties of holding her hand, wiping her brow, feeding her ice chips, and encouraging her progress. The doctor, a competent woman in her forties, checked Callie and declared her nearly ready. The nurses filed in. Jolie drifted to the back of the room, near Heath. Together, they watched mutely.

One minute bled into the next until the contractions seemed never-ending. Callie panted, trying to regulate her breathing. Sean worked through the pattern with her. Thorpe took up position behind her. The three of them had an almost wordless communication. The men understood that her happiness and comfort came before all else and never spoke unless it furthered that cause.

For the few seconds between contractions, Sean brushed a kiss on her damp forehead. Thorpe patted her with cool cloths and stroked her hair. They both told her they loved her and were proud of her every single day.

When the next contraction seized her petite frame, Thorpe braced himself behind her. Sean counted breaths. Callie grunted and bore down.

"The baby is crowning. A few more pushes!" the doctor announced.

Moments later, another contraction grabbed hold of Callie's

entire frame, this one seemingly on top of the last. She grabbed Sean's hand as Thorpe supported her. A grunt became a scream as she struggled to give her baby life.

"Just a bit more . . ."

"I can't." As the contraction let up, Callie flopped back, exhausted. "It hurts so much . . ." She burst into tears. "I gained too much weight and my body looks like something even a whale would be ashamed of."

Sean repressed a smile and kissed her again. "You're perfect, lovely."

Thorpe scowled. "He's right. You wouldn't have to beat us off with a stick so often if we didn't find you completely, stunningly beautiful."

The doctor regarded Callie with compassion. "You're not the first mother to feel this way. You won't be the last. Right now, you're hormonal and don't recognize your body. But you'll recover after the baby comes. Give it time." She checked Callie's progress again. "Now, c'mon. I think you can do this in one more push."

"I'm so tired." But she nodded.

"It was all that 'nesting' last night," Sean said, gently chiding.

"Next time you climb the kitchen cabinets to rearrange every pot and pan we have, make sure one of us is there to help you." *Or there will be hell to pay.* Jolie heard that subtext in Thorpe's voice. Then his stern tone softened more than she'd imagined possible. "You needed rest. We worry."

"I know . . ." she said miserably. "I couldn't sleep."

Jolie had never seen her friend anything less than bubbly and optimistic, and a potent combination of hormones and exhaustion probably drove this weepy mood. Still, Jolie's heart went out. "You can do this. You've got gumption, woman. And you're about to have a baby who needs its mommy. We're all here for you."

"See?" Sean murmured. "We're almost parents now. You can't give up, lovely. We've been waiting for the day our three would become four. Just a bit more."

"Dig deep, pet," Thorpe encouraged.

As another contraction gripped her, she looked to her men as if she needed them to be her pillars. Wordlessly, they gave their support, stalwart and strong, as she worked up her energy and courage to give one more mighty push. Then the wailing cry of the baby filled the air.

Jolie couldn't see much around all the people and equipment, but she could feel the miracle in the air. A new life began. Hope. Future. And as the doctor set the baby on Callie's chest, tears streamed down her rosy cheeks.

"Meet your son," the doctor said to the trio softly.

Instantly, Callie held the boy against her body. Thorpe and Sean both looked on, stroking his little head, soothing his cries with a glide down his chubby leg. To her shock, both men cried openly, too.

"He's beautiful." Callie's voice shook. She was unable to stop looking at the boy with a thatch of pitch-black hair and blue eyes.

"Amazing," Thorpe whispered.

Sean smiled. "Welcome to the world, Asher Daniel Mackenzie-Thorpe."

The doctor took the baby. Nurses weighed and cleaned him. After a swaddle, they presented him to Callie again. "Seven pounds, eight ounces. Nineteen inches. Congratulations."

The threesome didn't speak for long moments, just held one another as they marveled over the life they had created together.

Jolie's perspective tilted on its side. This was love in its purest form and she felt it charging the air, closing up her throat.

For the last thirty years, she'd valued all the wrong things for all the wrong reasons.

Life wasn't about work or balance sheets or making it from one day to the next. It was about savoring every moment of precious existence and sharing her most profound moments with loved ones. For so long, she'd strived to be as insular as possible, figuring that if she never let anyone close, she would never have to feel the pain of disappointment, sorrow, or hurt. Now she saw that her life had been empty because she'd been too afraid to truly live it. She'd devoted her existence to proving herself worthy of a father who would never love her, in walling herself off so she could never feel crushed again.

But without pain, she couldn't feel joy or amazement, hope or true love . . . Nothing that made life worth living.

Suddenly, her world turned blurry. She wiped at her cheeks, weirdly stunned to find them drenched with tears. Beside her, Heath looked choked up, too. Then he slipped his hand in hers.

Chapter Twelve

Rule for success number twelve:
Make plans . . . but always be ready for change.

IT was nearly ten P.M. when Heath let Jolie into the darkened house that Axel owned in Dallas. On a quiet street in an older, eclectic neighborhood, the Craftsman cottage fit the man—wide, open, almost an extension of nature—Heath noted absently, as he flipped on the lights and locked the doors behind them.

Jolie had been too quiet on the drive from the hospital. He didn't have to guess what she was thinking. The miracles of birth, of love, had hit her as profoundly as they had gobsmacked him. Now he wasn't certain what to say. Or do. Something about watching a life emerge into the arms of adoring parents had been overwhelming. That baby represented their deep devotion, the circle of life at work. Yes, he knew people had babies every day, but experiencing Asher's birth firsthand filled Heath with emotions now clamoring to be heard, even as logic fluttered in a dizzying whirl of circular thoughts before vanishing into disarray.

"I doubt Axel has anything in the refrigerator. He's been gone for months," he murmured, standing beside the gleaming appliance without much interest. "Shall I call for food?"

Jolie set her purse on the counter beside him and stared, looking a bit lost. "I'm not hungry."

In truth, he wasn't, either, at least not for food. He wasn't merely hungry for sex, per se. But he craved *her*—her touch, her tenderness, her open arms, her willingness to receive him in every way a woman could accept a man.

Bloody hell, he sounded like a mad sap, bleating on about the tripe of his feelings. But wishing he didn't have them hardly made them less real or insistent.

He pocketed the house keys. The powerful hush of the moment seemed too sacred for words. Just above it, he heard her breathing. The soft sound made him so aware that Jolie stood close and vulnerable and female.

For reasons he couldn't understand or explain, he knew unequivocally that she belonged to him now. The moment he acknowledged that, new, positively mad desires frothed in his brainpan, loud, insistent, urgent.

"Jolie?"

She froze as if she sensed his next words could change everything. "Yes."

He heard more than mere acknowledgment. Her voice resounded with total acceptance. "You don't know what I'm going to—"

"I do," she argued. "It's the same thing I've been thinking. And yes, I want what you want."

Did she realize he meant to start their future now? "Are we allowing the remarkable moment we witnessed to carry us away?"

Jolie hesitated for such a long moment, he wasn't certain she heard. But he needed her reply. He couldn't be alone in this irrational yearning for connection and sharing and the future.

"I think watching Asher's birth simply made things clearer to me. I've spent my entire life hating a man who isn't worth my energy and fearing that I'd become a woman I can't respect. I've devoted all my thoughts and waking hours to things like contempt and revenge. And after today, it seems so . . . petty. I don't need to prove to Carrington Quinn that I'm worthy. I simply need to be the best person I can be and live my life in whatever way fulfills me."

"That's insightful." And Heath was so proud of Jolie for figuring that out. "And you're utterly right."

"If I only worry about beating my father at his game, what sort of empty victory have I achieved if I win but I've forgotten my dreams along the way? Betti is mine. It's for me. Because I wanted to accomplish something I believed in and I love what I do. But today I also realized that life isn't work. Karis tried to tell me that. I've intentionally pushed people away so they couldn't hurt me." She sighed. "In some ways, I haven't lived at all."

"I stopped living years ago. Losing Anna was . . ." He frowned and hung his head to hide his face, to conceal his guilt. Every day, he still felt as if, by failing to avenge her, he'd wronged her.

Jolie stepped closer. "I'm sure it's the most difficult thing you've ever endured."

"The losing her was hard, yes. The living without her has been much harder. I'm afraid I haven't done a very good job of it. I welcomed the numbness long ago. I gave up believing I'd have a tomorrow that mattered. I've taken jobs in the past with a high probability for death because I didn't think my life mattered anymore. After seeing Callie and her son, I understand how my mother must have felt the moment she first held me. Suicide by terrorist or crime boss would have been an easy end to my pain and a horribly cruel way to add to hers. I would never do that now. And I don't think my life will be complete until I experience what Thorpe and Sean did today for myself."

"Yeah." She nodded, and he could see the million emotions on her face that neither of them had to speak.

They both simply knew.

"I'm not merely talking about having a child someday with some nameless woman. I'm talking about you. Us." He raked a hand through his hair. "This is abrupt. I never expected this. I—"

"Neither did I." She stepped close. "I didn't want this."

He paced in her direction, meeting her in the middle of the kitchen. "Nor did I. At all. You've changed my life so quickly and completely."

Jolie took the last step closer, then cupped his cheek. "Same. Even believing this is right, I'm scared to death."

"Because everything is so hectic with Betti now?"

She shook her head. "Work will always be important. Even though Karis tried to tell me it isn't life, that I should value people and relationships, I couldn't fathom why or how until you."

"Are you worried I'll hurt you?"

"No, that I'm not ready. That I won't do anything right." She lowered her hand and drew in a shuddering breath. "That I'll let you down."

"If you simply be yourself, you can't." He hesitated. "How could we have met less than a week ago and already be talking about the rest of our lives?"

She bit her lip. Her brow wrinkled. Jolie did that when she thought, and he'd found watching her keen mind work somewhere between fascinating and endearing. Now he held his breath.

"Maybe . . ." She shook her head. "Maybe we had to experience what we don't want out of life to understand what we actually do."

She was right. It wasn't the fact that he'd loved and lost that Heath lamented. Anna would always be a warm memory for him, and at the time he'd loved her dearly. It was the choices he'd made after her passing he truly regretted. It was the life he'd been living for the past six years he despised.

"I'm scared to death, too," he admitted.

"That I can't be what you need?"

"You already are," he assured. "I'm worried I won't be there to protect you if something truly dangerous happens. I couldn't bear to let you down."

"I have total faith in you."

Heath reached for her, cupped her shoulder, her face, sidling closer until he looked down into her eyes. "I intend to marry you."

A dry smile curled up the corner of her lips. "I never imagined I would be anyone's wife. I didn't understand why people settled down, spit kids out, bought a house in the 'burbs, and lived for the weekends. I realize now they're not settling for mediocrity or following the herd. They're sacrificing and compromising because they found someone who called to their soul and they had the courage to merge their lives in every way. The job and the commute, the soccer leagues and the PTA . . . It's all part and parcel of what people do in order to live with the person they love and create the next generation together." She frowned. "And wow, do I sound ridiculously profound. That was my long-winded way of saying yes."

They both stared at one another for timeless moments. They'd both agreed to something momentous that neither had seen coming. Heath wasn't sure what to say, how to proceed.

Jolie made the first move, launching herself against him, lips parted in welcome. Heath didn't hesitate, thrusting his fingers in her hair and tugging back to take possession of her mouth like he intended to claim the rest of her. She tugged at his T-shirt. He pulled at her top. She kicked off her shoes. He struggled out of his combat boots. She grabbed at his zipper. He unflicked the hooks of her bra.

His cock sprang free as he bared her breasts and broke their kiss to suck her nipple into his mouth with a desperate hunger he couldn't hold back. Bloody hell, this was happening. His heart chugged like a train. Need thundered through him with a ground-shaking boom. Tenderness gathered and swelled around his heart.

And nothing would stop him from making Jolie Quinn completely his and showing her just how well he could love her.

As he kicked his jeans away, he shoved her pants down her hips, still teasing the stiff bud of her breast with his tongue, his teeth. Sucking her in, then releasing her. Her taste, her texture, her flavor . . . everything felt perfect to him. He'd made a living by his gut. He simply knew this was right.

Jolie wriggled and kicked at her pants, stepping until she managed to work her way free. Then they were both blessedly naked, and Heath couldn't wait another moment. He shoved her back until the island stopped them. In one movement, he lifted her, spread her, grabbed her hips, and penetrated her.

"God, you feel so good." He gave a primal groan as his bare flesh slid inside her. "I'll spend every day and night giving you bliss, love. I'll strip you bare, show you how much I want you and . . . Oh, fuck."

Heath melted as he plunged in again and lost his ability to speak.

As she tilted her hips up, he took her thighs into the crooks of his arms and thrust again. Then he found a rhythm. Jolie leaned back on her hands and spread her legs wider, staring back as he claimed the woman who belonged to him in the most basic way.

She looked beautiful, breasts thrust out at him, her mouth open in pleasure as she tightened on his cock.

"More," she whimpered. "Every time you touch me, I think this need will go away but . . . I only want you deeper, harder. I want you more."

He clamped onto her hips and pounded ferociously inside her.

"I need this. I need you." He panted, breaths sawing, heart chugging, blood churning. The moment felt so pure and raw and natural. "Jolie. Jolie . . . love."

She gave a hard, mewling cry. "So close. So . . . God, I've never ached so badly." She keened out again, tightened, clamped. "Please . . ."

"I'm not wearing a condom," he reminded her.

If they meant to take this crazy forever gamble, they would do it together with their eyes wide open.

"I know." Her eyes willed him to give her everything—the moment, the future. "I'm well aware."

"And you want this?"

"Yes," she cried.

"You want this now? You want to share a life and a child and a home with me?"

A week ago, Heath wouldn't have believed he'd be uttering these words at all, much less holding his breath and hoping like hell that she'd say yes.

"Everything. I want all of it. I want it now."

A vision of taking her hand in his as they spoke vows, as they brought life into the world, as they ended their days together exploded in his head. Yes. A million times yes. The electric need to make that future theirs now rolled through his brain, took root in his chest, and sent the direct impulse straight to his cock.

The violent urge to mark her wouldn't be denied. He buried his face in her neck and jackhammered deep inside her, feeling her tighten more with every thrust until he had to fight his way into her slick depths. But that didn't stop him. Nothing would. He was going to do his best to plant his seed and let this woman—and the rest of the world know—they belonged to each other.

Suddenly, Jolie gasped, tensed, then he felt her convulse around him with a throaty scream.

That unraveled Heath entirely. For the first time in his life, he climaxed inside a woman without barriers, without any feeling except the profoundest desire to please her, share love, and make life.

Last night, he'd believed himself to be happy. And he had been—in a way that amazed him to the core. Now he had a better understanding of what true happiness was, and he never intended to let her go.

* * *

AFTER their searing, frenzied sex on the kitchen island, Heath found a pizza place that delivered until eleven P.M. When the steaming pie arrived, they ate out of the box, still mostly naked, not saying much that couldn't be said through touches or smiles.

With sated stomachs, they gathered their clothes and made their way to the bedroom. The room was mostly brown and utilitarian and it definitely looked like a man's space. Just like the rest of the house, it had a relaxed vibe. Being here with Heath while completely bare in every way felt natural.

The sheets had been stripped from the big mattress at some point, and they found a fresh set in a closet in the hallway. After making the bed, they fell into the cloud of blankets and rolled toward one another as if propelled by a gravity of their own.

Heath's lips found hers, his tongue sliding deep as he possessed her mouth. Their joining wasn't the same urgent dash to completion as before but something thoughtful, deliberate—a lingering promise blooming with springlike newness, rooting love deeper in their hearts.

After a hot shower, they crawled back into bed. Jolie curled against Heath, using his chest as a pillow. He cradled her in his arms.

"When I took this job, I'd planned to use the couple of weeks I dedicated to this assignment and decide if I want to remain in Dallas or move elsewhere again. I had no idea you would change everything."

"I didn't want to hire a security person. But the neighborhood burglar hit two doors down, plus I work enough late nights alone in the office that Karis convinced me I was putting myself at risk." She propped her chin on her hands and peered at him. "When we first met, I was admittedly attracted."

"I was, as well, despite you being a real ballbuster." He laughed. "Definitely not my usual type."

"You have a type?" It dismayed Jolie to think that she didn't fit his mold.

"That night you tracked me down in the bar, you pegged me right. I typically like the doe-eyed ones I could take care of." He shrugged. "I'm a protector at heart, and you seemed to have everything together. I knew within ten seconds of meeting you that you're the last woman who would ever stand about, looking to a man for answers."

"And that bothered you?" An anxiety she didn't like needled her, but Heath couldn't change himself to suit her any more than she could remake her psyche to please him.

"To my surprise, no. Your independence intrigued me." He cradled her head and stroked her hair. "You fascinated me, in fact. I love watching your mind work. I love that sometimes I know exactly what you'll do. Other times, you're completely unpredictable. You're probably the smartest person in the room more often than not. And I appreciate the fact that you're with me because you want to be with me, not because you find the real world difficult without my guidance. It's unexpectedly sweeter."

A big smile spread across Jolie's face, even as warmth seeped into every corner of her body. He saw her and understood. And he appreciated the parts of her that had scared away or turned off other men. "Good. I never imagined being the sort of woman who gave up any control to a man. I've seen how well that works out for my mother, in an endless cycle over and over."

"She chooses her husbands and lovers poorly."

"Every time." Jolie nodded.

"You're not her. You could never be her."

"I've worked hard not to be," she admitted. "In fact, I've never done a single romantically impulsive thing in my life . . . until you."

"I realize how much trust you've given me, love. You placed a great deal in me when you gave me control in the bedroom." When she blushed, he smiled. "You liked it that first night."

"I loved it," she admitted. "I juggle so many responsibilities and rarely think about my sex life beyond the one I can manage with my battery-operated boyfriend. I never thought I could handle surrendering in any capacity. But I can let go and know you'll catch me."

"Always. It only works because we've developed trust." He sighed and cupped his hands around her shoulders, urging her up his body. "I want you to know that I take nothing we've done tonight lightly."

"I know. I don't, either."

"I'm not certain precisely where we'll live next or what our lives will look like. But we'll make decisions together."

Jolie nodded. "Totally. I'm glad I didn't listen to my first instinct."

"Which was?"

"Well . . ." She grinned. "When I met you, I thought you were one of the hunkiest men I'd ever laid eyes on. I almost didn't hire you because I wanted to crawl over my desk and take your clothes off."

Heath let out a full-bodied laugh, which filled her with a mellow glow. "You hid your urges frighteningly well. I left that meeting certain that I had a job but worried you viewed me as useful, like an insect in a garden, but as appealing as pond scum."

"You're definitely more appealing than that." She winked. "Don't you feel better now?"

"Positively transformed." He sobered then. "Actually, I am. Before you, I hadn't moved on much after Anna's death. You made me want to try harder at life, actually enjoy it again."

His words humbled her, and Jolie blinked away stinging tears. "When I reamed you out at the bar, I had no idea you'd lost a wife. I got to my car and read the report my sister had stupidly compiled about you. That's when I found out you'd lost Anna. I felt terrible that I'd said anything about the way you dealt with your grief."

"But you were right; I wasn't dealing with it. Not well. You challenged me to look at myself. I needed that."

"I'm so sorry my sister poked into your background. I didn't read past the bullet points she put at the beginning. After I realized how deeply personal and intrusive it was, I forced myself to put away the rest. She spent hours compiling this report. There were pages . . ." Jolie wasn't sure how to say this, so she just blurted the words. "I think she was particularly interested in figuring out who killed Anna and why. I don't know why she thought she could put on her amateur sleuth hat and figure it out. Maybe because she devours mystery novels like they're M&M's.

"I wish she had." He sighed, and for the longest time didn't respond. Jolie winced and prepared to change the subject until he could discuss it with her without pain. Instead, he met it head-on. "That's one reason I've found moving forward difficult. I worked for weeks after I buried her, and I discerned a Russian named Yuri Garbanov made the hit. He dabbled in weapons. Mostly a lone wolf, though word on the street was that he'd begun providing the hardware and muscle for a drug cartel taking over the posh parts of London and littering it with designer drugs. We British have very different feelings about guns than our American cousins."

"Our second amendment at work," she quipped.

"Indeed. So I hunted him down and . . . it didn't end well for him. But the million dollar question is why. Why my wife? I knew of Garbanov when employed by MI5 but I had nothing to do with his investigation. One of my former peers, Kensforth, had responsibility for stopping his flow of guns into Britain, and the Russian proved all too slippery. Nothing went our way. Evidence even disappeared. So, despite no longer being employed by Her Majesty when I showed Garbanov his early grave, MI5 gratefully looked the other way. I tried to get the bastard to talk but . . . he knew he was a dead man either way and nothing I did to him could possibly be worse than the torture the drug lords would dish out. So I still have no idea why he targeted Anna."

"I'm sorry." They were simple words. Jolie wished she had something more eloquent with which to soothe Heath. But her empathy was sincere. She followed it up with a kiss. "I hope you get answers someday."

"Did your sister have any theories?"

"Maybe. Like I said, I didn't read it all." She reached for her phone and scrolled through her e-mails, forwarding the file Karis had sent her earlier in the week. "You take a look. And please ignore any hearts, flowers, and inferences that you might be her Prince Charming."

"Of course," he promised. "So now that we've cleared up our misconceptions and bared our souls, what shall we do tomorrow?"

"I should really drag out my laptop and try to figure out my financial situation, finagle a few extra months of float until I can find a new investor . . . something. But I have this crazy idea." She bit her lip. Would he think she'd gone completely batshit? Maybe she had. Still, this felt right. He'd mentioned this already, so . . .

"Crazy? You may be the sanest person I know." He tossed her a skeptical stare. "Tell me."

"How would you feel about a trip to Vegas tomorrow?"

"To gamble for the money to finance your expansion?" He sent her a glower. "I don't—"

"No. I don't like to play games when the odds are stacked against me." She dragged in a breath for courage. "We both know what we want out of our future. I could already be pregnant. I was just thinking . . . Why wait?"

She saw the moment understanding lit his face. He grinned. "Do you think Elvis would marry us?"

* * *

WHO knew a week could change his whole life?

Last Monday, Heath had begun a new but temporary job. The following Monday, he was beginning a completely different life as a married man. His wife of twelve hours slept beside him on the plane, her head propped on his shoulder.

He stared at their matching bands, purchased hastily when they'd reached Vegas Sunday afternoon. They'd found the county clerk's office, applied for a license, and been married by someone who looked like a medieval bishop in a fairy-tale ballroom. She'd worn a white summer dress she'd found at the back of her closet. He'd scrounged up a suit. They'd told no one what they planned and taken only a handful of pictures. This wedding had been purely for them.

This time when he spoke his vows, the words held far more meaning. Exchanging them with Anna had been easy. While standing in a field of flowers surrounded by their family and friends, he'd never believed that he would have to put those vows to the test so soon, especially the bit about death parting them. Speaking similar words with Jolie filled him with gravity, with love. Neither of them knew what tomorrow would bring but he was damn determined that he would hold on to her, be her faithful protector. Because he would never speak these vows again. They were forever.

Now satisfaction buzzed through his veins. He couldn't be happier that this amazing, talented, acerbic, complicated woman was his.

While she dozed—they hadn't bothered much with sleep—he scanned the dossier Karis had composed on him. Decent job for an amateur. She had included all the highlights, even learning about a school prank or two he'd all but forgotten. Cursory information about his parents, his sister, and his first marriage was tucked inside. Then onto Anna's death. She'd rightly pegged Garbanov as the one who'd executed the attack that resulted in Anna's fiery murder. Karis was also a bit of a conspiracy theorist because she felt sure that no one could pull off a public attack of that magnitude and manage never to be caught without help on the inside.

Heath had wondered about that himself. He and Myles had even speculated once or twice that, given the intel at their fingertips and the ensuing manhunt, catching the culprit should have been much simpler. Identifying the mastermind and bringing him to justice should never have proven impossible.

Karis went on to speculate that Kensforth may have had a hand in the murders of Anna and the other innocents, like Lucy, that day. He'd never been implicated, of course. He'd been too well connected. But a year after Anna's murder, he had died in a mysterious single-car crash, seemingly a million pounds richer than he had previously been.

Heath frowned. He'd heard about Kensforth's passing, had always thought the prick was the sort who cut corners and took shortcuts a bit too much because he was a sacred cow no one would ever sack. Had Kensforth taken money from Garbanov or the drug lords who employed him to look the other way? To destroy evidence and provide bureaucratic red tape? Had someone eliminated him because he'd suddenly grown a conscience . . . or because his usefulness had come to an end?

Either way, if that were the case, whoever had orchestrated the attack was still at large.

With a frown, Heath tucked his phone away.

After their flight landed, they swung by Axel's house to shower before heading to the office. Jolie had texted Karis earlier to say she'd be there shortly to explain.

While his new wife cleaned up, Heath called his parents to give them the news of his marriage. They might be a bit disappointed that he hadn't waited for them to attend the ceremony, but overall they were delighted and couldn't wait to meet Jolie.

Then he turned his mobile over in his hands a few times before finally deciding to call Myles.

"Fancy hearing from you twice in the same week," his old mate said by way of greeting. "How are things?"

"Quite well, actually."

"That sounds promising. Do tell."

"Well, I took your advice," Heath began, then spilled his happy news. "It feels great."

"Married? That's fantastic! I'm so thrilled for you. I'd like to meet her."

"I'm hoping to drag her away from the office during the holidays and pop over for a week or so, introduce her to my parents and all that. We'll have to make plans then."

"Absolutely! Couldn't be happier for you."

"Thanks." Heath fell quiet and paused, listening for the sounds of the water pipes to ensure Jolie was still in the shower. He didn't want to worry her unnecessarily if Karis's theory had no merit . . . or involve her if it did. "What do you know about Kensforth's death?"

"That old bastard? God, I haven't thought about him in five years. Shady prick. Supposedly died in a single-vehicle crash."

"I heard. Maybe I'm being sentimental or I've realized that I need closure, but I want to solve our first wives' murders. It won't bring Anna and Lucy back, I know, but you must have felt as if you failed them. I struggle with having let Anna down every day. Don't you want to know why it happened?"

"I won't deny that the past has been difficult." Myles choked up. "It's been a hard road to accept that I don't have any answers—and I may never. I don't have any new theories. I've come to realize that sometimes old regrets are best forgotten."

Heath didn't see it that way. "It's not possible to forget something that terrible. You were always a relentless bloke in chasing down the bad guys. We should solve this once and for all. I've always wondered if Kensforth was somehow involved or simply let it happen—for a price. To this day we don't know who perpetrated it or even why. Random violence doesn't make sense. The event was too well orchestrated."

"I suspect whoever planned the terrible deed had some drug-related murder in mind but he died in the fiery hail of gunfire, too. No one left to take responsibility. You eliminating Garbanov tied up the last of the loose ends."

And that seemed logical, given the players involved. Almost too logical. He and Myles had discussed this theory in the past. Then, like now, it didn't sit well in his gut. "Did you know Kensforth died with far more money in his bank account than he could possibly have made in his position while affording that nice West End place of his?"

"I'd heard some rumor to that effect. But didn't his wife come from money?"

"That's possible," Heath conceded. He hadn't known much about the bastard's personal life. It wasn't as if they'd been good mates. "I'll look into it and let you know what I find."

"Leave it. Please," Myles asked softly. "You want to understand that terrible day and don't mind rehashing it. I know I have no right to ask this of you but . . . stop. I can't relive that again. Hell, I can't go to that part of town without breaking into a fit of rage. Or depression. I love Camille and I'm grateful for her every day. But I can only be with her because I've made the choice to lock the past behind closed doors and toss the key in the recesses of my mind. I've said my last good-bye to Lucy and the child we never had. Don't dig this up and make me deal with that hell again."

Heath sat in stunned silence, feeling guilty as the devil. He'd assumed the closure he sought would benefit Myles, too. So they could both know they had found all the missing pieces of the past, put them together, then taped shut the boxes filled with tragedy. Hell, maybe he simply needed to understand so he could process what he'd done wrong and finally deal with his failure to protect Anna.

Never in a million years had Heath imagined that his best mate from those days would have such a different way of dealing with the trauma. He respected Myles's perspective, even if he didn't subscribe to it. But Heath couldn't simply let this go.

"Of course. I'm sorry. I had no idea . . ."

"Isn't that one of the reasons you left home? The constant memories? The seeing a familiar restaurant or person or even a bottle of wine that reminded you of her?"

He was right, and Myles hadn't been able to simply walk away from his job, his surroundings, his home. The man had always been the backbone of his family, supporting ailing parents and a freeloading brother. Heath winced, wishing he'd been more compassionate. "They're haunting, I know."

"And you know well that I can't leave. Camille and I have a comfortable life now. Things are coming together. It's hard but I accept that I lost Lucy to a senseless act of violence. Even if I knew the ultimate who and why, I'd never understand her death. So is there really any point in knowing who to hate?"

"It's different for you. I see. I won't bring it up again."

"That phrase 'let sleeping dogs lie'? Let them," he implored. "All the years I tried in vain to process what happened only led to struggles with depression and alcohol. So I've had to relegate that terrible day to the distant past and move on."

Heath stared out Axel's window into the blinding sunshine, blinking against a sudden onslaught of tears. He wasn't sure why precisely. He mourned Anna. He ached for the years of grief he and Myles had both endured very differently. He hurt for the loss of the friendship that seemed forever diminished by an act neither of them had perpetrated.

"Consider the subject closed."

Myles breathed a sigh of relief. "Thank you."

They rang off, and Jolie entered the room, putting on her simple diamond studs and elegant watch. Her wedding band winked in the light. "All okay?"

"Of course, love. I've called my parents. They're expecting us to spend Christmas in Liverpool now, mind you." He forced a smile. "You and Mum will get on well."

"I'm looking forward to meeting them. They weren't angry?"

"That I'd married without them there? They never expected me to marry again at all, so they're thrilled to bits." He rose and kissed her gently. "I'll take a quick shower and we'll be off."

Jolie grabbed his arm. "You seem a little quiet. Are you having second thoughts?"

Heath softened. He couldn't let his own regrets and worries about the past affect his rapport with Jolie. Maybe in some ways Myles was right. They had too many wonderful reasons to look forward for him to dwell in the past.

"Not at all. Make yourself some coffee, then we'll head to the office and surprise everyone."

Chapter Thirteen

Rule for success number thirteen:
Sometimes you'll get lucky . . . sometimes you won't.
Plan for both possibilities.

JOLIE jangled her keys nervously in her hands as she and Heath walked into Betti's suite, glancing around for her sister.

Rohan tapped away on the plug-in for the new website. Gerard looked positively inspired as he sketched in short, brisk strokes across the pad with an array of colors that made her heart happy. Wisteria smiled, inhaling the pungent bouquet of blooms on her desk, which told Jolie that her receptionist and the on-again-off-again man in her life were in another idyllic phase, which she hoped for their sake finally lasted. Arthur slapped papers on his desk in short jerks as he shifted through a stack of invoices.

Jolie frowned. No sign of Karis.

"Hi, everyone. Where's my sister?"

They all looked up when she walked in, then glanced at one another as if someone must know the answer but the question hadn't actually occurred to any of them.

Well, everyone except Arthur. "She went to an early lunch. Her bodyguard tagged along."

And her grumbling accountant didn't sound happy. Was he having a crappy Monday? Jolie shrugged and let out a sigh.

The buildup to telling her sister about her nuptials had been nerve-racking. The letdown now that Karis wasn't here seemed every bit as arduous. And she couldn't very well tell the rest of the office before she told her own family. So it would have to wait.

"Thanks. If anyone needs me, I'll be at my desk."

Jolie shut herself in her domain and sat, not certain where to start. So much had changed over the weekend, yet the problems here remained the same. Messages littered her desk. Gerard had left a few promising sketches. A tap on her computer revealed a bursting inbox. But nothing was more important than getting a new investor. She needed one and she needed the cash now. After her crazy, romantic, pleasure-filled weekend with Heath, she had to come down from her personal cloud nine to face reality again. And the truth was, Betti could well be a memory if she didn't find someone wealthy to believe in her vision and the bravery to stand back and let her fulfill it.

When she picked up her phone to start making phone calls, the stutter dial tone told her she had a voicemail. Hoping for good news, she punched in the code and listened.

"Jolie, it's Carrington. Your father. I'd like to schedule lunch next Tuesday to start discussing the terms of my takeover. I'm prepared to be generous and reward your hard work. Don't have your dippy receptionist call me to negotiate a time and location. I won't deal with small people simply because you'd like to avoid me or this inconvenient reality. Swallow your pride—it's a valuable skill to have in business—and call me personally. You need my help too badly to risk pissing me off."

Was he serious? She slammed the phone down so hard, Heath—and half the office—came running. Her glower sent all but her husband scampering off again.

"What is it?" he asked.

"The sperm donor wants to play hardball. Fine. There's no way I'm calling him to set up a lunch meeting so he can crush my dream.

I told him before that he could go fuck himself. Now I think I'll hire a skywriter to make sure he gets the message."

Heath shut the door, enclosing them in her office together. He looked as if he had something to say, then shook his head. "You're smart and determined. This will work out."

As agitated as Jolie felt, she had to give thanks for the blessings Heath had brought to her life. Her father had been absent, her mother more concerned with her various romances than her eldest daughter's accomplishments, her younger siblings had needed her guidance . . . She'd never had anyone in her corner simply because they believed in her.

"Thank you." She rose and wrapped her arms around him. "It means the world to me."

"You're welcome. Hungry?"

She opened her mouth to say that she was famished when the sunlight reflected off moving metal in her peripheral vision. Jolie turned to see Karis's car pulling into the lot. She drew in a shaking breath, not even sure why she was so nervous. Actually, she was. As much as she'd chastised her sister for her impulsive love life, Jolie felt pretty sure that Karis would have a few words for her in return. Hell, she probably deserved them. She'd jumped into marriage because it felt right.

How often had she heard her mother say that?

Even worse, after the divorces her mom would finally realize her most recent ex-husband had never loved her.

Jolie shook her head . . . until she realized she'd pledged her life to a man who'd never once said those words.

Had they jumped too fast, motivated by the intense experience of baby Asher's birth and their own emotional coupling? God, she hated second-guessing herself. She rarely did but business was far more cut-and-dried than matters of the heart.

"I think we should . . . I don't know, talk."

"All right." He frowned. "About what?"

Did she really doubt his commitment? His heart? No. Just because he hadn't said three little words was hardly proof he didn't feel the sentiment. She'd never known a better man than Heath Powell and refused to let a single moment of doubt derail her. She needed to get her head together, stop rethinking what was already done, and focus on Betti.

"On second thought, I'm just tired and a little nervous about Karis's reaction. I wish we didn't have to tell her our news in the office, but the longer I put this off, the more upset she'll be. Once I've advised her, I can call my mother." Because if she'd called her mom first, Diana would have called Karis immediately and spilled everything. "Gee, maybe if I tell my dad, he'll throw in a toaster with the screwing he's trying to give me."

Heath laughed. "You don't need his toaster."

"Damn right, I don't." She sighed and took his hand. "Shall we?"

"Absolutely. Karis will be happy for us. Don't worry."

Jolie sincerely hoped so.

Together, they walked out the door and headed into the crisp October sunlight, almost blinding in its blue beauty. It would have been a perfect day—warm with a gentle breeze and leaves so green the trees almost glowed—if she hadn't been so agitated.

And if someone hadn't chosen that moment to open fire on her in the parking lot.

* * *

WHEN the first shot rang through the air, Heath reacted instantly. He tackled Jolie to the ground and covered her, protecting her body with his own. Instinct kicked in, shutting down all functions except those necessary for survival. His vision sharpened. His hearing turned keener.

He became a hunter.

"Down!" he barked at the others.

Ten feet away, Cutter had already taken Karis to the blacktop, shielding her.

Heath's heart thrummed in his chest, amplifying the roaring in his ears. Adrenaline seared him as it jetted through his veins. He scanned Jolie's face in an urgent sweep. "You all right?"

She looked terrified and at a loss for words, but she nodded.

He wanted her to say something, but if she had taken multiple shots to the head or had concrete embed itself in her skin like shrapnel, as Anna had, she wouldn't be alive to even give him a bob of her head. Heath tried to tell himself to breathe and climb off the ledge of panic. All was well and he'd saved Jolie in time.

All he could think about was that if he hadn't reacted quickly enough, he might be burying another wife.

When he looked up, the car she'd been standing beside moments ago bore the indents of bullets in its frame, just above the window. His heart stopped.

Heath fucking well refused to grieve for the woman he loved again.

"Cutter, take the ladies inside."

"Roger that."

As Heath made to rise, Jolie grabbed his arm. "What are you doing?"

But the terror on her face said she knew.

"My job."

She was going to object. And he couldn't let her. Jolie had to understand that if something happened to her, it would crush him completely. Anna's loss had been beyond difficult. At first, he'd had entire weeks when he hadn't wanted to crawl out of a bottle. He hadn't been able to loosen the stranglehold of his rage. Finally, he'd found a reason to truly move on. So he'd married her.

The idea that one bullet could wipe Jolie from this earth and leave him to deal with the aftermath again filled him with a dark, icy fury.

Easing from her grasp, he crouched, darting across the lot hidden by shadow and foliage, chasing the glint of metal he'd glimpsed in the distance. The shooter had already likely escaped. But Heath hoped the guy had been slow escaping so he could cut down the bastard.

He pulled his weapon and searched the area, stealthing around the nearby industrial buildings, tiptoeing through bushes, scouting the shooter's position. When Heath stood in what he suspected was the same spot the would-be assassin had three minutes ago and looked back across the lane, dismay and an anger beyond anything he'd ever felt kicked him in the gut.

Karis's position had been blocked by a tree. No way the shooter had been aiming for her. Clearly, he'd meant to kill Jolie. An inch to the right, and Heath would be planning another funeral.

When the shooter had aborted, he'd left nothing behind, taking even spent shell casings and eradicating the imprints of his shoes from the dirt.

Professional.

Heath studied his surroundings, trying to decide where the culprit would have run, but once he'd hit concrete, Heath saw too many directions and possibilities to follow. A dead end.

The trained operative in him seethed to hunt this prick down. The man inside him just wanted to reach his wife and hold her close.

"Bloody fucking son of a bitch." He pounded a fist into the nearby fence and marched back to Betti.

Inside, chaos reigned. The police were on their way—again. Karis was crying hysterically, but Cutter looked calm in the face of her drama. Gerard paced the room with sweeping hand gestures and mutterings in French. Rohan blinked as if he couldn't believe violence had come to his workplace twice in less than a week. Arthur just sat and stared numbly.

He didn't see his wife. Heath's heart stopped. "Where's Jolie?"

"Bathroom," Cutter supplied, holding Karis awkwardly while she wailed. "I escorted her there and made sure the coast was clear."

Heath took off running, slamming his way through the door into the women's room. Yes, he knew someone else in the building might be using this restroom and he didn't care. "Jolie?"

He heard the sound of her heaving stomach. She hadn't eaten since last night so she didn't have anything to vomit up. The adrenaline crash had clearly imbalanced her system in the worst way. Hearing her suffering tore at his heart.

Without a second thought, he kicked open the door to the wide stall in back and rushed to her. "Love?"

She looked pale and shaky, like she was desperately trying to hold herself together.

"I won't let anything happen to you," he swore.

Then he realized she had no reason to believe him. She knew precisely how Anna had died and that he hadn't saved her.

Jolie blinked at him as she rose and splashed cold water from the sink into her mouth and onto her face. "I know. Cutter dragged me into the office, away from the windows—"

"As he should have."

"But I couldn't see you. I didn't know what had happened. I . . ." She threw herself against him.

Heath wrapped his arms around her, beyond humbled. Someone had shot at her and she had been worried about him?

He cupped her face in his hands. "I wasn't the target. You understand that?"

"They missed. I don't know why someone would take a shot at me but—"

"We need to go over potential suspects again."

"I know. But I can't stop thinking . . . what if the shooter had hurt you instead?"

"Shh. I'm fine. Remember, this is my job. Deep breath, love. Let's go."

"Just a minute." She panted. "Cutter had to help me here. My legs are shaking."

Heath felt his heart twist in his chest again as he bent to lift Jolie in his arms, cradling her against his chest.

"I'll get you out of here."

"The police . . ."

"Cutter can fill them in. They can call us later. Right now I'm worried about you."

Jolie didn't object again, just buried her face in his neck as he carried her through the office. That told him again just how rattled she'd been.

As they passed the reception area, she caught sight of her sister. "You all right?"

Karis was too busy sobbing to answer.

"She's fine," Cutter supplied. "Shaken up. As soon as we're done with the police, I'll take her home."

"I'll text you an address. Bring her there," Heath insisted. "We should work together, examine this from angles we haven't considered before and start figuring things out."

The two men nodded at each other, and Heath left Jolie inside while he checked her car and the lot for anything possibly dangerous before he brought her car around. Though as a good Brit he didn't relish driving on the opposite side of the road, he'd done it before. He'd manage.

Minutes later, he parked the car by the door, engine idling. He led her to the passenger seat, shielding her from the street and any potential danger with his own body. Then he settled her in the car, jogged around to his seat, and took off down the road.

His knuckles were white as he gripped the wheel. "Someone in your life wants not merely to scare you but to harm you. We need to take a hard look at *everyone* you know."

She gave him a shaky nod. "I'm ruling out my mother and sister. Mom is in Kilgore, which is in East Texas. She's a good three hours away . . . and really, why? She gains nothing if I'm hurt or dead except the loss of emergency cash."

Heath nodded in agreement. "I also agree that your sister has no involvement. She's not the violent sort, and she doesn't value money above all."

"As long as she has a decent roof and enough to eat, Karis is happy.

She's a fairly typical Millennial. She doesn't care if her accessories are Tiffany or Chanel. She wants tech gadgets. Everything else just needs to be functional and sturdy."

That was Heath's assessment as well. "Your father?"

The question had her chest buckling. It was already difficult enough for her to understand how the asshole could tell a young child that she was his stupidest mistake and walk out for twenty-five years, but to imagine that he could want her dead . . . Jolie clearly had difficulty processing it. Still, she tried to be as logical as possible.

"I don't think so. Mostly because he's trying to buy the company out from under me and his number one goal is always money. If I died, Karis would get everything, not him. And she knows how I feel. She would dissolve Betti before she sold it to him. Besides, Carrington Quinn isn't the sort to get his hands dirty. Oh, he likes to attack when there's financial blood in the water. But I seriously doubt he'd actually resort to anything as physical as murder."

As much as Heath despised the man he'd never met, he saw her logic. "He could hire someone but that makes almost no sense now. He still thinks he has the upper hand in your negotiations, so resorting to murder could actually undermine his position. We'll scratch him off the list. We know from Gardner's sister that the man's injuries were too extensive for him to be the perpetrator."

That assessment, however, meant Heath was back to square one.

"Right. And like we said, he's hardly the sort to throw a rock through my window. Besides, he barely knows Karis, so the strange gifts for her make no sense."

Heath sighed. "Let's look at the bigger pattern here. Gifts for your sister, a break-in targeting your computer, vandalism, then . . ." That horrific shot he could still hear echoing in his head making his gut clench with every retort of the sniper rifle. "Then today's incident."

They were very different methods, and he couldn't imagine what her tormenter was trying to accomplish except to confuse him.

"I don't see a pattern."

"The notes he left for Karis provided the most information. This man wants to be with her. And seems to think you'll stand in his way. Enough to kill you, I don't know."

"Why would I stand . . ." She trailed off. "Okay, I have chased off several of Karis's would-be boyfriends in the past."

"Maybe it's one of them?" He frowned. "But you said yourself that you haven't brushed any aside recently."

"Right. So why now? And why push his agenda violently? Maybe someone is pissed about my anti-dating policy among the staff. If that's the case, I know who's responsible."

"Arthur? Do you think he's actually unstable enough to resort to attempted murder?"

"I don't know. He comes off socially awkward but does that mean he would try to kill me?" Her mind seemed to race, then she sighed. "No. Can't be him. He was inside the office when the gunfire started from across the street."

"Even if Arthur hadn't been standing in plain sight, I would already know he hadn't pulled the trigger. I doubt he's capable of the cool head and skill required to handle a weapon of that caliber. But it's possible he hired someone professional."

"How? I doubt he has either the money or the connections."

"Maybe he knows a guy," Heath tossed back ironically.

She scoffed. "Seriously."

"All kidding aside, perhaps he found someone online willing to do it for cheap. Or in exchange for another favor."

"Like doing their taxes? Beating their video game?"

Heath nodded. "No, you're right. It doesn't add up."

"Besides, if he wants to date my sister, let's face it . . . Killing me isn't the way to her heart."

"Unless Arthur is more twisted than we imagined, you're right. Let's keep thinking."

She still looked white and shaky, and Heath resented every one of the twelve miles he had to drive between Betti's offices and Axel's house. He reached across the console and took her hand in his. She gave him a weak squeeze in return.

"In all the excitement, we never had the chance to tell my sister our news."

"We will," he promised.

He understood why that was important to her, but keeping Karis in the loop on their romantic life was the least of Heath's concerns now. The only thing that mattered was figuring out why someone wanted to hurt Jolie, why they'd stepped up their game to attempted murder today, and how to keep her alive so they could have a chance to live happily ever after.

* * *

HEATH forced her to drink water and lie down once they reached Axel's house. He spooned her, made sure she took some deep breaths, and held her until the doorbell rang.

At the sound, he sprang up. His heart revved as he withdrew his gun from his holster and dashed through the house to peer out the front window.

He sighed, his tension bleeding out. "It's Karis and Cutter."

His wife was right behind him and reached for the knob. Heath beat her to it and nudged her behind both the door and him, scanning the street as the duo filed in.

"Anyone follow you?" he asked.

Cutter shook his head as he ushered Karis inside and followed, blocking her body with his own. "All clear."

"Jolie." Karis rushed at her, and the two women hugged with great love and relief.

Twice in the last five days the sisters had been in danger. That was two times too many, in Heath's estimation.

"Are you okay?" Jolie stepped back enough to scan her sister's face.

"Fine. No one took a shot at me," Karis pointed out. "I'm worried about you."

Heath locked the door and eased the women toward the living room where no one could have possible sight lines inside unless they prowled around the backyard. But then he would see them, as well. "Let's not linger near windows."

They filed deeper into the house and everyone sat, Karis and Cutter on the two oversized chairs. Jolie sank onto the sofa and Heath sat beside her, reaching for her hand. He had scarcely known her for a week. Already he felt as if he had a place he belonged in life, a partner by his side. She glanced his way, and for all she'd been through today, her expression still said that she felt safe with him. She glowed with trust.

That both slayed and humbled him.

"Did you take care of the police?" Heath asked.

"Yeah. They haven't been able to figure anything out. And of course it's not related to the break-in at Jolie's office last week or the rock that went through her window on Saturday."

"Of course not." Heath rolled his eyes. *Imbeciles.* "If they're going to be more hindrance than help, I'll simply go around them."

"No one was hurt, and they didn't find enough physical evidence there was even a shooter. One of the suits suggested that Jolie's been through a lot lately, so she may be a little . . . excitable. It was probably something else, like an older car backfiring."

Heath clenched his fists. "That's utter shit. I know the difference between those sounds."

"So do I, and I argued." He shook his head. "But they don't agree there was an incident at all, so the case isn't high on their totem pole."

"Bloody hell." Heath held his wife closer, vowing to keep her safe from the would-be assassin—and anyone else who meant to harm her.

Cutter peered over at Jolie. "The question is, why would someone want to hurt you?"

It was the same question Heath had asked repeatedly.

She shrugged. "I'm drawing a blank. I certainly can't think of anyone who benefits from my death."

"Oh, I don't know. The girls at SweetieBow would love for you to die a horrible death in the next ten minutes," Karis quipped.

"One of our competitors," she supplied. "Well, the SweetieBow sisters live in Minneapolis, so it would be tough for them to get here and cause this much trouble."

"If they're serious, they could have hired someone to pull the trigger today." Cutter again marched over the ground Heath and Jolie had trampled earlier.

"That's true. But even if they believe I'm keeping them from success, they wouldn't be giving Karis presents."

"What if we're dealing with more than one person?" Heath mused beside her. "What if someone is responsible for the gifts and veiled threats? Another broke in last Wednesday and shot at Jolie today . . . That would explain the different methods and degrees of danger."

Karis frowned. "You mean, like, some guy really admired me in a secret way and left me cool stuff with typed notes, while someone totally different tried to scare Jolie off?"

"That's what I've been thinking, too," Cutter said. "I suggest we move all the random offerings Karis has received—my money is on Arthur being your admirer, by the way—and focus on the events we know the least about yet have been the most dangerous."

"Arthur?" Karis reared back as the possibility of their accountant/video game nerd being a romantic interest had never occurred to her.

"Good thinking." Heath nodded, ignoring her. "Let's review what we know."

"I'm not sure how much help I'll be," Jolie admitted. "I still can't believe someone would want me dead. *Me*. First, during the break-in, this person wanted my computer and whatever was on it. Then he . . . what? Called me names by throwing a rock through my window. What purpose did that serve? Then today, he tried to kill me. It's like he wanted to scare me off, and when that didn't work, he got pissed off. Except the rock is way more juvenile than the other acts."

"She has a point." Cutter nodded. "The rock feels like someone's frustration. Let's set that aside for the moment, too. Can you think of what someone might want to scare you from?"

"Before Friday night, I would have said securing an investor. But since someone tried to shoot me *after* Gardner and I very publicly parted ways—"

"That's putting it mildly," Heath cut in with a proud grin. "Some of the Tweets were quite funny."

Jolie rolled her eyes. "I can't imagine what else this guy wants me to cower from."

"Maybe a competitor simply wants to distract you and jar your operations," Karis suggested.

"By shooting at me? That's more than a distraction. And why would he go from a serious crime like breaking and entering, decide next to throw a rock through my living room window, then attempt murder? The sequence of events doesn't build from petty to life threatening. I feel like I'm playing a game of 'which one of these things is not like the other,' you know?"

Heath nodded. "So perhaps we focus more specifically on who would want to halt your production. Or someone who might resent your success."

"We've been over this." She stood and began to pace restlessly. "I can't think of anyone. Yes, my goal is world domination someday, but I'm not there yet. I can't possibly have made that many enemies on my way up."

It didn't seem that way to Heath, either. The whole situation had him scratching his head.

"Would you ladies mind seeing if you can find me a bottle of water somewhere?" Cutter asked.

Karis raised a brow. "The kitchen is less than twenty steps away. You need both of us to get you a drink?"

Cutter sighed. "How else am I going to talk about you without you hearing?"

Heath had to smile. Neither of the sisters took subtle hints well.

"Fine." Jolie grabbed Karis's hand and tugged her toward the kitchen. "We'll give you guys some space."

Silence fell as the men waited for the women to reach the kitchen. No wall separated them, so they could both keep an eye on their charges. Cutter watched Karis with a surgical stare.

"How are you two getting along?" Heath dropped his voice.

The other man shrugged. "She resents me in her personal space. You and Jolie both warned me that she'd make a pass at me. So far, she has done her utmost to keep distance between us."

Heath frowned. "I would have thought you would be pleased with that."

Cutter hesitated. "It's just . . . she seems as if she's going through a hard time right now. I'm not sure why. I'm sorry to make her situation more difficult but—"

"Her safety comes first. Always."

"Right." Cutter glanced down at the band on Heath's left ring finger. "When did you and Jolie get married? And why doesn't Karis know?"

"Yesterday. We were going to tell her today, then bedlam ensued."

"It surely did. Look . . ." Cutter sighed. "Karis shared with me the report she compiled on you."

Bloody hell, did everyone now know about his personal life?

"I'm sorry to pry. I didn't want to read it," Cutter assured. "But . . . she had this zany idea and I had to see if there was any chance it had validity."

Karis having a zany idea wasn't a stretch. She thought outside the box because the box didn't really exist for her.

"Go on," Heath prompted.

"After reading the dossier she'd compiled, I could see her point. Hear me out. What if . . ." He sighed and sat back as if trying to decide how to impart a potentially uncomfortable thought. "Well, is it possible that everything that's happened to Jolie in the past week has nothing to do with Betti and everything to do with you?"

That shocked Heath. "Me? What do you mean?"

"The unpleasant crap started happening when you came to work for her, right?"

"I grant you that, but none of my friends or family have met her. Until this morning, they didn't know she was in my life."

"But your past . . . Your late wife's unsolved murder . . . No one actually tried to kill Jolie until you married her."

Heath froze. He couldn't imagine anyone caring that he'd remarried. "Who would decide to make my life miserable by eliminating her? Besides, if that was their goal, why try to steal her computer? Why throw a rock through her window calling her something less than kind?"

"I don't know. Nothing makes sense now but the answer is right there. I can feel it. I know we're overlooking some pertinent detail or clue."

Cutter was probably right, and the truth was just beyond Heath's reach.

"Let's dig a bit, have a chat with Arthur. If he's Karis's 'admirer,' then we can put those incidents aside and focus on the events that threaten Jolie most."

Before Heath could continue, his phone dinged. Stone Sutter arrived at Betti to help with the final installation of the card readers but no one in the office knew where Heath had gone. He texted the man Axel's address and asked him to come by with Arthur and Jolie's computer in tow.

After a chipper reply, Heath settled in to wait for some answers. He only hoped what he found didn't worry him more.

Chapter Fourteen

Rule for success number fourteen:
Lead from the front.

"WHAT do you think they're talking about?" Karis whispered next to the refrigerator, glancing back at the men.

Who's trying to kill me. "They obviously didn't want us in on it, but whatever. It's been a long damn day already. I'm opening a bottle of wine."

She didn't wait for her sister's reply, just found an unopened box of wheat crackers in the pantry and snagged two glasses from a nearby cupboard. It wasn't gourmet but it might settle her shaky nerves.

"Merlot okay?" Jolie sauntered to the wine cabinet.

"Um . . . it's two o'clock in the afternoon. The business day isn't over."

"I don't care." She'd awakened earlier this morning in a gorgeous hotel room in Vegas as a newlywed. She'd started her morning as a bride, supposedly starting her fantastic life with the man of her dreams. This afternoon, if things had gone differently, she would have ended her day on a cold slab in the morgue. Adding stink to the pile of shit was the fact that if she didn't find a new investor soon, her business would be gobbled up by her asshole of a father. So wine sounded great about now. "Are you drinking or not?

Karis shrugged. "If you're game, sure."

Jolie gripped the wine bottle with her left hand and with the other rummaged around in a nearby drawer for the corkscrew.

Her younger sister gasped, staring at her finger. "Oh my . . . You didn't. Did you?" Karis darted toward the men, stopping to stare down at Heath's hand. "Oh my god. You did!"

Jolie closed her eyes. Damn. After the shooter had shaken her and chaos had ensued, she hadn't had the chance to sit Karis down and spill the news.

"We did." Jolie crossed the room. "Heath and I went to Vegas over the weekend and got married."

Karis grabbed her wrist and dragged her back to the kitchen, away from the men. "I'm happy for you, but would it have hurt you to call me? To call any of the family who loves you and ask . . . oh, I don't know, maybe if we'd like to be there to share your special day?"

No. She tried to picture Karis standing beside her at the altar, wearing a simple but lovely bridesmaid's dress, her mother dabbing at tears in the front pew of a simple church. A pang of regret twisted her chest if she'd hurt anyone's feelings, but she and Heath hadn't wanted pomp and ceremony.

"I understand but we did this for us. Because we were ready to be happy together."

With a shrug, her sister conceded the point. "Sorry. That was the selfish part of me talking. I wanted to be important enough to you to share your momentous day with me."

"You are. We didn't elope to prevent anyone from attending our wedding, KK. We just didn't want to wait. If it makes you happy, you can plan us a reception around Thanksgiving. Austin will be home then," she said of their brother, who lived in Los Angeles. "It'll be great."

"Sure." Karis still looked confused. "But . . . why rush to get married. You've always told me that if someone cares about you enough, they'll wait until you're sure. I mean, I just never thought you'd leap so quickly after all the times Mom has."

Jolie didn't know how to explain to her sister that she'd simply known marrying Heath was right. She'd use all the words and phrases her mother did every time she wound up with a new man who would eventually treat her like dirt and break her heart.

"I never thought I would, either," she said softly. "That should explain to you how I feel. He's amazing, supportive, kind, sexy, smart."

A bit of envy crossed Karis's young face. "Hell, I'd settle for sane, showered, and steadily employed right now."

"You have time," Jolie promised. "Someone will come along. The right someone . . . Still nothing between you and Cutter?"

"No." She leaned against the kitchen counter. "I've overheard snatches of his phone calls. It sounds like he's embroiled in some love triangle. Whoever she is, he loves her terribly."

Now Karis sounded downright wistful. Jolie took her hands. "It'll happen. In the meantime, focus on you. Figure out what you want out of life so when he enters the picture, you'll know whether or not he fits in the frame."

Her sister sighed. "You're right. Should we call Mom and give her the good news?"

Jolie hated to talk about getting married when Diana was in the middle of a divorce but . . . "Let's do it."

* * *

THE doorbell rang about an hour later. A lean stranger with buzzed hair, ink coloring his bountiful muscles, and a dangerous look stood at the portal, carrying her computer. Arthur lingered beside him, holding a box.

Her husband turned. "Jolie, meet Stone Sutter. He's an amazing tech expert who will finish installing the database logs so we can launch your office security system. I'd also like him to take a look at your computer, see if we can upgrade those defenses as well."

"Stone, Jolie is my wife. We got married yesterday."

"Congratulations, man!" Stone stuck out his hand. "As a guy who recently joined the marital state, it's bliss. Enjoy . . ."

"How is Lily, then?" Heath asked, letting the men into the house.

"Great. She's started a support group for teen victims of rape and their families. She's really glad to be making a difference. We're trying to get pregnant. She's ready, so . . . good times." He raised two thumbs.

"Excellent. Give her my regards."

"Why am I here?" Arthur asked, standing awkwardly in the entryway, holding a battered cardboard box with a chemical company's logo emblazoned across the top, held together with two kinds of tape.

"Because I asked Stone to bring you," Heath supplied. "Why are you holding that box?"

"It mysteriously appeared in one of the cubicles earlier. It didn't look like anything the FedEx guy had dropped off because someone had ordered cool stuff online."

Stone was right. It looked patched together, battered, maybe even dangerous.

"Everyone else at the office seemed afraid the box might be suspicious." Stone shrugged. "So I brought it out here. I figured we're more equipped to handle it than the web developer, the crazy Frenchman, and your sobbing receptionist."

So Wisteria and her boyfriend were already off again? Jolie sighed.

Heath turned to Arthur. "Was that on Karis's desk?"

He swallowed. "I . . . um, yeah. I wasn't there, so no idea who left it."

"Of course not," Heath quipped caustically. "Let's try this again, shall we? You left Karis this box—and all the other recent gifts."

Arthur paled. "I don't know what you mean."

"Rubbish. You do." Heath cocked a brow. "It would be better for all if you confessed now."

The accountant huffed, risking a glance at Karis before jerking his gaze away. "All right, damn it! I intended to talk to Jolie about the policy that didn't allow me to date coworkers, but after what happened in the file room last week, I wondered if the policy was even relevant anymore. You two are married now? I guess that answers my question."

Jolie wished she had handled her relationship with Heath better around the office but she didn't regret a moment of her time with him.

"You're the one who's been leaving me gifts?" Karis gaped. "The tulips?"

"Of course. I'd hoped they would convey what I was too tongue-tied to say face-to-face. Why you thought he gave them to you, I can't imagine." Arthur gestured toward Heath.

"About that, you and I are equally perplexed, I assure you," Heath returned. "The candy?"

"Yes."

"The candle, too?" Karis asked.

Jolie wondered if he knew that he wasn't her sister's type. Karis liked them buff and slick and full of charisma, just like their mother.

"Who else would it have been?" Arthur implored. "I've been paying attention to your likes and dislikes. When you and Ben split up a while back, I thought . . . maybe, here's my chance. So I studied you for weeks. I wanted to show you that I'm more than a number cruncher and a gaming geek. I can be thoughtful and romantic." With a tsk, he turned back to Heath and Jolie. "But you two kept reading the most menacing meanings into my notes."

"They all but threatened Jolie, so yes. We were concerned." Heath sized him up. "The rock through her window Saturday with 'bitch' painted in red letters?"

Arthur paused, lips pressed together in a stubborn line. Then regret furrowed his brow. "I was angry. I'm sorry. I'll pay for the damages. It's just . . . I could have been spending the weekend with Karis. My worry that she would never love me might already be over if you had simply talked to me about the policy."

"You're right, and I regret that I didn't take time for you." Jolie frowned. "But you made me believe someone was out to do me bodily harm."

"No. *You* two decided that. If I didn't know otherwise, I'd say you're unromantic people."

"Why didn't you even try to ask me out?" Karis asked.

"I wanted to." He looked away. "I'm not always good with words."

"You spent all this time getting to know me, and I'm flattered. But how was I supposed to fall in love with you if you never let me know you?"

Arthur looked at Karis as if that had never occurred to him. "It's . . . I, um— I guess I hoped you might give me a try if you knew I could be caring."

Karis shook her head. "Buttering me up won't do you any good. All my life, I've watched my mom fall for the wrong men. And it always ends horribly. Ben was the last guy I let sweet-talk me. I woke up one day to find him sexting someone else while I was lying right beside him. I let myself feel heartbroken for a while. When the burglar had me cornered in the office the other night and I worried I could die, I decided it was time to be more like my older sister than my mother. I resolved to get my life together." She turned to Jolie. "Yesterday, I enrolled in college. I start after the holidays. I'll be attending classes at night. I'm ready to make something of my life. And someday, my Prince Charming will come. But I won't need him to complete me. I'll be a complete person all on my own."

Jolie swelled with pride. It was weirdly maternal but also like the thrill she'd feel for a good friend.

"I'm so proud of you." She grabbed her sister into a big bear hug and felt her eyes sting with tears.

"I really am sorry about everything," Arthur offered. "I thought I was being smart but . . . I see your point. Can we start over, Karis? Maybe go to dinner? That is, if our boss will lift the anti-dating policy and I still have a job."

The old her would have fired him on the spot. The new her had a vastly different approach. "Everyone is human. We make mistakes. Consider this your second—and last chance. You're on probation for ninety days. But if there are no more problems, mysterious boxes in the office, or rocks through my window, then you're still employed. You're a great asset, and I'd hate to lose you. Whatever happens between you and my sister is up to you two."

Karis hesitated. "Maybe we'll start as friends, see where it leads."

It wasn't the answer Arthur wanted to hear but he accepted it with grace. "I'd like that."

* * *

A few hours later, Karis and Arthur had disappeared into a theater room with a big screen and hooked up his console so the accountant could introduce her to the postapocalyptic world he gamed in. No one had seen them for hours, so Heath guessed they were hitting it off. Jolie worked quietly at the kitchen table with her pad of paper and her mobile, making one phone call after another, beating the bushes for a new investor.

Heath focused on his job—keeping her alive. Arthur had owned up to everything except the two most troublesome events: the break-in and the attempted shooting. If Heath couldn't point the finger at the accountant for those, he wasn't sure where else to cast his suspicion.

Stone tapped away on Jolie's computer, the grooves bracketing his frown growing deeper with every moment. "Okay, this is bad."

"What?" Heath really didn't want more bad news. He simply wanted to take his wife to their bed, shut the door, and forget about the rest of the world.

"Last Wednesday evening, someone got onto your wife's system and started installing a whole bunch of data mining software and tracking cookies. Basically, they wanted to know her every keystroke and query." Stone shook his head. "Whoever started the download didn't finish, though."

"We interrupted them. When Jolie and I first approached during the break-in, we beat the police there. Karis was inside, by herself."

"She was scared," Cutter supplied. "She told me."

"Absolutely. Jolie was afraid for her, and I promised to get Karis out alive. But when we arrived, we found a man typing on her computer. We interrupted him, so he tried to steal the machine."

"There's something on here that he wants badly."

Heath paced, teeth gritted. "We have no idea what. At first we assumed something business related but—"

"I'm not sure about that." Stone tapped a few more keys. Then a couple more. His confusion turned to concern. "He seems most interested in her browsing history for the seven-day period before and after Wednesday. She searched for something on the Internet and he seems focused on those queries."

"Such as?" Fabrics? Trends? Loans? Investment advice?

Stone leveled a hard glance at him. "The most searched item during that period of time was you."

Cutter grunted. "I hate to say I told you so . . ."

Heath tried to absorb that news but it didn't make sense. Yes, Karis had apparently used her sister's computer to make inquiries about him but who was left to care? Anna's parents probably had the most legitimate reason to hate him. He'd failed to protect their only daughter. But they had died before she had. His only other suspect, Kensforth, was gone, too. Hell, he would even suspect Myles . . . except the man was a continent away, trying to get on with his life. Of course he had the connections to hire someone to kill Jolie but why her? Why now? He'd lost even more than Heath had that day and still seemed to be grieving in his own way.

Who did that leave?

The mastermind of the attacks that killed Anna and Lucy. That nameless, faceless shadow of a figure who seemed more elusive than smoke. Heath cursed. He had to solve this mystery—for himself, for Anna, for his future with Jolie—before it was too late.

"Can you get anything else from the computer that might give us more information? How the burglar intended to watch Jolie's Internet searches? Any hint of affiliation or identity or—"

"No, sorry. Like I said, he started the work. He didn't finish it. There's not enough here for me to go on, just a few files he downloaded from a known hacker site using Jolie's own Wi-Fi."

So no cyber fingerprints, as it were. The noose of fate and panic twisted together, slowly strangling him. "Thank you for trying."

Stone tossed down a couple of business cards. "Call me if you think of anything else or have more questions."

"Thanks. Any other suggestions?"

"Yeah, load your guns. I have a bad feeling about this."

Heath did, too. "I'm going to follow up with Sean on the one loose end I've got. The burglar who broke into Betti escaped on foot. But we're still waiting to hear from the city about any traffic cam footage they may have captured.

"I'm sure he's had his hands full with the baby. They came home from the hospital yesterday," Stone said.

"Callie texted me pictures," Jolie supplied. "He's precious. I hope I can visit them soon."

Once this case was solved and the danger had come to an end? "Of course. In the meantime, I'll put a call into Sean tonight and see if he's learned anything new."

But he got Sean's voicemail before the device even rang.

With a sigh, he hung up and figured they'd start fresh tomorrow. His stomach was rumbling from lack of lunch. Jolie hunched over her mobile, her eyes squinting as if they'd become strained. Regardless of how tired they were or what else was going on, his need to hold her had risen slowly throughout the day. He had to have her, like air, like food.

Like love.

When Stone departed, dragging Arthur with him, Karis and Cutter retired to separate bedrooms upstairs. Heath approached Jolie, took her hand, and eased her to her feet. "Come with me, wife."

Chapter Fifteen

Rule for success number fifteen:
Celebrate your wins.

HEATH'S voice made her entire body tingle. Four simple words, and Jolie was absolute putty.

On shaking legs, she stood and put her hand in his and sent him a saucy sideways glance. "Where are we going?"

She knew but she ached to hear him say it.

"Our bed. Leave your phone on the table." His voice had gone low, commanding.

Jolie shivered. She was in the terrible habit of taking her phone with her at all times, even when she was supposed to be sleeping. It often dinged in the middle of the night with e-mails, important news stories, even Twitter notifications about mentions of Betti. But as he had since she'd met him, Heath reordered her priorities, making it impossible to think only about work.

"All right." With a shiver, she rose and turned her back on the device.

As he led her down the hall, toward the master bedroom, he slipped an arm around her waist. His palm burned a trail down her body, straight to her ass. He cupped her cheek, bent to nibble at her neck, and backed her into the wall.

"I don't know if I can wait to find the bed, love." He sounded gruff, impatient. "I need to touch you and ensure you're all right and still mine." Cradling her face in his big hands, he kissed her, a deep claiming of her lips before he backed away with a pained frown. His grip tightened on her. "You must know what I was thinking when I heard that gunshot."

Jolie knew exactly and she could only imagine the worry and adrenaline, his fear that history could repeat itself. "Nothing tragic happened. I'm here. I'm yours."

She sealed her words with another kiss, and he held her tighter, dragging his lips across her jaw, to her ear, dropping to her neck, tasting, nipping, savoring. When he lifted his head again and seized her mouth once more, she was panting and tugging at his shirt, desperate to feel him inside her.

"Now . . ." She wasn't asking.

"Not yet. I need you to do something for me, love." He let out a ragged breath. "Trust me."

"I do."

"With every part of you. I want to try . . . Damn it." Heath pressed their foreheads together as if he couldn't get close enough to her. "Today I felt entirely out of my mind when those shots were aimed at you. We've been piecing the facts together all bloody day and nothing makes sense. None of this is within my ability to control. I need something that is. Surrender yourself to me—your pleasure, your body, your will."

Mentally, Jolie found it tough to allow anyone dominion over her. Surprisingly, the one time she'd tackled the mental hurdle and let go with Heath in bed, she'd loved it. But this time would be harder. He'd want everything. The hunger in his eyes made that clear.

She wasn't even sure she was capable of surrendering her whole self, but she loved him too much not to try.

"I'll do my best to give you anything you need."

"Anything?"

"I trust you." She cupped his face. He would never hurt her like Carrington Quinn. Or crush her like Mom's thoughtless, cheating exes.

"I haven't topped anyone in seven years. I've seen it, been around others exchanging power. Most of my worldly belongings are still at Thorpe's club. But I haven't trusted anyone or cared enough to try since Anna. Does that change anything for you?"

"Does that make me trust you less because . . . what? You're out of practice?" She shook her head. "No. I'm touched that you chose me, that you trust me, too."

He smiled as he hoisted her against his body. She wasn't used to anyone lifting her. Everyone saw her as ballsy and capable and strong. But she ached for this man to cherish her, to treat her as if she was the most special, fragile woman in his world.

When he carried her to the bed and lay her down, their clothes melted away with long kisses, sweeping touches, and soft strokes of his fingertips. She assisted him, ensuring that with each passing moment, he bared as much skin as she did.

When they were naked and panting, he cradled her cheek and stared. Then his demeanor turned hard. His voice dropped to something almost forbidding. "Give me your hands."

Jolie didn't question him or the thudding of her heart. She simply did as he commanded.

He kissed each palm, then stretched one arm flat against the mattress, toward the corner of the bed, before fastening it in a padded cuff she hadn't noticed previously. He attached the cuff to something on the bedframe she couldn't see. He repeated the process with the other. Her breath caught when ankle cuffs followed.

Suddenly, she was naked, spread out for his pleasure, waiting. Though he'd done nothing more than strap her down, Jolie's heart revved. Her breathing quickened. Her insides began to melt.

"Where did you get the restraints?" She managed to breathe out the question.

"It's Axel's house," he said as his lips wandered across her skin. "He works security at Dominion, so he has a few of his own . . . proclivities."

"Oh." But the question burning uppermost in her mind had nothing to do with Axel. "What about yours? You like restraining a woman?"

He shuddered. "I used to enjoy having total control. With you, it's . . . so much more. I had Anna's trust from day one. She wanted guidance, so I gave it to her. Guiding you can be like herding a cat, somewhere between difficult and impossible."

Jolie had to laugh because she knew it was true.

"Most often, you don't want my interference," he went on. "You don't need it."

"But I need you more than you know," she confessed.

"When your life is in danger—"

"It's about more than that. You understand me and that's more epic than you can imagine."

"The fact you're choosing to give your will and strength to me—because I've earned your trust, not simply because surrendering is in your nature—means the world."

Jolie smiled up at him, feeling as if she glowed. Her body softened every bit as much as her heart. "What now?"

"Take me and everything I need to give you."

She arched her back and flowered her knees open in offering. "I'm yours."

Heath started at the top, filtering his fingers through her hair, as he kissed her—cheeks, jaw, lips, neck—working his way down to her breasts. Once there, he pinched, licked, sucked, nipped. Jolie didn't recall her nipples being so sensitive. He toyed with them back and forth, tonguing them, drawing them deep in his mouth. The suction made her clit ache. She wriggled, feeling slick and swollen, wishing he would thrust inside her, plunge deep, so they would be as close as two people possibly could.

But he made her wait. He lavished every bit of his devotion on her, sliding his lips under the curve of her breasts, over her belly until he licked his way to her navel and dropped lower, hovering over the pad of her pussy.

Warmth turned to liquid heat when he breathed out a hungry sigh. "I've wanted to taste you again for days."

"We've been busy."

"I don't have any illusions. We're always going to be busy, love. But I need you under my tongue. I need to drive you to pleasure and watch you come apart for me."

He nudged her sensitive clit with his tongue then, jolting her with instant sensation. He reached up her body with his long arms, cupping her breasts with one hand while he tormented her pussy with his mouth.

"Yes!" she cried out.

Heath worked her slowly, as if he had all day, as if nothing would ever be more important than her build to ecstasy. He never let her fall over, just sent her spiraling up. Jolie's impatience soared. She wanted to wrap her arms and legs around him, urge him inside her—anything to end the torment. Anything to feel him deep.

"Stop fighting me," he murmured against her thigh. "I'll take you in my time, in my way. You're mine to control. Let go."

Any other man she would have scoffed at and told him to fuck himself. But Heath . . . She yearned to surrender every part of herself to him because she cared about his needs more than her own.

When had that happened? And rather than being terrified, she embraced the closeness, the intimacy, the amazing buzz of euphoria she always felt with him.

After another wriggle and more straining against her bonds, Jolie realized she wasn't going anywhere—and she didn't really want to. Instead, she dragged in a deep breath, let it fill her lungs, run through her bloodstream, and calm her mind. She was giving her body and her will to this man. He didn't want to steal it from her. He shouldn't have to wrest it away.

Zeroing in on the teasing drift of his lips over her skin, the prod of his tongue between her legs, the hard draw on her clit when he sucked her flesh in, she melted, reveling in his sensual torture as he bent her to his will.

Jolie couldn't control when or how he lavished these sensations on her. He seemed utterly content to taste and torment, driving her up toward the precipice of pleasure, closer to the scalding heat that drugged her veins, making her pant and tense and sweat. She certainly had no say over where he touched her, how long he lingered. Definitely not over whether she came. He exercised that authority over her repeatedly, lifting her to the edge of bliss, skimming her with its rush of heat, letting her almost experience satisfaction, before he directed his attention away from her clit or nipples, both so hard now that they throbbed.

Then he backed away, plying her with drugging kisses until she again simmered just below a boil. When the urge to climax eased from a sharp, painful ache to a slow burn and she lost herself in his kiss until the meshing of their lips became its own pleasure, then he skimmed down her body and resumed the sultry torment of his tongue on her sensitive nubbin, repeating the agonizing cycle once more.

She couldn't help twisting against her bonds and begging. "Heath . . ."

"Yes, love? What is it?"

He had to ask? No, this was part of the teasing. This was him enjoying his power over her body.

"I want to come."

"I know you want to. But you don't yet *need* to. And it's my say when you come, isn't it? You gave me that right." He pinned her hips to the mattress, taking away what little freedom of movement she'd had.

"I'm not ready yet." He grinned at her, mischief toying with the corners of his lips. "But feel free to plead your case as loudly as you'd like."

Jolie pressed her lips together. The stubborn part of her that didn't like losing control absolutely hated his speech and wanted to scratch his eyes out. Yes, that was probably her sexual frustration talking. But he wasn't merely messing with her body. He fucked with her head, too.

Jolie wasn't anything like his late wife; she refused to do whatever Anna would have done. Whether Heath knew it or not, he wanted more than that, too. He sought to test her like a sturdy sapling. He yearned to bend—but never break—her. He liked the cat-and-mouse foreplay of asserting his will until he coaxed or seduced her into submission.

Fighting for control was way more her speed, too. Even if she lost in the end, she'd win.

Jolie smiled. "Forget it. I won't do it."

"Really?" He thumbed one of her nipples already so sensitive from his toying and sucking. That act forced her to bite back a gasp. "So there's nothing I could do to make you beg me?"

Jolie gritted her teeth. Probably more of that would do the trick. God knew that if he put his tongue on her clit again, it might drive her to plead for his mercy—and his cock. But damn it, she'd bite her tongue if she had to. She would not give in without a fight.

"Nope. I was choosing to give you something I thought you wanted but if you're going to be an arrogant bastard about it . . ." She looked away with a little shrug.

His deep laugh warmed her. "You haven't yet seen arrogant bastard, love. That was me gently toying with you."

"Really? That was as gentle as a hammer. You're not as subtle as you think."

"Maybe not, but you're a terrible liar." His lips whispered over the pad of her pussy.

She tried not to shiver.

"Look at you . . ." He caressed broad hands over her breasts, lingering on her nipples. "So flushed. So tense." He raked his tongue between her folds again. "So swollen and wet."

"I didn't say you couldn't arouse me. I said you couldn't break me."

"Don't challenge me. I intend to hear you beg for me before I give you release. We won't leave this bed until you do."

Jolie smiled secretly. *Goody* . . . "I have a very strong will."

"You also have a very loose tongue that makes you say words I'll ensure you eat."

"Whatever . . ." She tried to seem as if she were rolling her eyes. But really, they were falling into the back of her head with pleasure.

His body tightened. His gaze sharpened. She saw the predator in him rear his head, ready to play hard. Everything about him and this moment made her blood race. Her heart spin.

"The trick to a woman is to find out exactly where she's sensitive and exploit it. Over the past week, I've learned quite a bit about you, wife." He slid up her body, covering her with his own.

Already, Jolie was sensitive but this skin-to-skin contact now made her feel as if every inch of her surface was a pleasure receptor. The mere hint of friction while he rubbed against her had her body tightening, her breath accelerating. Then he ramped up the sensations by burying his head in her neck and simply breathing.

"You're sensitive here," he whispered under her ear. Then he nipped at her lobe. "Here, too."

Involuntarily, she trembled under him.

"Hmm," he murmured against her flesh. "You like this, as well."

He kissed his way across her jaw before brushing his lips over hers, hovering, breathing, teasing but never quite kissing her. So close . . . but so far away. Desperate for more, Jolie tried to fight back, raise her head, force the kiss.

He reared back with a scolding scowl. "This is for me to give you, not for you to take."

"You either want me or you don't." She prodded at him.

"Oh, I think we both know how fucking much I want you." He pressed the steely ridge of his erection directly between her legs, proving it in case she wasn't sure.

Before Jolie could stop herself, she exhaled a sigh of pleasure.

"Just like we both know you want me." He nudged her again with his cock, unerringly rubbing against her most sensitive spot.

Jolie bit her lip to hold in a groan. Her toes curled. She grabbed the sheets.

"The question is, what will it take for you to surrender every part of yourself?"

So close. Already she was damn close to eschewing this push-pull struggle for the momentous orgasm she knew waited on the other side.

But as she looked up at him, his eyes gleamed. He looked alive. In the moment. Happy. He was enjoying the hell out of this.

She dug deep for resistance.

"You may never know," she tossed back.

He laughed as if to say he found her delusion adorable. "Oh, I will. Often."

What a sweet threat.

Holding in a sigh, she smiled up at him. "I'm waiting."

He grabbed one of the discarded pillows strewn around the bed and shoved it under her hips before he adjusted something just out of her line of sight, providing a little slack in the attachment of her cuffs to the bed. He bent her knees wider, opening her completely. "Not very patiently."

With those words swimming in her brain, he found her slick opening with the head of his cock and pushed in with a force and a will that had her dragging in a shocked breath. In this position, he stretched her almost to her limit. She felt him invade every part of her, drag each inch of his shaft against her nerve endings, electrify her entire body.

Above her, he clenched his eyes shut tightly and froze. "Bloody fucking hell."

His voice shook, and knowing she affected him made Jolie try that much harder.

Beneath him, she clamped down, swung her hips, kissed her way across his shoulder and up his neck before settling at his ear. "Do I feel good around you all tight and bare? Do you think about this during the day? Late at night? Do you imagine how I'll sound when I cry out for you just before you release inside me?"

Heath swore then, something terse and crude that highlighted his struggle for control.

"I imagine how I'll strip you down and make you beg," he growled as he thrust deep. "Only then will I give you what you crave before I come inside you."

Jolie had no opportunity to answer before he began stroking his way deeper. If he had pushed in with all the finesse of a jackhammer, she probably could have resisted resuming the sweet climb to orgasm. Maybe. But once again, he proved how well he knew her by inching in with a molasses slide. He dragged his way to almost complete withdrawal before he slid back in with a smooth glide and a rough sigh.

The effort cost him, she could tell. He tensed. His breathing turned irregular. His fingers on her thighs tightened. But he displayed incredible control, not rushing, not banging, utilizing every opportunity to make her feel every inch of him.

Over and over, he eased back, surging deep, establishing a rhythm so slow, it magnified every sensation. He had her restrained completely, so she couldn't claw at him or wrap her legs around him. She couldn't even throw her hips up to him in silent pleading because he weighted her down with his big body, controlling her in every way.

Jolie could only tense beneath him, toss her head, and struggle to hold back a litany of pleas for him to end this searing torment.

He captured her lips, his tongue mimicking the rhythm of his thrusts and setting her completely ablaze. They were connected everywhere—lips, bodies, souls. She'd never felt more filled with another human being than she did right now.

She'd never felt closer.

He picked up the pace, gripping the edges of the bed and using the leverage to push his way deeper into her. His muscles bulged. He grunted with effort. Then he looked down into her eyes. He might want her to beg him but everything on his face entreated Jolie for her love and devotion. A week ago, she wouldn't have known what true yearning looked like, but he wore his need with naked honesty. No fronting or trying to hide. Sure, he'd play games. They both enjoyed them. But at the end, he simply wanted to be with her.

She couldn't imagine wanting to be anywhere but with him for the rest of her life.

It was the thought of ever being without him again that had her parting her lips and surrendering. "Please, Heath. Please . . ." She couldn't look away from the endless wells of his dark eyes, forever sucking her deeper into his depths. "Give me what I need."

"An orgasm?" He was challenging her, seeing what this pleasure meant to her.

"You," she breathed. "Be with me. Stay with me. Care."

He groaned. "I do, love. Take me—and everything I give you."

"That's all I want."

He thrust in harder, finally faster, now hitting a spot deep that had her writhing under him, twitching with the pending explosion, keening. Just one more breath, one more kiss, one more stroke . . .

"Heath!" Jolie couldn't hold it together anymore. "I want you. Always. Please . . ."

Then the pleasure crested and erased everything holding her back—pride, fear, insecurity. He replaced that with the heat of his passion and the steadiness of his devotion. She felt him pour into her, pistoning as he let out a long groan and let go.

When they stilled, only the sounds of their panting filled the room. He stroked her hair away from her face, staring at her as if she was a wonder. He kissed her so gently, tears leaked from her eyes. His tenderness felt palpable, the moment timeless and defining.

Being raw with him was moving, beautiful.

He swallowed hard. "I love you."

"I love you, too. I've never said that to a man in my life. But I'll love you forever."

Emotion softened Heath's face. He released her hands and flattened one of her palms to his chest, over the steady beat of his heart. "I hope you do. I'll love you that long and more."

* * *

JOLIE sat behind the sleek glass desk in her office and hung up the phone, still blinking in shock. The timing of the call had been amazing. Perfect. So fortuitous.

It must be serendipity.

Every other part of her life was sparkling and spectacular. Heath, of course, was the brightest spot. Even Karis was making better decisions for her future. It looked as if she and Arthur were cautiously developing something. And while her accountant had totally screwed up, he was still a huge step above most of her sister's boyfriends.

And now this phone call made her entire life complete.

She bolted to her feet and ran into the reception area to find Heath bent over Wisteria's computer, installing the last of the database files to make the card readers on the office doors fully functional.

"Heath?"

He turned. She must have been wearing an expression that conveyed all the shock she was feeling because he leapt to his feet. "What's wrong?"

"Nothing. It's good news. I . . ." She smiled until he caught on and returned the expression. "Everything's going to be all right. With Betti, I mean. I just received a call from a consortium of European funds, Quantum. Somehow they heard that I've been seeking an investor and asked if I was still looking for capital. I talked to this guy, Clarke Winston, for almost an hour. I've done some cursory research, and they look legitimate. He's already sent me paperwork with an investor agreement I can wholeheartedly sign. They want to be silent partners and don't expect to see any return on funds for five years. It's like a dream. Can you believe it?"

"You're happy, then?"

"Ecstatic. These are better terms than I'd hoped for. Best of all, they can wire me the funds right away. I can call my vendors and manufacturers and give them the good news. We can get started on the next phase of Betti. This is so amazing! It's the answer to my prayers."

Heath gathered her in his arms and kissed her forehead. "It couldn't have happened to a more deserving person. Congratulations."

"I'll work hard to make the most of this."

"Of that, I have no doubt, love. You never cease to amaze me."

She smiled and cupped his face. "We should celebrate tonight."

Heath leaned closer, his dark eyes drilling into her. "What did you have in mind? If you're open to suggestions, I've got a few."

"I'll bet you do. Later. My to-do list is a mile long after this phone call . . ." She shook her head, still in disbelief. "I'm not altogether sure how or why this group zeroed in on me, but I'm not looking a gift horse in the mouth."

"Maybe it was the *D Magazine* article," he suggested. "They made you sound like the second coming of clothes, you know."

"Maybe. It was pretty awesome press."

"Well, off with you, then. I'm still installing and testing all this equipment. You get busy now so we can get busy later." He winked.

"You got it. So excited! I can't wait to get the paperwork signed and the money in place. The moment that's done, I'm going to make two phone calls. The first to Richard Gardner telling him that I hope his penis is blistered for life so he can't screw some other unsuspecting businesswoman. The second phone call will be to my sperm donor to let him know that I don't need him, I've never needed him, and—in case he forgot—he can go fuck himself."

"Perfect." Heath beamed proudly at her, and Jolie wasn't just thrilled for Betti but for them.

Together they would have a bright future. And having such an understanding husband who was strong enough not to be threatened by her success, who didn't need to meddle because he believed she could accomplish her goals all on her own . . . That meant everything to her.

"Isn't it?" She couldn't stop smiling. Success felt fabulous. It would also be the best revenge. Richard Gardner didn't matter now. Carrington Quinn would never matter again.

Screw feeling vindicated. Jolie felt free.

Peeking around the office, Heath cupped her shoulders and turned her around. Everyone else was either away from their desks or had their heads buried in something. "Go." He gave her ass a light swat. "You can tell me everything you've got planned tonight after a great dinner. Naked."

With a laugh, Jolie left to find Karis and the rest of the staff and let them know they apparently had a savior.

* * *

EARLY the following morning, the buzzing of Heath's phone woke him from a sound sleep. He groaned and rolled over, relaxing instantly when he found Jolie beside him, barely stirring with the intrusive vibration of his mobile.

He'd awakened her more than once last night to make love to her again. Not being able to get enough of her didn't surprise him. He loved sex. They were newlyweds. She was fascinating. What prompted him to reach for her again and again was the closeness. It wasn't merely growing but multiplying so quickly that every time he touched her, he found it harder to catch his breath. They were entangled on every level, entwined all the way down to their souls.

Bloody hell, he sounded ridiculous, bleating on about matters of the heart. But that didn't change the fact that every moment with her only had him falling deeper in love.

The phone buzzed again, and he groped for it with a groan. He'd ten times rather be awakened by his passion for his wife than whoever wanted to disturb their peace.

"What?" he barked.

"It's Sean. Sorry I couldn't get back to you sooner. This baby is exhausting. Why does he only sleep two hours at a time?"

Despite the dire reason for the voicemail he'd left Sean the other day, Heath grinned, rolling out of bed and tossing on his jeans. "You sound beyond weary."

"Because I am. Callie is doing all she can but she needs rest. She's got a fever we're watching. Thorpe and I are trying to change diapers and understand swaddling. We're walking Asher, talking and cooing to him, taking turns sleeping so we can care for him . . . Fuck, I should have paid more attention when the Santiago brothers told me how difficult parenting an infant was."

Despite how doggedly tired the man sounded, Heath still envied him. "He's a beautiful baby."

"Amazing. Watching Callie give birth was something I'll never forget and I wouldn't trade it for all the sleep in the world."

That's what Heath suspected. "Congratulations."

"Thank you. But I didn't call to bitch about needing a nap. I finally got some info back on the street cam footage. Does the name Jim Dulin mean anything to you?"

"No." He frowned as he headed for the coffeemaker. "Should it?"

"He's your burglar. By the way, he's not the guy who's been hitting Betti's neighborhood businesses, either. They caught that guy breaking into a Condom Sense store last night."

"I'll bet he wasn't stealing computers from them."

Sean laughed. "No. Anyway, Jim Dulin is a thug for hire with a rap sheet so long if he wound it around a cardboard husk of toilet paper, it would be an extra jumbo roll. Lots of burglary and trespassing, some B and E, and assault. Aggravated robbery, of course. Unlawful possession of a firearm."

"Is there such a charge in Texas?"

"If you're a convicted felon. He also had some army training as a sniper back in the day."

Making it entirely possible he'd been the one who had tried to shoot Jolie. "Damn it."

"I don't think he's had time to burrow too deep underground. The police are trying to track down his last known address but I worked an angle and came up with this." He rattled off a street number and name. "Dulin was last seen there yesterday. It's in a seedy part of town. Surprise, surprise. It's a rent-by-the-week joint."

"Thanks. I'll start there. I appreciate it."

"No problem. I once risked everything to keep Callie alive. I know how that worry feels. I hope you find this guy fast."

They rang off, and Heath returned to the bedroom to find his wife rolling over and stretching. "Who was that?"

He explained. "I'm going to go over there and see what I can find. Stay with Cutter. He'll take you and Karis to the office. Unless I could persuade you to stay here and work today?"

"Can't do it. I'm the boss. I've got a staff to lead and a business to run."

"I knew you would say that." Heath sighed.

"Do you think there's any chance Monday's shooting was an accident or a fluke or—"

"Honestly, no. I wish it had been. I would sleep more and worry less. Remember what I said, stay with Cutter." He bent to kiss her. "I won't be gone long. Be a good girl today so I can treat you like a very bad girl tonight."

When he winked, she laughed. He loved that sight. Jolie had had so little to laugh about in her life.

"You got it." Jolie grabbed his arm, looking at him with troubled eyes. "Be safe."

"Of course." He kissed her forehead.

Heath didn't spare the time for a shower. He just shoved on the rest of his clothes, had a quick exchange with Cutter about the situation, then hopped on his bike.

The morning air bit his skin as he traveled to the address Sean had given him. It was only a few miles away but it might as well have been a whole world. Prostitutes milled around, most leaving the motel after what was probably a debauched evening of johns and drugs. Junkies were passed out on the concrete stairs leading to the upper floors, seemingly oblivious to the morning chill and the noisy traffic on the nearby street. Management looked the other way, as evidenced by the big tattooed guy in a rumpled dress shirt wiping his bald head with a sweat towel as he ambled from the office to a beat-up truck at the edge of the lot, ignoring the carnage around him.

Heath shook his head. How did one wind up here, serving the dregs of society with no hope for the future?

That could have been him, he realized. If he hadn't pulled himself out of his rage, hadn't forced himself to pick up and move on. He would have stopped caring and merely kept subsisting day to day, hoping life took him someplace where he could disappear because nothing mattered anymore.

Thankfully, he'd persisted. Or he would never have met Jolie.

Heath headed up the littered staircase. An old man was drinking a bottle of cheap wine as he urinated off the side of the balcony, onto someone's car below. A hooker who looked old beyond her youth buried her face in shadow as she passed, but that didn't hide the bruising. Even if she needed his interference, she wouldn't appreciate it.

He scowled and forged ahead, locating the room number Sean had given him. Drapes drawn. No signs of movement inside.

He found a tired woman in her forties shoving a housekeeping cart from door to door as if she were pushing a boulder uphill.

"A moment, please?" he asked.

She looked at him as if he'd lost his mind. "What'chu want?"

"I'm looking for a missing person," he improvised.

And it was true in a sense. According to Sean, no one had seen Jim Dulin for about twenty-four hours.

"I can't help you. You'll have to talk to Eddie, the day manager."

He would prefer to avoid management. Besides, this woman would benefit far more from his desperation. "Are you sure?" He pulled out a hundred dollars. "I simply need to peek into a room and see if I can find my missing someone."

"You a cop?" She scowled.

"Private eye." *Of a sort.* "I have a very concerned client."

She spied the money, her eyes narrowed with suspicion. "You tryin' to get me fired?"

"Not at all. If you help me, I help you." He extended the money. "Your boss will never know and you will never hear from me again."

She looked around, then snatched the money from his hand, tucking it in the kerchief she had wrapped around her head. "What room?"

He whispered the number. "I only need a few minutes."

"I keep the master key on the chain hanging from my belt loop." Without moving her head, she cast her gaze down clandestinely. "If you was to swipe it, I might not notice for a few minutes since I'll be restocking my cart."

"Excellent. And because my fingers are slippery, I'm sure I'll drop it just outside that room where you'll easily find it."

She acknowledged him with a nod and walked away slowly. Heath thanked a bit of his misspent youth because he'd learned to pickpocket for fun. Relieving the maid of her room key and snagging a pair of latex gloves from the cart was a breeze.

Clinging to the shadows, he made his way to Dulin's room and let himself in.

He knew something was wrong instantly. Despite the air conditioning being on full blast, the atmosphere was too still. No one rushed forward to ask why the hell he'd barged in. No one lay on the beds. The shower wasn't running. Nothing stirred.

Heath knew what death felt like—and it had come to visit here recently.

He crept through the room, past the second of the queen beds. There, wedged between the mattress and the wall lay the body of a man in his thirties. His face was white, waxy. Blood, probably from a bullet wound in the back of his head, pooled into the dirty, patterned carpet.

Just looking at the state of the body, the guy had probably been dead somewhere between eight and twelve hours. The killer had turned the AC on high so the decomposing body wouldn't smell right away but the stench was beginning to pervade the room now.

Grimacing, Heath thrust on the latex gloves and bent to the body. This was no theft gone wrong. The wallet in his back pocket still had a few hundred dollars tucked inside. And a driver's license. He was, indeed, James Dulin. The picture and description matched.

Damn it, he could no longer ask the petty criminal questions about why he'd broken into Betti and whether he'd been the one to shoot at Jolie. The fact that Dulin had been murdered was unsettling enough. Maybe it was a coincidence that the man who had been paid to steal Jolie's computer, then later her life, had been killed himself.

During his years in MI5, Heath had found that coincidences were never quite as random as they first appeared.

He searched the rest of the body. A .22 sat in a holster. He'd shoved a few bullets in his pocket. Anything else he might have had in there was conveniently missing.

In his shoe, Dulin had tucked a thin key. Heath studied it, holding it up to the weak sunlight leaking under the limp blackout drapes that had seen better days. It wasn't to a safe deposit or a locker facility. It was smaller, maybe opening a suitcase.

Wedged under Dulin's hip, he found the guy's phone, as if it had been in his hand and fallen onto the floor just before he landed on top of it. He didn't have the mobile password protected, which told Heath that he hadn't used it much. Sure enough, he only had two people in his contacts, Barbara and Addison. The first was his sister, based on the information in the contact folder. Addison was his daughter, maybe seven or eight, living with her aunt Barbara. All the calls to and from the phone were to those two mobile numbers. The few pictures he had were of them both.

He sighed. The family left behind were often hit the hardest because they frequently knew their relative was a criminal but death finally dashed their hopes their loved one would turn his life around.

Heath tucked the phone under the body again, approximately where he'd found it. When investigators encountered Dulin's body, they'd want to contact the next of kin. That would be the easiest means to find them. But this man couldn't have operated without a connection to his shady underworld, and he wouldn't want to be traced.

Dulin had a burner phone somewhere, likely in the room. Heath simply had to locate it.

Nothing under the beds, in the bathroom, beneath the adjacent sink. The closet proved empty of all but clothes and a discarded suitcase. The drawers contained a few pairs of boxers and a Bible.

Heath headed to the kitchenette area and pulled open drawers, prowled inside cabinets. After finding nothing, he peeked in the oven. Inside a baking pan rested a little metal lockbox.

Sliding the oven rack out, he fished in his pocket for the key he'd found on Dulin's body. Sure enough, it fit into the small lock on the box. Heath frowned. It wasn't high security. Why had the criminal imagined he could hide anything here? Then again, perhaps he hadn't been terribly bright. Heath would never know now . . .

He pried the lid open and found about ten thousand in cash, three fake passports—all badly done because Dulin had actually looked far more like a redneck than a Russian diplomat—and a burner phone.

Plucking the disposable cell from the box, he scrolled through the calls. Most were to an overseas mobile, all reached with the dialing code 44. United Kingdom.

A flush of shock and anxiety hit his system. Cutter had been right. Everything happening to Jolie wasn't about her past, but his. He'd put away so many dangerous criminals in his decade with MI5. Any of them could have done their time or escaped and decided payback was in order.

But only one case had haunted him relentlessly for years. Only one case had the power to unnerve him.

Somehow, some way, this had to do with Anna's murder.

Swallowing, he looked at the call history. A slew of calls starting last Wednesday had culminated in one at ten a.m. on Monday morning. A silent period followed between that call and the final one Monday, at three in the afternoon—shortly after Jolie's attempted murder. Everything had been silent since, and Heath suspected he knew why.

This burner was his only link between himself and whoever wanted to do his wife harm.

He didn't hesitate.

Plucking through the buttons, he redialed the most frequently called number on the device and waited. On the third ring, a man answered with a guarded "What?"

The familiar voice chilled him. Heath didn't say a word. His thoughts raced, his palms sweated, his head spun with disbelief.

The man on the other end sighed. "You couldn't leave it alone, could you? I hope you have your funeral suit ready. You'll need it."

Fear detonated throughout Heath's body, the impact like a nuclear explosion in his gut. He had to get to Jolie now.

Heath wasn't sure what the man was up to or why he'd just threatened everything but no one would spill even a drop of Jolie's blood.

Hanging up the phone, Heath shoved everything back into place, darted out the door, and dropped the key as he went. On the mad dash to his bike, he texted Cutter that danger was coming. Then he shoved the burner phone in his pocket and the latex gloves into a nearby Dumpster.

It would take him half an hour—maybe more—to reach his wife. He only hoped he got to Jolie before anyone else did.

Chapter Sixteen

Rule for success number sixteen:
Be flexible and adaptable.

As the morning sun slanted through the front windows of Betti's suite, Jolie scanned the investor agreement for the third time. She'd made notes last night and e-mailed Clarke Winston for answers. They had been waiting for her bright and early this morning. She'd called an attorney she occasionally consulted with and asked him to glance at the document. To her shock, he'd called back within the hour to say it was a golden handshake of a deal and she would be a fool not to take it.

Today, she planned to do just that.

A moment later, Wisteria knocked, her long face appearing in the sidelight window next to the office door. Clearly, the poor woman had been crying again, and Jolie no longer wanted to tell her receptionist to avoid men. That would never work. Besides, she now understood the lure of romance. God, she loved Heath more every day—far more than she'd ever thought she'd love any man. He'd proven himself to be honorable. She trusted and respected him. And he reminded her to laugh. He wasn't a perfect man . . . but he was the perfect one for her. That's what Jolie wished Wisteria could find for herself.

Rising, she cracked the door. "Yes? I'm reading a contract. Emergencies only."

"It's kind of an emergency. You have a visitor." Wisteria pulled the door wide to reveal a man in a sharp navy suit, crisp shirt, stylish briefcase. Late thirties, blue eyes, hair somewhere between blond and brown, well-trimmed beard. Reasonably attractive. "He's here to talk to you about the Quantum Consortium thing."

Jolie paused. Clarke hadn't mentioned they were sending a representative. Was this surprise visit a hidden prerequisite? Did they want to interview her further? Inspect her operations?

"Hello, Ms. Quinn." He sounded very British as he stuck out his hand.

"Hello." She shook it. "Actually, I'm Mrs. Powell now. I recently married. But call me Jolie. Come in and sit. I had no idea you were coming. What's your name?"

She shut the door behind them, enclosing them in her office. As he crossed the room toward the guest chair she offered, he tripped spectacularly and sprawled on hands and knees, his briefcase tumbling across the carpet.

Jolie rushed to help him up. "Are you all right?"

He pushed his glasses up the bridge of his nose with a sheepish grin and collected himself. "After a recent injury, I'm a bit clumsy, I'm afraid. Thank you."

As he sat, Jolie rounded the desk to her own oversized leather seat. "So you're with Quantum?"

"Well, I have some information Clarke neglected to include in his conversations with you. I felt as if I had to discuss the bits of the agreement you might not be aware of."

"Such as . . .?"

He sized her up. Not like a sexual partner but as if trying to determine her capability. Jolie bristled. Clarke had been affable and easy to do business with. This man annoyed her.

"Do you know where the capital you're contemplating is coming from?"

The implications of his question made her frown. "Isn't it a general investment fund?"

He sighed as if deeply distressed. "It's as I suspected. You don't have the first clue. I can't let you remain in the dark."

"In the dark how?"

"Mr. Winston represents your investor because they're related."

Clarke hadn't mentioned that but he had been, in every other way, completely professional. She shrugged. "All right."

"Of course you don't understand. I'm botching this." He shook his head. "Mr. Winston is an investment broker married to your new husband's sister. Mr. Powell intended to fund your company expansion without advising you."

Jolie froze, shock sliding through her. "Clarke is Heath's brother-in-law?"

"Precisely."

"So Clarke doesn't represent Quantum Consortium?"

"He does, technically." He looked so sorry to be the bearer of bad news. "But I'm afraid it scarcely existed three days past."

Now she knew he was wrong. "I researched it. That fund was created eight years ago."

"On paper, yes. But it's been inactive. You might not have been able to locate documentation because the group was always privately owned, so few public records exist."

That had been Jolie's conclusion, too. But Clarke worked for a very reputable European brokerage. Never a hint of scandal or shady dealings. And of course she'd never imagined that Heath would use Quantum to dabble in her business without first talking to her. Hell, she hadn't even known he possessed that kind of money.

"And you think my husband intended to give me millions of dollars for Betti's expansion without my knowledge?"

"I'm afraid so."

Because he wanted make her dreams come true? Because, after Gardner's crap, Heath hoped she'd succeed? Or because he pitied her? Jolie wasn't sure. Why hadn't he told her his plans?

Did he think she couldn't achieve her dreams without his help?

That possibility raging through her head, Jolie wilted back into her chair. She tried not to believe that he'd discounted her. Betrayed her. He had never before lied to her, not even when it would have made his life easier. But why else would he congratulate her for finding a new investor if he knew who had provided the capital all along?

Then again, Jolie didn't know this man in her office. Maybe he was mistaken. Maybe he was stirring some shit pot she didn't understand.

"I don't believe you."

"Your loyalty is admirable. How much do you know about your new husband? Were you aware that he's a very wealthy man, worth around ten million pounds?"

Her jaw dropped. "Impossible. He would never have taken a job with me if he had that kind of money—"

"Yes, he would. He's done it for years. Following the death of his first wife, he inherited the sizeable estate Anna's parents left behind. He also collected a hefty life insurance policy. Both sums he rolled over into crafty investments, managed by his brother-in-law. I can only imagine why he hasn't touched that money until now."

"Who are you? How could you possibly know any of this?"

"I'm Myles Beaker."

Was that name supposed to mean something? "And?"

"I see Heath didn't mention me. I'm sure he would prefer to move on from his guilt." He sighed as if he harbored deep regret for coming here to burst her newlywed bubble. "I was Heath's partner when he worked with MI5."

"So you're not with Quantum?"

"I'm sorry, no. I needed an expedient story to ensure you would see me. I have to explain the truth. You see, Heath and I both lost wives on the same terrible day. Anna perished, which I presume you know. But my Lucy and our unborn child were murdered, too."

The man took a moment to collect himself, and Jolie couldn't help softening. "Take your time."

He shook his head, seemingly determined to forge ahead. "I've wracked my brain for years to figure out who killed them and why. A random attack simply didn't make sense. Somehow, those innocent women were at the epicenter of violence. Everything was well planned, professionally executed. I'm a grieving man. I want answers. I've struggled so much since that tragic day. I dug and investigated. I searched high and low. I've come to the conclusion that Heath must have killed Anna for the money. Lucy and our unborn child were simply collateral damage in the wake of his greed. And now, I fear, he's plotting the same fate for you."

Jolie's phone buzzed at that moment. She glanced at the screen. Heath. She nearly snatched up the device and started barking questions. Had he really intended to invest in Betti secretly? Why?

She didn't believe the stranger was right about Heath killing Anna. After all, he'd seemed so angry and torn when he'd discussed his first wife's death. Jolie's gut—and her heart—didn't want to believe he could fake all that. But she'd barely known Heath for a week. As much as she hated to contemplate his deception, she couldn't afford to be naive. She'd hear Beaker out, see where this theory led. That way, she'd know the right questions to ask her new husband in case his former partner could prove any part of it true.

Declining the call, she silenced her phone. "You're saying my husband killed his first wife for money and now wants to murder me for mine?"

"Precisely."

Time to review facts. She had initiated both sex and marriage . . .

but Heath had planted the suggestions in her head. Had she been too sure of herself to see a potential charlatan coming and leapt into marriage because, screw the consequences, he made her feel good? Because he'd given her the best sex of her life? Her mother had certainly succumbed to that ruse more than once—with disastrous results.

Nervous now, Jolie tapped her fingers on her desk. Certainly Heath wouldn't be so eager to get her pregnant if he meant to kill her. Unless he didn't intend to leave her alive long enough for that to matter.

Maybe Beaker was a desperate man, looking for someone to blame for his loss. Maybe he believed what he said and sought to "save" her from Anna's fate. Or maybe he was an asshole with an ax to grind.

"He's beyond mercenary," Beaker added.

"And he wants to take my money by first giving me money?" The absurdity of that hit her.

"Yes, by marrying you *and* investing in your company, he'll likely have every right to your funds when something happens to you. He would also have a very strong claim on Betti. I presume you don't have any sort of prenuptial agreement?"

"No." Until the last few years, she'd never had much money. Sometimes she forgot that she was no longer struggling to pay off student loans.

Beaker shot her a superior expression. "There you go. Whoever you've named in your will as a benefactor will have a devil of a time defending their position in court because Heath will be both your husband and your primary investor."

Laws varied from state to state . . . but she saw his point. "That's quite a theory."

"After the cold-blooded way he executed Anna, Lucy, and our baby, I have no doubt he's capable of killing you to more than double his wealth."

"He's never once mentioned money to me."

"Of course not. Why bother with small amounts here or there

when he could score big? What is Betti worth now? I've seen esti-
mates that you could sell it for upwards of thirty million dollars," he
said, his accent clipped. "Is that right?"

Her last valuation put her somewhere in that neighborhood. For
a man she'd never heard of, Beaker seemed well informed about her.
"Why do you want to know?"

"My point is, he's aware of this. And you're his next mark."

Jolie thought back over the last week, to all the amazing, touching, tender ways her husband had filled in the holes around her heart
and soul. Either he was the perfect man for her . . . or a con artist of
epic proportions. She hadn't looked closely into Heath's background
before she had hired him. Callie's devoted husband had recommended him. Sean was a sensible man with a good bullshit meter.
He wouldn't recommend a criminal, right? Not if he'd known.

"You look skeptical," Beaker cut into her thoughts. "I can prove
your husband intended to invest in Betti without your knowledge or
consent."

"Really?"

Myles withdrew his phone from his pocket and set it on the desk
between them. With a few taps of the screen, Jolie found herself listening to a familiar voice.

"Hi, Heath. Clarke here. I've had the chance to speak with your
new wife. Jolie is a lovely woman. Very sharp. I'm impressed. Your
sister is most excited to meet her. I don't know if I'll be able to contain Jane until Christmas. She quite wants to meet Jolie." He sounded
amused. "The good news is I've managed to liquidate everything you
requested. I'll contact her today to extend the offer and the contract.
I'll keep you informed along the way . . . unless you'd like to tell her
that you're her investor. I can't think subterfuge is the best way to
begin a marriage . . ."

Beaker tapped the screen to end the recording. But that didn't
stop shock from shredding Jolie's composure.

Heath truly had used his brother-in-law to give her money for

Betti without any intent to tell her. She sat back, stunned. What else had Beaker pegged correctly? Certainly not murder, right?

"How did you get that voicemail?"

He sent her an almost pitying expression. "I've spent too many years as a spy. I'm afraid some habits die hard."

Jolie didn't like the lengths he'd gone to in order to prove her husband guilty but she couldn't deny the recording sounded authentic. "It appears he deceived me about investing in Betti, I'll grant you. But it's a long way from investor to murderer."

"Your skepticism is understandable. I didn't want to believe it myself. We were partners and best mates. Our wives were very close. We trusted each other completely with our lives over and over. Believe me, no one was more surprised than me to realize Heath had blown everything up for his own ends."

She knew men could sometimes be selfish liars. Jolie had seen that truth in action over and over, repeating through her childhood like bad music in an elevator.

"If you can prove that Heath killed your pregnant wife, why haven't you gone to the proper authorities? You must know exactly who to contact in order to bring this matter to justice."

"Because Heath will kill me. Look at the call history on his phone. He's reached out twice in the last week, both times to threaten me. Few people have the skills to kill me, frankly. I'm not afraid of much. But your husband has a dangerous, ruthless side."

"Can't the authorities protect you?"

"Spoken like someone who still believes in a system that's both broken and corrupt." Beaker gave a bark of a laugh. "Heath has the money to pay off anyone. That's how he got away with it the first time, you know."

"Let's pretend I believe you. What do you want?"

He folded his hands in his lap, looking perplexed. "Nothing. I simply had to warn you."

"You don't know me."

"I wouldn't be able to live with myself if I stood by idly while another woman was cut down to serve his greed."

Her instinct kept flaring. Or was that her hope that romance and love could be both real and lasting? After all, why would he run the risk of hacking Clarke's phone when he claimed to be terrified of Heath? Her new husband had been a spy, too. He would know all the ways Beaker could obtain such recordings. He was thorough and would be watching for something like that if he had dark deeds to hide.

"I want to see your proof."

Her demand seemed to surprise him. "I don't have the rest here. You're welcome to come with me to my hotel 'round the corner. I'll bring everything down to the lobby if it makes you more comfortable and review the evidence with you."

Jolie shook her head. She wasn't going anywhere with a man she didn't know. "You'll have to bring it here."

Regret crossed his face instantly. "Impossible. The minute Heath returns, someone will tell him I've been to your office. He'll devise all manner of lies to put you at ease and make me sound somewhere between delusional and dangerous. Once he's discredited me, he'll ensure I never come within a mile of you again. Eventually, of course, it will be too late."

"I'm a grown woman who makes her own decisions. If you promise you'll return here with proof, nothing and no one will stop me from meeting you, least of all my husband. He's my partner in life, not my keeper. If you want me to hear you out, those are my terms."

"I took an enormous risk coming here at all. If I return, he'll certainly kill me." He sighed, stood, shaking his head sadly, as if he wished he could make her understand. "Good luck. Stay safe."

Beaker turned to leave. Jolie didn't want to risk her business or her life but she'd met this stranger ten minutes ago. How was she supposed to believe him over the man she had vowed to love forever?

As he reached the door, he glanced back. "I hope I'm wrong, Ms. Quinn. Maybe I am. After all, no one has tried to kill you since you married, so—"

"Someone has." The words popped out with a frown. "On Monday, outside my office. But Heath was standing beside me. He couldn't possibly have had anything to do with the attempt."

"Oh, my dear woman. He has accomplices. Without them, he couldn't possibly have managed the sort of 'attack' necessary to kill our first wives. He had another MI5 operative in on it with him, Kensforth. That ring a bell? No. I can prove that as well." Beaker looked so earnest. "He had a demolitions expert, several lookouts, and an assassin. He probably used the same shooter a few days ago, though I'm surprised the man missed. He was deadly accurate with Anna and Lucy. Ten minutes. Please."

Something in her gut kept telling Jolie to resist. "Come back here and I'll look at it."

"I know you want to believe the man you married is a perfect husband and devoted lover. But certainly you've met a charming man or two in your past, perhaps were even taken in by him? Been deceived by him? Heath is the consummate professional. He'll tell you precisely what you want to hear in order to earn your trust. I watched him with Anna. I know firsthand."

Jolie frowned. Taken in by a charming man? No, she never had been. But her mother had fallen prey to men with looks and charisma repeatedly. As a child, Jolie had sworn she would be smarter, would never trust blindly or be duped by a lying snake. She had sworn to question everything if she ever decided to get serious about a man so she would never be blindsided and crushed because she was too in love to ask the right questions.

Looking back over the last week, Jolie realized she'd broken her promise to herself. She had trusted without question, lost herself in the moment, and stopped thinking about anything except how good it felt to be in love.

Jolie hated to consider that she'd made a colossal mistake, but if she didn't look at Beaker's evidence, would she always wonder if he'd been right? Would she even get to live with the regret of ignoring him?

If he could prove all his claims in a public place in ten minutes, what did she have to lose?

"All right. Which hotel?"

Beaker gave her the name, and she sent a quick text to Cutter. Odd that he didn't acknowledge her message right away but he could also be tied up with Karis.

With a shrug, Jolie grabbed her phone and shoved it in her purse, which she slung over her shoulder. "I'll take my own car and meet you in the lobby."

He looked relieved. Reenergized. "Splendid. I'll prove everything. You'll see."

She really hoped he couldn't. Finding out that Heath had deceived her in every way would kill her.

Dread biting her belly, she followed Beaker out of her office. Wisteria wasn't at her desk. Gerard had tuned out the world with his earbuds and sketchpad again. Rohan, Karis, and Arthur should be in a development meeting. No worries. Cutter knew where she was going.

In the parking lot, Beaker's car was parked next to hers. He walked beside her, scanning the lot carefully, looking this way and that. Like he was expecting trouble.

When they reached the door to her vehicle, he paused behind her. "I think it would be best if you rode with me."

"No. I'll take my own transpor—"

"Get in the fucking car." The gentle concern and grieving cry in his voice were gone, replaced by a hard growl. He emphasized his point by sticking the barrel of his gun in her back. "Now."

Jolie's heart stopped. This couldn't be happening. A glance over her shoulder confirmed that he had absolutely no compunction about killing her. "C-Cutter knows I'm leaving here with you."

Myles scoffed. "Cutter had an unfortunate accident in the men's room. He won't be telling anyone anything."

Panic tried to overwhelm her, followed quickly by regret. She wished like hell she'd listened to her instinct, that she'd taken Heath's earlier call. Was she too cynical to believe in love, in the man she'd married?

How would she escape this mess without dying?

"I won't get in the car with you. You'll have to kill me here in the lot." Because if he had the balls to start shooting, someone in the building would come running. Yeah, she'd be injured, maybe even killed. But he wouldn't be able to rape or torture her. He couldn't hold her over Heath's head to make her husband dance to his will.

"If you don't get in, I will blow up everyone inside Betti's offices, including your sister, with the bomb I planted last night."

A new wave of horror swept over her. "I don't believe you."

Beaker yanked on her hair and tilted her face back to look up at him. "Care to try me?"

No. No, she didn't. She couldn't risk everyone else on her hunch. "I'll go with you."

"I rather thought you might. There's a good girl." He opened the door. "Now let's make your husband suffer, shall we?"

Chapter Seventeen

Rule for success number seventeen:
Decide to succeed.

HEATH weaved in and out of rush hour traffic as he headed toward Betti's office as quickly as he dared. Sweat ran from his brow, dripped down his temple. His heart raced. Why hadn't Jolie answered her phone? Why hadn't Cutter responded, either? Wisteria wasn't at her desk. He'd tried to call Karis, who hadn't answered. Instead, she'd texted back that she was busy with Arthur, taking advantage of the file room, followed by a winky icon. She hadn't responded to his emergency text in return.

Heath stopped at a light with a curse and pulled out his phone again. The blinding sunlight overhead made the screen hard to see as he tried to track Jolie's phone. It showed her at a static location just off Central Expressway, now about five miles north of Betti's offices. Why would she go there? Early lunch? Doctor appointment? Shopping? Why hadn't she told him any of that?

Only one reason made sense: Somehow, Myles had Jolie in his grip.

Bloody hell, he had to get to her. He hated to panic, but now that Myles knew Heath had pieced together at least some of the puzzle of their past, he wouldn't hesitate to move in for the kill. Because he clearly hadn't hesitated seven years ago. Heath quickly rang Hunter Edgington in Lafayette.

"Hey, man," the former SEAL greeted. "Everything okay with Cutter?"

"He's not answering his phone. No one at Betti is. I'm stranded on the fucking freeway at rush hour and I'm fairly certain the man who killed my first wife is trying to kill my second."

"Wait. *You* got married again? Okay, not important. Who is your second wife?"

"Jolie," he gritted his teeth. "My former partner at MI5, Myles Beaker, has her, I suspect. I've just realized he was responsible for killing Anna and now . . ."

Heath swallowed, not sure he could finish that sentence. Thankfully, he didn't have to.

"I got the picture," Hunter said. "Any idea where to find them?"

"Not really. Do you know anyone who can be here quickly? Beaker is a crafty bastard. He knows I have information about him so he'll likely want to trade my silence for Jolie's life. But he hasn't contacted me yet. I think we have time . . . but not much."

"You need backup." Hunter assessed the situation immediately. "Let me . . . Logan!" he called out to his younger brother, also a former SEAL. "Text Xander and ask him if we can borrow his plane again. Emergency."

"On it."

"Plane?" Who was Xander that he had a plane at his disposal?

Heath knew it would take time for the Edgington brothers to arrive but they got results.

"Yeah, Xander Santiago and his brother, Javier, own a defense contracting company, so they have a jet. I think we use it for missions as much as they use it for business," Hunter quipped. "It's really fucking handy. I'm coming to Dallas. Logan is in, too. We'll get together as many as we can to help."

"Xander says the plane is ours," Logan called out in the background.

"Awesome," Hunter replied. "We're on our way."

Heath felt his first glimmer of hope. "How soon can you be here?"

"Louisiana is just next door. Two hours max."

"Text me the name of the airport and I'll have a car ready." Heath wasn't sure how he'd manage that but he would make it work.

"No need. Xander keeps a fleet ready there. He comes to Dallas often."

"Thank you." From the bottom of his heart. A weight had been lifted from his soul. No, Jolie wasn't safe yet, but with these men, she had a much better chance of survival.

"You're welcome. I've got my go bag in hand. So does Logan. We've texted the wives that we're leaving. I'll pick up Tyler Murphy on the way. He's in, too. Let us know when you hear from Beaker."

Heath both anticipated and dreaded that moment. "Will do."

"Xander's plane has Wi-Fi, so we can receive texts. You can tell us where to rendezvous."

As soon as the call ended, Heath tried to decide how to proceed. Follow Jolie's phone, which hadn't moved since the last time he'd pinged the device, or go to Betti. Figuring the police would soon be at her office, he followed her mobile.

When he reached the location, he found an abandoned building beside the freeway. The car park was empty. He didn't see her vehicle or any hint of the woman herself. But he found her phone discarded on the asphalt, as if someone had thrown the device, maybe from a moving car because it could be tracked.

Fresh fear gripped Heath.

He retrieved the mobile with the edge of his shirt to prevent marking it with his fingerprints. As he stared at the shattered screen, Heath's blood to turned to ice again. Jolie would never cut herself off from the outside world intentionally. She always wanted to be in contact—for her business, for her sister, for emergencies. But Myles would certainly know that a man who'd lost one wife once would be paranoid about the safety of a new one and do everything possible to keep an eye on her when he couldn't be there to do it himself.

Heath pictured Myles wresting the cell from her hands and throwing her lifeline to safety out his window. He could imagine the abject terror she would feel. It almost debilitated him. Guilt followed closely. How could he have failed Jolie? How could he have overlooked the possibility—for so long—that Myles was a killer?

Then again, what grieving widower imagines that his best mate would go so far as to kill his own wife and unborn baby? And for what? Heath had no clue.

Shoving down his horror, Heath called 911. "There's a kidnapping in progress."

No, he didn't know what car Myles was driving or what he was wearing or where he might take her. Maybe someone at Betti had seen them or overheard something? The dispatcher said that police were en route to the location in question and that if he had new information, he should advise those units when he arrived.

Heath raced to get there. He couldn't endure this again—the loss, the despair, the feeling of failure. The engulfing guilt. But worse, he couldn't lose Jolie. She wasn't merely a wife he guided and doted on and cared for. She was a partner, his equal, his intellectual challenge. She motivated him to live again and be better than ever.

What the fuck would he do if he lost her?

After a ten-minute detour, he screeched up to Betti. Barely bothering to park his bike, he vaulted off and ran into the suite. Just inside the door, he found Wisteria blinking in shock, Karis crying, Arthur trying to comfort her, Gerard and Rohan arguing about who could have done what to stop this, and Cutter being taken away on a stretcher with a rapidly reddening bandage wrapped around his head.

A uniformed officer approached. "Who are you?"

"I'm the person who called. My wife is missing. Jolie Quinn. Now Powell. Five foot six inches, brown hair, green eyes, thirty years old—"

"Her sister just filled us in. Where have you been?" the cop asked suspiciously.

Heath nearly groaned. The police almost always suspected the spouse in any kidnapping or murder, thinking it was some sort of domestic dispute. "I was late coming into work. I tried to call the office and everyone here on my way but got no response. That's very unlike my wife and her staff. We've had trouble here of late. A break-in, a shooting. I worried. And now she's gone. She may have been abducted by a man named Myles Beaker. He's MI5."

"Huh? He's what?"

Heath tried not to lose his patience. "It's the British equivalent of the FBI. He's very dangerous and he's got a vendetta against me. Five foot ten inches, sandy hair, blue eyes. I'm not sure what he's driving or where he'll be taking her. I fear he means to kill her. We need to find them."

"I understand, sir. You need to calm down. If we don't know anything about his vehicle or his destination, that makes things a bit trickier—"

"If this was your wife, your mother or daughter, your loved one in the hands of someone you knew had killed before, how would you respond?"

The fortysomething cop drew in a long breath, then nodded. "We'll do everything we can."

Heath hoped it would be enough, hoped his backup from Louisiana made it soon. If not, he would be attending Jolie's funeral . . . and burying himself with her.

* * *

JOLIE stumbled, barely managing to keep her balance as Beaker gave her a merciless shove forward. "Keep moving."

She couldn't see anything since he'd blindfolded her and cuffed her wrists half an hour ago, shortly after he'd tossed her phone out the window of his Jeep. She had no idea where he'd taken her or what was next.

He grabbed her, stopped her short. A door opened, then he pushed her through and released her. Jolie's instinct told her to kick him, run—do something. But she stood, wrists tied behind her back, unable to see anything around her. He jabbed the gun into her spine.

God, she couldn't just stand here and die. "Where are we?"

He ripped off her blindfold to reveal what looked like an abandoned industrial building. Some antique conveyer belt system wound through the cavernous structure. It was dark. The place looked filthy. A few cracks in the roof let in limited sunlight. The quiet, except for the scurry of what was probably rodents she didn't want to identify, sounded eerie.

Beaker led her to an old office, complete with a rusty desk and a pair of grimy chairs. He shot her an impatient look as he urged her into one of the seats. "Nowhere anyone will find you. Please don't try to be a heroine. I've been chasing and capturing some of the most prolific and shrewd criminals in the world for fifteen years. They haven't outsmarted me, and you won't either."

"So you chose to become one of them?"

"Don't be daft." He scowled as he sat. "I'm not some ridiculous serial killer who slaughters for the thrill. I never wanted to kill Anna."

Jolie stared at him in complete horror. So Heath's former partner had killed his first wife? Did her husband even know that? "Oh my god . . ."

"I see I've shocked you. I did him a favor, you know. Anna wasn't his equal. She was a simpering little thing. Beautiful, yes. But void of a brain or any hint of intrepid spirit. I was most surprised when I began digging into you, Ms. Quinn. Or rather, Powell. You're quite different."

And because he hadn't liked Anna, Beaker had decided she deserved to die? "So you have the same end planned for me?"

"As it happens, I would prefer not to hurt you. I think you could do great things in life. That should make you feel better, eh?"

It didn't because she didn't believe him. "What do you want from me?"

"Nothing, actually. I want to hear from your husband. We have unfinished business. A few days ago I told him to stop poking around in the past. I'll bet he wishes now that he had listened to me." Beaker sighed. "He really was one of my best friends. Shame . . ."

Because the madman meant to kill him? She had to break free, warn Heath. Jolie had no illusions. Beaker would use her as leverage, and Heath would let him because losing another wife would destroy him.

Jolie cursed herself for not trusting her first instinct about this asshole—and for not believing in Heath's love enough to conquer her inner cynic. "There was no bomb in Betti's offices, was there?"

"No, but I had to make it sound good." He smiled, obviously pleased with himself. "You, my dear, have only two weaknesses. Well, three now. Initially, I knew your Achilles' heel was your business and your sister. By threatening both, I figured I would easily sway you. But I think you love your new husband a great deal and would do most anything for him."

She refused to give Beaker anything else to use against her. "We married impulsively a few days ago. He's great in bed. I'd like to have a baby someday. He was game." She shrugged through the lies. "Marriage seemed like a good idea. I'm thirty. It was time."

He shot her a chastising glare. "If you're going to lie, you'll have to do a far better job. I've looked into your background, profiled you a bit. After your mother's rocky up-and-down love life, I think only real love would tempt you to the altar. You're a driven career woman in the throes of expansion. I rather thought that revealing Heath's secret plot to invest in Betti as a way to earn your trust was a stroke of genius." He patted himself on the back. "You might want a child but you still have time. So any childbearing you want now would only be because you've found someone you want to spend your life with. Do you have a better lie to run past me?"

"Do you want money?"

"No. If that were my sole motivation, I would have found some way to bilk Heath out of his. Or better yet, organize criminals and steal millions. I know quite well how to do it. I've learned from some of the best masterminds over the years. But as it happens, I'm not a thief. I believe in earning my money and devoting my skills when the time is right."

Jolie didn't understand this man at all. Not a killer? Not a thief? "Why the hell did you murder Anna?" She gasped as something truly awful occurred to her. "You also killed your own pregnant wife?"

"It was a difficult but unfortunate necessity. I never wanted to hurt her, but . . . she left me no other option. Your husband should be calling soon." He glanced at his phone. "I do hope he uses his common sense, rather than his bravado. He doesn't need to save the world, just you. Hungry?" He opened a cooler she hadn't noticed on the floor beside the desk. "Ham sandwich?"

Eating was the last thing on her mind now. "No."

"Then we'll wait. Heath is really very smart. I'm sure it will occur to him to call and—" His mobile rang then, and Beaker glanced down at the screen. "Excellent."

Jolie wished she could reach through the phone and tell Heath not to talk to Beaker, not to get involved or put himself in danger. But that was her husband. He would protect her a hundred times over before he would lift a finger to shield himself. He would never let her stay at this man's mercy if he could save her.

"I wondered when you would call," Myles said, putting the line on speaker.

"Let her go, you motherfucker! Don't hurt her. She's done nothing to you."

Hearing her husband's voice, Jolie's heart caught in her throat. "Heath!"

"Shut up," Beaker snapped at her, then turned his attention back to her husband. "As it happens, I quite agree with you, Powell."

"Let me talk to her."

"Soon. Now I don't have much time because I'm certain you have the authorities recording and tracing this. Don't insult my intelligence by insisting otherwise. So here's what you're going to do: Head toward the West End. In thirty minutes, I'll text you an address. You will have another ten minutes to find it. At that point, you will receive a package. I'll call you with further instructions. Come alone. Record nothing. Fail any of these demands and I fear for your lovely bride. Do you understand?"

Heath said nothing for a long moment, then he growled as if barely restraining his temper. "If you want money or information, I'll need to start gathering it now."

"Nothing like that. Really, I thought you knew me better."

"Clearly I don't know you at all. How could you kill Anna, Lucy, and your own baby?"

Beaker didn't answer. "Watch for my text in thirty minutes."

"I need an hour. I don't have a car."

Jolie frowned. Anyone on her staff would lend him a car. Why was he stalling?

Her captor gave a long-suffering sigh. "Don't take me for an idiot. I've done my legwork. I know you have a motorcycle. I know your wife has plenty of people who will drive you to and fro. I'm sure you've also established some connections in Dallas. Isn't your wife friends with that heiress from Chicago who just had a baby? Callindra Howe? Isn't her husband former FBI?" Beaker tsked at Heath. "Don't treat me like a fool. Thirty minutes. I'm hanging up."

"Wait! I want to talk to Jol—"

Beaker ended the call and set the phone on his desk. "I've disabled location services on this phone, and by the time the authorities triangulate the towers the phone pinged during our call, this ordeal will be long over. So . . . not hungry, eh?"

Not in the least. "Why are you tormenting someone who used to be your friend?"

"Patience. It shouldn't be much longer now . . ."

Chapter Eighteen

Rule for success number eighteen:
Learn to cooperate—when it suits you.

Heath bought a burner phone in case Myles had figured out how to duplicate his personal device. With it, he contacted Hunter Edgington as soon as Myles rang off. The former SEAL texted back immediately that they were still forty minutes out. They would leave the airport and drive directly to the West End so they could be in position whenever Heath got his next set of instructions.

Trying to keep his calm and hope that Jolie was safe, he acknowledged them, then headed for his bike.

Karis followed, tears streaming down her face. "Please bring her back safely."

He found it hard to meet the woman's gaze. If he had kept his distance from Jolie, if he had just kept living his gray existence, if he hadn't blithely assumed that the danger to his new wife stemmed from some element of *her* life, none of this would be happening. But no, he'd blazed ahead, claiming Jolie because she made him happy. He'd sought closure on Anna's death because he had told himself he deserved to finally be rid of the albatross of his guilt and start living again. After all, he had to understand where he'd gone wrong in the past so he didn't make the same mistakes twice. Not once had he imagined that yearning would jeopardize Jolie's life.

Now here he was, terrified he would be looking down at an open grave as he tossed earth on top of his wife's casket again.

"I'm going to do everything I can," he vowed.

"I know." Karis threw herself against him, sobbing with all the fear and heartbreak inside her. "I just . . . She's always taken care of everyone, kept our family together. We would have a terrible void without her. I don't know whether to call my mother and brother or . . ."

"You might need them now for comfort. Holding vigil while you wait for answers alone is difficult." That was an understatement. He had waited hours to hear whether Anna had died in the violence. He'd last seen Jolie less than four hours ago and it already felt like a lifetime. "Regardless of what happens, stay close to them. They will help you through anything."

Another lesson Heath had learned the hard way after shutting so many people out of his life.

Karis let him go and nodded. "Thanks. I don't know what's happening or why, but she loves you." She gripped his shoulders. "You're the best thing that ever happened to her."

Heath knew damn well that wasn't true, and if Jolie made it out of this alive, he would do her the favor of leaving her. Being alone was what he deserved. He refused to put her in danger again.

"I've got to go."

"I feel so terrible that I was too wrapped up in my own life this morning to see what was happening with hers." She nodded, tears filling her eyes again. "Please keep me posted."

"Of course."

Then Heath straddled his motorbike, checked the bullets in his SIG, and extracted the keys from his pocket. He zoomed into the late morning breeze, knowing this would be over by nightfall.

He prayed Jolie would still be alive.

When he reached the West End, he parked in a mostly vacant lot. The area had once been industrial, then revitalized as a tourist haven, only to fall on hard times again in the past few years. The remnants of bars and restaurants lingered. A few businesses had survived, making a living off the folks who worked in nearby areas downtown and tourists who wandered off the beaten path after visiting the Sixth Floor Museum at Dealey Plaza. But for the most part, the area was quiet.

Heath glanced at his phone. The first text should come at any moment.

As if on cue, his mobile dinged. The message came from an unfamiliar local number, likely a burner phone.

On the corner of Market and Munger, you will find a small Segway tour company. Inside, tell the receptionist you need to talk to Bill. When the phone rings, answer it. Advise now.

Understood, Heath replied, then texted the update to Hunter via his disposable phone. Once done, he headed toward the corner Myles had advised him to locate.

Inside, he found a pretty young blonde who wore a bright smile that matched her vivid blue T-shirt advertising the tour company. "Can I help you?"

Heath wondered if she had any idea what she'd agreed to be a party to.

"I need to speak with Bill."

Her smile faded, replaced by a blank expression. As hard as she tried to be nonchalant, Heath knew she had zero idea who or what she'd become involved with. He sighed, hating Myles all over again for dragging more innocents into whatever twisted game he played. For the life of him, Heath couldn't figure out the man's motive. What the fuck did he want?

She handed him a package. "Here you are. According to the courier who dropped this off, Bill will contact you shortly."

With a curt nod, Heath thanked her. Now he had ten minutes to wait.

Exiting the building out the back, he looked around cautiously, aware this could be one giant trap and that Myles could easily have hired a sniper to pick him off at any moment.

Wending his way through shadows and staying behind whatever cover he could find, Heath ducked beneath the deep overhang of an abandoned storefront. To shoot him in this secluded area, someone would have to stand directly in front of him. Heath didn't see anyone in the empty lot across the street except a parking attendant with his buds in his ears, bopping to the beat of whatever tune he played from his phone.

Watching for anyone else who looked as if they had murder on their minds, he couldn't help but think about how beautiful the day was, far too blue and perfect for anyone to die.

The phone in his hands rang on schedule. He picked up the call after the first ring.

"Where is she, Myles?"

The man didn't acknowledge his query. "At the corner of Ross and Griffin, you'll find a 7-Eleven. Go inside and locate the men's toilet. Look around. You'll know what to do next."

He didn't like the way this was going down, with Myles holding all the cards. But of course the man had Jolie, so he had everything. "I want to know that my wife is still alive."

"Of course. I wouldn't kill my insurance policy. Say hello," he instructed.

"Heath?"

The sound of her shaking voice drowned him in a surge of relief. She might be afraid, but she was still on this earth, breathing, her heart beating. Heath intended to keep it that way. "Are you all right?"

He knew just how adept the bastard was at torturing to extract information. In fact, he thought of all the methods he'd seen his former partner use on enemy combatants—soldiers and spies who had voluntarily signed up for a covert war, knowing death or disfigurement were likely if caught. Jolie had merely tried to grow a business, get married, live her life . . . For falling in love with him, she could suffer the ultimate price.

"I'm fine. Don't put yourself in danger. Don't—"

"Your wife thinks she can save you. It's a sweet but foolish notion," Myles drawled.

"She doesn't know anything. Leave her alone."

"Really, I expected more from you than the typical response. When has demanding anything like that ever worked?"

Myles was right. He had to stop behaving like a distraught man in love and start playing the game like a spy.

Heath listened to the call with a sharp ear. He heard Jolie's voice in the background. Myles had taken her someplace industrial. The echo was obvious, and there were plenty of abandoned factories downtown. No other extraneous sounds came through, like the airplane he now heard overhead. So Jolie wasn't very close, damn it. But he did hear heavy traffic noise through their connection. He'd bet that put her on the south edge of downtown somewhere, farther away from Love Field, closer to the Mix Master.

The 7-Eleven Myles wanted him to find was a bit on the north edge of downtown.

"I'm on foot. I'll need a bit." Hopefully, stalling would give the Edgington brothers enough time to get here.

Myles sighed with impatience. "Stop treating me like an idiot. You have wheels. Get to the next location. You have fifteen minutes."

Then Beaker hung up. Heath cursed. The accelerated timetable kept everything in Myles's control. Heath's head spun as he glanced at his phone. The Edgington brothers and the rest of the posse would still be fifteen minutes away when he had to arrive at the convenience store.

Bloody hell. He texted Hunter the information about Myles's demands, as well as his observations about the sounds he'd heard during the call. The former SEAL wrote back immediately.

We'll fan out. Go to the mini-mart and play along. We'll search the south edge of the downtown corridor for likely locations as soon as we get there. We're hitting the cars now, so it won't be long.

As much as Heath didn't like that plan, he didn't see another choice.

Jogging back to his motorbike, he traveled the few blocks to the corner Myles had indicated, circling a few times to see if he could catch sight of his former mate or anyone who looked out of place. While he saw some gangbanger and drug-dealing types, most people simply seemed in a hurry to get whatever they needed from this little corner of hell so they could be gone. Heath wished he could do the same. The last thing he wanted to do was walk directly into Myles's trap. He didn't know precisely what the man intended in forcing him to follow these clues, but Beaker had a particular endgame scenario in mind.

Finally seeing nothing of concern in the little mart, Heath parked and meandered inside, casing the interior. He spotted nothing suspicious as he walked the edges of the room around the coolers. The attendants up front looked blankly efficient. The woman working the register on the right had to be at least seventy, five feet tall, and weighed a hundred pounds. The kid working beside her looked gangly and anxious, as if this might be his first job.

With time running out, Heath headed toward the back—and the loo.

His phone buzzed. The crew from Louisiana was getting in position. That made Heath feel a bit better. They were smart and seasoned. If there was a way to save Jolie, they would help him find it.

Heath loitered in the hall outside the toilet for a minute or two. No one approached.

With a bad feeling rolling in his gut, he walked inside and locked the door, then began searching the place. Quickly, he found an envelope with his name taped to the porcelain under the basin.

LEAVE THE TOILET NOW.

With anxiety gripping his gut, Heath shoved the note in his pocket, washed his hands, texted Hunter the latest development, then exited. As soon as he opened the door, Myles stood outside in a heavy coat, despite the warm autumn day. The man looked as if he'd aged fifteen years in the last seven. And he was hiding the barrel of his gun behind the bulk of the coat.

"Hello, old friend." Myles gave him a bland smile. "Let's go."

Chapter Nineteen

Rule for success number nineteen:
Choose your partners wisely.

I'M not going anywhere until I know Jolie is safe," Heath vowed to Myles.

"You can set her free yourself once we arrive at our destination. All you have to do is come with me."

"Don't take me for a fool. You kidnapped her so you could kill her and torment me again." He lunged into Myles's face, snarling. "You decided that I'd done something to earn your hate and you wanted to make me pay. Since the grief and guilt nearly killed me the first time, you thought you would simply do it again and see if that would finish me off."

"I'm hurt that you didn't assign me some more complex and interesting motive. And why would I have killed my own wife and unborn child simply to torment you? You think rather a lot of your importance if you imagine I would do that."

"Then what the fuck is going on?"

"Do you remember the kill list of homegrown terrorists the

Home Secretary floated through the service that summer before Anna and Lucy died?"

Yes, they'd both been on a task force to hunt down combatants who had trained overseas in terror camps and come home to launch attacks on British soil. Her Majesty's government would never admit it, but MI5 agents had been tasked with hunting these people down once they returned to the UK and assassinating them.

"Of course."

"As you'll recall, we split the list. But Lucy and I were trying to get pregnant, so you covered my responsibilities while I spent time with my wife."

"Yes." That had kept him beyond busy, constantly on edge.

"As it happens, I located one of my targets. Or rather, he found me. He said he wanted to explain his beef with the British government and the Western world, so I listened."

"And he converted you to his brand of terror?" The thought horrified Heath all over again.

"Of course not. I have no interest in someone's mission serving another god. But they had cash, and I needed some." He paused, reluctant to speak. "I'd run into a bit of bad luck gambling online."

Heath had wondered back then what was troubling his former partner. He'd simply thought Lucy's desire for a baby had proven more difficult than they had expected. Then, after Myles's wife had conceived, Heath had assumed his friend's stress had to do with her difficult pregnancy. He had never seen any sort of addictive behavior.

"You had a gambling problem?"

Myles nodded. "I've since gotten treatment. It's under control now. I haven't bet on anything in at least five years." He sounded proud of himself.

Heath stared in horror. "So you killed off your wife—and mine—because a terrorist paid you to?"

"It's nothing that simple." Myles shoved the gun in his gut.

"Enough chitchat. Move out. And before you think about trying to take me down here, you should know we're not alone in this convenience store."

Myles had accomplices? Heath couldn't scan the little place again since Myles and a wall blocked his view. But when he had last looked at the store's patrons . . .

"I don't believe you."

"Your folly, then. If I don't return in the next ten minutes, the accomplice I have watching your wife will shoot her. Now give me your gun." He held out his hand expectantly.

Heath had no way of refuting that assertion, and he feared testing it. He looked for some way out. Any way. But Myles had thought everything through. Yes, he could be lying again. But Heath couldn't take the risk of Jolie dying because he'd been stubborn. Better him dead than her.

He reached in and extracted his weapon, giving it over to Myles clandestinely and praying the Edgington brothers could pull magic out of their hat.

"Excellent. My car is over there." He pointed and headed outside. "I'll explain then."

Blinding sun glared overhead. The young guy behind the cash register barely noticed them but the older lady watched with a suspicious frown. Heath didn't expect them to be any help and didn't want to put innocent bystanders in danger. Instead, he allowed Myles to lead him to the vehicle . . . while looking for his opportunity.

Beaker settled him into the passenger's seat of his rental and cuffed his wrist to a handle in the door before settling in the driver's side.

"I'll make this quick. I'm explaining because it involved you and I can see why you would insist on knowing the details and motives." Myles backed out of his parking spot and merged with the traffic on the road, heading south and east. "I haven't told your wife because I'm presuming you'd like to keep her alive."

Which meant that Beaker intended to kill him. Frankly, Heath wasn't surprised.

"I'm listening."

"So . . . my gambling addiction. Before the attack, I owed nearly a hundred thousand pounds. This group of British nationals with foreign training on our kill list were willing to pay me to overlook their names. At first, that was enough. But the pressure became too great. Remember what a prick Evans was about checking every name off?"

Heath remembered Jonathan Evans being a tough director general and demanding that more suspects be purged from the list more quickly before innocent civilians were caught in the crosshairs. While no one had ever taken responsibility for the attack that killed Anna and Lucy, he had wondered if some combatant had known his name was on that list and decided to strike back. But Heath had never found any proof. Other than locating a few underlings—Myles's accomplices, apparently—he'd run into one dead end after another.

"So they had you help them plan an incident for more money?"

"Exactly. I resisted. God, did I. After all, it was the sort of crime I try to prevent from ever happening. I did my best to divert the group of school children wandering through. It was a relief to lose only two, though several were scarred for life. Pity . . ."

Heath could scarcely believe any of the remorseless words coming from Myles's mouth. "If you had been stupid enough to mount up gambling debts and the choice between killing innocents or letting your bookie end you came about, I rather think you should have chosen the latter."

Myles rolled his eyes. "Always the hero. Always doing the 'right thing.' You realize that will get you killed? I wasn't ready to die. I knew that if I could get my gambling problem under control, I could do more to keep the UK safe than anyone who died that day. It all would have gone swimmingly with fairly minimal casualties." He sighed. "But Lucy caught on to the fact that I'd accepted money from these terrorists. She invited Anna to lunch that day to tell your wife that I'd gone rogue and to persuade Anna to plead for your help so she could both leave me and turn me in. What kind of disloyal wife is that? Killing her in our home would raise too many questions, so I decided I'd be far better off suggesting the two women have lunch at a new bistro in the open-air market. Lucy had no idea that I'd caught wind of what she plotted, so she took my suggestion."

"And you killed her for what she knew. Why Anna, then? Why take my wife?"

"Because I'm fairly certain she knew more than she should by that point. I didn't want to give her the opportunity to divulge anything to you. You'll find this odd, but I loved you like a brother, so the last thing I wanted to do was kill you. Ending Lucy was difficult, and it hurt me deeply to lose the baby. But I promised myself that I would find someone again someday. Camille is a far better partner. More understanding. And I did you a favor that day as well. Jolie is your equal. She is a wife worthy of you. Anna . . ." Myles shook his head. "She was a simpering girl. I think you could have been far happier with Jolie. But I digress. I didn't want to have to kill you back then, so I ensured that your wife took whatever she knew to her grave."

"How? You didn't pull the trigger or set off the explosives."

"Kensforth, the greedy bastard, helped me to arrange all that and the cover-up. I intentionally stayed by your side that day and acted appropriately shocked and saddened by our mutual loss so that no suspicion would ever come my way. It worked perfectly, and you later killed all the contractors Kensforth had hired. Thank you, by the way. Those were loose ends we needed to eliminate, and you saved us the trouble." He sent Heath a smug smile. "Then a few months later, I made sure that Kensforth met an unfortunate end.

That should have been everything. You were clearly in the dark about the details, so I stepped back, let you be. I'd hoped that would be the end of it. But your new wife simply had to dig through your past. She poked into your background, and that investigation extended in some part to me. Somehow, she extracted old phone records that tied me to the extremists I was supposed to be eliminating. I had to find out exactly what she might be looking for."

Jolie hadn't looked into his background, not that Heath recalled. Then . . . he remembered that Karis had. Using Jolie's computer.

Myles had always been paranoid about his paperwork on the job. It made sense that he would be doubly paranoid about any cyber trail he left behind.

"How did you even know about those Internet searches?"

"I have little alarms that trigger whenever anyone searches for certain parameters or digs into particular files. Every so often, people stumble into such things, which often forces me to hunt them down and place tracking software on their computers. Sometimes they'll believe they've suffered a computer virus. Or if it's serious, a break-in. If I have to go in person, I often remove an item or two to make it look good. Then I'll watch the user's cyber traffic. If, based on their other searches, it's clear they have no interest in me or anything I've done, I move on. I would have done the same with Jolie but you interrupted me that night I sneaked into Betti before I could complete the software install. Most of what I gleaned from looking at the queries on your wife's computer was that she was quite interested in her company and courting a potential investor. But she was incredibly interested in you. I wanted to scare her away from digging deeper into me by association. When you turned up on the scene, I knew I needed to distract you. You were already paranoid with her safety. In the following days, I could see by watching your interactions through open windows and whatnot that you were smitten with her. Really, you should consider that I did you a favor by eliminating Anna so that you could upgrade your wife . . ."

Heath didn't feel anything but sick. "So you had Dulin shoot at her the other day and miss on purpose, hoping it would keep us busy."

"Quite. I tried to show mercy, Heath. You must know I could have killed her twenty times over if I had wanted to. I even begged you to leave it alone." He sighed, heading through a green light and turning south again. "You chose not to listen, and I know you too well to believe any speech you'd give now to persuade me you'll keep my secret. Your conscience won't let you be anything but a hero, so you'll never stay silent about innocent blood spilling."

Myles was right. "So what do you have planned next?"

"It should be obvious." Myles sounded disappointed that he hadn't yet figured it out.

Heath had—and he wished like hell there was something he could do to stop it. "You're a fucking despicable prick and I hope you pay for everything you've done."

"Perhaps I will someday but it won't be by your hand."

"And Jolie?"

"Your wife is a pragmatist. She'll keep her mouth closed, I think."

He hoped so. She would know that Myles had killed him. Perhaps she was even aware that Beaker had murdered their first wives. For her sake, he prayed she kept that secret.

"Likely so. She doesn't have a violent bone in her body."

"I know how to manipulate her. She won't want to risk her business or her sister. Understand, I'm taking a risk by letting her live. That's my favor to you, because we were best mates. When you see her, convince her to accept my leniency and move on."

Heath would try. But Jolie had always had a mind of her own, just one of the many things he loved about her. "How were you able to kidnap her?"

"You deciding to invest in her business without her knowledge really was a boon. It helped me gain her trust long enough to walk out Betti's door with her. Her mother's terrible history with men gave me an edge, too. All I had to do was prove you were playing her and persuade her that I had more incriminating evidence. She's so insistent that no man take her for a fool."

Myles had figured out Jolie quickly. He had known exactly how to dig under her defenses and gouge her soft spot. It disappointed Heath that after all they'd shared—the closeness, the soul baring, their spontaneous marriage—that she would suspect him of having underhanded motives for wanting to invest in Betti. He'd hoped that she could trust him and believe that he had invested in *her*. But she had never seen any examples of solid, stable men in her life. Jolie liked empirical evidence with which to make decisions, and when it came to men with long-term staying power, she had none.

His former partner had also concluded that she would stand down to protect those she loved—another good guess. Heath wanted her to keep on living, grow Betti, steady Karis, maybe—if they'd been fortunate—raise whatever child they might have conceived together.

From a side street, Myles pulled into the car park of an abandoned factory. It was ghost-town eerie, the quiet. People had once worked here. It had been a bustling environment. Today, the big building was a sprawling lot of emptiness with faded signs pointing employees long gone to a security door. Utter silence.

Myles killed the engine and leapt from the car, darting around to the other side. Slowly, he opened the door and pointed the gun in Heath's face with one hand, while handing him the cuff key with the other. "Unlock yourself and come with me."

Heath did. If Jolie wasn't trapped inside the building with another potential killer waiting for time to run down so he could pull the trigger, Heath would have played dirty and beat the stuffing out of the bastard while he waited for the Edgingtons and their backup to arrive.

But he refused to risk his wife. No matter what she thought of his surprise investment or whether she hated him for accidentally dragging her into this mess, he loved her. He always would. And if fate gave him the chance, he would make certain she knew it before he left her in safety and peace.

"Key, please." Myles held out his palm as soon as Heath had finished removing the cuffs.

After shutting and locking the vehicle, Myles jabbed the gun into Heath's back and prodded him toward the employee entrance. Heath walked, taking one last look around at the sunny day, at the steel marvels of the buildings mankind had erected with time and ingenuity. He hated that, barring a miracle, he wouldn't see what came next in humanity's chapter, that his parents and sister would mourn him and likely feel incomplete for the rest of their lives. Mostly, he wanted to watch Jolie walk to safety so he could die in peace and know he'd finally saved someone he loved.

A movement on the far side of the lot caught his attention. He flicked his gaze in that direction and caught the rustle of a bush grown wild after the factory had been abandoned. The glint of metal hit the sun for an instant before disappearing.

Hunter and his team had managed to figure out the location of the lair and were in place.

To distract Myles, he turned and asked, "What's your endgame?"

"After I'm through with you, I'll watch your widow for a few days to ensure she understands the rules. Then I'll go home and back to work. Camille is due in January, so I'll have that to look forward to. Simple, really."

As he'd expected. Myles had already done his explaining, so the instant Jolie left this warehouse, Heath would be a dead man. Oh, his traitorous mate might enjoy another moment of gloating or sneer that Heath had a moral stick too far up his bum. But then Beaker would pull the trigger. The one silver lining? The Edgington brothers and their cohorts would get Jolie to safety in case Myles had a change of heart and decided to end her, too. They would also make Beaker pay for his sins. Heath wished he could be around to see that.

Myles dug out a key from his pocket. The door squeaked when it opened. The inside was musty. Dust motes played. Dead, dry leaves covered the floor. Nothing here had been touched for at least twenty years. A rusting desk sat empty except for an old telephone. Paper clips were strewn across the surface, nearly buried under inches of dust and grime. An old rack of time cards littered the wall and the floor beside the door to the factory floor. The ancient time clock looked like a relic. Everywhere he looked, windows had been busted out. Parts of the metal roof looked as if they'd been rusted by the elements or had simply blown away.

"Through this door." Myles gave him a shove, then yanked another portal open before pushing him in the back once more, sending him stumbling into the big open space of the factory.

Other than some long-forgotten machinery, he saw nothing inside. The power had been turned off for years, and if it hadn't been for sunlight, the place would be pitch-black. Thankfully, golden rays managed to reach the center of the space and cast a little glow on a cascade of dark curls brushing a woman's shoulders and drifting down to brush the back of the chair. Jolie. Thank god she was still alive. She was the only thing that mattered now.

She'd been cuffed to a lone metal desk chair in the middle of the room. A pang cramped his chest and rage fueled his blood when he saw his wife restrained, terrorized, and in danger. What he didn't see was another accomplice who would have killed Jolie, as Myles had threatened. Fuck.

"Jolie!" he called out and ran for her.

Myles pulled him back, pointing a gun at her head. "You have three minutes. Use them wisely."

At the sound of his voice, his wife craned around to look at him, but he ran to her side and skidded to a stop in front of her, taking her face in his hands. She looked no worse for the wear. A little smudge of mascara where she might have cried. But no bruises or cuts, no signs that Myles had used blunt force on her.

"Heath! You shouldn't be here. How did he catch you?"

"He's exchanging his life for yours," Myles barged in. "He's going to give you some instructions. I suggest you follow them or you and your loved ones will meet a similar fate."

Jolie searched Heath's face for the truth. Heath didn't hide from her. He merely nodded, so bloody sad that he wouldn't spend any more days or nights with this fascinating woman, see how they could have raised children or balanced their lives and grown old together.

"You can't do that! You can't surrender to him and let—" She shook her head, unwilling to finish that sentence.

He bent and softly kissed her lips. "It's done. I'm at peace because you'll be safe. But you have to follow my instructions to ensure that." If Myles didn't uphold his end of the bargain, Heath would fight him to the death. Myles might have a weapon but Heath had superior hand-to-hand combat skills—and they both knew it. "Once you leave here, keep walking. Don't stop until you've reached safety. Do you understand? Don't turn around or come back or try to be heroic. I've lived hard and well, and I leave knowing I kept the person I love most safe."

Her lip trembled and the stoic woman who almost never cried looked on the verge of tears. "I can't . . . I don't want to live without you. I love you."

"Then respect my last wishes." He brushed another kiss across her lips, aching to hold on to this sweetness for eternity. "Once you're safe and back at Betti, forget all this. Don't seek revenge. Don't tell anyone about Myles or whatever you may know about his past misdeeds. All you know is that your husband skipped out on you and hasn't come back." Because he had little doubt Myles would dispose of his body in some thorough manner to ensure no one ever found it.

"Then he's getting away with everything he's ever done. The murders, the violence."

"But he's sparing you. That's all I want. Take the money I gave you for Betti and accomplish great things. Do that for me. You've always dreamed big. Now soar high."

The tears that welled in her eyes spilled onto her cheeks. "I can't lose you. I won't just give you up and walk away."

"Then we'll die together, and that will be the biggest regret of my life. I already carry such terrible guilt for allowing Anna to die when she trusted me to keep her safe. Please don't add to my sorrow. Grant me this last wish."

Jolie looked speechless for once in her life. "Hold me."

Heath looked to Myles with a raised brow. "Just once."

The man sighed and trudged in their direction. "I'm so glad Camille isn't this emotional." But he uncuffed Jolie, still keeping the gun trained on her, inches from her temple.

Briefly, Heath thought about jumping the man and wresting the gun from him. He stood a fighting chance of taking the weapon from Myles. But he also would most likely pull the trigger first and kill Jolie instantly.

Heath backed up a step, waiting patiently until Jolie was free. Once Myles had pocketed the key and wrenched the cuffs off her wrists, she stood on shaky legs. Heath charged directly for her, then scooped her up in his arms, holding her tight and lifting her from the ground. He slanted his mouth across her soft lips, delving deep. Their last kiss. There wouldn't be another. His three minutes were up and, given his former partner's loud sigh, Myles's patience was at an end.

He tasted her desperation, her love, her sorrow and devotion, her confusion, and her wish that she could stop time and figure out some way to free them both. Heath shared her sentiment but anything that risked her was a nonstarter for him. So now he had to be strong and send her to safety, watch her leave, then face his end. Even if the

Edgington posse was right outside the door, they probably wouldn't be able to save him. Even if Heath fought back, Myles wouldn't tarry.

Odd to think that in less than two minutes Jolie would be a widow.

With another taste of her lips and one last squeeze of her body against his, he set her down and eased back, putting space between them. "Go. Live well. Be happy. Stay safe. For me."

She reached out for him, but Heath couldn't give her what she wanted so he took another step back and looked at Myles. "Let her go. It's time."

Chapter Twenty

Rule for success number twenty:
Never be afraid to commit when the circumstance is right.

JOLIE couldn't stop looking back at Heath through her watery tears for another last glance. She'd found love. She finally knew what it meant to be accepted, adored, understood. Whatever the reason Heath had chosen to invest in Betti without telling her, it hadn't been to undermine her. Maybe he had wanted to surprise her. Maybe he had sought to help her in a way that wouldn't leave her feeling guilty or beholden. Being hung up on his reason seemed ridiculous now. He'd done it for her. And she regretted like hell that she hadn't simply believed in him. He wasn't like anyone her mother had ever shacked up with. Heath had only ever tried to lift her up.

The consequences for allowing her past to barge in and her hang-ups to come between them would probably be fatal.

"Go on." Myles prodded her in the back with his gun.

After he'd cuffed Heath to a giant piece of machinery bolted into the concrete floor, the bastard had urged her toward the door. She stumbled, stalling for time, trying to find some way to save the man who had sacrificed everything for her, the husband who would bury her heart with him.

How crushing that it had taken this terrible tragedy to finally crack her cynical shell.

If she survived this day, she intended to open herself up to new people and new experiences. She would talk to her mother about the scars the woman's romances had left on her childhood, the respect it had killed . . . and the new understanding she had about how love could make a person do crazy things. They would heal. She would tell her father to leave her alone once and for all. She would guide Karis as much as the headstrong girl needed, but acknowledge that her sister had a pretty good head on her shoulders. Jolie would run Betti with every ounce of her passion and scale to the business heights she'd always dreamed. She would eventually learn to laugh again, savor life. She would hope that she and Heath had created life. Above all, she would live.

But she would rather do all that with Heath by her side. And she would never forget him or simply give up without doing *something* to save him now.

With one last look over her shoulder, her husband lifted his hand in a final good-bye. Jolie blew him a kiss and tried to stay strong. She didn't have time to wallow in grief. She had to get clever and save him.

Then Myles pushed her into the ante office, around the corner, out of Heath's sight.

She feared she would never see him again.

"Stop pushing me."

"Move faster. Knowing your husband, he didn't walk into this slaughterhouse without some backup plan. I'd like to finish my part quickly and be gone."

In other words, kill Heath.

"I can persuade him not to tell anyone about what happened with Lucy and Anna and—"

"No. I'm afraid there's a bit more to it than that. Oh, he might stay silent for a time, long enough to secure you and your loved ones. But he believes too much in God, country, and doing the right thing. He would come after me someday—probably soon. It's better if our battle to the finish ends in one tiny bang rather than an epic war that drags our remaining loved ones into the fray. I simply want to bury my past, return to my job, my wife, and the business of forgetting all the rest. Now, out you go."

He held open the door to the parking lot of the big factory and gave her another nudge. Jolie grabbed the frame so he couldn't close the door.

"Let go or I'll be forced to shoot you. Think of how disappointed he'll be to see that his sacrifice was so wasted. He loves you. Of that I'm sure. Pity. You two probably made a wonderful couple." He shrugged dismissively. "I'll give you until the count of three to take your hands off the door and let him die in peace."

Jolie swallowed. Her thoughts raced. She wanted to honor Heath and his wishes . . . but she refused to walk away while he died. If she perished trying to save him, then she would leave this earth in peace and meet him on the other side with an apology and a heart full of love.

Myles glowered. "One . . . two . . ."

"I'm going." Jolie did her best to sound dejected. She made a show of slowly releasing the doorframe, of fighting her tears, and bowed her head with slumped shoulders—a pose of defeat.

"It's better this way," Myles assured.

Jolie violently disagreed but waited for the right moment. As he reached for the rusty door handle, she readied herself to strike.

Then a big boom followed by a spewing plume of fire burst across the lot, on the far side of the roof. The ground shook, making her stumble back. Myles jerked around with a curse, obviously trying to figure out what the hell was happening.

She used that moment to ram her knee into Beaker's balls as hard as she could. Down to his knees he dropped, clutching his genitals. He looked pale and sick, instantly sweaty. But when she went to kick him again, he grabbed her ankle in a surprisingly harsh grip. Then he pointed the gun in her face with a snarl of evil that had her wanting to back up.

"Stupid, stupid bitch! Why are people always too stubborn to accept my mercy?"

She shoved at his elbow, disrupting his aim, then grabbed him by the hair and pounded his head into the door. "Fuck your mercy."

He wrenched free and snarled up at her, eyes glowing with hate, teeth bared. "I will make you pay, bitch."

Before he could pounce, shots rang out in the distance. Bullets pinged off the metal structure and concrete floor inches from Myles's face. He let her go and rolled away.

Jolie jerked and dived inside for cover. The shots had come from behind her. Instinctively, she turned, wondering who was shooting and whose side they were on. Maybe it was Heath's backup Beaker had mentioned.

"I will come back for you," he vowed. "I'll end your life and I'll make it hurt."

Then he shoved her outside again, slammed the door between them, and locked it. On the far side of the warehouse, the flames still shot high. Smoke spewed up. The bullets behind her had stopped completely.

She darted toward the fire. Maybe the explosion had blown a hole in the wall so she could get inside. Something. She had to find a way inside and help Heath. Impossible to dial 911 without a phone. It would take them too long to arrive anyway.

Before she rounded the corner of the warehouse, a man she'd never met melted out of the shadows. "I'm Tyler Murphy. Your husband called my buddies to get him out of a tight spot. There are three of us. Well, four, including that sniper asshole, One-Mile. He came along at the last minute. We've all got a position around the exterior perimeter and—"

"We have maybe thirty seconds before Myles kills Heath."

"Tell me anything about the inside of this place that might help."

"Heath is cuffed to some machinery in the middle of the factory floor. He's a sitting duck. If someone can aim a round through one of the broken windows . . ."

"Yeah, I must be out of practice," he grimaced, rubbing the back of his neck. "Three little boys will eat up your time at the shooting range. I'm glad I didn't hit you but pissed as hell I didn't whack that Brit. Sorry." He pulled out a radio. "Can anyone get a view inside one of the windows?"

"Roger that. Looking now," a voice crackled over the radio.

"Ten-four, Logan."

Jolie appreciated that they meant to do something but she feared it wouldn't be fast enough. She looked around—for a nearby window to jump in, a way to pick the lock on the door.

Then she caught sight of someone hauling ass in a big black truck toward them. He screeched to a stop, window down. "I just found out what was going down and raced over here. What's the sitch?"

Stone. Thank goodness. "I think I know what to do. Please trust me. Can I have your truck?"

The former ex-con shifted into Park and scooted into the passenger's seat. "All yours."

Jolie slid behind the wheel. "I hope you're not too attached to this vehicle. You might want to get out. This will be dangerous."

Stone put on his seat belt and shrugged. "I'm good."

She didn't acknowledge him. Her sole focus was on Heath. "Then hold on."

Heart thumping wildly, she stomped on the gas. The truck leapt into action, burning rubber before surging forward. Jolie drove around the side of the building, where the wall was hopefully compromised by fire. She had to hope that she remembered the layout of the factory and that she wasn't too late. But she couldn't think of another way to save him.

As soon as she found the fiery side of the warehouse, she spotted a wall crumbling under the heat and gunned the vehicle toward it.

A crunch of metal and a jolt told her they'd made impact. A sheet of metal blocked her view for a terrifying second. Hoping she'd made the right call, she fought the urge to close her eyes and wait for the danger to pass. Instead, she forced herself to stay in the moment, relieved when the steel siding fell away and she could see out the windshield again.

Twenty feet in front of her she spotted Myles bearing down on Heath, gun in hand, pointing the weapon directly at her husband's head.

Her heart stopped—but she didn't. Jolie laid on the horn and the gas at once, doing her best to startle or distract the rogue agent. But he didn't flinch.

In seconds, he would have to choose between ending Heath or saving himself.

She drove closer and closer, fearing she would be too late. Her only consolation would be that she would end Myles, too. And she would have avenged the man she loved.

He made his choice, stood his ground. In the final second, he said something to Heath, then tightened his finger on the trigger.

Jolie heard the retort of a gun reverberate through the air. Her throat tightened. She watched Heath in horror, holding her breath until the moment she had to watch his blood splatter before he crumpled to the ground, gone to her forever.

Instead, Myles collapsed in a heap, the gun falling from his lifeless hand.

Her husband was still standing, tall and very much alive.

Stomping on the brakes, Jolie threw the car in Park and leapt out of the vehicle, rushing over to Myles. Stone and Tyler were right behind her, as was another man with dark hair and intense blue eyes taking in the scene as he vaulted through a window. Seconds later, another man with a chiseled face, dark aviators, and a high-powered scoped rifle in his hands dashed through the hole in the side of the building.

"Stop!" they all shouted at once to her.

"Love, no!" Heath added his growl to the mix.

Jolie wasn't listening to any of them. She had to know if Myles was dead.

She had to know if the threat was over.

When she reached the traitorous spy, she fell to her knees and looked into his sightless eyes. Blood pooled from under his head. Someone had planted a bullet right between his eyes with military precision.

Myles Beaker would never hurt anyone again. She finally exhaled. Then sent the rest of the crowd a shaky nod.

The stranger carrying the rifle cocked his head and studied Myles's body with a clinical gaze. "Nailed him right where I wanted to on the first shot. Damn, that makes me happy." He moved his big combat boot out of the way just before the pool of blood spread under his feet. "God, I love hollow-point rounds. Pinprick at the front. Gaping hole at the back. Perfect for taking out assholes."

Who was this guy?

"Shut up, Pierce." The blue-eyed man gritted his teeth.

"Don't be an asshole, Logan. And never call me Pierce again," he growled in return.

Jolie barely listened to their squabbling. With a sob, she reached into Myles's pockets, frantically searching for the handcuff key. She had to get Heath free, feel his arms around her now, see for herself that he was all right. When she finally extracted it with shaking fingers, she jumped to her feet and closed the distance between them.

Jolie approached, her eyes fastened on her husband. He watched her in return, gratitude and love all over his face.

She still shook with the adrenaline churning through her blood as she fumbled with the little key. Finally, she managed to shove it in the hole, turn it, and wrench him free.

Instantly, Heath took her into his arms and pressed her close, burying his face in her neck and breathing her in. "You saved me."

"You're alive." Jolie trembled all over.

Never had she loved anyone more. Until him, she had never taken chances, never believed in anything she couldn't accomplish by herself, never known what it was to be half of a solid unit that would stand forever.

Now, knowing they had a future together, she could finally really live.

"Love . . . You didn't have to risk yourself to—"

"Yes, I did. You sacrificed yourself to save me. How could I do less for you?" She peppered his jaw with kisses. "Now we'll have the chance to spend our lives together and—"

"I almost got you killed. I couldn't have lived with myself if I'd been your undoing." He held her tighter—then abruptly let her go. "I'm not worthy."

Jolie's heart plummeted to her feet. She stared at him, blinked, tried to read between the lines. "Not worthy? You are the best man. Everything to me . . ."

"I can't live in a world where you don't exist, and I only know one way to make sure you're safe from my past."

What was he saying, that he intended to leave her for her own good? "I need you beside me."

He shook his head, his dark eyes filling with moisture. "You nearly died because of my blind foolishness. I never imagined Myles would have been the one—"

"Who in their right mind would?" she argued, reaching for his hands and refusing to let go. "You believed he was your friend. But you saved me. You sacrificed for me. I understand now that you gave your life's savings to me because you believe in me."

Heath nodded. "Of course. I know you'll achieve great things. You may not like the method I chose, and I'm sorry for that. But I never did it to deceive you, simply to provide what you needed and deserved in a way that allowed you free rein."

His words touched her so deeply. Never had a man been more perfect for her. Never would she find another one like him. Never would she love again.

Even if he left a million times over for her "own good," she would hunt him down and bring him back.

"I didn't understand at first. I spent so much time trying not to be duped and used by men, like my mother. I couldn't believe that anyone would really want to invest in me simply because they thought I could achieve good things. You're the first one. The only one."

"I'll always believe in you." He looked as if he wanted to touch her so badly but didn't allow himself.

Jolie wasn't having any of that. "Then believe in us. Because I believe in you, too. I believe in how good and strong and just you are. I believe you're the other half of my soul. And if you leave, Myles will have won after all. You don't want to bury me, live in a world without me? I don't want to lose you, live my life without the perfect man for me by my side." Tears filled her eyes and spilled down her cheeks as she pressed closer to him, willing him to understand. "Stay."

Heath didn't say anything for a terrible, timeless moment. He searched her face, his thoughts clearly racing.

Finally, someone else cleared his throat and broke into the conversation. Tyler. "Dude, do it. Just say yes. Take it from someone who tried to deny how much he loved his wife for way too long. That walking-away-to-be-the-better-man shit never works out. You'll wind up with her again and be so damn over the moon that you decided to give forever another chance. Seriously." Tyler shrugged. "C'mon. Kiss and make up."

The other men laughed, except One-Mile, who rolled his eyes and sighed. "You're all pussy whipped."

No one listened to him.

Hope and wonder spread across Heath's face. "You forgive me? You really want me to stay?"

"Of course!" She sent him a saucy stare. "You said you liked a challenge. Here I am."

A grin finally cut through his despair and he eased closer. "Yes, living with you will be, I'm certain. I wouldn't want it any other way."

"Well, I would never want to bore you," she drawled.

"You never could, Jolie Powell. I love you."

"I love you, too. Now will you kiss me so we can live happily ever after?" she sniffled through her tears.

He leaned in and put his arms around her, holding on tighter than ever. "I'd like nothing more . . ."

Epilogue

December

CUTTER Bryant stepped through the wrought iron door and into bedlam. Voices and laughter resounded just over the din of holiday music in the massive foyer of what could only be called a mansion. Polished travertine gleamed, blending perfectly with the rich cream plaster walls. The soft color highlighted the intricate crown molding that rimmed the ceiling and every doorway in sight. A festive garland wrapped the soaring columns and elaborate handrails up both sides of the double staircase in fresh pine, scenting the room. Twinkling white lights and big red bows added to the holiday cheer. An enormous chandelier illuminated every corner with a warm glow, centered above a Christmas tree that had to be twenty feet tall.

Holy shit. How much did a place like this cost?

You're a long way from the double-wide . . .

Callie Mackenzie scurried up to him, wearing a stunning red dress, killer black heels, and a welcoming smile. "Hi, Cutter. Glad you could come to the party. Merry Christmas!"

He smoothed a palm down his well-worn jeans, feeling distinctly underdressed. "Merry Christmas to you, too, Mrs. Mackenzie. The sign on the door said to come in . . ."

"Totally. And please, call me Callie." She paused to look around him. "Where's your plus one?"

"She couldn't make it," he managed to say with a smile.

The truth still felt like a hot poker in his chest.

"Sorry to hear that, but I guess that just means more eggnog for the rest of us." She winked. "Come join the party. The caterers set up the food in the dining room but we're all hanging around the kitchen."

"Thanks. This is for you." He handed her a bottle of merlot. God, the woman probably had a cellar full of expensive vino. He knew shit about wine and hoped she'd find this more palatable than a cross between Boone's Farm and Drano.

She took it, looking genuinely touched. "Thank you. You didn't have to bring me anything. I just wanted your company."

So Sean had said when he'd texted the invite. Cutter still couldn't figure out exactly why they had asked him to join their party, but he followed Callie down their airy, window-lined hallway, past a formal living room with a baby grand, a stunning office with an imposing mahogany desk and towering bookshelves filled with hardbound tomes, then finally a formal dining room laden with food and another chandelier so dazzling it looked as if it belonged in the middle of a Neiman Marcus flagship store.

The voices grew louder. Over the murmur of conversation, Cutter picked out the teasing note of Logan Edgington telling his brother to go fuck himself. Hunter gave a hearty laugh. A moment later, he heard Lily Sutter's polite, high-pitched thanks for a fresh bottle of water. Mitchell Thorpe told the girl she was welcome. He had a smile in his voice when he called her Sweet Pea.

They rounded the corner, and Cutter paused in the wide arch of the entry. Thank goodness the kitchen was massive. There had to be thirty people in here, drinks in hand. Happiness brimmed. Cutter spotted Jolie, who stood beside Heath, holding his hand. Karis relayed something that made them all smile.

"Drink?" Callie asked, playing the good hostess.

"I'll take a beer, if you've got one."

She pranced past a wall of tall white cabinets, to a floor-to-ceiling Sub-Zero refrigerator, and pulled open the door. "Stella, Blue Moon, Heineken, Shiner Bock, Coors, Bud, Miller Lite, Corona . . ."

"Whatever's easiest to grab. I'm not picky."

When she turned back, she popped off the cap and planted an ice-cold Stella in his hand. "Glass?"

He shook his head. "I'm good. Thanks."

"No, thank you. You helped Heath keep safe the woman who's like a sister to me, so if I can do anything to make you happy or comfortable, just let me know."

Was she really lauding him for getting whacked unconscious in the bathroom at Betti? "I was just doing my job. I wish I'd done it better."

"Without you, Jolie and Karis might not be here today. You're brave. The Edgington brothers say you can be damn funny. And my husband thinks the world of you. That makes you as good as family in my book." Callie hugged him.

Slowly, he embraced the woman. Two minutes ago he'd been feeling deeply out of place. With a few words, she'd made him one of the gang. Usually he preferred to be alone. Now, he liked the crowd, was warming to the sense of belonging.

"You're very gracious. The Edgington brothers are not only bosses but friends. And I owe your husband a debt of gratitude for giving me a chance."

She smiled. "Mingle. Eat, drink, and be merry. If you, um . . . ever want to talk about what happened with your 'plus one,' I'm a willing ear. I might even know a thing or two about complicated relationships."

Bless her, but Cutter couldn't think of anything he wanted to talk about less than the clusterfuck of his love life.

Before he could form a gentle excuse, Mitchell Thorpe sidled up and planted a kiss on his submissive's temple, then reached out to shake his hand. "Cutter, good to see you."

"You, too. Thanks for the invite, man."

"Our pleasure. Let me introduce you to anyone you haven't met."

That would take a while. He didn't know most of the room.

Beer in hand, Thorpe led him over to a stunning redhead.

"Hi. I'm Morgan Cole." Her blue eyes sparkled as she looked across the room on tiptoes. "I belong to the big, bad Cajun, Jack."

Cutter had met the man once or twice and agreed with his wife's assessment. "And you live in Lafayette?"

"Yeah. I think you're only a couple of miles from us." She gave him a big smile. "Hey, if you like kids, I'm always looking for a qualified babysitter. Our son, Brice, is an adorable terror who will grow up to be just like his father. And our daughter—"

"Lacey is a lovely baby with her mama's hair," Thorpe cut in.

"And her daddy's temper." Morgan laughed. "But she's precious."

"Absolutely." Thorpe gave her a fond grin.

Cutter had never pictured the dungeon owner as the type who liked kids, but he guessed that having a son could have changed the man's outlook.

"I'm afraid I know more about handguns than kids, ma'am," he told Morgan.

"Oh, god. Ma'am is my mother. I'm not old enough for that. Call me Morgan or I'll have my husband call you something hideous in French. But it will sound beautiful. Don't worry."

Cutter couldn't help but laugh. Maybe coming here really had been a good idea. Beat the shit out of being alone and wishing he hadn't fucked everything up.

Just then, Jack Cole sidled up and shook his hand. "Hey there. Good to see you."

"You, too."

"How did a smart man like you end up working for my dumbass competitors?" Jack teased.

Cutter had to smile. "They were smart enough to hire me first."

Everyone laughed.

"Touché," Jack shot back. "If you ever change your mind—"

"We've got him under contract, asshole," Hunter Edgington butted in, holding his wife's hand. "You're a day late and a dollar short."

"I'm sure you're doing just fine without me," Cutter drawled to Jack.

"Well, there seems to be enough business to go around."

"And then some. Not sure if that's a good thing . . ." Hunter shook his head, then turned to Cutter. "I don't think you've officially met my other half. Kata, this is Cutter Bryant."

"I've heard a lot about you. Nice to finally meet you," the gorgeous Latina with curves for days said.

"You, too."

"Hey, we're having a New Year's party at our house, and you're officially invited."

"Are you going to suggest I babysit, too?" he poked at Morgan.

"Hell no. Despite being a baby, I can already tell that our son, Phoenix, is going to be a man's man. Between his father and his uncles, he doesn't need more male influence. Besides, I'm going to do what Callie did for this party and hire a couple of babysitters. It's great having the kids upstairs so we can pop up and check on them while enjoying the evening."

Cutter figured spending New Year's with this crowd would suck way less than spending it alone with his regrets. Besides, this bunch made him smile for the first time in weeks. "I'd love to."

"Great. I'll have Hunter give you the details." Kata turned to Jack. "And you're bringing that awesome gumbo, right? Please . . ."

"Happy to." Jack nodded her way. "Morgan's brother Brandon, his wife Emberlin, and their beautiful bundle of joy who is probably being born right about"—he glanced at his watch—"now will be visiting from Houston, so they'll probably be with us. Is that all right?"

"The more the merrier!" Kata assured.

"Cutter!" A hand slapped his back, and he turned to see Hunter's brother, Logan.

"Hey." A new smile stretched across Cutter's face.

"You doing all right?" The man looked concerned.

Tonight, Cutter wanted to forget everything weighing him down. Resisting the urge to rub at his neck, he nodded Logan's way. Why the fuck had he gotten drunk last week and spilled his shit? "Fine."

"You're a terrible liar," Logan said just loud enough for Cutter to hear. "See that pretty redhead over there?" He motioned to a petite beauty with eyes only for her husband. "I pined for that one for an eternity before I got smart enough to marry her. Maybe you should do the same."

It would be a cold day in hell.

Logan's wife joined them. "Hi. You must be Cutter. Tara Edgington."

"Happy to meet you." He bit back the urge to call her ma'am. He doubted she would like it any better than Morgan, but it was hard to cast off his Texas upbringing.

"Did you check on the twins?" Logan asked his wife.

"Mandy is asleep. Macy, predictably, is causing trouble." She shook her head ruefully. "She's trying to keep up with Luc and Alyssa's little one."

"Those two are going to be running buddies, aren't they?" Logan shook his head as if that possibility was something to fear.

A drop-dead gorgeous blonde in wicked heels and a dress designed for seduction strolled up with a grin. "I'll just apologize now. Chloe was born a troublemaker, and it's bound to rub off."

"I blame you," teased a man with inky hair and laughing dark eyes who wrapped his arm around the blonde.

Cutter frowned. The guy looked familiar, but he couldn't place the man.

Thorpe jumped in. "Do you know Luc and Alyssa Traverson?"

"I don't believe I do." Cutter held out his hand at Luc. "But I recognize you. You're a famous chef, right?"

"TV strikes again." He laughed. "Do you cook?"

A smile cracked Cutter's face. "Not a lick."

Luc laughed. "You work for Hunter and Logan, right?"

"I do." Cutter sipped his beer.

"Poor bastard," Alyssa jumped in with an affectionate grin. "And don't feel bad about your lack of culinary expertise. Compared to Luc, I can barely boil water. But it's all right; he likes to feed everyone. In fact, he made some of the desserts for tonight."

"Everything I've seen you cook on TV is amazing, so I'll look forward to that."

"I know Callie is." Thorpe grinned and turned him back toward the rest of the revelry. "That woman loves her sweets."

"I'm looking forward to something else sweet, sugar," Cutter heard Luc mutter softly to his wife.

A glance over his shoulder revealed Alyssa stepping up to kiss her husband with a passion he envied.

"You've met Kimber?" Thorpe asked as he plucked up a plump shrimp and dipped it in the cocktail sauce.

Cutter followed suit and nodded at his bosses' younger sister. "A few times, yes. How are you?"

"Great. Good to see you again." The lanky knockout with auburn hair smiled. As imposing as her brothers could be, Kimber was all easy-breezy welcome.

The same couldn't be said about her husband.

"Deke." The man held out his hand but his stare warned Cutter not to visually linger on his wife.

"Don't be such a caveman." Kimber rolled her eyes. "He's not going to jump on me in the next two seconds."

"He might, kitten." Deke shrugged. "I want to."

"You always want to." She shook her head with a smirk.

Deke winked. "Damn straight.

She tried not to show that his possessiveness amused her. "The kids okay upstairs?"

"Cal, Seth, and Chase are all in the same room. I'm thinking we'll be lucky if the house is still standing by the end of the night." Deke winced.

"You think it's bad now? Wait until puberty." Kimber pointed out. "How's Sierra?"

The smile that scrawled across Deke's face was almost a little love-drunk. "Our girl is pretty as usual. She was getting sleepy and probably wanting kisses from mommy."

"On it," Kimber vowed. "Nice to see you, Cutter." She waved as she turned to leave the kitchen.

Sean Mackenzie passed her as he sauntered into the room and made a beeline for Thorpe. "The sitters are putting all the infants to bed. Callie and I just tucked Ash into his crib, if you want to give him a goodnight kiss."

"Wouldn't miss the opportunity to tuck our little man into bed. Would you finish introducing Cutter to everyone?" Thorpe filled Sean in on the folks he'd already met. "Back soon."

After the dungeon owner hustled out of the kitchen, Sean led Cutter over to a pair of urbane Hispanic guys who looked so much alike, they had to be brothers. Between them stood a luscious blonde beauty. They both held one of her hands and hovered protectively.

"How can you possibly think the Saints are going to be in the Super Bowl this year?" The elder brother chided a big blond hulk of a man with a brawny arm wrapped around a pretty brunette.

"Because they're better than the fucking Rams." The beefy guy scoffed back.

"And I think the Cowboys will beat them all," Sean cut in.

"In your dreams." The younger suave-suited brother rolled his eyes.

The women just looked at one another, obviously determined to get off the sports talk and onto something more interesting.

"You told me parenting wasn't easy. I thought it would be so much simpler with three of us." The blonde shook her head ruefully.

"Ha! I'll see your infant girl and raise you three rambunctious boys under the age of four." The brunette anchored a hand on her hip and grinned back. "Seth was already a handful. Chase upped the chaos times twenty. But when Blake was born a few months back? I gave up on anything that looked like peace and quiet forever. If I get twenty minutes a week in my spa tub, I call that a win."

The attractive blonde winced. "Never mind coffee next week. How about a drink?"

Their men all erupted with laughter.

"This is Cutter Bryant," Sean said to the group, then turned to him. "Meet the Santiagos. Javier and Xander own a defense contracting company. This is their lovely wife, London."

"Great to put a face with a name." Cutter eagerly shook their hands. "You lent Hunter and Logan your plane so they could reach Jolie in time to save her. I can't thank you enough. If it hadn't been for you guys . . ."

Sean smiled. "They've lent more than one of us lovesick saps their jet so we can bring back our woman in one piece. If not for them, I don't know if I'd have found Callie again. And I'd be a lost man."

His wife joined him then and pressed a kiss to his lips before bumping shoulders with the elder Santiago brother. "We're all grateful, guys. But at the time Sean and Thorpe hunted me down, I was cursing your names."

"Just repaying you for all the times you stuck your tongue out at everyone, brat," Xander teased.

She repeated the gesture with a sassy smile.

They laughed, then Sean added, "The sitters are settling Dulce into her playpen if you want to join them."

"Thanks," London murmured. "Cutter, if you're willing to talk about anything but football, I hope we can chat again after I tuck my daughter in."

"We'll come, too, belleza." Xander followed with a hand at the small of her back.

"Merry Christmas." Javier nodded his way.

"Same to you." Cutter watched them leave, both men touching their curvaceous wife again. He marveled at them, just as he did Callie, Sean, and Thorpe. Making love work with two people was hard enough. He couldn't imagine how difficult it would be to get three people on the same page.

Sean directed Cutter to the other couple nearby. "Tyler and Delaney Murphy. If you're looking for trouble, he's the guy you want."

"Did Luc tell you to say that?" The blond hulk narrowed his eyes.

"No." Sean's face danced with mirth. "Lys did."

That made Delaney laugh. "Guess she hasn't forgiven you for all your 'cockzilla' antics."

Cutter, who had just taken another sip of his designer beer, nearly spit it out. "Cockzilla?"

Tyler actually looked a little uncomfortable. "I might have, um . . . gotten around a little before Del and I married." He wrapped his arm around his wife and brought her close. "Lucky for me, all it takes is the love of an amazing woman to change everything."

Cutter had once thought the same thing. But it hadn't worked that way for him.

Delaney looked almost smug. "I'd say you're damn lucky."

Tyler kissed her soundly. "You got that right."

When he dove into his wife's kiss for seconds, Sean elbowed them. "Hey, no conceiving baby number four on my kitchen floor."

They broke apart, and Delaney blushed. "On that note, I'll go kiss Blake."

"I'll try to calm Seth and Chase down," Tyler offered. "Stop them from huffing and puffing and blowing the house down."

"What are you going to sing them tonight, daddy?" She shot her husband a fond smile.

"I'm taking requests . . ."

As they left the room, Sean directed Cutter to a familiar foursome. He shook Joaquin Muñoz's hand. The former NSA agent was on the quiet side, but more than fair and damn fine to work for. His ballerina bride, Bailey, flashed her blue eyes and a welcoming expression.

"Good to see you." Cutter nodded their way.

"You, too, man. Nice to get in a few words out of the office." Joaquin clapped him on the shoulder.

"Cutter," the eldest Edgington greeted.

He turned to Caleb with a respectful nod. "Colonel. How are you and your lovely wife?"

"Carlotta and I just came back from a South Pacific cruise. I'm liking this retirement gig."

"We had a lovely time," Joaquin's mother added. "I have never seen water so blue. It was the honeymoon we could not have when Caleb was working."

"That sounds fantastic." Cutter would love to see the world with someone he adored someday but . . . Yeah, not going to happen, and he was sounding like a weeping pansy, lamenting his loneliness, blah, blah, blah.

She's gone. Move on, dumbass.

"You enjoying working for our sons?" Caleb gave him a lopsided grin, clearly knowing he asked a loaded question.

Cutter glanced at Joaquin, then turned back to the colonel. "I am."

Caleb barked out a laugh. "Good P.C. answer. How about the truth?"

"If I had to guess . . ." Joaquin drawled. "None of us are you, and he'd really been looking forward to learning from your experience. Is that about right?"

Cutter had to laugh. "Yep. No offense."

"None taken," Joaquin assured.

Sean led Cutter away. With relief, he glanced at the cluster of familiar faces sitting at the breakfast nook table. "I think I've got it from here. That's a lot of people to meet in one night. My introverted soul might have to crawl in a corner for a decade before I recover."

Sean laughed. "The shy thing won't last long in this crowd. And that's not even everyone we invited. Gia and Jason Denning are at a holiday party with her family across town tonight. Decker McConnell called for a rain check since his wife, Rachel, has the flu. Jesse McCall took his bride, Bristol, with him on his farewell tour. I think they're in Mexico City tonight. Tough gig, huh?"

Now he was impressed. "Wow, McCall is a mega star."

"He's also Kimber's former fiancé. Deke wouldn't mind if someone tied a boulder around the guy's neck and dropped him in the ocean, but everyone else says the singer has changed and his new wife is a doll." Sean shrugged. "If there's one thing we all believe in, it's second chances."

Meaning no one was going to hold against him the fact that he'd gotten his skull bashed in while peeing. But Cutter was all too aware that in their business, mistakes cost lives. If he had a do-over on that day, he'd gladly take it. But talking about that debacle was pointless, so he nodded.

"All right, then. I'll leave you to it." Sean gave him a nod.

"Thanks for the introductions. I'll meander to the corner. I know all the folks over there." He pointed to Jolie, Heath, and the folks clustered around the table.

"Need a fresh beer?"

Plenty left in this bottle, and he'd driven himself tonight. Cutter shook his head. "One is my limit."

"Let us know if you need anything else. And welcome, man."

"Thanks." Cutter couldn't help but feel as if Sean had welcomed him not just to the party, but to their close-knit cluster of friends. And weirdly, despite all the committed relationships and the love hanging heavy in the air, he didn't feel out of place.

With another sip of brew, he headed for Jolie and Heath. They both leapt up from their seats to give him a warm welcome. They'd replaced their hastily purchased wedding bands with something more substantial. Diamonds winked from Jolie's left hand. Ribbed titanium banded Heath's finger. They looked incredibly happy.

"I was hoping we'd see you tonight." She hugged him.

Stone Sutter pulled up a chair for him. Heath all but shoved him into it.

Karis gave him a soft smile. He wished now there could have been some spark between them. She would never have ripped him in two. But they'd talked about their lack of chemistry after Jolie and Heath's rescue. Neither felt a vibe other than friendship.

"Hey," she called softly.

"How's my favorite brown-eyed girl today?" he asked softly. "And where's Arthur?"

She shook her head. "It wasn't going to last. He was a whim. I wanted to like him more than I actually did. He left Betti, took a job in Denver. How about you? I heard you're engaged now."

"Yeah." Other than the clipped word, Cutter kept his face carefully blank. He didn't want anyone knowing that the last few weeks had utterly gutted him. They had enough on their plates, and talking changed nothing. "Brea and I are planning a January wedding."

"Where is she?"

"With her family." He didn't want to say more. Karis already looked suspicious enough, studying him with big eyes.

"You're hurting. I'm sorry."

He wished to hell she'd stop being so perceptive. "I'll be fine. Hey, Brea is going skiing for the holidays with her parents. Maybe . . . Would you come to Hunter and Kata Edgington's New Year's party with me?"

"Neither of us would have to spend the holiday alone. Score," she tried to joke.

But her expression looked nearly as sad as he felt. She wanted someone, wanted to be in love. At twenty-three, she had plenty of time to find someone for her heart to call home. He just hoped that when Karis found that someone, he didn't rip the beating organ from her chest with a few awful words.

Cutter stopped his march down Maudlin Lane. "I'd appreciate it."

She reached for his hand and squeezed. "That's what friends are for."

They fell silent, and he homed in on the conversation the rest of the women around the table were whispering.

"Exactly!" Mystery Dillon leaned against her big brick of a husband, Axel. They'd gotten hitched in a posh ceremony six weeks ago. "I get up some mornings and I feel great. Others . . . it's like I can barely roll out of bed before the nausea hits."

Lily Sutter wrinkled her nose. "Right? And when that nausea lasts all day?"

Both women groaned.

"It gets better after the first trimester, right?" Mystery put in. "Please tell me it does."

Stone placed a bracing hand on his wife's shoulder before Lily nodded. "It did for me the first time. I'm hoping that holds true again. One thing I am realizing?" She yawned, then laughed. "I was a lot less tired all the time when I did this pregnancy thing as a teenager. This baby is sucking out all my vitamins." She cradled her still-flat belly. "I feel like a twenty-three-year-old grandma. I go to bed at eight thirty now."

Everyone laughed.

Nice to see the ladies, formerly rivals for Axel's affection, bonding like fast friends over their coming babies.

"I feel the same. Twenty-five going on seventy-five," Mystery swore. "Some days are just wretched, and yet I'm so excited to experience everything about this pregnancy, even having my stomach announce my arrival before I actually make it into a room. What's your due date?"

"August sixth. You?"

Mystery laughed. "August fourth. Looks like we'll be doing this together."

Lily reached for her hand. "Thank goodness."

Stone and Axel exchanged a glance that silently asked when their brides had become best buddies. But neither objected. They just shrugged and clinked beer bottles.

"Well . . ." Jolie put in. "I won't be living vicariously through you two."

Cutter whipped his stare around to the incredibly busy owner of Betti.

"You're pregnant?" Karis asked, clearly holding her breath.

"We found out this morning," Heath supplied, giving his wife's shoulder a squeeze.

Karis squealed and jumped out of her chair. Jolie rose, and the sisters met halfway for a heartfelt hug.

It was nice to know that good things still happened to good people. Cutter stuck out his hand to Heath. "Congrats, man."

"Thanks. We're beyond thrilled."

Jolie nodded. "It's the best week ever. Before the baby news, the TV promos of Shealyn West in my spring collection started airing."

Cutter's heart clutched but he kept his expression flat.

"Orders are already exploding. The press lauded the line. I simply had to hire a permanent head of security." Jolie's megawatt smile said that all her dreams were coming true. Then she glanced up at her husband as if he was her most treasured blessing.

"You made certain I couldn't say no to that position—or any other—love," Heath ribbed.

She blushed.

"That's great," Cutter told them. "Congratulations."

"It helps that Shealyn West looks good in everything."

She looks even better in absolutely nothing.

Cutter swallowed back the thought and gave Jolie a vague smile. "I'm really happy for you. For all of you." He finished off the last of his beer and set it on the counter. "But I have to head back to Lafayette tonight, so I'm going to hit the road."

Karis grabbed his arm. "If you leave, I'm the only other sad sack single in the place. Please . . ."

"You're going to be fine, little gypsy." He kissed her forehead.

Before he could make his getaway, the conversations fell to whispers, then died to a sudden hush. Cutter turned to the opening of the kitchen. His fingers curled into fists.

Who the fuck had invited One-Mile?

The guy clambered in wearing combat boots and a sneer. As usual, those dead dark eyes gave away nothing as he scanned the crowd. Their eyes met. Cutter felt the blast of hate from across the kitchen.

"Whoa," Stone said under his breath.

As if sensing the rising tension, Logan's wife grabbed Callie by the hand. Together, the two of them led the sniper to the far side of the room.

All the more reason to leave. If Cutter stayed, he'd want to avenge Brea. After all, he was going to marry her, and he didn't think for an instant that Callie would forgive him for committing murder on her kitchen floor.

"I'll catch you all later." He nodded at everyone, then snagged Sean's attention. "Thanks for everything. I had a great time."

"Can you stay for three more minutes? Callie hosted this party for a reason."

Cutter sighed. The woman had been nothing but gracious. Nearly everyone in this room had been. He could shelve his animosity for a bit. "Sure."

As if sensing the sudden undercurrent in the room could get

ugly fast, Callie rose and clinked a fork against her glass of champagne. Sean headed for his wife and flanked her left. Thorpe had already taken up residence at her right. Everyone gave her their attention, even Pierce the pus-bleeding asswipe.

"Thorpe, Sean, and I are so happy everyone could come for this holiday celebration with us. Some of you are actually family, but as you know, I was unfortunate enough to lose mine years ago. Same with Sean and Thorpe. We've made our own little family together. Most of you have married and done the same." She laughed. "The sheer number of babies between all of us is crazy."

"Twelve." Thorpe shook his head. "With two more on the way. We need to figure out what's causing that."

"And do it again." Sean winked.

Everyone laughed.

"Make that three more on the way," Heath cut in, smoothing a hand down Jolie's belly.

Well wishes resounded around the room before everyone turned back to Callie again.

"Clearly, we're pretty good at expanding our family," she teased, then sobered. "That's what tonight is about. We're not conventional and never have been. But we have big hearts, loyalty a mile wide, and love to spare. We've helped one another, shared joy, tears, good times and bad. Besides significant others, we've found our 'people' in this group. We've learned how to become each other's brothers, sisters, cousins, neighbors, best friends, confidantes . . . We've become a big, wonderful extended family. I couldn't think of better people to make my way through life with." She teared up. "And now I'm going to cry. Just know that you're the family we've chosen. We love you as if you shared our blood. We wish you the very merriest of Christmases and the happiest of New Years."

"Hear, hear!" Everyone raised their glasses and toasted the Mackenzie-Thorpe trio before hugs began all around.

Cutter found himself wrapped up in a soft, feminine hug or the recipient of a hearty slap on the back. The joy was contagious. He found himself smiling, sharing a moment, even opening a little of his shell.

Until he spied Pierce Walker across the room.

Heath grabbed his arm. "Let it go."

Never. "Sure. Great to see you, man. Let's get together soon."

The Brit nodded but he clearly wasn't fooled. "You have my number."

If he wanted to talk? Nope. This was probably one situation that would only be solved with violence.

But Cutter kept that to himself. He shook Heath's hand, hugged Jolie and Karis, brushed a kiss across Callie's cheek, then headed for the door.

The sound of loud boots clomped behind him. "Hey, fucker! You're not marrying Brea."

Cutter ignored One-Mile's spew of crap and slammed the door between them. Not for a second did he think this was over. But for the night he was determined to ignore the asshole and focus on the holiday spirit, along with the new, extended family he'd surprisingly been adopted into. He had a feeling all their experience, positive vibes, and love would help him through this trial—and anything else that gave him hell.

With that bit of unexpected reassurance, he climbed in his car and drove into the night . . .

About the Author

Shayla Black is the *New York Times* and *USA Today* bestselling author of about fifty novels. For over fifteen years, she's written contemporary, erotic, paranormal, and historical romances via traditional, independent, foreign, and audio publishers. Her books have sold millions of copies and been published in a dozen languages.

Raised an only child, Shayla occupied herself with lots of daydreaming, much to the chagrin of her teachers. In college, she found her love for reading and realized that she could have a career publishing the stories spinning in her imagination. Though she graduated with a degree in Marketing/Advertising and embarked on a stint in corporate America to pay the bills, her heart has always been with her characters. She's thrilled that she's been living her dream as a full-time author for the past seven years.

Shayla currently lives in North Texas with her wonderfully supportive husband, her teenage daughter, and a very spoiled cat. In her "free" time, she enjoys reality TV, reading, and listening to an eclectic blend of music.